Samuel Thompson

Reminiscences of a Canadian Pioneer for the Last Fifty Years

An autobiography

Samuel Thompson

Reminiscences of a Canadian Pioneer for the Last Fifty Years
An autobiography

ISBN/EAN: 9783337013097

Printed in Europe, USA, Canada, Australia, Japan

Cover: Foto ©Raphael Reischuk / pixelio.de

More available books at **www.hansebooks.com**

REMINISCENCES

OF A

CANADIAN PIONEER

FOR

THE LAST FIFTY YEARS.

AN AUTOBIOGRAPHY.

BY

SAMUEL THOMPSON,

Formerly Editor of the " Toronto Daily Colonist." the " Parliamentary Hansard," &c., &c

----

Toronto:

HUNTER, ROSE & COMPANY.

MDCCCLXXXIV.

PREFACE.

IT was in consequence of a suggestion by the late S. J. Watson, Librarian of the Ontario Legislature—who urged that one who had gone through so many experiences of early Canadian history as myself, ought to put the same on record—that I first thought of writing these " Reminiscences," a portion of which appeared in the *Canadian Monthly Magazine.* For the assistance which has enabled me to complete and issue this volume, I am obliged to the kind support of those friends who have subscribed for its publication; for which they will please accept my grateful thanks.

In the space at my disposal, I have necessarily been compelled to give little more than a gossiping narrative of events coming under my own observation. But I have been careful to verify every statement of which I was not personally cognizant; and to avoid everything of a controversial character; as well as to touch gently on those faults of public men which I felt obliged to notice.

It has been a labour of love to me, to place on record many honourable deeds of Nature's gentlemen, whose lights ought not to be hidden altogether "under a bushel," and whose names should be enrolled by Canada amongst her earliest worthies. I have had the advantage, in several cases, of the use of family records, which have assisted me materially in rendering more complete several of the earlier chapters, particularly the account of Mackenzie's movements while in the neighbourhood of Gallows Hill; also the sketches of the "Tories of Rebellion Times;" as well as the history of the Mechanics' Institute, in which though a very old member, I never occupied any official position.

Since the first part of these pages was in type, I have had to lament the deaths of more than one comrade whose name is recorded therein; amongst them Dr. A. A. Riddel—my "Archie"—and my dearest friend Dr. Alpheus Todd, to whom I have been indebted for a thousand proofs of generous sympathy.

THE AUTHOR.

CONTENTS.

Chap.		Page

REMINISCENCES

OF

A CANADIAN PIONEER.

CHAPTER I.

THE AUTHOR'S ANTECEDENTS AND FORBEARS.

THE writer of these pages was born in the year 1810, in the City of London, and in the Parish of Clerkenwell, being within sound of Bow Bells. My father was churchwarden of St. James's, Clerkenwell, and was a master-manufacturer of coal measures and coal shovels, now amongst the obsolete implements of by-gone days. His father was, I believe, a Scotsman, and has been illnaturedly surmised to have run away from the field of Culloden, where he may have fought under the name and style of Evan McTavish, a name which, like those of numbers of his fellow clansmen, would naturally anglicise itself into John Thompson, in order to save its owner's neck from a threatened

Hanoverian halter. But he was both canny and winsome, and by-and-by succeeded in capturing the affections and "tocher" of Sarah Reynolds, daughter of the wealthy landlord of the Bull Inn, of Meriden, in Warwickshire, the greatest and oldest of those famous English hostelries, which did duty as the resting-place of monarchs *en route*, and combined within their solid walls whole troops of blacksmiths, carpenters, hostlers, and many other crafts and callings. No doubt from this source I got my Warwickshire blood, and English ways of thinking, in testimony of which I may cite the following facts : while living in Quebec, in 1859-60, a mason employed to rebuild a brick chimney challenged me as a brother Warwickshire man, saying he knew dozens of gentlemen there who were as like me " as two peas." Again, in 1841, a lady who claimed to be the last direct descendant of William Shakespeare, of Stratford-upon-Avon, and the possessor of the watch and other relics of the poet, said she was quite startled at my likeness to an original portrait of her great ancestor, in the possession of her family.

My grandfather carried on the business of timber dealer (we in Canada should call it lumber merchant), between Scotland and England, buying up the standing timber in gentlemen's parks, squaring and teaming it southward, and so became a prosperous man. Finally, at his death, he left a large family of sons and daughters, all in thriving circumstances. His second son, William, married my mother, Anna Hawkins, daughter of the Rev. Isaac Hawkins, of Taunton, in Somersetshire, and his wife, Joan Wilmington, of Wilmington Park, near Taunton. My grandfather Hawkins was one of John Wesley's earliest converts, and was by him ordained to the ministry. Through my mother, we are understood to be descended from Sir John Hawkins, the world-renowned buccaneer, admiral, and founder of the English Royal Navy, who was honoured by being associated with her most sacred Majesty Queen Elizabeth, in a secret partnership in the profits of piratical raids undertaken in the name and for the behoof of Protestant Christianity. So at least says the historian, Froude.

One word more about my father. He was a member of the London trained-bands, and served during the Gordon riots, described by Dickens in "Barnaby Rudge." He personally rescued a family of Roman Catholics from the rioters, secreted them in his house on Holborn Hill, and aided them to escape to Jamaica, whence they sent us many valuable presents of mahogany furniture, which must be still in the possession of some of my nephews or nieces in England. My mother has often told me, that she remembered well seeing dozens of miserable victims of riot and drunkenness lying in the kennel in front of her house, lapping up the streams of gin which ran burning down the foul gutter, consuming the poor wretches themselves in its fiery progress.

My father died the same year I was born. My dear mother, who was the meekest and most pious of women, did her best to teach her children to avoid the snares of worldly pride and ambition, and to be contented with the humble lot in which they had been placed by Providence. She was by religious profession a Swedenborgian, and in that denomination educated a family of eleven children, of whom I am the youngest. I was sent to a respectable day-school, and afterwards as boarder to a commercial academy, where I learnt the English branches of education, with a little Latin, French, and drawing. I was, as a child, passionately fond of reading, especially of Homer's Iliad and Odyssey, and of Sir Walter Scott's novels, which latter delightful books have influenced my tastes through life, and still hold me fascinated whenever I happen to take them up.

So things went on till 1823, when I was thirteen years old. My mother had been left a life-interest in freehold and leasehold property worth some thirty thousand pounds sterling ; but, following the advice of her father and brother, was induced to invest in losing speculations, until scarcely sufficient was left to keep the wolf from the door. It was, therefore, settled that I must be sent to learn a trade, and, by my uncle's advice, I was placed as apprentice to one William Molineux, of the Liberty of the Rolls, in the district of Lincoln's Inn, printer. He was a hard master, though not an unkind man. For seven long years was I kept at press and case, working eleven hours a day usually, sometimes sixteen, and occassionally all night, for which latter indulgence I got half a crown for the night's work, but no other payment or present from year's end to year's end. The factory laws had not then been thought of, and the condition of apprentices in England was much the same as that of convicts condemned to hard labour, except for a couple of hours' freedom, and too often of vicious license, in the evenings.

.

CHAPTER II.

HISTORY OF A MAN OF GENIUS.

THE course of my narrative now requires a brief account of my mother's only brother, whose example and conversation, more than anything else, taught me to turn my thoughts westwards, and finally to follow his example by crossing the Atlantic ocean, and seeking "fresh fields and pastures new" under a transatlantic sky.

John Isaac Hawkins was a name well known, both in European and American scientific circles, fifty years ago, as an inventor of the most fertile resource, and an expert in all matters relating to civil engineering. He must have left England for America somewhere about the year 1790, full of republican enthusiasm and of schemes of universal benevolence. Of his record in the United States I know very little, except that he married a wife in New Jersey, that he resided at Bordenton, that he acquired some property adjacent to Philadelphia, that he was intimate with the elder Adams, Jefferson, and many other eminent men. Returning with his wife to England, after twenty-five years' absence, he established a sugar refinery in Titchfield Street, Cavendish square, London, patronized his English relatives with much condescension, and won my childish heart by great lumps of rock-candy, and scientific experiments of a delightfully awful character. Also, he borrowed my mother's money, to be expended for the good of mankind, and the elaboration of the teeming offspring of his inexhaustible inventive faculty. Morden's patent lead pencils, Bramah's patent locks, and, I think, Gillott's steel pens were among his numerous useful achievements, from some or all of which he enjoyed to the day of his death a small income, in the shape of a royalty on the profits. He assisted in the perfecting of Perkins's steam-gun, which the Duke of Wellington condemned as too barbarous for civilized warfare, but which its discoverer, Mr. Perkins, looked upon as the destined extirpator of all warfare, by the simple process of rendering resistance utterly impossible. This appalling and destructive weapon has culminated in these times in the famous mitrailleuses of Napoleon III, at Woerth and Sedan, which, however, certainly neither exterminated the Prussians nor added glory to the French empire.

At his home I was in the habit of meeting the leading men of the Royal Society and the Society of Arts, of which he was a member, and of listening

to their discussions about scientific novelties. The
eccentric Duke of Norfolk, Earl Stanhope, the inventor of the Stanhope press, and other noble amateur scientists, availed themselves of his practical
skill, and his name became known throughout
Europe. In 1825 or thereabouts, he was selected
by the Emperor Francis Joseph, of Austria, to design
and superintend the first extensive works erected in
Vienna for the promotion of the new manufacture
of beet-root sugar, now an important national industry throughout Germany. He described the intercourse of the Austrian Imperial-Royal family
with all who approached them, and even with the
mendicants who were daily admitted to an audience
with the Emperor at five o'clock in the morning, as
of the most cordial and lovable character.

From Vienna my uncle went to Paris, and performed the same duties there for the French Government, in the erection of extensive sugar works.
The chief difficulty he encountered there, was in
parrying the determination of the Parisian artisans
not to lose their Sunday's labour. They could not,
they said, support their families on six days' wages,
and unless he paid them for remaining idle on the
Sabbath day, they must and would work seven days
in the week. I believe they gained their point,
much to his distress and chagrin.

His next exploit was in the construction of the Thames tunnel, in connection with which he acted as superintendent of the works under Sir Isambert Brunel. This occupied him nearly up to the time of my own departure for Canada, in 1833. The sequel of his story is a melancholy one. He made fortunes for other men who bought his inventions but himself sank into debt, and at last died in obscurity at Rahway, New Jersey, whither he had returned as a last resort, there to find his former friends dead, his beloved republic become a paradise for office-grabbers and sharpers, his life a mere tale of talents dissipated, and vague ambition unsatisfied.*

* Since writing the above, I find in *Scribner's Monthly* for November 1880, the following notice of my uncle, which forms a sad sequel to a long career of untiring enthusiasm in the service of his fellow-creatures. It is the closing paragraph of an article headed " Bordentown and the Bonapartes," from the pen of Joseph B. Gilder :

"It yet remains to say a few words of Dr. John Isaac Hawkins—civil engineer, inventor, poet, preacher, phrenologist and 'mentor-general to mankind,'—who visited the village towards the close of the last century, married and lived there for many years ; then disappeared, and, after a long absence, returned a gray old man, with a wife barely out of her teens. 'This isn't the wife you took away, doctor,' some one ventured to remark. 'No,' the blushing girl replied, 'and he's buried one between us.' The poor fellow had hard work to gain a livelihood. For a time, the ladies paid him to lecture to them in their parlours ; but when he brought a bag of skulls, and the heart and windpipe of his [adopted] son preserved in

After his return from Vienna, I lived much at my uncle's house, in London, as my mother had removed to the pleasant village of Epsom in Surrey. There I studied German with some degree of success, and learnt much about foreign nations and the world at large. There too I learnt to distrust my own ability to make my way amidst the crowded industries of the old country, and began to cast a longing eye to lands where there was plenty of room for in-

---

spirits, they would have nothing more to do with him. As a last resort, he started the 'Journal of Human Nature and Human Progress,' his wife 'setting up' for the press her husband's contributions in prose and rhyme. But the 'Journal' died after a brief and inglorious career. Hawkins claimed to have made the first survey for a tunnel under the Thames, and he invented the 'ever-pointed pencil,' the 'iridium-pointed gold pen,' and a method of condensing coffee. He also constructed a little stove with a handle, which he carried into the kitchen to cook his meals or into the reception-room when visitors called, and at night into his bedroom. He invented also a new religion, whose altar was erected in his own small parlour, where Dr. John Isaac Hawkins, priest, held forth to Mrs. John Isaac Hawkins, people. But a shadow stretched along the poor man's path from the loss of his only [adopted] son —'a companion in all of his philosophical researches,' who died and was dissected at the early age of seven. Thereafter the old man wandered, as 'lonely as a cloud,' sometimes in England, sometimes in America; but attended patiently and faithfully by his first wife, then by a second, and finally by a third, who clung to him with the devotion of Little Nell to her doting grandfather."

dividual effort, and a reasonable prospect of a life unblighted by the dread of the parish workhouse and a pauper's grave.

CHAPTER III.

SOME REMINISCENCES OF A LONDON APPRENTICE.

HAVING been an indulged youngest child, I found the life of a printer's boy bitterly distasteful, and it was long before I could brace myself up to the required tasks.   But time worked a change; I got to be a smart pressman and compositor; and at eighteen the foremanship of the office was entrusted to me, still without remuneration or reward. Those were the days of the Corn Law League. Col. Peyronnet Thompson, the apostle of Free Trade, author of the " Catholic State Waggon " and other political tracts, got his work done at our office. We printed the *Examiner*, which brought me into contact with John and Leigh Hunt, with Jeremy Bentham, then a feeble old man whose life was passed in an easy chair, and with his *protegé* Edwin Chadwick ; also with Albany Fonblanque, Sir John Morland the philanthropist, and other eminent men.

Last but not least, we printed " Figaro in London,"
the forerunner of " Punch," and I was favoured with
the kindest encouragement by De Walden, its first
editor, afterwards Police Magistrate. I have known
that gentleman come into the office on the morning
of publication, ask how much copy was still wanted,
and have seen him stand at a desk, and without
preparation or hesitation, dash off paragraph after
paragraph of the pungent witticisms, which the same
afternoon sent all London into roars of laughter at
the expense of political humbugs of all kinds, whether friends or foes. These were not unhappy days
for me. With such associations, I became a zealous
Reformer, and heartily applauded my elder brother,
when he refused, with thousands of others, to pay
taxes at the time the first Reform Bill was rejected
by the House of Lords.

At this period of my life, as might have been expected from the nature of my education and the
course of reading which I preferred, I began to try
my hand at poetry, and wrote several slight pieces
for the Christmas Annuals, which, sad to say, were
never accepted. But the fate of Chatterton, of
Coleridge, and other like sufferers, discouraged me ;
and I adopted the prudent resolution, to prefer
wealth to fame, and comfort to martyrdom in the
service of the Muses,

With the termination of my seven years' apprenticeship, these literary efforts came also to an end. Disgusted with printing, I entered the service of my brother, a timber merchant, and in consequence obtained a general knowledge of the many varieties of wood used in manufactures, which I have since found serviceable. And this brings me to the year 1831, from which date to the present day, I have identified myself thoroughly with Canada, her industries and progress, without for a moment ceasing to be an Englishman of the English, a loyal subject of the Queen, and a firm believer in the high destinies of the Pan-Anglican Empire of the future.

CHAPTER IV.

WESTWARD, HO !

"MARTIN DOYLE," was the text-book which first awakened, amongst tens of thousands of British readers, a keen interest in the backwoods of what is now the Province of Ontario. The year 1832, the first dread year of Asiatic cholera, contributed by its terrors to the exodus of alarmed fugitives from the crowded cities of the old country.   My brothers Thomas and Isaac, both a few years older than myself, made up their minds to emigrate, and I joyously offered to join them, in the expectation of a good deal of fun of the kind described by Dr. Dunlop. So we set seriously to work, "pooled" our small means, learnt to make seine-nets, economized to an unheard of extent, became curious in the purchase of stores, including pannikins and other primitive tinware, and at length engaged passage in the bark *Asia*, 500 tons, rated A. No. 1, formerly an East Indiaman, and now bound for Quebec, to seek a cargo of white pine lumber for the London market.   So sanguine were we of returning in the course of six or seven years, with plenty of money to enrich, and perhaps bring back with us, our dear mother and unmarried sisters, that we scarcely realized the pain of leave-taking, and went on board ship in the St. Catherine's Docks, surrounded by applauding friends, and in the highest possible spirits.

Our fellow-passengers were not of the most desirable class.   With the exception of a London hairdresser and his wife, very respectable people, with whom we shared the second-cabin, the emigrants were chiefly rough countrymen, with their wives and numerous children, sent out by the parish authorities from the neighbourhood of Dorking, in Surrey, and more ignorant than can readily be conceived. Helpless as infants under suffering, sulky and even savage under privations, they were a troublesome charge to the ship's officers, and very ill-fitted for the dangers of the sea which lay before us. Captain Ward was the ship's master; there were first and second mates, the former a tall Scot, the latter a short thick-set Englishman, and both good sailors. The boatswain, cook and crew of about a dozen men and boys, made up our ship's company.

All things went reasonably well for some time. Heavy head-winds detained us in the channel for a fortnight, which was relieved by landing at Torbay, climbing the heights of Brixham, and living on fresh fish for twenty-four hours. Then came a fair wind, which lasted until we got near the banks of Newfoundland. Head-winds beset us again, and this time so seriously that our vessel, which was timber-sheathed, sprang a plank, and immediately began to leak dangerously. The passengers had taken to their berths for the night, and were of course ignorant of what had happened, but feared something wrong from the hurry of tramping of feet overhead, the vehement shouts of the mates giving orders for lowering sail, and the other usual accom-

paniments of a heavy squall on board ship. It was
not long, however, before we learned the alarming
truth. "All hands on deck to pump ship," came
thundering down both hatchways, in the coarse
tones of the second mate. We hurried on deck
half-dressed, to face a scene of confusion affrighting
in the eyes of landsmen—the ship stripped to her
storm-sails, almost on her beam-ends in a tremendous sea, the wind blowing "great guns," the deck
at an angle of at least fifteen degrees, flooded with
rain pouring in torrents, and encumbered with
ropes which there had not been time to clew away,
the four ship's pumps manned by twice as many
landsmen, the sailors all engaged in desperate efforts
to stop the leak by thrumming sails together and
drawing them under the ship's bows.

Captain Ward told us very calmly that he had
been in gales off the Cape of Good Hope, and thought
nothing of a " little puff " like this; he also told us
that he should keep on his course in the hope that
the wind would abate, and that we could manage
the leak; but if not, he had no doubt of carrying us
safely back to the west coast of Ireland, where he
might comfortably refit.

Certainly courage is infectious. We were twelve
hundred miles at sea, with a great leak in our ship's
side, and very little hope of escape, but the master's

coolness and bravery delighted us, and even the weakest man on board took his spell at the pumps, and worked away for dear life. My brother Thomas was a martyr to sea-sickness, and could hardly stand without help; but Isaac had been bred a farmer, accustomed to hard work and field sports, and speedily took command of the pumps, worked two spells for another man's one, and by his example encouraged the grumbling steerage passengers to persevere, if only for very shame. Some of their wives even took turns with great spirit and effect. I did my best, but it was not much that I could accomplish.

In all my after-life I never experienced such supreme comfort and peace of mind, as during that night, while lying under wet sails on the sloping deck, talking with my brother of the certainty of our being at the bottom of the sea before morning, of our mother and friends at home, and of our hope of meeting them in the great Hereafter. Tired out at last, we fell asleep where we lay, and woke only at the cry, "spell ho!" which summoned us again to the pumps.

The report of "five feet of water in the hold—the ballast shifted!" determined matters for us towards morning. Capt. Ward decided that he must put about and run for Galway, and so he did. The sea had by daylight gone down so much, that the cap-

tain's cutter could be lowered and the leak examin-
ed from the outside. This was done by the first
mate, Mr. Cattanagh, who brought back the cheering news that so long as we were running before the
wind the leak was four feet out of water, and that
we were saved for the present. The bark still remained at the same unsightly angle, her ballast,
which was chiefly coals, having shifted bodily over to
leeward; the pumps had to be kept going, and in
this deplorable state, in constant dread of squalls,
and wearied with incessant hard work, we sailed for
eight days and nights, never sighting a ship until
nearly off the mouth of the Shannon, where we hail-
ed a brig whose name I forget. She passed on,
however, refusing to answer our signals of distress.

Next day, to our immense relief, the *Asia* entered Galway Bay, and here we lay six weeks for
repairs, enjoying ourselves not a little, and forgetting past danger, except as a memorable episode in
the battle of life.

CHAPTER V.

CONNEMARA AND GALWAY FIFTY YEARS AGO.

THE Town of Galway is a relic of the times when Spain maintained an active commerce with the west of Ireland, and meddled not a little in the intrigues of the time. Everybody has read of the warden of Galway, who hanged his son outside a window of his own house, to prevent a rescue from justice by a popular rising in the young man's favour. That house still stood, and probably yet stands, a mournful memento of a most dismal tragedy. In 1833 it was in ruins, as was also the whole long row of massive cut stone buildings of which it formed part. In front there was a tablet recording the above event; the walls were entire, but the roof was quite gone, and the upper stories open to the winds and storms. The basement story appeared to have been solidly arched, and in its cavernous recesses, and those of the adjoining cellars along that side of the street, dwelt a race of butchers and of small hucksters, dealing in potatoes, oats, some groceries and rough wares of many kinds. The first floor of a brick store opposite was occupied by a hair-dresser with whom our London fellow-passenger claimed acquaintance. One day we were sitting at his window, looking across at the old warden's house, when a singular scene was enacted under our astonished eyes. A beggarman, so ragged as barely to comply with the demands of common decency, and bearing an old sack suspended over his shoulder on a short cudgel, came lounging along the middle of the street seeking alms. A butcher's dog of aristocratic tastes took offence at the man's rags, and attacked him savagely. The old man struck at the dog, the dog's owner darted out of his cellar and struck at the beggar, somebody else took a part, and in the twinkling of an eye as it were, the narrow street was blocked up with men furiously-wielding shillelaghs, striking right and left at whoever happened to be most handy, and yelling like Dante's devils in full chorus. Another minute, and a squad of policemen in green uniforms—peelers, they are popularly called —appeared as if by magic, and with the effect of magic; for instantly, and with a celerity evidently the result of long practice, the crowd, beggarman, butcher, dog and all, vanished into the yawning cellars, and the street was left as quiet as before, the police marching leisurely back to their barracks.

We spent much of our time in rambling along the shore of Galway Bay, a beautiful and extensive harbour, where we found many curious specimens of sea-weeds, particularly the edible dilosk, and rare shells and minerals. Some of our people went out shooting snipe, and were warned on all hands to go in parties, and to take care of their guns, which would prove too strong a temptation for the native peasantry, as the spirit of Ribbonism was rife throughout Connemara. Another amusement was, to watch the groups of visitors from Tuam and the surrounding parts of Clare and other counties, who were attracted by the marvel of a ship of five hundred tons in their bay, no such phenomenon having happened within the memory of man. At another time we explored the rapid river Corrib, and the beautiful lake of the same name, a few miles distant. The salmon weirs on the river were exceedingly interesting, where we saw the largest fish confined in cribs for market, and apparently quite unconscious of their captivity. The castle of one of the Lynch family was visible from the bay, an ancient structure with its walls mounted with cannon to keep sheriffs' officers at a distance. Other feudal castles were also in sight.

Across the bay loomed the rugged mountains of Clare, seemingly utterly barren in their bleak nakedness. With the aid of the captain's telescope we could see on these inhospitable hills dark objects, which turned out to be the mud cabins of a numerous peasantry, the very class for whom, in this present year of 1883, Mr. Gladstone and his colleagues are trying to create an elysium of rural contentment. We traversed the country roads for miles, to observe the mode of farming there, and could find nothing, even up to the very streets of Galway, but mud cabins with one or two rooms, shared with the cow and pigs, and entrenched, as it were, behind a huge pile of manure that must have been the accumulation of years. Anything in the shape of valuable improvements was conspicuously absent.

Everything in Connemara seems paradoxical. These rough-coated, hard-worked, down-trodden Celts proved to be the liveliest, brightest, wittiest of mankind. They came in shoals to our ship, danced reels by the hour upon deck to a whistled accompaniment, with the most extravagant leaps and snapping of fingers. It was an amusing sight to see women driving huge pigs into the sea, held by a string tied to the hind leg, and there scraping and sluicing the unwieldy, squealing creatures until they came out as white as new cream. These Galway women are singularly handsome, with a decidedly Murillo cast of features, betokening plainly their Iberian ancestry. They might well have sat as models to the chief of Spanish painters.

In the suburbs of Galway are many acres of boggy land, which are cultivated as potato plots, highly enriched with salt sea-weed manure, and very productive. These farms—by which title they are dignified—were rented, we were told, at three to four pounds sterling per acre. Rents in the open country ranged from one pound upwards. Yet we bought cup potatoes at twopence per stone of sixteen lbs.; and for a leg of mutton paid sixpence English.

Enquiring the cause of these singular anomalies, we were assured on all hands, that the system of renting through middlemen was the bane of Ireland. A farm might be sub-let two or three times, each tenant paying an increased rental, and the landlord-in-chief, a Blake, a Lynch, or a Martin, realizing less rent than he would obtain in Scotland or England. We heard of no Protestant oppressors here; the gentry and nobility worshipped at the same altar with the humblest of their dependents, and certainly meant them well and treated them considerately.

We attended the English service in the ancient Gothic Abbey Church. The ministrations were of the strictest Puritan type; the sculptured escutcheons and tablets on the walls—the groined arches and bosses of the roof—were almost obliterated by thick coat upon coat of whitewash, laid on in an iconoclastic spirit which I have since seen equalled in the

Dutch Cathedral of Rotterdam, and nowhere else. Another Sunday we visited a small Roman Catholic chapel at some distance. It was impossible to get inside the building, as the crowd of worshippers not only filled the sacred edifice, but spread themselves over a pretty extensive and well-filled churchyard, where they knelt throughout morning prayer, lasting a full hour or more.

The party-feuds of the town are quite free from sectarian feeling. The fishermen, who were dressed from head to foot in hoddengray, and the butchers, who clothed themselves entirely in sky-blue—coats, waistcoats, breeches, and stockings alike, with black hats and shoes—constituted the belligerent powers. Every Saturday night, or oftener, they would marshal their forces respectively on the wide fish-market place, by the sea-shore, or on the long wharf extending into deep water, and with their shillelaghs hold high tournament for the honour of their craft and the love of fair maidens. One night, while the *Asia* lay off the wharf, an unfortunate combatant fell senseless into the water and was drowned. But no inquiry followed, and no surprise was expressed at a circumstance so trivial.

By the way, it would be unpardonable to quit Connemara without recording its "potheen." Every homestead had its peat-stack, and every peat-stack might be the hiding-place of a keg of illicit native spirits. We were invited, and encouraged by example, to taste a glass; but a single mouthful almost choked us; and never again did we dare to put the fiery liquid to our lips.

Our recollections of Galway are of a mixed character—painful, because of the consciousness that the empire at large must be held responsible for the unequal distribution of nature's blessings amongst her people—pleasant, because of the uniform hospitality and courtesy shown to us by all classes and creeds of the townsfolk.

CHAPTER VI.

MORE SEA EXPERIENCES.

IN the month of July we were ready for sea again. In the meantime Captain Ward had got together a new list of passengers, and we more than doubled our numbers by the addition of several Roman Catholic gentlemen of birth and education with their followers, and a party of Orangemen and their families, of a rather rough farming sort, escaping from religious feuds and hostile neighbours. A blooming widow Culleeney, of the former class, was added to the scanty female society on board; and for the first few hours after leaving port, we had fun and dancing on deck galore. But alas, sea-sickness put an end to our merriment all too soon. Our new recruits fled below, and scarcely showed their faces on deck for several days.   Yet, in this apparently quiet interval, discord had found her way between decks.

We were listening one fine evening to the comical jokes and rich brogue of the most gentlemanly of the Irish Catholics above-mentioned, when suddenly a dozen men, women and children, armed with sticks and foaming at the mouth, rushed up the steerage hatchway, and without note of warning or apparent provocation, attacked the defenceless group standing near us with the blindness of insanity and the most frantic cries of rage. Fortunately there were several of the ship's officers and sailors on deck, who laid about them lustily with their fists, and speedily drove the attacking party below, where they were confined for some days, under a threat of severe punishment from the captain, who meant what he said. So this breeze passed over. What it was about, who was offended, and how, we never could discover; we set it down to the general principle, that the poor creatures were merely ' blue-mowlded for want of a bating."

Moderately fair breezes, occasional dead calms, rude, baffling head-winds, attended us until we reached the Gulf of St. Lawrence. After sailing all day northward, and all night southerly, we found ourselves next morning actually retrograded some thirty or forty knots. But we were rewarded sometimes by strange sights and wondrous spectacles. Once a shoal of porpoises and grampuses crossed our course, frolicking and turning summersets in the air, and continuing to stream onwards for full two hours. Another time, when far north, we had the most magnificent display of aurora borealis. Night after night the sea became radiant with phosphorescent light. Icebergs attended us in thousands, compelling our captain to shorten sail frequently ; once we passed near two of these ice-cliffs which exceeded five hundred feet in height, and again we were nearly overwhelmed by the sudden break-down of a huge mass as big as a cathedral. Near the Island of Anticosti we saw at least three hundred spouting whales at one view. I have crossed the Atlantic four times since, and have scarcely seen a single whale or shark. It seems that modern steamship travel has driven away the inhabitants of the deep to quieter seas, and robbed " life on the ocean wave " of much of its romance.

CHAPTER VII.

UP THE ST. LAWRENCE.

THE St. Lawrence River was gained, and escaping with a few days' quarantine at Grosse Isle, we reached Quebec, there to be transferred to a fine steamer for Montreal. At Lachine we were provided with large barges, here called batteaux, which sufficed to accommodate the whole of the *Asia's* passengers going west, with their luggage. They were drawn by Canadian ponies, lively and perfectly hardy little animals, which, with their French-Canadian drivers, amused us exceedingly. While loading up, we were favoured with one of those accidental historical "bits"—as a painter would say—which occur so rarely in a lifetime. The then despot of the North-West, Sir George Simpson, was just starting for the seat of his government *via* the Ottawa River. With him were some half-dozen officers, civil and military, and the party was escorted by six or eight Nor'-West canoes—each thirty or forty feet long, and manned by some twenty-four Indians, in the full glory of war-paint, feathers, and most dazzling costumes. To see these stately boats, and their no less stately crews, gliding with measured stroke, in gallant procession, on their way to the vasty wilderness of the Hudson's Bay territory, with the British flag displayed at each prow, was a sight never to be forgotten. And as they paddled, the woods echoed far and wide to the strange weird sounds of their favourite boat-song :—

> " A la claire fontaine,
>   M'en allant promener,
>   J'ai trouvé l'eau si belle,
>   Que je m'y suis baigné.
> Il y a longtemps que je t'aime,
> Jamais je ne t'oublirai."

From Lachine to the Coteau, thence by canal and along shore successively to Cornwall, Prescott, and Kingston, occupied several days. We were charmed to get on dry land, to follow our batteau along well-beaten paths, gathering nuts, stealing a few apples now and then from some orchard skirting the road ; dining at some weather-boarded way-side tavern, with painted floors, and French cuisine, all delightfully strange and comical to us ; then on board the batteau again at night. Once, in a cedar swamp, we were enraptured at finding a dazzling specimen of the scarlet *lobelia fulgens*, the most brilliant of wild flowers, which Indians use for making red ink.   At another time, the Long Sault rapids, up which was steaming the double-hulled steamer *Iroquois*, amazed us by their grandeur and power, and filled our minds with a sense of the vastness of the land we had come to inhabit. And so we wended on our way until put aboard the Lake Ontario steamer *United Kingdom* for Little York, where we landed about the first week in September, 1833, after a journey of four months. Now-a-days, a trip to England by the Allan Line is thought tedious if it last ten days, and even five days is considered not unattainable. When we left England, a thirty mile railway from Liverpool to Manchester was all that Europe had seen. Dr. Dionysius Lardner pronounced steam voyages across the Atlantic an impossibility, and men believed him. Now, even China and Japan have their railways and steamships; Canada is being spanned from the Atlantic to the Pacific by a railroad, destined, I believe, to work still greater changes in the future of our race, and of the world

CHAPTER VIII.

MUDDY LITTLE YORK.

WHEN we landed at York, it contained 8,500 inhabitants or thereabouts, being the same population nearly as Belleville, St. Catharines, and Brantford severally claimed in 1881. In addition to King street the principal thoroughfares were Lot, Hospital, and Newgate streets, now more euphoniously styled Queen, Richmond and Adelaide streets respectively; Church, George, Bay and York streets were almost without buildings; Yonge street ran north thirty-three miles to Lake Simcoe, and Dundas street extended westward a hundred miles to London. More or less isolated wooden stores there were on King and Yonge streets; taverns were pretty numerous; a wooden English church; Methodist, Presbyterian, and Roman Catholic churches of the like construction; a brick gaol and court-house of the ugliest architecture: scattered private houses, a wheat-field where now stands the Rossin House; beyond it a rough-cast Government House, brick Parliament Buildings uglier even than the gaol, and some government offices located in one-story brick buildings twenty-five feet square,—comprised the lions of the Toronto of that day. Of brick private buildings, only Moore's hotel at the corner of Market square; J. S. Baldwin's residence, now the Canada Company's office; James F. Smith's grocery (afterwards the *Colonist* office), on King street; Ridout's hardware store at the corner of King and Yonge streets, occur to my memory, but there may have been one or two others. So well did the town merit its muddy soubriquet, that in crossing Church street near St. James's Church, boots were drawn off the feet by the tough clay soil; and to reach our tavern on Market lane (now Colborne street), we had to hop from stone to stone placed loosely along the roadside. There was rude flagged pavement here and there, but not a solitary planked footpath throughout the town.

To us the sole attraction was the Emigrant Office. At that time, Sir John Colborne, Lieut. Governor of Upper Canada, was exerting himself to induce retired army officers, and other well-to-do settlers, to take up lands in the country north and west of Lake Simcoe. U. E. rights, *i.e.*, location tickets for two hundred acres of land, subject to conditions of actual settlement, were easily obtainable. We purchased one of these for a hundred dollars, or rather for twenty pounds sterling—dollars and cents not being current in Canada at that date—and forthwith booked ourselves for Lake Simcoe, in an open waggon without springs, loaded with the bedding and cooking utensils of intending settlers, some of them our shipmates of the *Asia*. A day's journey brought us to Holland Landing, whence a small steamer conveyed us across the lake to Barrie. The Holland River was then a mere muddy ditch, swarming with huge bullfrogs and black snakes, and winding in and out through thickets of reeds and rushes. Arrived at Barrie, we found a wharf, a log bakery, two log taverns—one of them also a store—and a farm house, likewise log. Other farmhouses there were at some little distance, hidden by trees.

Some of our fellow travellers were discouraged by the solitary appearance of things here, and turned back at once. My brothers and myself, and one other emigrant, determined to go on ; and next afternoon, armed with axes, guns, and mosquito nets, off we started for the unknown forest, then reaching, unbroken, from Lake Simcoe to Lake Huron. From Barrie to the Nottawasaga river, eleven miles, a road had been chopped and logged sixty-six feet wide ; beyond the river, nothing but a bush path existed.

C

CHAPTER IX.

A PIONEER TAVERN.

WE had walked a distance of eight miles, and it was quite dark, when we came within sight of the clearing where we were advised to stop for the night. Completely blockading the road, and full in our way, was a confused mass of felled timber, which we were afterwards told was a wind-row or brush-fence. It consisted of an irregular heap of prostrate trees, branches and all, thrown together in line, to serve as a fence against stray cattle. After several fruitless attempts to effect an entrance, there was nothing for it but to shout at the top of our voices for assistance.

Presently we heard a shrill cry, rather like the call of some strange bird than a human voice; immediately afterwards, the reflection of a strong light became visible, and a man emerged from the brush-wood, bearing a large blazing fragment of resinous wood, which lighted up every object around in a picturesque and singular manner. High over head, eighty feet at least, was a vivid green canopy of leaves, extending on all sides as far as the eye could penetrate, varied here and there by the twinkling of some lustrous star that peeped through from the dark sky without, and supported by the straight trunks and arching branches of innumerable trees—the rustic pillars of this superb natural temple. The effect was strikingly beautiful and surprising.

Nor was the figure of our guide less strange. He was the first genuine specimen of a Yankee we had encountered—a Vermonter—tall, bony and awkward, but with a good-natured simplicity in his shrewd features ; he wore uncouth leather leggings, tied with deer sinews—loose mocassins, a Guernsey shirt, a scarlet sash confining his patched trowsers at the waist, and a palmetto hat, dragged out of all describable shape, the colour of each article so obscured by stains and rough usage, as to be matter rather of conjecture than certainty. He proved to be our landlord for the night, David Root by name.

Following his guidance, and climbing successively over a number of huge trunks, stumbling through a net-work of branches, and plunging into a shallow stream up to the ankles in soft mud, we reached at length what he called his tavern, at the further side of the clearing. It was a log building of a single apartment, where presided " the wife," a smart, plump, good-looking little Irishwoman, in a stuff gown, and without shoes or stockings. They had been recently married, as he promptly informed us, had selected this wild spot on a half-opened road, impassable for waggons, without a neighbour for miles, and under the inevitable necessity of shouldering all their provisions from the embryo village we had just quitted: all this with the resolute determination of "keeping tavern."

The floor was of loose split logs, hewn into some approach to evenness with an adze; the walls of logs entire, filled in the interstices with chips of pine, which, however, did not prevent an occasional glimpse of the objects visible outside, and had the advantage, moreover, of rendering a window unnecessary; the hearth was the bare soil, the ceiling slabs of pine wood, the chimney a square hole in the roof; the fire literally an entire tree, branches and all, cut into four-feet lengths, and heaped up to the height of as many feet. It was a chill evening, and the dancing flames were inspiriting, as they threw a cheerful radiance all around, and revealed to our curious eyes extraordinary pieces of furniture—a log bedstead in the darkest corner, a pair of snow-shoes, sundry spiral augers and rough tools, a bundle of dried deer-sinews, together with some articles of feminine gear, a small red framed looking-glass, a clumsy comb suspended from a nail by a string, and other similar treasures.

We were accommodated with stools of various sizes and heights, on three legs or on four, or mere pieces of log sawn short off, which latter our host justly recommended as being more steady on the uneven floor. We exchanged our wet boots for slippers, mocassins, or whatever the good-natured fellow could supply us with. The hostess was intently busy making large flat cakes; roasting them, first on one side, then on the other; and alternately boiling and frying broad slices of salt pork, when, suddenly suspending operations, she exclaimed, with a vivacity that startled us, " Oh, Root, I've cracked my spider ! "

Inquiring with alarm what was the matter, we learned that the cast-iron pan on three feet, which she used for her cookery, was called a "spider," and that its fracture had occasioned the exclamation. The injured spider performed "its spiriting gently" notwithstanding, and, sooth to say, all parties did full justice to its savoury contents.

Bed-time drew near. A heap of odd-looking rugs and clean blankets was laid for our accommodation and pronounced to be ready. But how to get into it ? We had heard of some rather primitive practices among the steerage passengers on board ship, it is true, but had not accustomed ourselves to " uncase " before company, and hesitated to lie down in our clothes. After waiting some little time in blank dismay, Mr. Root kindly set us an example by quietly slipping out of his nether integuments and turning into bed. There was no help for it; by one means or other we contrived to sneak under the blankets ; and, after hanging up a large coloured quilt between our lair and the couch occupied by her now snoring spouse, the good wife also disappeared. ·

In spite of the novelty of the situation, and some occasional disturbance from gusts of wind stealing through the " chinks," and fanning into brightness the dying embers on the hearth, we slept deliciously and awoke refreshed.

CHAPTER X.

A FIRST DAY IN THE BUSH.

BEFORE day-break breakfast was ready, and proved to be a more tempting meal than the supper of the night before. There were fine dry potatoes, roast wild pigeon, fried pork, cakes, butter, eggs, milk, " China tea," and chocolate—which last was a brown-coloured extract of cherry-tree bark, sassafras root, and wild sarsaparilla, warmly recommended by our host as " first-rate bitters." Declining this latter beverage, we made a hearty meal.

It was now day-break. As we were new comers, Root offered to convoy us " a piece of the way," a very serviceable act of kindness, for, in the dim twilight we experienced at first no little difficulty in discerning it.   Pointing out some faint glimmerings of morning, which were showing themselves more and more brightly over the tall tree-tops, our friend remarked, "I guess that's where the sun's calc'lating to rise."

The day had advanced sufficiently to enable us to distinguish the road with ease. Our tavern-keeper returned to his work, and in a few minutes the forest echoed to the quick strokes of his lustily-wielded axe. We found ourselves advancing along a wide avenue, unmarked as yet by the track of wheels, and unimpeded by growing brush-wood. To the width of sixty-six feet, all the trees had been cut down to a height of between two and three feet, in a precisely straight course for miles, and burnt or drawn into the woods; while along the centre, or winding from side to side like the course of a drunken man, a waggon-track had been made by grubbing up smaller and evading the larger stumps, or by throwing a collection of small limbs and decayed wood into the deeper inequalities. Here and there, a ravine would be rendered passable by placing across it two long trunks of trees, often at a sharp angle, and crossing these transversely with shorter logs; the whole covered with brush-wood and earth, and dignified with the name of a "corduroy bridge."

At the Nottawasaga River, we found a log house recently erected, the temporary residence of Wellesley Richey, Esq., an Irish gentleman, then in charge of the new settlements thereabouts. Mr. Richey received us very courteously, and handed us over to the charge of an experienced guide, whose business it was to show lands to intending settlers—a very necessary precaution indeed, as after a mile or two the road ceased altogether.

For some miles further, the forest consisted of Norway and white pine, almost unmixed with any other timber. There is something majestic in these vast and thickly-set labyrinths of brown columnar stems averaging a hundred and fifty feet in height, perhaps, and from one to five in thickness, making a traveller feel somewhat like a Lilliputian Gulliver in a field of Brobdignagian wheat. It is singular to observe the effect of an occasional gust of wind in such situations. It may not even fan your cheek; but you hear a low surging sound, like the moaning of breakers in a calm sea, which gradually increases to a loud boisterous roar, still seemingly at a great distance; the branches remain in perfect repose, you can discover no evidence of a stirring breeze, till, looking perpendicularly upwards, you are astonished to see some patriarchal giant close at hand—six yards round and sixty high—which alone has caught the breeze, waving its huge fantastic arms wildly at a dizzy height above your head.

There are times when the hardiest woodman dares not enter the pine woods; when some unusually severe gale sweeping over them bends their strong but slender stems like willow wands, or catches the wide-spreading branches of the loftier trees with a force that fairly wrenches them out by the roots, which creeping along on the surface of the soil, present no very powerful resistance. Nothing but the close contiguity of the trees saves them from general prostration. Interlocked branches are every moment broken off and flung to a distance, and even the trunks clash, and as it were, whet themselves against each other, with a shock and uproar that startles the firmest nerves.

It were tedious to detail all the events of our morning's march: How armed with English fowling pieces and laden with ammunition, we momentarily expected to encounter some grisly she-bear, with a numerous family of cubs; or at the least a herd of deer or a flock of wild turkeys: how we saw 'nothing more dangerous than woodpeckers with crimson heads, hammering away at decayed trees like transmigrated carpenters; how we at last shot two partridges sitting on branches, very unlike English ones, of which we were fain to make a meal, which was utterly detestable for want of salt ; how the government guide led us, helter-skelter, into the untracked woods, walking as for a wager, through thickets of ground hemlock,* which

---

* Taxus Canadensis, or Canadian Yew, is a trailing evergreen shrub which covers the ground in places. Its stems are as strong as cart-ropes, and often reach the length of twenty feet,

entangled our feet and often tripped us up ; how we were obliged to follow him over and under wind-falls, to pass which it was necessary to climb sometimes twenty feet along some half-recumbent tree ; how when we enquired whether clay or sand were considered the best soil, he said some preferred one, and some the other ; how he showed us the front of a lot that was bad, and guessed that the rear ought to be better; how we turned back at last, thoroughly jaded, but no wiser than when we set out—all this and much more, must be left to the reader's imagination.

It was drawing towards evening. The guide strode in advance, tired and taciturn, like some evil fate. We followed in pairs, each of us provided with a small bunch of leafy twigs to flap away the mosquitoes, which rose in myriads from the thick, damp underbrush.

"It will be getting dark," said the guide, "you must look out for the blaze."

We glanced anxiously around. "What does he mean?" asked one of the party, "I see no blaze."

The man explained that the blaze (query, blazon ?) was a white mark which we had noticed on some of the trees in our route, made by slicing off a portion of the bark with an axe, and invariably used by surveyors to indicate the road, as well as divisions and sub-divisions of townships. After a time this mark loses its whiteness and becomes undistinguishable in the dusk of evening, even to an experienced eye.

Not a little rejoiced were we, when we presently saw a genuine blaze in the form of a log fire, that brilliantly lighted up the forest in front of a wigwam, which, like everything else on that eventful day, was to us delightfully new and interesting. We found, seated on logs near the fire, two persons in blanket coats and red sashes, evidently gentlemen; and occupying a second wigwam at a little distance, half-a-dozen axemen. The gentlemen proved to be the Messrs. Walker, afterwards of Barrie, sons of the wealthy owner of the great shot-works at Waterloo Bridge, London, England. They had purchased a tract of a thousand acres, and commenced operations by hiring men to cut a road through the forest eight or ten miles to their new estate, which pioneering exploit they were now superintending in person. Nothing could exceed the vigour of their plans. Their property was to be enclosed in a ring fence like a park, to exclude trespassers on their game. They would have herds of deer and wild horses. The river which intersected their land was to be cleared of the drift logs, and made navigable. In short, they meant to convert it into another England. In the meanwhile, the elder brother had cut his foot with an axe, and was disabled for the present; and the younger was busily engaged in the unromantic occupation of frying pancakes, which the axemen, who were unskilled in cookery, were to have for their supper,

Nowhere does good-fellowship spring up so readily as in the bush. We were soon engaged in discussing the aforesaid pancakes, with some fried pork, as well as in sharing the sanguine hopes and bright visions which accorded so well with our own ideas and feelings.

We quitted the wigwam and its cheerful tenants with mutual good wishes for success, and shortly afterwards reached the river whence we had started, where Mr. Richey kindly invited us to stay for the night. Exhausted by our rough progress, we slept soundly till the morning sun shone high over the forest.

CHAPTER XI.

A CHAPTER ON CHOPPING.

IMAGINE yourself, gentle reader, who have perhaps passed most of your days between the wearisome confinement of an office or counting-house, and a rare holiday visit of a few days or weeks at your cousin's or grandfather's pleasant farm in the country—imagine yourself, I say, transplanted to a " home " like ours. No road approaches within ten miles; no footpath nearer than half that distance; the surveyor's blaze is the sole distinctive mark between the adjoining lots and your own; there are trees innumerable—splendid trees—beech, maple, elm, ash, cherry—above and around you, which, while you are wondering what on earth to do with them, as you see no chance of conveying them to market for sale, you are horrified to hear, must be consumed by fire—yea, burnt ruthlessly to ashes, and scattered over the surface of the earth as "good manure"; unless indeed—a desperately forlorn hope—you may "some day" have an opportunity of selling them in the shape of potash, "when there is a road out" to some navigable lake or river.

Well, say you, let us set to work and chop down some of these trees. Softly, good sir. In the first place, you must underbrush. With an axe or a strong, long handled bill-hook, made to be used with both hands, you cut away for some distance round—a quarter or half an acre perhaps—all the small saplings and underwood which would otherwise impede your operations upon the larger trees. In "a good hard-wood bush," that is, where the principal timber is maple, white oak, elm, white ash, hickory, and other of the harder species of timber—the "underbrush" is very trifling indeed; and in an hour or two may be cleared off sufficiently to give the forest an agreeable park-like appearance—so much so that, as has been said of English Acts of Parliament, any skilful hand might drive a coach and six through.

When you have finished "under-brushing," you stand with whetted axe, ready and willing to attack the fathers of the forest—but stay—you don't know how to chop? It is rather doubtful, as you have travelled hither in a great hurry, whether you have ever seen an axeman at work. Your man, Carroll, who has been in the country five or six years, and is quite *au fait*, will readily instruct you. Observe—you strike your axe, by a dexterous swing backwards and round over your shoulder,—take care there are no twigs near you, or you may perhaps hurt yourself seriously—you strike your axe into the tree with a downward slant, at about thirty inches from the ground; then, by an upward stroke you meet the former incision and release a chip, which flies out briskly. Thus you proceed, by alternate downward and upward or horizontal strokes on that side of the tree which leans over, or towards which you wish to compel it to fall, until you have made a clear gap rather more than half way through, when you attack it in rear.

Now for the reward of your perspiring exertions —a few well-aimed blows on the reverse side of the tree, rather higher than in front, and the vast mass " totters to its fall,"—another for the *coup-de-grace* —crack! crack! cra-a-ack!—aha!—away with you behind yon beech—the noble tree bows gently its leafy honours with graceful sweep towards the earth—for a moment slowly and leisurely, presently with giddy velocity, until it strikes the ground, amidst a whirlwind of leaves, with a loud *thud*, and a concussion both of air and earth, that may be *felt* at a considerable distance. You feel yourself a second David, who has overthrown a mightier Goliath.

Now do you step exultingly upon the prostrate trunk, which you forthwith proceed to cut up into about fourteen-foot lengths, chopping all the branches close off, and throwing the smaller on to your brush piles. It is a common mistake of new immigrants, who are naturally enough pleased with the novel spectacle of falling trees, to cut down so many before they begin to chop them into lengths, that the ground is wholly encumbered, and becomes a perfect chaos of confused and heaped-up trunks and branches, which nothing but the joint operation of decay and fire will clear off, unless at an immense waste of time and trouble. To an experienced axeman, these first attempts at chopping afford a ready text for all kinds of ironical comments upon the unworkmanlike appearance of the stumps and "cuts," which are generally—like those gnawn off by beavers in making their dams—haggled all round the tree, instead of presenting two clear smooth surfaces, in front and rear, as if sliced off with a knife. Your genuine axeman is not a little jealous of his reputation as a " clean cutter "-his axe is always bright as burnished silver, guiltless of rust or flaw, and fitted with a handle which, with its graceful curve and slender proportions, is a tolerable approach to Hogarth's "line of beauty;" he would as soon think of deserting his beloved "bush" and settling in a town ! as trust his keen weapon in the hands of inexperience or even mediocrity. With him every blow tells—he never leaves the slightest chip in the "cut," nor makes a false stroke, so that in passing your hand over the surface thus left, you are almost unable to detect roughness or inequality.

But we must return to our work, and take care in so doing to avoid the mishap which befel a settler in our neighbourhood. He was busy chopping away manfully at one of those numerous trees which, yielding to the force of some sudden gust of wind, have fallen so gently among their compeers, that the greater portion of their roots still retains a powerful hold upon the soil, and the branches put forth their annual verdure as regularly as when erect. Standing on the recumbent trunk, at a height of five or six feet from the ground, the man toiled away, in happy ignorance of his danger, until having chopped nearly to the centre on both sides of the tree, instead of leaping off and completing the cut in safety on terra firma, he dealt a mighty stroke which severed at once the slight portion that remained uncut—in an instant, as if from a mortar, the poor fellow was launched sixteen feet into the air, by the powerful elasticity of the roots, which, relieved from the immense weight of the trunk and branches, reverted violently to their natural position, and flung their innocent releaser to the winds. The astonished chopper, falling on his back, lay stunned for many minutes, and when he was at length able to rise, crawled to his shanty sorely bruised and bewildered. He was able, however, to return to his work in a few days, but not without vowing earnestly never again to trust himself next the root.

There are other precautions to be observed, such as whether the branches interlock with other trees, in which case they will probably break off, and must be carefully watched, lest they fall or are flung back upon oneself—what space you have to escape at the last moment—whether the tree is likely to be caught and twisted aside in its fall, or held upright, a very dangerous position, as then you must cut down others to release it, and can hardly calculate which way it will tend: these and many other circumstances are to be noted and watched with a cool judgment and steady eye, to avoid the numerous accidents to which the inexperienced and rash are constantly exposed. One of these mischances befel an Amazonian chopper of our neighbourhood, whose history, as we can both chop and talk, I shall relate.

Mary —— was the second of several daughters of an emigrant from the county of Galway, whose family, having suffered from continual hardship and

privation in their native land, had found no difficulty in adapting themselves to the habits and exi-
gencies of the wilderness.

Hardworking they were all and thrifty. Mary
and her elder sister, neither of them older than
eighteen, would start before day-break to the nearest store, seventeen miles off, and return the same
evening laden each with a full sack flung across the
shoulder, containing about a bushel and a half, or
90lbs. weight of potatoes, destined to supply food
for the family, as well as seed for their first crop.
Being much out of doors, and accustomed to work
about the clearing, Mary became in time a "first-
rate" chopper, and would yield to none of the new
settlers in the dexterity with which she would fell,
brush and cut up maple or beech; and preferring
such active exercise to the dull routine of household
work, took her place at chopping, logging or burning, as regularly and with at least as much spirit as
her brothers. Indeed, chopping is quite an accom-
plishment among young women in the more remote
parts of the woods, where schools are unknown, and
fashions from New York or Philadelphia have not
yet penetrated. A belle of this class will employ
her leisure hours in learning to play—not the piano-
forte—but the dinner-horn, a bright tin tube sometimes nearly four feet in length, requiring the lungs
of that almost forgotten individual, an English mail-
coach-guard; and an intriguing mamma of those

parts will bid her daughter exhibit the strength of
her throat and the delicacy of her musical ear,
by a series of flourishes and "mots" upon her graceful "tooting-weapon." I do not mean, however,
that Mary possessed this fashionable acquirement,
as the neighbourhood had not then arrived at such
an advanced era of musical taste, but she made up
in hard work for all other deficiencies; and being
a good-looking, sunny-faced, dark-eyed, joyous-
hearted girl, was not a little admired among the
young axe-men of the township. But she preferred
remaining under her parents' roof-tree, where her
stout-arm and resolute disposition rendered her
absolute mistress of the household, to the indignity
of promising to "obey" any man, who could wield
no better axe than her own. At length it was
whispered that Mary's heart, long hard as rock-elm,
had become soft as basswood, under the combined
influence of the stalwart figure, handsome face and
good axe of Johnny, a lad of eighteen recently
arrived in the neighbourhood, who was born in one
of the early Scotch settlements in the Newcastle
District—settlements which have turned out a race
of choppers, accustomed from their infancy to
handle the axe, and unsurpassed in the cleanness
of their cut, the keenness of their weapon, or the
amount of cordwood they can chop, split and pile in
a day.

Many a fair denizen of the abodes of fashion might have envied Mary the bright smiles and gay greetings which passed between her and young Johnny, when they met in her father's clearing at sunrise to commence the day's work. It is common for axemen to exchange labour, as they prefer working in couples, and Johnny was under a treaty of this kind with Patsy, Mary's brother. But Patsy vacated his place for Mary, who was emulous of beating the young Scotch lad at his own weapon; and she had tucked up her sleeves and taken in the slack, as a sailor would say, of her dress—Johnny meanwhile laying aside his coat, waistcoat and neckcloth, baring his brawny arms, and drawing tight the bright scarlet sash round his waist—thus equipped for their favourite occupation, they chopped away in merry rivalry, at maple, elm, ash, birch and basswood—Johnny sometimes gallantly fetching water from the deliciously-cold natural spring that oozed out of the mossy hill-side, to quench Mary's thirst, and stealing now and then a kiss by way of guerdon—for which he never failed to get a vehement box on the ear, a penalty which, although it would certainly have annihilated any lover of less robust frame, he seemed nowise unwilling to incur again and again. Thus matters proceeded, the maiden by no means acknowledging herself beaten, and the young man too gallant to outstrip overmuch his fair opponent—until the harsh sound of the breakfast or dinner horn would summon both to the house, to partake of the rude but plentiful mess of " colcannon " and milk, which was to supply strength for a long and severe day's labour.

Alas! that I should have to relate the melancholy termination of poor Mary's unsophisticated career. Whether Johnny's image occupied her thoughts, to the exclusion of the huge yellow birch she was one day chopping, or that the wicked genius who takes delight in thwarting the course of true love had caught her guardian angel asleep on his post, I know not; but certain it is, that in an evil hour she miscalculated the cut, and was thoughtlessly continuing her work, when the birch, overbalancing, split upwards, and the side nearest to Mary, springing suddenly out, struck her a blow so severe as to destroy life instantaneously. Her yet warm remains were carried hastily to the house, and every expedient for her recovery that the slender knowledge of the family could suggest, was resorted to, but in vain. I pass over the silent agony of poor Johnny, and the heart-rending lamentations of the mother and sisters. In a decent coffin, contrived after many unsuccessful attempts by Johnny and Patsy, the unfortunate girl was carried to her grave, in the same field which she had assisted to clear, amid a concourse of simple-minded, coarsely-clad, but kindly sympathising neighbours, from all parts of the surrounding district. Many years have rolled away since I stood by Mary's fresh-made grave, and it may be that Johnny has forgotten his first love ; but I was told, that no other had yet taken the place of her, whom he once hoped to make his " bonny bride."

By this time you have cut down trees enough to enable you fairly to see the sky ! Yes, dear sir, it was entirely hidden before, and the sight is not, a little exhilarating to a new " bush-whacker." We must think of preparing fire-wood for the night.. It is highly amusing to see a party of axemen, just returning from their work, set about this necessary task. Four " hands " commence at once upon some luckless maple, whose excellent burning qualities ensure it the preference. Two on each side, they strike alternate blows—one with the right hand, his " mate " with the left—in a rapid succession of strokes that seem perfectly miraculous to the inexperienced beholder—the tree is felled in a trice—a dozen men jump upon it, each intent on exhibiting his skill by making his " cut " in the shortest possible time. The more modest select the upper end of the tree—the bolder attack the butt—their bright axes, flashing vividly in the sunbeams, are whirled around their heads with such velocity as to elude the eye—huge chips a foot broad are thrown off incessantly—they wheel round for the " back cut " at the same instant, like a file of soldiers facing about upon some enemy in rear—and in the space of two or three minutes, the once tall and graceful trunk lies dissevered in as many fragments as there are choppers.

It invariably astonishes new comers to observe with what dexterity and ease an axeman will fell a tree in the precise spot which he wishes it to occupy so as to suit his convenience in cutting it up, or in removing it by oxen to the log-pile where it is destined to be consumed. If it should happen to overhang a creek or "swale" (wet places where oxen cannot readily operate), every contrivance is resorted to, to overcome its apparently inevitable tendency. Choosing a time when not a breath of air is stirring to defeat his operations, or better still, when the wind is favourable, he cuts deeply into the huge victim on the side to which he wishes to throw it, until it actually trembles on the slight remaining support, cautiously regulating the direction of the "cut" so that the tree may not overbalance itself—then he gently fells among its branches on the reverse side all the smaller trees with which it may be reached —and last and boldest expedient of all, he cuts several "spring poles"—trimmed saplings from twenty to forty feet in length and four to eight inches thick—which with great care and labour are set up against the stem, and by the united strength and weight of several men used as spring levers, after the manner in which ladders are employed by firemen to overthrow tottering stacks of chimneys ; the squared end of these poles holding firmly in the rough bark, they slowly but surely compel the unwilling monster to obey the might of its hereditary ruler, man. With such certainty is this feat accomplished, that I have seen a solitary pine, nearly five feet thick and somewhere about a hundred and seventy feet in height, forced by this latter means, aided by the strength of two men only, against its decided natural bearing, to fall down the side of a mound, at the bottom of which a saw-pit was already prepared to convert it into lumber. The moment when the enormous mass is about yielding to its fate, is one of breathless interest—it sways alarmingly, as if it must inevitably fall backward, crushing poles and perhaps axemen to atoms in its overwhelming descent—ha! there is a slight cat's paw of air in our favour—cling to your pole—now! an inch or two gained !—the stout stick trembles and bends at the revulsive sway of the monstrous tree but still holds its own—drive your axe into the back cut—that helps her—again, another axe! soh, the first is loose—again !—she *must* go—both axes are fixed in the cut as immovably as her roots in the ground—another puff of wind—she sways the wrong way—no, no! hold on—she cracks—strike in again the slackened axes—bravo! one blow more—quick, catch your axe and clear out !—see! what a sweep —what a rush of wind—what an enormous top— down! down! how beautifully she falls—hurrah! *just in the right place !*

CHAPTER XII.

LIFE IN THE BACKWOODS.

WE had selected, on the advice of our guide, a tolerably good hard-wood lot in the centre of the Township of Sunnidale, part of which is now the site of the village of New Lowell, on the Northern Railway. To engage a yo"ng Scotch axeman from the County of Lanark, on the Ottawa river; to try our virgin axes upon the splendid maples and beeches which it seemed almost a profanation to destroy; to fell half an acre of trees; to build a bark wigwam for our night's lodging; and in time to put up a substantial log shanty, roofed with wooden troughs and " chinked " with slats and moss—these things were to us more than mortal felicity. Our mansion was twenty-five feet long and eighteen wide. At one end an open fire-place, at the other sumptuous beds laid on flatted logs, cushioned with soft hemlock twigs, redolent of turpentine and health. For our provisions, cakes made of flour; salt pork of the best; tea and coffee without milk; with the occasional luxury of a few partridges and pigeons, and even a haunch of venison of our own shooting; also some potatoes. We wanted no more. There were few other settlers within many miles, and those as raw as ourselves; so we mended our own clothes, did our own cooking, and washed our own linen.

Owing to the tedious length of our sea voyage, there was no time for getting in crops that year; not even fall wheat; so we had plenty of leisure to make ourselves comfortable for the winter. And we were by no means without visitors. Sometimes a surveyor's party sought shelter for the night on their way to the strangely-named townships of Alta and Zero—now Collingwood and St. Vincent. Among these were Charles Rankin, surveyor, now of London; his brother, Arthur Rankin, since M.P. for Essex; a young gentleman from England, now Dr. Barrett, late of Upper Canada College. By-and-by came some Chippawa Indians, *en route* to or from the Christian Islands of Lake Huron; we were great friends with them. I had made a sort of harp or zittern, and they were charmed with its simple music. Their mode of counting money on their fingers was highly comical—" one cop, one cop, one cop, three cop !" and so on up to twenty, which was the largest sum they could accomplish. At night, they wrapped their blankets round them, lay down on the bare earthen floor near the fire, and slept quietly till day-break, when they would start on their way with many smiles and hand-shakings. In fact, our shanty, being the only comfortable shelter between Barrie and the Georgian Bay, became a sort of half-way house, at which travellers looked for a night's lodging; and we were not sorry when the opening of a log-tavern, a mile off, by an old Scotchwoman, ycleped Mother McNeil, enabled us to select our visitors. This tavern was a curiosity in its way, built of the roughest logs, with no artificial floor, but the soil being swaley or wet—a mud-hole yawned just inside the door, where bull-frogs not unfrequently saluted the wayfarer with their deepest diapason notes.

I must record my own experiences with their congeners, the toads. We were annoyed by flies, and I noticed an old toad creep stealthily from under the house logs, wait patiently near a patch of sunshine on the floor, and as soon as two or three flies, attracted by the sun's warmth, drew near its post, dart out its long slender tongue, and so catch them all one after another. Improving upon the hint, we afterwards regularly scattered a few grains of sugar, to attract more flies within the old fellow's reach, and thus kept the shanty comparatively clear of those winged nuisances, and secured quiet repose for ourselves in the early mornings. Another toad soon joined the first one, and they became so much at home as to allow us to scratch their backs gently with a stick, when they would heave up their puffed sides to be scrubbed. These toads swallow mice and young ducks, and in their turn fall victims to garter and other snakes.

During the following year, 1834, the Government opened up a settlement on the Sunnidale road, employing the new immigrants in road making, chopping and clearing, and putting up log shanties; and gave them the land so cleared to live on, but without power of sale. In this way, two or three hundred settlers, English, Irish and Highland Scotch, chiefly the latter, were located in Sunnidale. A Scottish gentleman, a Mr. H. C. Young, was appointed local immigrant agent, and spent some time with us. Eventually it was found that the laud was too aguish for settlement, being close to a large cedar swamp extending several miles to the Nottawasaga River; and on the representation of the agent, it was in 1835 determined to transfer operations to the adjoining township of Nottawasaga, in which the town of Collingwood is now situated.

It was about this time that the prospect of a railway from Toronto to the Georgian Bay was first mooted, the mouth of the Nottawasaga River being the expected terminus. A talented Toronto engineer whose name I think was Lynn, published a pamphlet containing an outline route for the railroad, which was extended through to the North-West. To him, doubtless, is due the first practical suggestion of a Canadian Pacific Railway. We, in Sunnidale, were confidently assured that the line would pass directly through our own land, and many a weary sigh at hope deferred did the delusion cost us.

CHAPTER XIII.

SOME GATHERINGS FROM NATURAL HISTORY.

I NEED not weary the reader with details of our farming proceedings, which differed in no respect from the now well-known routine of bush life. I will, however, add one or two notices of occurrences which may be thought worth relating. We were not without wild animals in our bush. Bears, wolves, foxes, racoons, skunks, mink and ermine among beasts; eagles, jays, many kinds of hawks, wood-peckers, loons, partridges and pigeons, besides a host of other birds, were common enough. Bears' nests abounded, consisting of a kind of arbour which the bear makes for himself in the top of the loftiest beech trees, by dragging inwards all the upper branches laden with their wealth of nuts, upon which he feasts at leisure. The marks of his formidable claws are plainly visible the whole length of the trunks of most large beech-trees. In Canada West the bear is seldom dangerous. One old fellow which we often encountered, haunted 'a favourite raspberry patch on the road-side; when anybody passed near him he would scamper off in such haste that I have seen him dash himself violently against any tree or fallen branch that might be in his way.

Once we saw a bear roll himself headlong from the forks of a tree fully forty feet from the ground, tumbling over and over, but alighting safely, and " making tracks " with the utmost expedition.

An Englishman whom I knew, of a very studious temperament, was strolling along the Medonte road deeply intent upon a volume of Ovid or some other Latin author, when, looking up to ascertain the cause of a shadow which fell across his book, he found himself nearly stumbling against a huge brown bear, standing erect on its hind legs, and with formidable paw raised ready to strike. The surprise seems to have been mutual, for after waiting a moment or two as if to recognise each other's features should they meet again, the student merely said " Oh ! a bear !" coolly turned on his heel, plunged into his book again, and walked slowly back toward the village, leaving Bruin to move off at leisure in an opposite direction. So saith my informant.

Another friend, when a youth, was quail-shooting on the site of the City of Toronto, which was nothing but a rough swampy thicket of cedars and pines mixed with hardwood. Stepping hastily across a rotten pine log, the lad plumped full upon a great fat bear taking its siesta in the shade. Which of the two fled the fastest is not known, but it was probably the animal, judging by my own experience in Sunnidale.

Wolves often disturbed us with their hideous howlings. We had a beautiful liver and white English setter, called Dash, with her two pups. One night in winter, poor Dash, whom we kept within doors, was excited by the yelping of her pups outside, which appeared to be alarmed by some intruder about the premises. A wolf had been seen prowling near, so we got out our guns and whatever weapon was handy, but incautiously opened the door and let out the slut before we were ourselves quite dressed. She rushed out in eager haste, and in a few seconds we heard the wolf and dog fighting, with the most frightful discord of yells and howls that ever deafened the human ear. The noise ceased as suddenly as it had begun. We followed as fast as we could to the scene of the struggle, but found nothing there except a trampled space in the snow stained with blood, the dog having evidently been killed and dragged away. Next morning we followed the track further, and found at no great distance another similar spot, where the wolf had devoured its victim so utterly, that not a hair, bone, nor anything else was left, save the poor animal's heart, which had been flung away to a little distance in the snow. Beyond this were no signs of blood. We set a trap for the wolf, and tracked him for miles in the hope of avenging poor Dash, but without effect. This same wolf, we heard afterwards, was killed by a settler with a handspike, to our great satisfaction.

Among our neighbours of the Sunnidale settlement was a married couple from England, named Sewell, very well-conducted and industrious. They had a fair little child under two years old, named Hetty, whom we often stopped to admire for her prettiness and engaging simplicity. They also possessed, and were very proud of, several broods of newly-hatched chickens, some of which had been carried off by an immense falcon, which would swoop down from the lofty elm-trees still left standing in the half-chopped clearing, too suddenly to be easily shot. One day Hetty was feeding the young chickens when the hawk pounced upon the old hen, which struggled desperately; whereupon little Hetty bravely joined in the battle, seized the intruder by the wings from behind and held him fast, crying out loudly, "I've got him, mother!" It turned out, after the hawk was killed, that it had been blind of one eye.

In the spring of 1834, we had with infinite labour managed to clear off a small patch of ground, which we sowed with spring wheat, and watched its growth with the most intense anxiety, until it attained a height of ten inches, and began to put forth tender ears. Already the exquisite pleasure of eating bread the product of our own land, and of our own labour, was present to our imaginations, and the number of bushels to be reaped, the barn for storage, the journeys to mill, were eagerly dis-

cussed. But one day in August, occurred a hail-
storm such as is seldom experienced in half a century. A perfect cataract of ice fell upon our hapless wheat crop. Flattened hailstones measuring
two and a half inches in diameter, seven and a half
in circumference, covered the ground several inches
deep. Every blade of wheat was utterly destroyed,
and with it all our sanguine hopes of plenty for that
year. I have preserved a tracing which I made at
the time, of one of those hailstones. The centre was
spherical, an inch in girth, from which laterally radi-
ated lines three fourths of an inch long, like the
spokes of a wheel, and outside of them again a wavy
border resembling the undulating edge of pie crust.
The superficial structure of the whole, was much
like that of a full blown rose. A remarkable hail-
storm occurred in Toronto, in the year 1878, but the
stones, although similar in formation, were scarcely
as bulky.

It was one night in November following, when
our axeman, William Whitelaw, who had risen from
bed at eleven o'clock to fetch a new log for the fire
shouted to us to come out and see a strange sight.
Lazily we complied, expecting nothing extraordinary ; but, on getting into the cold frosty air outside, we were transfixed with astonishment and admiration. Our clearing being small, and the timber
partly hemlock, we seemed to be environed with a
dense black wall the height of the forest trees, while

E

over all, in dazzling splendour, shone a canopy of the most brilliant meteors, radiating in all directions from a single point in the heavens, nearly over-head, but slightly to the north-west. I have since read all the descriptions of meteoric showers I could find in our scientific annals, and watched year after year for a return of the same wonderful vision, but neither in the records of history nor otherwise, since that night, have I read of or seen anything so marvellously beautiful. Hour after hour we gazed in wonder and awe, as the radiant messengers streamed on their courses, sometimes singly, sometimes in starry cohorts of thousands, appearing to descend amongst the trees close beside us, but in reality shooting far beyond the horizon. Those who have looked upwards during a fall of snow will remember how the large flakes seem to radiate from a centre. Thus I believe astronomers account for the appearance of these showers of stars, by the circumstance that they meet the earth full in its orbit, and so dart past it from an opposite point, like a flight of birds confronting a locomotive, or a storm of hail directly facing a vessel under full steam. No description I have read has given even a faint idea of the reality as I saw it on that memorable night. From eleven p.m. to three in the morning, the majestic spectacle continued in full glory, gradually fading away before the appeoach of daybreak.

We often had knotty and not very logical discussions about the origin of seeds, and the cause of the thick growth of new varieties of plants and trees wherever the forest had been burnt over. On our land, and everywhere in the immediate neighbourhood, the process of clearing by fire was sure to be followed by a spontaneous growth, first of fire-weed or wild lettuce, and secondly by a crop of young cherry trees, so thick as to choke one another. At other spots, where pine-trees had stood for a century, the outcome of their destruction by fire was invariably a thick growth of raspberries, with poplars of the aspen variety. Our Celtic friends, most of whom were pious Presbyterians, insisted that a new creation of plants must be constantly going on to account for such miraculous growth. To test the matter, I scooped up a panful of black soil from our clearing, washed it, and got a small tea-cupful of cherry-stones, exactly similar to those growing in the forest. The cause of this surprising accumulation of seed was not far to find. A few miles distant was a pigeon-roost. In spring, the birds would come flying round the east shore of Lake Huron, skirting the Georgian Bay, in such vast clouds as to darken the sun; and so swiftly that swan-shot failed to bring them down unless striking them in rear; and, even then, we rarely got them, as the velocity of their flight impelled them far into the thicket before falling. These beautiful creatures attacked our crops with serious results, and devoured all our young peas. I have known twenty-five pigeons killed at a single shot ; and have myself got a dozen by firing at random into a maple-tree on which they had alighted, but where not one had been visible.

The pigeon-roost itself was a marvel. Men, women and children went by the hundred, some with guns, but the majority with baskets, to pick up the countless birds that had been disabled by the fall of great branches of trees broken off by the weight of their roosting comrades overhead. The women skinned the birds, cut off their plump breasts, throwing the remainder away, and packed them in barrels with salt, for keeping. To these pigeons we were, doubtless, indebted for our crop of young cherry-trees.

Where there was so much seed, a corresponding crop might be expected ; and dense thickets of choke-cherry trees grew up in neglected clearings accordingly. Forcing my way through one of these, I found myself literally face to face with a garter snake five feet long, which was also in search of cherries, and had wriggled its way to the upper branches of a young tree ten feet high. Garter snakes, however, are as harmless as frogs, and like them, are the victims of a general persecution. In some places they are exceedingly numerous. One summer's evening I was travelling on foot from Holland Landing to Bradford, across the Holland river, a distance of three miles, nearly all marsh, laid with cedar logs placed crosswise, to form a passable road. The sun was nearing the horizon ; the snakes—

garter chiefly, but a few copperhead and black— glided on to the logs to bask apparently in the sunshine, in such numbers, that after vainly trying to step across without treading on them, I was fain to take to flight, springing from log to log like some long-legged bird, and so escaping from the unpleasant companionship.*

One of the most perplexing tasks to new settlers is that of keeping cows. " Bossy " soon learns that the bush is "all before her where to choose," and she indulges her whims by straying away in the most unexpected directions, and putting you to half-a-day's toilsome search before she can be captured. The obvious remedy is the cow-bell, but even with this tell-tale appendage, the experienced cow contrives to baffle your vigilance. She will ensconce herself in the midst of a clump of underbrush, lying perfectly still, and paying no heed to your most endearing appeals of " Co' bossy, co' bossy," until some fly-sting obliges her to jerk her head and betray her hiding-place by a single note of the bell. Then she will deliberately get up, and walk off straight to the shanty, ready to be milked.

---

* It is affirmed that in two or three localities in Manitoba, garter snakes sometimes congregate in such multitudes as to form ropes as thick as a man's leg, which, by their constant writhing and twining in and out, present a strangely glittering and moving spectacle.

CHAPTER XIV.

OUR REMOVAL TO NOTTAWASAGA.

IN the autumn of 1835, we were favoured with a
visit from Mr. A. B. Hawke, chief emigrant
agent for Upper Canada, and a gentleman held in
general esteem, as a friend to emigrants, and a
kind-hearted man. He slept, or rather tried to
sleep, at our shanty. It was very hot weather, the
mosquitoes were in full vigour, and the tortures they
inflicted on the poor man were truly pitiable. We
being acclimatised, could cover our heads, and lie
perdu, sleeping in spite of the humming hosts outside. But our visitor had learnt no such philosophy.
He threw off the bedclothes on account of the heat;
slapped his face and hands to kill his tormentors;
and actually roared with pain and anger, relieving
himself now and then by objurgations mingled with
expletives not a little profane. It was impossible
to resist laughing at the desperate emphasis of his
protests, although our mirth did not help much to
soothe the annoyance, at which, however, he could
not help laughing in turn.

Mosquitoes do not plague all night, and our friend
got a little repose in the cool of the morning, but
vowed, most solemnly, that nothing should induce
him to pass another night in Sunnidale.

To this circumstance, perhaps, were we indebted for the permission we soon afterwards obtained, to exchange our Sunnidale lot for one in Nottawasaga, where some clearing had been done by the new settlers, on what was called the Scotch line; and gladly we quitted our first location for land decidedly more eligible for farm purposes, although seventeen miles further distant from Barrie, which was still the only village within reasonably easy access.

We had obtained small government contracts for corduroying, or causewaying, the many swampy spots on the Sunnidale road, which enabled us to employ a number of axemen, and to live a little more comfortably; and about this time, Mr. Young being in weak health, and unequal to the hardships of bush life, resigned his agency, and got my brother Thomas appointed temporarily as his successor; so we had the benefit of a good log-house he had built on the Nottawasaga road, near the Batteau creek, on which is now situated the Batteau station of the Northern Railway. We abode there until we found time to cut a road to our land, and afterwards to erect a comfortable cedar-log house thereon.

Here, with a large open clearing around us, plenty of neighbours, and a sawmill at no great distance, we were able to make our home nearly as comfortable as are the majority of Canadian farm-houses of to-day. We had a neat picket-fenced garden, a large double log barn, a yoke of oxen, and plenty of poultry. The house stood on a handsome rising eminence, and commanded a noble prospect, which included the Georgian Bay, visible at a distance of six miles, and the Christian Islands, twenty miles further north. The land was productive, and the air highly salubrious.

Would some of my readers like to know how to raise a log barn? I shall try to teach them. For such an undertaking much previous labour and foresight are required. In our case, fortunately, there was a small cedar swamp within a hundred paces of the site we had chosen for our barn, which was picturesquely separated from the house by a ravine some thirty feet deep, with a clear spring of the sweetest and coldest water flowing between steep banks. The barn was to consist of two large bays, each thirty feet square aud eight logs high, with a threshing floor twelve feet wide between, the whole combined into one by an upper story or loft, twenty by seventy-two feet, and four logs high, including the roof-plates.

It will be seen, then, that to build such a barn would require sixty-four logs of thirty feet each for the lower story; and sixteen more of the same length, as well as eight of seventy-two feet each, for the loft. Our handy swamp provided all these, not from standing trees only, but from many fallen patriarchs buried four or five feet under the surface in black muck, and perfectly sound. To get them out of the mud required both skill and patience. All the branches having been cleared off as thoroughly as possible, the entire tree was drawn out by those most patient of all patient drudges, the oxen, and when on solid ground, sawn to the required length. A number of skids were also provided, of the size and kind of the spring-poles already described in chapter XI., and plenty of handspikes.

Having got these prime essentials ready, the next business was to summon our good neighbours to a "raising bee." On the day named, accordingly, we had about thirty practised axemen on the ground by day-break, all in the best of spirits, and confident in their powers for work. Eight of the heaviest logs, about two feet thick, had been placed in position as sleepers or foundation logs, duly saddled at the corners. Parallel with these at a distance of twenty-feet on either side, were ranged in order all the logs required to complete the building.

Well, now we begin. Eight of the smartest men jump at once on the eight corners. In a few minutes each of the four men in front has his saddle ready—that is, he has chopped his end of the first log into an angular shape, thus $\wedge$. The four men in rear have done the same thing no less expeditiously, and all are waiting for the next log. Meanwhile, at the ends of both bays, four several parties of three men each, stationed below, have placed their skids in a sloping position—the upper end on the rising wall and the lower on the ground —and up these skids they roll additional logs transversely to those already in position. These are received by the corner-men above, and carefully adjusted in their places according to their " natural lie," that is, so that they will be least likely to render the wall unsteady ; then turned half-back to receive the undercut, which should be exactly an inverse counterpart of the saddle. A skilful hand will make this undercut with unerring certainty, so that the log when turned forward again, will fit down upon its two saddles without further adjustment. Now for more logs back and front ; then others at the ends, and so on, every log fitted as before, and each one somewhat lighter than its predecessor. All this time the oxen have been busily employed in drawing more logs where needed. The skids have to be re-adjusted for every successive log, and a supply of new logs rolled up as fast as wanted. The quick strokes of eight axes wielded by active fellows perched on the still rising walls, and balancing themselves dexterously and even gracefully as they work, the constant demand for " another log," and the merry voices and rough jokes of the workers, altogether form as lively and exciting a picture as is often witnessed. Add to these a bright sky and a fresh breeze, with the beautiful green back-ground of the noble hardwood trees around— and I know of no mere pleasure party that I would rather join.

Breakfast and dinner form welcome interludes. Ample stores of provender, meat, bread, potatoes, puddings various, tea and coffee, have been prepared and are thoroughly enjoyed, inasmuch as they are rare luxuries to many of the guests. Then again to work, until the last crowning effort of all—the raising of the seventy-two-foot logs—has to be encountered. Great care is necessary here, as accidents are not infrequent. The best skids, the stoutest handspikes, the strongest and hardiest men, must be selected. Our logs being cedar and therefore light, there was comparatively little danger; and they were all successfully raised, and well secured by cross-girders before sundown.

Then, and not till then, after supper, a little whiskey was allowed. Teetotalism had not made its way into our backwoods; and we were considered very straightlaced indeed to set our faces as we did against all excess. Our Highland and Irish neighbours looked upon the weak stuff sold in Canada with supreme contempt; and recollecting our Galway experience, we felt no surprise thereat.

The roofing such a building is a subsequent operation, for which no "bee" is required. Shingles four feet long, on round rafters, are generally used for log barns, to be replaced at some future day by more perfect roofing. A well-made cedar barn will stand for forty years with proper care, by which time there should be no difficulty in replacing it by a good substantial, roomy frame building.

CHAPTER XV.

SOCIETY IN THE BACKWOODS.

SIR JOHN COLBORNE, as has been mentioned already, did all in his power to induce well-to-do immigrants, and particularly military men, to settle on lands west and north of Lake Simcoe. Some of these gentlemen were entitled, in those days, to draw from three to twelve hundred acres of land in their own right ; but the privilege was of very doubtful value. Take an example. Captain Workman, with his wife, highly educated and thoroughly estimable people, were persuaded to select their land on the Georgian Bay, near the site of the present village of Meaford. A small rivulet which enters the bay there, is still called " the Captain's creek." To get there, they had to go to Penetanguishene, then a military station, now the seat of a Reformatory for boys. From thence they embarked on scows, with their servants, furniture, cows, farm implements and provisions. Rough weather obliged them to land on one of the Christian Islands, very bleak spots outside of Penetanguishene harbour, occupied only by a few Chippewa Indians. After nearly two weeks' delay and severe privation, they at length reached their destination, and had then to camp out until a roof could be put up to shelter them from the storms, not uncommon on that exposed coast.

We had ourselves, along with others, taken up additional land on what was called " the Blue Mountains," which are considered to be a spur of the Alleghanies, extending northerly across by Niagara, from the State of New York. The then newly-surveyed townships of St. Vincent and Euphrasia were attracting settlers, and amongst them our axeman, Whitelaw, and many more of the like class. To reach this land, we had bought a smart sail-boat, and in her enjoyed ourselves by coasting from the Nottawasaga river north-westerly along the bay. In this way we happened one evening to put in at the little harbour where Capt. Workman had chosen his location. It was early in the spring. The snows from the uplands had swelled the rivulet into a rushing torrent. The garden, prettily laid out, was converted into an island, the water whirling and eddying close to the house both in front and rear, and altogether presenting a scene of wild confusion. We found the captain highly excited, but bravely contending with his watery adversary; the lady of the house in a state of alarmed perplexity; the servants at their wits' end, hurrying here and there with little effect. Fortunately, when we got there the actual danger was past, the waters subsiding rapidly during the night. But it struck us as a most cruel and inconsiderate act on the part of the Government, to expose tenderly reared families to hazards which even the rudest of rough pioneers would not care to encounter.

After enduring several years of severe hardship, and expending a considerable income in this out-of-the-world spot, Captain Workman and his family removed to Toronto, and afterwards returned to England, wiser, perhaps, but no richer certainly, than when they left the old country.

A couple of miles along the shore, we found another military settler, Lieutenant Waddell, who had served as brigade-major at the Battle of Waterloo ; with him were his wife, two sons, and two daughters. On landing, the first person we encountered was the eldest son, John, a youth of twenty years—six feet in stature at least, and bearing on his shoulder, sustained by a stick thrust through its gills, a sturgeon so large that its tail trailed on the ground behind him. He had just caught it with a floating line. Here again the same melancholy story : ladies delicately nurtured, exposed to rough labour, and deprived of all the comforts of civilized life, exhausting themselves in weary struggle with the elements. Brave soldiers in the decline of life, condemned to tasks only adapted to hinds and navvies. What worse fate can be reserved for Siberian exiles ! This family also soon removed to Toronto, and afterwards to Niagara, where the kindly, excellent old soldier is well remembered ; then to Chatham, where he became barrack-master, and died there. His son, John Waddell, married into the Eberts family, and prospered ; later he was member for Kent ; and ultimately met his death by drowning on a lumbering excursion in the Georgian Bay. Other members of the family now reside at Goderich.

Along the west shore of Lake Simcoe, several other military and naval officers, with their households, were scattered. Some, whose names I shall not record, had left their families at home, and brought out with them female companions of questionable position, whom, nevertheless, they introduced as their wives. The appearance of the true wives rid the county of the scandal and its actors.

Conspicuous among the best class of gentlemen settlers was the late Col. E. G. O'Brien, of Shanty Bay, near Barrie, of whom I shall have occasion to speak hereafter. Capt. St. John, of Lake Couchiching, was equally respected. The Messrs. Lally, of Medonte ; Walker, of Tecumseth and Barrie ; Sibbald, of Kempenfeldt Bay ; are all names well known in those days, as are also many others of the like class. But where are the results of the policy which sent them there ? What did they gain—what have their families and descendants gained—by the ruinous outlay to which they were subjected ? With one or two exceptions, absolutely nothing but wasted means and saddest memories.

It is pleasant to turn to a different class of settlers
—the hardy Scots, Irish, English, and Germans, to
whom the Counties of Simcoe and Grey stand indebted for their present state of prosperity. The Sunnidale settlement was ill-chosen, and therefore a failure. But in the north of that township, much better land and a healthier situation are found, and
there, as well as in Nottawasaga adjoining, the true
conditions of rational colonization, and the practical
development of those conditions, are plainly to be
seen.

The system of clearing five acre lots, and erecting
log shanties thereon, to be given to immigrants without power of sale, which was commenced in Sunnidale, was continued in Nottawasaga. The settlement
was called the Scotch line, nearly all the people being from the islands of Arran and Islay, lying off
Argyleshire, in Scotland. Very few of them knew
a word of English. There were Campbells, McGil-
livrays, Livingstons, McDiarmids, McAlmons, Mc-
Nees, Jardines, and other characteristic names. The
chief man among them was Angus Campbell, who
had been a tradesman of some kind in the old country, and exercised a beneficial influence over the rest.
He was well informed, sternly Presbyterian, and often
reminded us of " douce Davie Deans " in the "Heart
of Midlothian." One of the Livingstons was a school-
master. They were, one and all, hardy and industrious folk. Day after day, month after month,

year after year, added to their wealth and comfort.
Cows were purchased, and soon became common.
There were a few oxen and horses before long.
When I visited the township of Nottawasaga some
years since, I found Angus Campbell, postmaster and
justice of the peace; Andrew Jardine, township clerk
or treasurer; and McDiarmids, Livingstons, Shaws,
&c., spread all over the surrounding country, possessing large farms richly stocked, good barns well-filled, and even commodious frame houses comfortably
furnished.   They ride to church or market in handsome buggies well horsed; have their temperance
meetings and political gatherings of the most zealous
sort, and altogether present a model specimen of a
prosperous farming community.   What has been
said of the Scotch, is no less applicable to the Irish,
Germans and English, who formed the minority in
that township.   I hear of their sons, and their sons'
sons, as thriving farmers and storekeepers, all over
Ontario.

Our axeman, Whitelaw, was of Scottish parentage,
but a Canadian by birth, and won his way with the
rest. He settled in St. Vincent, married a smart and
pretty Irish lass, had many sons and daughters, acquired a farm of five hundred acres, of which he
cleared and cultivated a large portion almost single-
handed, and in time became able to build the finest
frame house in the township; served as reeve, was
a justice of peace, and even a candidate for parlia-

F

ment, in which, well for himself, he failed. His excessive labours, however, brought on asthma, of which he died not long since, leaving several families of descendants to represent him.,

I could go on with the list of prosperous settlers of this class, to fill a volume. Some of the young men entered the ministry, and I recognise their names occasionally at Presbyterian and Wesleyan conventions. Some less fortunate were tempted away to Iowa and Illinois, and there died victims to ague and heat.

But if we "look on this picture and on that;" if we compare the results of the settlement of educated people and of the labouring classes, the former withering away and leaving no sign behind—the latter growing in numbers and advancing in wealth and position until they fill the whole land, it is impossible to avoid the conclusion, that except as leaders and teachers of their companions, gentlefolk of refined tastes and of superior education, have no place in the bush, and should shun it as a wild delusion and a cruel snare.

CHAPTER XVI.

MORE ABOUT NOTTAWASAGA AND ITS PEOPLE.

AMONG the duties handed over to my brother Thomas, by his predecessor in the emigrant agency, was the care of a large medicine chest full of quinine, rhubarb, jalap, and a host of other drugs, strong enough for horses as well as men, including a long catalogue of poisons, such as arsenic, belladonna, vitriol, &c. To assist in the distribution of this rather formidable charge, a copy of " Buchan's Domestic Medicine " was added. My brother had no taste for drugs, and therefore deputed the care of the medicine chest to me. So I studied " Buchan " zealously, and was fortunate enough to secure the aid of an old army sergeant, an Irishman who had been accustomed to camp hospital life, and knew how to bleed, and treat wounds. Time and practice gave me courage to dispense the medicines, which I did cautiously, and so successfully as to earn the soubriquet of "Doctor," and to be sought after in cases both dangerous and difficult. As, however, about this time, a clever, licensed practitioner had established himself at Barrie, thirty-four miles distant, I declined to prescribe in serious cases, except in one or two of great urgency. A Prussian soldier named

Murtz, had received a gun-shot wound in the chest at the battle of Quatre Bras, under Marshal Blücher, and had frequently suffered therefrom.   One day in winter, when the thermometer ranged far below zero, this man had been threshing in our barn, when he was seized with inflammation of the chest, and forced to return home.   As it appeared to be a case of life and death, I ventured to act boldly, ordered bleeding, a blister on the chest, and poultices to the feet —in fact, everything that Buchan directed.   My brave serjeant took charge of the patient; and between us, or perhaps in spite of us, the man got over the attack.   The singular part of the case was, that the old bullet wound never troubled him afterwards, and he looked upon me as the first of living physicians.

In 1836, a band of Potawatomie Indians, claiming allegiance to the Queen, was allowed to leave the State of Michigan and settle in Canada.   They travelled from Sarnia through the woods, along the eastern shore of Lake Huron, and passed through Nottawasaga, on their way to Penetanguishene.   Between the Scotch line and Sunnidale, near the present village of Stayner, lived an old Highland piper named Campbell, very partial to whiskey and dirt. There were two or three small clearings grouped together, and the principal crop was potatoes, nearly full grown.   The old man was sitting sunning himself at his shanty-door.   The young men were all

absent at mill or elsewhere, and none but women
and children about, when a party of Indians, men
and squaws with their papooses, came stealing from
the woods, and very quietly began to dig the potatoes with their fingers and fill their bags with the
spoil. The poor old piper was horribly frightened
and perplexed ; and in his agitation could think of
nothing but climbing on to his shanty roof, which
was covered with earth, and there playing with all
his might upon his Highland pipes, partly as a sum-
mons for assistance from his friends, partly to terrify
the enemy. But the enemy were not at all terrified.
They gathered in a ring round the shanty, laughed,
danced, and enjoyed the fun immensely ; nor would
they pass on until the return of some of the younger
settlers summoned by the din of the bagpipes, relieved the old piper from his elevated post. In the
meantime, the presence and efforts of the women of
the settlement sufficed to rescue their potato crop.

<hr>

CHAPTER XVII.

A RUDE WINTER EXPERIENCE.

THE chief inconvenience we sustained in Nottawasaga arose from the depth of snow in
winter, which was generally four feet and sometimes more. We had got our large log barn well

filled with grain and hay. Two feet of snow had fallen during the day, and it continued snowing throughout the night. Next morning, to our great tribulation, neither snow nor roof was to be seen on the barn, the whole having fallen inside. No time was to be lost. My share of the work was to hurry to the Scotch line, there to warn every settler to send at least one stout hand to assist in re-raising the roof. None but those who have suffered can imagine what it is to have to walk at speed through several feet of soft snow. The sinews of the knees very soon begin to be painfully affected, and finally to feel as if they were being cut with a sharp knife. This is what Indians call " snow evil," their cure for which is to apply a hot cinder to the spot, thus raising a blister. I toiled on, however, and once in the settlement, walked with comparative ease. Everybody was ready and eager to help, and so we had plenty of assistance at our need, and before night got our barn roof restored.

The practice of exchanging work is universal in new settlements; and, indeed, without it nothing of importance can be effected. Each man gives a day's work to his neighbour, for a logging or raising-bee; and looks for the same help when he is ready for it. Thus as many as twenty or forty able axemen can be relied upon at an emergency.

At a later time, some of us became expert in the use of snow-shoes, and took long journeys through

the woods, not merely with ease but with a great
deal of pleasure.   As a rule, snow is far from being
considered an evil in the backwoods, on account of
the very great facility it affords for travelling and
teaming, both for business and pleasure, as well as
for the aid it gives to the hunter or trapper.

My own feelings on the subject, I found leisure to
embody in the following verses:

THE TRAPPER.

Away, away! my dog and I;
  The woodland boughs are bare,
The radiant sun shines warm and high,
  The frost-flake* gems the air.

---

* On a fine, bright winter morning, when the slight
feathery crystals formed from the congealed dew, which
have silently settled on the trees during the night, are
wafted thence by the morning breeze, filling the translu-
cent atmosphere with innumerable minute, sparkling
stars; when the thick, strong coat of ice on the four-foot
deep snow is slightly covered by the same fine, white
dust, betraying the foot-print of the smallest wild animal—on such a morning the hardy trapper is best able
to follow his solitary pursuits.   In the glorious winters
of Canada, he will sometimes remain from home for
days, or even weeks, with no companions but his dog
and rifle, and no other shelter than such as his own
hands can procure—carried away by his ardour for the
sport, and the hope of the rich booty which usually rewards his perseverance.

Away, away ! thro' forests wide
    Our course is swift and free ;
Warm 'neath the snow the saplings hide—
    Its ice-crust firm pace we.

The partridge* with expanded crest
    Struts proudly by his mate ;
The squirrel trims its glossy vest,
    Or eats its nut in state.

Quick echoes answer, shrill and short,
    The woodcock's frequent cry ;
We heed them not—a keener sport
    We seek—my dog and I.

Far in the woods our traps are set
    In loneliest, thickest glade,
Where summer's soil is soft and wet,
    And dark firs lend their shade.

Hurrah ! a gallant spoil is here
    To glad a trapper's sight—
The warm-clad marten, sleek and fair,
    The ermine soft and white ;

---

* The partridge of Canada—a grey variety of grouse —not only displays a handsome black-barred tail like that of the turkey, but has the power of erecting his head-feathers, as well as of spreading a black fan-like tuft placed on either side of his neck. Although timid when alarmed, he is not naturally shy, but at times may be approached near enough to observe his very graceful and playful habits—a facility of access for which the poor bird commonly pays with his life.

Or mink, or fox—a welcome prize—
  Or useful squirrel grey,
Or wild-cat fierce with flaming eyes,
  Or fisher,* meaner prey.

On, on ! the cautious toils once more
  Are set—the task is done ;
Our pleasant morning's labour o'er,
  Our pastime but begun.

Away, away ! till fall of eve,
  The deer-track be our guide,
The antler'd stag our quarry brave,
  Our park the forest wide.

At night, the bright fire at our feet,
  Our couch the wigwam dry—
No laggard tastes a rest so sweet
  As thou, good dog, and I.

---

* Dr. Johnson, in one of his peculiar moods, has described the *fitchew* or *fitchat*, which is here called the "fisher" as "*a stinking little beast that robs the hen-roost and warren*"—a very ungrateful libel upon an animal that supplies exceedingly useful fur for common purposes.

CHAPTER XVIII.

THE FOREST WEALTH OF CANADA.

HAVING been accustomed to gardening all my life, I have taken great pleasure in roaming the bush in search of botanical treasures of all kinds, and have often thought that it would be easy to fill a large and showy garden with the native plants of Canada alone.

But of course, her main vegetable wealth consists in the forests with which the Provinces of Quebec and Ontario were formerly clothed. In the country around the Georgian Bay, especially, abound the very finest specimens of hardwood timber. Standing on a hill overlooking the River Saugeen at the village of Durham, one sees for twenty miles round scarcely a single pine tree in the whole prospect. The townships of Arran and Derby, when first surveyed, were wonderfully studded with noble trees. Oak, elm, beech, butternut, ash and maple, seemed to vie with each other in the size of their stems and the spread of their branches. In our own clearing in St. Vincent, the axemen considered that five of these great forest kings would occupy an acre of ground, leaving little space for younger trees or underbrush.

I once saw a white or wainscot oak that measured fully twelve feet in circumference at the butt, and eighty feet clear of branches. This noble tree must have contained somewhere about seven thousand square feet of inch boarding, and would represent a value approaching one hundred and thirty pounds sterling in the English market. White and black ash, black birch, red beech, maple and even basswood or lime, are of little, if any, less intrinsic worth. Rock elm is very valuable, competing as it does with hickory for many purposes.

When residing in the city of Quebec, in the year 1859–60, I published a series of articles in the Quebec *Advertiser*, descriptive of the hardwoods of Ontario. The lumber merchants of that city held then, that their correspondents in Liverpool was so wedded to old-fashioned ideas, that they would not so much as look at any price-list except for pine and the few other woods for which there was an assured demand. But I know that my papers were transmitted home, and they may possibly have converted some few readers, as, since then, our rock elm, our white ash, and the black birch of Lower Canada, have been in increased demand, and are regularly quoted at London and Liverpool. But even though old country dealers should make light of our products, that is no reason why we should undervalue them ourselves.

Not merely is our larger timber improvidently wasted, but the smaller kinds, such as blue beech, ironwood or hornbeam, buttonwood or plane tree, and red and white cedar, are swept away without a thought of their great marketable value in the Old World.*

It seems absolute fatuity to allow this waste of our natural wealth to go on unheeded. We send our pine across the Atlantic, as if it were the most valuable wood that we have, instead of being, as it really is, amongst the most inferior. From our eastern seaports white oak is shipped in the form of staves chiefly, also some ash, birch and elm. So far well. But what about the millions of tons of hardwood of all kinds which we destroy annually for fuel, and which ought to realize, if exported, four times as many millions of dollars?

Besides the plain, straight-grained timber which we heedlessly burn up to get it out of the way, there are our ornamental woods—our beautiful curled and

---

-* I have myself, when a youth, sold red cedar in London at sixpence sterling per square foot, inch thick. Lime (or basswood) was sold at twopence, and ash and beech at about the same price. White or yellow pine was then worth one penny, or just half the value of basswood. These are retail prices. On referring to the London wholesale quotations for July 1881, I find these statements fully borne out. It will be news to most of my readers, that Canadian black birch has been proved by test, under the authority of the British Admiralty, to be of greater specific gravity than English oak, and therefore better fitted for ships' flooring, for which purpose it is now extensively used. Also for staircases in large mansions.

bird's eye maple, our waved ash, our serviceable butternut or yellow walnut, our comely cherry, and even
our exquisite black walnut, all doomed to the same
perdition. Little of this waste would occur if once
the owners of land knew that a market could be got
for their timber. Cheese and butter factories for
export, have already spread over the land—why not
furniture factories also?   Why not warm ourselves
with the coal of Nova Scotia, of Manitoba, and, by-
and-by, of the Saskatchewan, and spare our forest
treasures for nobler uses? Would not this whole
question be a fitting subject for the appointment of
a competent parliamentary commission?

To me these reflections are not the birth of to-day,
but date from my bush residence in the township of
Nottawasaga. If I should succeed now in bringing
them effectively before my fellow Canadians ere it is
too late, I shall feel that I have neither thought nor
written in vain.

CHAPTER XIX.

A MELANCHOLY TALE.

THE Scottish settlers in Nottawasaga were respectable, God-fearing, and though somewhat
stern in their manners, thoroughly estimable people
on the whole. They married young, had numerous

families, and taught their children at an early age
the duties of good citizenship, and the religious
principles of their Presbyterian forefathers.

Among them, not the prettiest certainly, but the
most amiable and beloved, was Flora McDiarmid, a
tall, bright-complexioned lass of twenty, perhaps,
who was the chief mainstay of her widowed father,
whose log shanty she kept in perfect order as far as
their simple resources permitted, while she exercised
a vigilant watch over her younger brothers and sisters, and with their assistance contrived to work
their four acre allotment to good advantage.

Wherever there was trouble in the settlement, or
mirth afoot, Flora was sure to be there, nursing the
sick, cheering the unhappy, helping to provide the
good things for the simple feast,—she was, in fact,
the life of the somewhat dull and overworked community. Was the minister from afar to be received
with due honour, was the sober church service to be
celebrated in a shanty with becoming propriety—
Flora was ever on hand, at the head of all the other
lassies, guiding and directing everything, and in so
kindly and cheerful a way that none thought of
disputing her behests or hesitating at their fulfil-
ment.

Such being the case, no wonder that Malcolm Mc-
Almon and other young fellows contended for her
hand in marriage. But Malcolm won the preference,
and blithely he set to work to build a splendid log

shanty, twenty-five feet square, divided into inner compartments, with windows and doors, and other unequalled conveniences for domestic comfort new to the settlement; and when it was ready, and supplied with plenishings of all kinds, Flora and Malcolm were married amid the rejoicings of the whole township, and settled quietly down to the steady hard work of a life in the extreme backwoods, some miles distant from our clearing.

The next thing I heard of them was many months afterwards, when Malcolm was happy in the expectation of an heir to his two hundred acre lot, in the ninth or tenth concession of the township. But alas! as time stole on, accounts were unfavourable, and grew worse and worse. The nearest professional man lived at Barrie, thirty-four miles distant. A wandering herb doctor, as he called himself, of the Yankee eclectic school, was the best who had yet visited the township, and even he was far away at this time. There were experienced matrons enough in the settlement, but their skill deserted them, or the case was beyond their ability. And so poor Flora died, and her infant with her.

The same day her brother John, in deep distress, came to beg us to lend them pine boards enough to make the poor dead woman a coffin. Except the pine tree which we had cut down and sawn up, as related already, there was not a foot of sawn lumber in the settlement, and scarcely a hammer or a nail either, but what we possessed ourselves. So, being very sorry for their affliction, I told them they should have the coffin by next morning; and I set to work myself, made a tolerably handsome box, stained in black, of the right shape and dimensions, and gave it to them at the appointed hour. We of course attended the funeral, which was conducted with due solemnity by the Presbyterian minister above-mentioned. And never shall I forget the weeping bearers, staggering under their burthen through tangled brushwood and round upturned roots and cradle holes, and the long train of mourners following in their rear, to the chosen grave in the wilderness, where now I hear stands a small Presbyterian church in the village of Duntroon.

CHAPTER XX.

FROM BARRIE TO NOTTAWASAGA.

FOR nearly three years we continued to work on contentedly at our bush farm. In the summer of 1837, we received intelligence that two of our sisters were on their way to join us in Canada, and soon afterwards that they had reached Toronto, and expected to meet us at Barrie on a certain day. At the same time we learnt that the bridge across the Nottawasaga river, eleven miles from Barrie, had given way, and was barely passable on foot, as it lay floating on the water. One of our span of horses had been killed and his fellow sold, so that we had to hire a team to convey our sisters' goods from Barrie to the bridge where it was necessary to meet them with our own ox-team and waggon. I walked to Barrie accordingly, and found my sisters at Bingham's tavern, very glad to see me, but in a state of complete bewilderment and some alarm at the rough ways of the place, then only containing a tavern or two, and some twenty stores and dwellings. My fustian clothes, which I had made myself, and considered first-rate, they "laughed at consumedly." My boots! they were soaked and trod out of all fashionable proportions. Fortunately, other people in Barrie were nearly as open to criticism as myself, and as we had to get on our way without loss of time, I forgot my eccentricities of dress in the rough experiences of the road.

From Barrie to Root's tavern was pleasant travelling, the day being fine and the road fairly good. We took some rest and refreshment there, and started again, but had not gone two miles before a serious misfortune befel us. I have mentioned corduroy-bridges before; one of these had been thrown across a beautifully clear white-paved streamlet know to travellers on this road as "sweet-

I

water." The waggon was heavily laden with chests and other luggage, and the horses not being very strong, found it beyond their power to drag the load across the bridge on account of its steepness. Alarmed for my eldest sister, who was riding, I persuaded her to descend and walk on. Again and again, the teamster whipped his horses, and again and again, after they had almost scaled the crest, the weight of the load dragged them backward. I wanted to lighten the load, but the man said it was needless, and bade me block the wheels with a piece of broken branch lying near, which I did ; the next moment I was petrified to see the waggon over-balance itself and fall sideways into the stream seven or eight feet beneath, dragging the horses over with it, their forefeet clinging to the bridge and their hind feet entangled amongst the spokes of the wheels below.

My elder sister had gone on. The younger bravely caught the horses' heads and held them by main force to quiet their struggles, while the man and I got out an axe, cut the spokes of the wheels, and so in a few minutes got the horses on to firm ground, where they stood panting and terrified for some minutes. Meanwhile, to get the heavy sea-boxes out of the water and carry them up the face of a nearly perpendicular bank, then get up the waggon and reload it, was no easy task, but was accomplished at last.

The teamster, being afraid of injury to his horses' legs, at first refused to go further on the road. However, they had suffered no harm; and we finished our journey to the bridge where my brother awaited us. Here the unlucky boxes had to be carried across loose floating logs, and loaded on to the ox-waggon, which ended our hard work for that day.

Two days longer were we slowly travelling through Sunnidale and into Nottawasaga, spending each night at some friendly settler's shanty, and so lightening the fatigues of the way.

CHAPTER XXI.

FAREWELL TO THE BACKWOODS.

MY sisters had come into the woods fresh from the lovely village of Epsom, in Surrey, and accustomed to all the comforts of English life. Their consternation at the rudeness of the accommodations which we had considered rather luxurious than otherwise, dispelled all our illusions, and made us think seriously of moving nearer to Toronto. I was the first to feel the need of change, and as I had occasionally walked ninety miles to the city, to draw money for our road contracts, and the same distance back again, and had gained some friends there, it took me very little time to make up my mind. My brothers and sisters remained throughout the following winter, and then removed to a rented farm at Bradford.

Not that the bush has ever lost its charms for me. I still delight to escape thither, to roam at large, admiring the stately trees with their graceful outlines of varied foliage, seeking in their delicious shade for ferns and all kinds of wild plants, forgetting the turmoil and anxieties of the business world, and wishing I could leave it behind for ever and aye. In some such mood it was that I wrote—

"COME TO THE WOODS." *

Come to the woods—the dark old woods,
   Where our life is blithe and free ;
No thought of sorrow or strife intrudes
   Beneath the wild woodland tree.

Our wigwam is raised with skill and care
   In some quiet forest nook ;
Our healthful fare is of ven'son rare,
   Our draught from the crystal brook.

In summer we trap the beaver shy,
   In winter we chase the deer,
And, summer or winter, our days pass by
   In honest and hearty cheer.

---

* These lines were set to music by the late J. P. Clarke, Mus. Bac. of Toronto University, in his " Songs of Canada."

And when at the last we fall asleep
On mother earth's ancient breast,
The forest-dirge deep shall o'er us sweep,
And lull us to peaceful rest.

CHAPTER XXII.

A JOURNEY TO TORONTO.

TO make my narrative intelligible to those who are not familiar with the times of which I am about to write, I must revert briefly to the year 1834. During that year I made my first business visit to Toronto, then newly erected into a city. As the journey may be taken as a fair specimen of our facilities for travelling in those days, I shall describe it.

I left our shanty in Sunnidale in the bright early morning, equipped only with an umbrella and a blue bag, such as is usually carried by lawyers, containing some articles of clothing. The first three or four miles of the road lay over felled trees cut into logs, but not hauled out of the way. To step or jump over these logs every few feet may be amusing enough by way of sport, but it becomes not a little tiresome when repeated mile after mile, with scarcely any intermission, and without the stimulus

of companionship. After getting into a better
cleared road, the chief difficulty lay with the im-
perfectly "stubbed" underbrush and the frequency
of cradle-holes—that is, hollows caused by up-turned
roots—in roughly timbered land. This kind of
travelling continued till mid-day, when I got a substantial dinner and a boisterous welcome from my
old friend Root and his family. He had a pretty
little daughter by this time.

An hour's rest, and an easy walk of seven miles
to Barrie, were pleasant enough, in spite of stumps
and hollows. At Barrie I met with more friends,
who would have had me remain there for the night ;
but time was too valuable. So on I trudged, skirting round the sandy beach of beautiful Kempenfeldt
Bay, and into the thick dark woods of Innisfil,
where the road was a mere brushed track, easily
missed in the twilight, and very muddy from recent
rains. Making all the expedition in my power, I
sped on towards Clement's tavern, then the only
hostelry between Barrie and Bradford, and situated
close to the height of land whence arise, in a single
field, the sources of various streams flowing into the
Nottawasaga, the Holland, and the Credit Rivers.
But rain came on, and the road became a succession
of water-holes so deep that I all but lost my boots,
and, moreover, it was so dark that it was impossible
to walk along logs laid by the roadside, which was
the local custom in daylight.

I felt myself in a dilemma. To go forward or backward seemed equally unpromising. I had often spent nights in the bush, with or without a wigwam, and the thought of danger did not occur to me. Suddenly I recollected that about half a mile back I had passed a newly chopped and partially-logged clearing, and that there might possibly be workmen still about. So I returned to the place, and shouted for assistance; but no person was within hearing. There was, however, a small log hut, about six feet square, which the axe-men had roughly put up for protection from the rain, and in it had left some fire still burning. I was glad enough to secure even so poor a shelter as this. Everything was wet. I was without supper, and very tired after thirty miles' walk. But I tried to make the best of a bad job: collected plenty of half-consumed brands from the still blazing log-heaps, to keep up some warmth during the night, and then lay down on the round logs that had been used for seats, to sleep as best I might.

But this was not to be. At about nine o'clock there arose from the woods, first a sharp snapping bark, answered by a single yelp; then two or three yells at intervals. Again a silence, lasting perhaps five minutes. This kept on, the noise increasing in frequency, and coming nearer and again nearer, until it became impossible to mistake it for aught but the howling of wolves. The clearing might be five or six acres. Scattered over it were partially or

wholly burnt log heaps.   I knew that wolves would
not be likely to venture amongst the fires, and that
I was practically safe.   But the position was not
pleasant, and I should have preferred a bed at
Clement's, as a matter of choice.   I, however, kept up
my fire very assiduously, and the evil brutes continued their concert of fiendish discords—sometimes
remaining silent for a time, and anon bursting into a
full chorus *fortissimo*—for many long, long hours,
until the glad beams of morning peeped through the
trees, and the sky grew brighter and brighter ; when
the wolves ceased their serenade, and I fell fast
asleep, with my damp umbrella for a pillow.

With the advancing day, I awoke, stiffened in
every joint, and very hungry.   A few minutes' walk
on my road showed me a distant opening in the
woods, towards which I hastened, and found a new
shanty, inhabited by a good-natured settler and his
family, from whom I got some breakfast, for which
they would accept nothing but thanks.   They had
lately been much troubled, they said, with wolves
about their cattle sheds at night.

From thence I proceeded to Bradford, fifteen
miles, by a road interlaced with pine roots, with deep
water-holes between, and so desperately rugged as
to defy any wheeled vehicle but an ox-cart to
struggle over it.   Here my troubles ended for the
present.   Mr. Thomas Drury, of that village, had
been in partnership with a cousin of my own, as

brewers, at Mile End, London. His hospitable reception, and a good night's repose, made me forget previous discomforts, and I went on my way next morning with a light heart, carrying with me a letter of introduction to a man of whom I had occasionally heard in the bush, one William Lyon Mackenzie.

The day's journey by way of Yonge Street was easily accomplished by stage—an old-fashioned conveyance enough, swung on leather straps, and subject to tremendous jerks from loose stones on the rough road, innocent of Macadam, and full of the deepest ruts. A fellow-passenger, by way of encouragement, told me how an old man, a few weeks before, had been jolted so violently against the roof, as to leave marks of his blood there, which, being not uncommon, were left unheeded for days. My friend advised me to keep on my hat, which I had laid aside on account of the heat of the day, and I was not slow to adopt the suggestion.

Arrived in town, my first business was to seek out Mr. William Hawkins, well-known in those days as an eminent provincial land surveyor. I found him at a house on the south side of Newgate (now Adelaide) street, two or three doors west of Bay Street. He was living as a private boarder with an English family; and, at his friendly intercession, I was admitted to the same privilege. The home was that of Mr. H. C. Todd, with his wife and two sons. With them, I continued to reside as often as I visited Toronto, and for long after I became a citizen. That I spent there many happy days, among kind and considerate friends, numbers of my readers will be well assured when I mention, that the two boys were Alfred and Alpheus Todd, the one loved and lamented as the late Clerk of Committees in the Canadian House of Commons—the other widely known in Europe and America, as the late Librarian of the Dominion Parliament.

My stay in Toronto on that occasion was very brief. To wait upon the Chief Emigrant Agent for instructions about road-making in Sunnidale; to make a few small purchases of clothing and tea; and to start back again, without loss of time, were matters of course. One thing, however, I found time to do, which had more bearing upon this narrative, and that was, to present Mr. Drury's letter of introduction to William L. Mackenzie, M. P. P., at his printing-office on Hospital Street. I had often seen copies, in the bush, of the *Colonial Advocate*, as well as of the *Courier* and *Gazette* newspapers, but had the faintest possible idea of Canadian politics. The letter was from one whose hospitality Mackenzie had experienced for weeks in London, and consequently I felt certain of a courteous reception. Without descending from the high stool he used at his desk, he received the letter, read it, looked at me frigidly, and said in his singular, harsh Dundee dialect: "We must look after our own people before doing anything for strangers." Mr. Drury had told him that I wished to know if there were any opening for proof-readers in Toronto. I was not a little surprised to find myself ostracized as a stranger in a British colony, but, having other views, thought no more of the circumstance at the time.

This reminds me of another characteristic anecdote of Mackenzie, which was related to me by one who was on the spot where it happened. In 1820, on his first arrival in Montreal from Scotland, he got an engagement as chain-bearer on the survey of the Lachine canal. A few days afterwards, the surveying party, as usual at noon, sat down on a grassy bank to eat their dinner. They had been thus occupied for half an hour, and were getting ready for a smoke, when the new chain-bearer suddenly jumped up with an exclamation, "Now, boys, time for work! we mustn't waste the government money!" The consequence of which ill-timed outburst was his prompt dismissal from the service.

CHAPTER XXIII.

SOME GLIMPSES OF UPPER CANADIAN POLITICS.

IN the course of the years 1835,'6 and '7, I made many journeys to Toronto, sometimes wholly on foot, sometimes partly by steamboat and stage. I became very intimate with the Todd family and connections, which included Mrs. Todd's brother, William P. Patrick, then, and long afterwards, Clerk of the Legislative Assembly; his brother-in-law, Dr. Thomas D. Morrison, M.P.P.; Thomas Vaux, Accountant of the Legislature ; Caleb Hopkins, M. P. P., for Halton; William H. Doel, brewer; William C. Keele, attorney, and their families. Nearly all these persons were, or had been, zealous admirers of Wm. L. Mackenzie's political course. And the same thing must be said of my friend Mr. Drury, of Bradford; his sister married Edward Henderson, merchant tailor, of King Street west, whose father, E. T. Henderson, was well known amongst Mackenzie's supporters. It was his cottage on Yonge Street (near what is now Gloucester Street), at which the leaders of the popular party used often to meet in council. The house stood in an orchard, well fenced, and was then very rural and secluded from observation.

Amongst all these really estimable people, and at their houses, nothing of course was heard disparaging to the Reformers of that day, and their active leader. My own political prejudices also were in his favour. And so matters went on until the arrival, in 1835, of Sir Francis Bond Head, as Lieutenant-Governor, when we, in the bush, began to hear of violent struggles between the House of Assembly on the one side, and the Lieutenant-Governor supported by the Legislative Council on the other. Each political party, by turns, had had its successes and reverses at the polls. In 1825, the majority of the Assembly was Tory; in 1826, and for several years afterwards, a Reform majority was elected; in 1831, again, Toryism was successful; in 1835, the balance veered over to the popular side once more, by a majority only of four. This majority, led by Mackenzie, refused to pass the supplies; whereupon, Sir Francis appealed to the people by dissolving the Parliament.

What were the precise grounds of difference in principle between the opposing parties, did not very clearly appear to us in the bush. Sir Francis Head had no power to grant " Responsible Government," as it has since been interpreted. On each side there were friends and opponents of that system. Among Tories, Ogle R. Gowan, Charles Fothergill, and others, advocated a responsible ministry, and were loud in their denunciations of the " Family Compact." On the Reform side were ranged such men as Marshall

S. Bidwell and Dr. Rolph, who preferred American Republicanism, in which "Responsible Government" was and is utterly unknown. We consequently found it hard to understand the party cries of the day. But we began to perceive that there was a Republican bias on one hand, contending with a Monarchical leaning on the other; and we had come to Canada, as had most well-informed immigrants, expressly to avoid the evils of Republicanism, and to preserve our British constitutional heritage intact.

When therefore Sir Francis Head threw himself with great energy into the electoral arena, when he bade the foes of the Empire " come if they dare ! " when he called upon the "United Empire Loyalists," —men, who in 1770 had thrown away their all, rather than accept an alien rule—to vindicate once more their right to choose whom they would follow, King or President—when he traversed the length and breadth of the land, making himself at home in the farm-houses, and calling upon fathers and husbands and sons to stand up for their hearths, and their old traditions of honour and fealty to the Crown, it would have been strange indeed had he failed.

The next House of Assembly, elected in 1837, contained a majority of twenty-six to fourteen in favour of Sir F. B. Head's policy. This precipitated matters. Had Mackenzie been capable of enduring defeat with a good grace ; had he restrained his natural irritability of temper, and kept his skirts cautiously clear of all contact with men of Republican aspirations, he might and probably would have recovered his position as a parliamentary leader, and died an honoured and very likely even a titled veteran ! But he became frantic with choler and disappointment, and rushed headlong into the most passionate extremes, which ended in making him a mere cat's-paw in the hands of cunning schemers, who did not fail, after their manner, to disavow their own handiwork when it had ceased to serve their purposes.

CHAPTER XXIV.

TORONTO DURING THE REBELLION.

IN November, 1837, I had travelled to Toronto for the purpose of seeking permanent employment in the city, and meant to return in the first week of December, to spend my last Christmas in the woods. But the fates and William Lyon Mackenzie had decided otherwise. I was staying for a few days with my friend Joseph Heughen, the London hairdresser mentioned as a fellow-passenger on board the *Asia*, whose name must be familiar to most Toronto citizens of that day. His shop was near Ridout's hardware-store, on King Street, at the corner of Yonge Street.   On Sunday, the 3rd, we' heard that armed men were assembling at the Holland Landing and Newmarket to attack the city, and that lists of houses to be burned by them were in the hands of their leaders; that Samuel Lount, blacksmith, had been manufacturing pikes at the Landing for their use; that two or three persons had been warned by friends in the secret to sell their houses, or to leave the city, or to look for startling changes of some sort.   Then it was known that a quantity of arms and a couple of cannon were being brought from the garrison, and stored in the covered way under the old City Hall.   Every idle report was eagerly caught up, and magnified a hundredfold.   But the burthen of all invariably was, an expected invasion by the Yankees to drive all loyalists from Canada.   In this way rumour followed rumour, all business ceased, and everybody listened anxiously for the next alarm.   At length it came in earnest. At eleven o'clock on Monday night, the 4th of December, every bell in the city was set ringing, occasional gun-shots were fired, by accident as it turned out, but none the less startling to nervous people; a confused murmur arose in the streets, becoming louder every minute; presently the sound of a horse's hoofs was heard, echoing loudly along Yonge Street. With others I hurried out, and found at Ridout's corner a horseman, who proved to be Alderman John

Powell, who told his breathless listeners, how he had been stopped beyond the Yonge Street toll-gate, two miles out, by Mackenzie and Anderson at the head of a number of rebels in arms; how he had shot Anderson and missed Mackenzie; how he had dodged behind a log when pursued; and had finally got into town by the College Avenue.

There was but little sleep in Toronto that night, and next day everything was uproar and excitement, heightened by the news that Col. Moodie, of Richmond Hill, a retired officer of the army, who was determined to force his way through the armed bodies of rebels, to bring tidings of the rising to the Government in Toronto, had been shot down and inhumanly left to bleed to death at Montgomery's tavern. The flames and smoke from Dr. Horne's house at Rosedale, were visible all over the city; it had been fired in the presence of Mackenzie in person, in retaliation, it was said, for the refusal of discount by the Bank of Upper Canada, of which Dr. Horne was teller. The ruins of the still-burning building were visited by hundreds of citizens, and added greatly to the excitement and exasperation of the hour. By-and-by it became known that Mr. Robert Baldwin and Dr. John Rolph had been sent, with a flag of truce, to learn the wants of the insurgents. Many citizens accompanied the party at a little distance. A flag of truce was in itself a delightful novelty, and the street urchins cheered

J

vociferously, scudding away at the smallest alarm. Arrived at the toll-gate, there were waiting outside Mackenzie, Lount, Gibson, Fletcher and other leaders, with a couple of hundred of their men. In reply to the Lieutenant-Governor's message of inquiry, as to what was wanted, the answer was, "Independence, and a convention to arrange details," which rather compendious demand, being reported to Sir Francis, was at once rejected. So there was nothing for it but to fight.

Mackenzie did his best to induce his men to advance on the city that evening; but as most of his followers had been led to expect that there would be no resistance, and no bloodshed, they were shocked and discouraged by Col. Moodie's death, as well as by those of Anderson and one or two others. A picket of volunteers under Col. Jarvis, fired on them, when not far within the toll-gate, killing one and wounding two others, and retired still firing. After this the insurgents lost all confidence, and even threatened to shoot Mackenzie himself, for reproaching them with cowardice. A farmer living by the roadside told me at the time, that while a detachment of rebels were marching southwards down the hill, since known as Mount Pleasant, they saw a waggon-load of cordwood standing on the opposite rise, and supposing it to be a piece of artillery loaded to the muzzle with grape or canister, these brave warriors leaped the fences right and left like squirrels, and could by no effort of their officers be induced again to advance.

By this time the principal buildings in the city —the City Hall, Upper Canada Bank, the Parliament Buildings, Osgoode Hall, Government House, the Canada Company's office, and many private dwellings and shops, were put in a state of defence by barricading the windows and doors with two-inch plank, loopholed for musketry; and the city bore a rather formidable appearance. Arms and ammunition were distributed to all householders who chose to accept them. I remember well the trepidation with which my friend Heughen shrank from touching the musket that was held out for his acceptance; and the outspoken indignation of the militia sergeant, whose proffer of the firearm was declined. The poor hairdresser told me afterwards, that many of his customers were rebels, and that he dreaded the loss of their patronage.

The same evening came Mr. Speaker McNab, with a steamer from Hamilton, bringing sixty of the " men of Gore." It was an inspiriting thing to see these fine fellows land on the wharf, bright and fresh from their short voyage, and full of zeal and loyalty. The ringing cheers they sent forth were re-echoed with interest by the townsmen. From Scarborough also, marched in a party of militia, under Captain McLean.

It was on the same day that a lady, still living, was travelling by stage from Streetsville, on her

way through Toronto to Cornwall, having with her
a large trunk of new clothing prepared for a long
visit to her relatives. Very awkwardly for her, Mackenzie had started, at the head of a few men, from
Yonge Street across to Dundas Street, to stop the
stage and capture the mails, so as to intercept news
of Dr. Duncombe's rising in the London District.
Not content with seizing the mail-bags and all the
money they contained, Mackenzie himself, pistol in
hand, demanded the surrender of the poor woman's
portmanteau, and carried it off bodily. It was
asserted at the time that he only succeeded in evading capture a few days after, at Oakville, by dis-
guising himself in woman's clothes, which may explain his raid upon the lady's wardrobe; for which,
I believe, she failed to get any compensation whatsoever under the Rebellion Losses Act. This lady
afterwards became the wife of John F. Rogers, who
was my partner in business for several subsequent
years.

In the course of the next day, Wednesday, parties
of men arrived from Niagara, Hamilton, Oakville,
Port Credit and other places in greater or less numbers—many of them Orangemen, delighted with
their new occupation. The Lieutenant-Governor
was thus enabled to vacate the City Hall and take
up his headquarters in the Parliament Buildings;
and before night as many as fifteen hundred volunteers were armed and partially drilled. Among

them were a number of Mackenzie's former supporters, with their sons and relatives, now thoroughly ashamed of the man, and utterly alienated by his declared republicanism.

Next morning followed the "Battle of Gallows Hill," or, as it might more fitly be styled, the "Skirmish of Montgomery's Farm." Being a stranger in the city, I had not then formally volunteered, but took upon myself to accompany the advancing force, on the chance of finding something to do, either as a volunteer or a newspaper correspondent, should an opening occur. The main body, led by Sir Francis himself, with Colonels Fitzgibbon and McNab as Adjutants, marched by Yonge Street, and consisted of six hundred men with two guns; while two other bodies, of two hundred and a hundred and twenty men, respectively, headed by Colonels W. Chisholm and S. P. Jarvis, advanced by bye-roads and fields on the east and on the west of Yonge Street. Nothing was seen of the enemy till within half-a-mile of Montgomery's tavern. The road was there bordered on the west side by pine woods, from whence dropping rifle-shots began to be heard, which were answered by the louder muskets of the militia. Presently our artillery opened their hoarse throats, and the woods rang with strong reverberations. Splinters were dashed from the trees, threatening, and I believe causing worse mischief than the shots themselves. It is said that this kind of skirmishing continued for half-an-hour—to me it seemed but a few minutes. As the militia advanced, their opponents melted away. Parties of volunteers dashed over the fences and into the woods, shouting and firing as they ran. Two or three wounded men of both parties were lifted tenderly into carts and sent off to the city to be placed in hospital. Others lay bleeding by the road-side —rebels by their rustic clothing; their wounds were bound up, and they were removed in their turn. Soon a movement was visible through the smoke, on the hill fronting the tavern, where some tall pines were then standing. I could see there two or three hundred men, now firing irregularly at the advancing loyalists; now swaying to and fro without any apparent design. Some horsemen were among them, who seemed to act more as scouts than as leaders.

We had by this time arrived within cannon shot of the tavern itself. Two or three balls were seen to strike and pass through it. A crowd of men rushed from the doors, and scattered wildly in a northerly direction. Those on the hill wavered, receded under shelter of the undulating land, and then fled like their fellows. Their horsemen took the side-road westward, and were pursued, but not in time to prevent their escape. Had our right and left wings kept pace with the main body, the whole insurgent force must have been captured.

Sir Francis halted his men opposite the tavern, and gave the word to demolish the building, by way of a severe lesson to the disaffected. This was promptly done by firing the furniture in the lower rooms, and presently thick clouds of smoke and vivid flames burst from doors and windows. The battalion next moved on to perform the same service at Gibson's house, several miles further north Many prisoners were taken in the pursuit, all of whom Sir Francis released, after admonishing them to be better subjects in future. The march back to Toronto was very leisurely executed, several of the mounted officers carrying dead pigs and geese slung across their saddle-bows as trophies of victory.

Next day, volunteers for the city guard were called for, and among them I was regularly enrolled and placed under pay, at three shillings and nine pence per diem. My captain was George Percival Ridout; and his brother, Joseph D. Ridout, was lieutenant. Our company was duly drilled at the City Hall, and continued to do duty as long as their services were required, which was about four months. I have a vivid recollection of being stationed at the Don Bridge to look out for a second visit from Peter Matthews's band of rebels, eighty of whom had attempted to burn the bridge, and succeeded in burning three adjoining houses; also, of being forgotten and kept there without food or relief throughout a bitter cold winter's night and morning. Also, of doing duty as sentry over poor old Colonel Van Egmond, a Dutch officer who had served under Napoleon I., and who was grievously sick from exposure in the woods and confinement in gaol, of which he soon afterwards died. Another day, I was placed, as one of a corporal's guard, in charge of Lesslie's stationery and drug-store, and found there a saucy little shop-boy who has since developed into the portly person of Alderman Baxter, now one, and not the least, of our city notabilities. The guards and the guarded were on the best of terms. We were treated with much hospitality by Mr. Joseph Lesslie, late Postmaster of Toronto, and have all been excellent friends ever since. Our corporal, I ought to say, was Anthony Blachford, since a well-known and respected citizen.

Those were exciting times in Toronto. The day after the battle, six hundred men of Simcoe, under command of Lieutenant-Colonel Dewson, came marching down Yonge Street, headed by Highland pipers playing the national pibroch. In their ranks I first saw Hugh Scobie, a stalwart Scotsman, afterwards widely known as publisher of the *British Colonist* newspaper. With this party were brought in sixty prisoners, tied to a long rope, most of whom were afterwards released on parole.

A day or two afterwards, entered the volunteers from the Newcastle District, who had marched the whole distance from Brockville, under the command,

I think, of Lieutenant-Colonel Ogle R. Gowan. They were a fine body of men, and in the highest spirits at the prospect of a fight with the young Queen Victoria's enemies.

A great sensation was created when the leaders who had been arrested after the battle, Dr. Thomas D. Morrison, John G. Parker, and two others, preceded by a loaded cannon pointed towards the prisoners, were marched along King Street to the Common Jail, which is the same building now occupied as York Chambers, at the corner of Toronto and Court Streets. The Court House stood, and still stands, converted into shops and offices, on Church Street; between the two was an open common which was used in those days as the place of public executions. It was here that, on the 12th of April following, I witnessed, with great sorrow, the execution by hanging of Samuel Lount and Peter Matthews, two of the principal rebel leaders.

Sir F. B. Head had then left the Province.

The following narrative of circumstances which occurred during the time when Mackenzie was in command of the rebel force on Yonge Street, has been kindly communicated to me by a gentleman, who, as a young lad, was personally cognizant of the facts described. It has, I believe, never been published, and will interest many of my readers:

"It was on Monday morning, the 5th of December, 1837, when rumours of the disturbances that had broken out in Lower Canada were causing great excitement throughout the Home District, that the late James S. Howard's servant-man, named Bolton, went into his master's bed-room and asked if Mr. H. had heard shots fired during the night. He replied that he had not, and told the man to go down to the street and find out what was the matter. Bolton returned shortly with the news, that a man named Anderson had been shot at the foot of the hill, and that his body was lying in a house near by. Shortly after came the startling report of the death of poor Col. Moodie, which was a great shock to Mrs. Howard, who knew him well, and was herself a native of Fredericton, where the Colonel's regiment (the old Hundred and Fourth) had been raised during the war of 1812. Mr. Howard immediately ordered his carriage, and started for the city, from whence he did not return for ten days. About nine o'clock, a man named Pool, who held the rank of captain in the rebel army, called at Mr. Howard's house, to ask if Anderson's body was there. Being told where it was said to be, he turned and went away. Immediately afterwards, the first detachment of the rebel army came in sight, consisting of some fifteen or twenty men, who drew up on the lawn in front of the house. Presently, at the word of command they wheeled round and went away in search of the dead rebel. Next came three or four men (loyalists) hurrying down the road, who said that there were five hundred rebels behind them. Then was heard the report of fire arms, and anon more armed men showed themselves along the brow of Gallows Hill, and took up ground near the present residence of Mr. Hooper. About eleven o'clock, another detachment appeared, headed by a man on a small white horse, almost a pony, who turned out to be the commander-in-chief, Mackenzie himself. He wore a great coat buttoned up to the chin, and presented the appearance of being stuffed.

In talking among themselves, the men intimated that he had on a great many coats, as if to make himself bullet proof. To enable the man on the white pony to enter the lawn, his men wrenched off the fence boards ; he entered the house without knocking, took possession of the sitting room where Mrs. and Miss Howard and her brother were sitting, and ordered dinner to be got ready for fifty men. Utterly astonished at such a demand, Mrs. Howard said she could do nothing of the kind. After abusing Mr. Howard for some time—who had incurred his dislike by refusing him special privileges at the Post Office—Mackenzie said Howard had held his office long enough, and that it was time somebody else had it. Mrs. Howard at length referred him to the servant in the kitchen ; which hint he took, and went to see about dinner himself. There happened to be a large iron sugar-kettle, in which was boiling a sheep killed by dogs shortly before. This they emptied, and refilled with beef from a barrel in the cellar. A baking of bread just made was also confiscated, and cut up by a tall thin man, named Eckhardt, from Markham. While these preparations were going on, other men were busy in the tool house mending their arms, which consisted of all sorts of weapons, from chisels and gouges fixed on poles, to hatchets, knives and guns of all descriptions. About two o'clock there was a regular stampede, and the family were left quite alone, much to their relief ; with the exception of a young Highland Scotchman mounting guard. He must have been a recent arrival from the old country, as he wore the blue jacket and trowsers of the sea-faring men of the western isles. Mrs. Howard seeing all the rest had left, went out to speak to him, saying she regretted to see so fine a young Scotchman turning rebel against his Queen. His answer was, "Country first, Queen next." He told her that it was the flag of truce which had called his comrades away. About half-past three they all returned, headed by the commander-in-chief, who demanded of Mrs. Howard whe-

ther the dinner he had ordered was ready ?   She said it
was just as they had left it.   Irritated at her coolness he
got very angry, shook his horse-whip, pulled her from her
chair to the window, bidding her look out and be thank-
ful that her own house was not in the same state.   He
pointed to Dr. Horne's house at Blue Hill, on the east
side of the road, which during his absence he had set on
fire, much to the disappointment of his men, whom,
though very hungry, he would not allow to touch anything, but burnt all up.   There was considerable grumbling among the men about it.   Poor Lount, who was with
them, told Mrs. Howard not to mind Mackenzie, but to
give them all they wanted, and they would not harm her.
They got through their dinner about dusk, and returned
to the lawn, where they had some barrels of whiskey.
They kept up a regular—or rather an irregular firing all
night.   The family were much alarmed, having only one
servant woman with them ; the man Bolton had escaped
for fear as he said of being taken prisoner by the rebels.
There the men remained until Wednesday, when they
returned to Montgomery's tavern, a mile or two up the
street, where is now the village of Eglinton.   About
eleven o'clock in the morning, the loyalist force marched
out to attack the rebels, who were posted at the Paul
Pry Inn, on the east side of the road, with their main
body at Montgomery's, some distance further north.   It
was a very fine sunny day, and the loyalists made a formidable appearance, as the sun shone on their bright
musket-barrels and bayonets.   The first shot fired was
from the artillery, under the command of Captain Craig ;
it went through the Paul Pry under the eaves and out of
the roof.   The rebels took to the woods on each side of the
road, which at that time were much nearer than at present.   Thomas Bell, who had charge of a company of
volunteers, said that on the morning of the battle, a
stranger asked leave to accompany him.   The man wore
a long beard, and was rumoured to have been one of

Napoleon's officers. Mr. Bell saw him take aim at one of the retreating rebels, who was crouching behind a stump, firing at the loyalists. Nothing could be seen but the top of his head. The stranger fired with fatal effect. The dead man turned out to be a farmer of the name of Widman, from Whitchurch. Montgomery's tavern, a large building on the hill-side of the road, was next attacked, and was quickly evacuated by the flying rebels, who got into the woods to the west and dispersed. It was then that Mackenzie made his escape. The tavern having been the rebel head-quarters, and the place from which Col. Moodie was shot, was set on fire and burned down. The house of Gibson, another rebel rendezvous, about eight miles north, was also burnt. With that small effort the rebellion in Upper Canada was crushed. A few days after, some fifty or sixty rebel prisoners from about Sharon and Lloydtown, were marched down to the city, roped together, two and two in a long string ; and shortly afterwards a volunteer corps—commanded by Colonels Hill and Dewson, raised amongst the log-cabin settlers, in the County of Simcoe, came down in sleighs to the city, where they did duty all winter. It was an extraordinary fact, that these poor settlers, living in contentment in their log-cabins, with their potato patches around, should turn out and put down a rebellion, originated among old settlers and wealthy farmers in the prosperous County of York. Mackenzie early lost the sympathies of a great proportion of his followers. One of them, named Jacob Kurtz, swore most lustily, the same winter, that if he could catch his old leader he would shoot him. While retreating eastward, a party of the rebels attempted to burn the Don Bridge, and would have succeeded, but for the determined efforts of a Mrs. Ross, who put out the fire, at the expense of a bullet in her knee; the ball was extracted by the late Dr. Widmer, who was very popular about Yorkville and the east end of the city."

CHAPTER XXV.

THE VICTOR AND THE VANQUISHED.

IT is now forty-five years since the last act of the rebellion was consummated, by the defeat of Duncombe's party in the London district, the punishment of Sutherland's brigands at Windsor, and the destruction of the steamer *Caroline* and dispersal of the discreditable ruffians, of whom their "president," Mackenzie, was heartily sick, at Navy Island. None of these events came within my own observation, and I pass them by without special remark.

But respecting Sir Francis Bond Head and his antagonist, I feel that more should be said, in justice to both. It is eminently unfair to censure Sir Francis for not doing that which he was not commissioned to do. Even so thorough a Reformer and so just a man as Earl Russell, had failed to see the advisability of extending "responsible government" to any of Her Majesty's Colonies. Up to the time of Lord Durham's report in 1839, no such proposal had been even mooted; and it appears to have been the general opinion of British statesmen, at the date of Sir Francis Head's appointment, that to give a responsible ministry to Canada was equivalent to

offering her independence. In taking it for granted
that Canadians as a whole were unfit to have conferred on them the same rights of self-government
as were possessed by Englishmen, Irishmen and
Scotchmen in the old country, consisted the original
error. This error, however, Sir Francis shared with
the Colonial Office and both Houses of the Imperial
Parliament. Since those days the mistake has been
admitted, and not Canada alone, but the Australian
colonies and South Africa have profited by our advancement in self-government.

As for Sir Francis's personal character, even
Mackenzie's biographer allows that he was frank,
kindly and generous in an unusual degree. That he
won the entire esteem of so many men of whom all
Canadians of whatever party are proud—such men
as Chief Justice Robinson, Bishop Strachan, Chief
Justices Macaulay, Draper and McLean, Sir Allan
N. McNab, Messrs. Henry Ruttan, Mahlon Burwell,
Jno. W. Gamble and many others, I hold to be in-
dubitable proof of his high qualities and honest intentions. Nobody can doubt that had he been sent
here to carry out responsible government, he would
have done it zealously and honourably. But he was
sent to oppose it, and, in opposing it, he simply did
his duty.

A gentleman* well qualified to judge, and who
knew him personally, has favoured me with the fol-

---

* The late lamented Dr. Alpheus Todd, librarian of the
Dominion Parliament.

lowing remarks apropos of the subject, which I have pleasure in laying before my readers :

" As a boy, I had a sincere admiration for his [Sir Francis's] devoted loyalty, and genuine English character; and I have since learnt to respect and appreciate with greater discriminatiou his great services to the Crown and Empire. He was a little Quixotic perhaps. He had a marked individuality of his own. But he was as true as steel, and most staunch to British law and British principle in the trying days of his administration in Canada. His loyalty was chivalrous and magnetic ; by his enlightened enthusiasm in a good cause he evoked a true spirit of loyalty in Upper Canada, that had well-nigh become extinct, being overlaid with the spirit of ultra-radicalism that had for years previously got uppermost among our people. But Upper Canada loyalty had a deep and solid foundatiou in the patriotism of the U. E. Loyalists, a noble race who had proved by deeds, not words, their attachment to the Crown and government of the mother land. These U. E. Loyalists were the true founders of Upper Canada ; and they were forefathers of whom we may be justly proud—themselves 'honouring the father and the mother '—their sovereign and the institutions under which they were born—they did literally obtain the promised reward of that 'first commandment with promise,' viz.: length of days and honour."

William Lyon Mackenzie was principally remarkable for his indomitable perseverance and unhesitating self-reliance. Of toleration for other men's opinions, he seems to have had none. He did, or strove to do, whatsoever he himself thought right, and those who differed with him he denounced in the most unmeasured terms. For example, writing of the Imperial Government in 1837, he says:

" Small cause have Highlanders and the descendants of Highlanders to feel a friendship for the Guelphic family. If the Stuarts had their faults, they never enforced loyalty in the glens and valleys of the north by banishing and extirpating the people ; it was reserved for the Brunswickers to give, as a sequel to the massacre of Glencoe, the cruel order for depopulation. I am proud of my descent from a rebel race ; who held borrowed chieftains, a scrip nobility, rag money and national debt in abomination. . . . Words cannot express my contempt at witnessing the servile, crouching attitude of the country of my choice. If the people felt as I feel, there is never a Grant or Glenelg who crossed the Tay and Tweed to exchange high-born Highland poverty for substantial Lowland wealth, who would dare to insult Upper Canada with the official presence, as its ruler, of such an equivocal character as this Mr. what do they call him—Francis Bond Head."

Had Mackenzie confined himself to this kind of vituperation, all might have gone well for him, and for his followers. People would only have laughed at his vehemence. The advocacy of the principle of responsible government in Canada would have been and was taken up by Orangemen, U. E. Loyalists, and other known Tories. Ever since the day when the manufacture of even a hob-nail in the American colonies was declared by English statesmen to be intolerable, the struggle has gone on for colonial equality as against imperial centralization. The final adoption of the theory of ministerial responsi-

K

bility by all political parties in Canada, is Mackenzie's best justification.

But he sold himself in his disappointment to the republican tempter, and justly paid the penalty. That he felt this himself long before he died, will be incontestably shown by his own words, which I copy from Mr. Lindsey's "Life of Mackenzie," vol. ii., page 290:

"After what I have seen here, I frankly confess to you that, had I passed nine years in the United States before, instead of after, the outbreak, I am very sure I would have been the last man in America to be engaged in it."

And, again, page 291 :

"A course of careful observations during the last eleven years has fully satisfied me that, had the violent movements in which I and many others were engaged on both sides of the Niagara proved successful, that success would have deeply injured the people of Canada, whom I then believed I was serving at great risks; that it would have deprived millions, perhaps, of our own countrymen in Europe of a home upon this continent, except upon conditions which, though many hundreds of thousands of immigrants have been constrained to accept them, are of an exceedingly onerous and degrading character. . . . There is not a living man on this continent who more sincerely desires that British Government in Canada may long continue, and give a home and a welcome to the old countryman, than myself."

Of Mackenzie's imprisonment and career in the United States, nothing need be said here. I saw him once more in the Canadian Parliament after his return from exile, in the year 1858. He was then remarkable for his good humour, and for his personal independence of party. His chosen associates were, as it seemed to me, chiefly on the Opposition or Conservative side of the House.

Before closing this chapter, I cannot help referring to the unfortunate men who suffered in various ways. They were farmers of the best class, and of the most simple habits. The poor fellows who lay wounded by the road side on Yonge Street, were not persons astute enough to discuss political theories, but feeble creatures who could only shed bitter tears over their bodily sufferings, and look helplessly for assistance from their conquerors. There were among them boys of twelve or fifteen years old, one of whom had been commissioned by his ignorant old mother at St. Catharines, to be sure and bring her home a check-apron full of tea from one of the Toronto groceries.

I thought at the time, and I think still, that the Government ought to have interfered before matters came to a head, and so saved all these hapless people from the cruel consequences of their leaders' folly. On the other hand, it is asserted that neither Sir Francis nor his Council could be brought to credit the probability of an armed rising. A friend has told me that his father, who was then a member of the Executive Council, attended a meeting as late as nine o'clock on the 4th December, 1837. That he returned home and retired to rest at eleven. In half an hour a messenger from Government House came knocking violently at the door, with the news of the rising ; when he jumped out of bed exclaiming, " I hope Robinson will believe me next time." The Chief Justice had received with entire incredulity the information laid before the Council, of the threatened movement that week.

CHAPTER XXVI.

RESULTS IN THE FUTURE.

WHATEVER may be thought of Sir Francis B. Head's policy—whether we prefer to call it mere foolhardiness or chivalric zeal—there can be no doubt that he served as an effective instrument in the hands of Providence for the building up of a " Greater Britain " on the American continent. The success of the outbreak of 1837 could only have ended in Canada's absorption by the United States, which must surely have proved a lamentable finale to the grand heroic act of the loyalists of the old colonies, who came here to preserve what they held to be their duty alike to their God and their earthly sovereign. It is certain, I

think, that religious principle is the true basis, and
the one only safeguard of Canadian existence.   It
was the influence of the Anglican, and especially of
the Methodist pastors, of 1770, that led their flocks
into the wilderness to find here a congenial home.
In Lower Canada, in 1837, it was in like manner
the influence of the clergy, both Roman Catholic
and Protestant, that defeated Papineau and his Republican followers.   And it is the religious and
moral sentiment of Canada, in all her seven Provinces, that now constitutes the true bond of union
between us and the parent Empire.   Only a few
years since, the statesmen of the old country felt no
shame in preferring United States amity to Colonial
connection.   To-day a British premier openly and
even ostentatiously repudiates any such policy as
suicidal.

That Canada possesses, in every sense of the word,
a healthier atmosphere than its Southern neighbour,
and that it owes its continued moral salubrity to the
defeat of Mackenzie's allies in 1837-8, I for one confidently hold—with Mackenzie himself.   That this
superiority is due to the greater and more habitual
respect paid to all authority—Divine and secular—
I devoutly believe.   That our present and future
welfare hangs, as by a thread, upon that one inherent, all-important characteristic, that we are a
religious community, seems to me plain to all who
care to read correctly the signs of the times.

The historian of the future will find in these con-
siderations his best clue to our existing status in
relation to our cousins to the south of us. He will
discover on the one side of the line, peaceful industry,
home affections, unaffected charity, harmless recre-
ations, a general desire for education, and a sincere
reverence for law and authority. On the other, he
may observe a heterogeneous commixture of many
races, and notably of their worst elements ; he will
see the marriage-tie degraded into a mockery, the
Sabbath-day a scoffing, the house of God a rostrum
or a concert-hall, the law a screen for crime, the
judicial bench a purchasable commodity, the patri-
mony of the State an asylum for Mormonism.

I am fully sensible that the United States possesses
estimable citizens in great numbers, who feel, and
lament more than anybody else, the flagrant abuses
of her free institutions. But do they exercise any
controlling voice in elections ? Do they even hope
to influence the popular vote ? They tell us themselves that they are powerless. And so—we have
only to wish them a fairer prospect; and to pray
that Canada may escape the inevitable Nemesis that
attends upon great national faults such as theirs.

CHAPTER XXVII.

A CONFIRMED TORY.

MY good friend and host, Henry Cook Todd, was one of the most uncompromising Tories I ever met with. He might have sat for the portrait of Mr. Grimwig. in "Oliver Twist." Like that celebrated old gentleman, "his bark was aye waur than his bite." He would pour out a torrent of scorn and sarcasm upon some luckless object of his indignation, public or private; and, having exhausted the full vials of his wrath, would end with some kind act toward, perhaps, the very person he had been anathematizing, and subside into an amiable mood of compassion for the weaknesses of erring mankind generally.

He was a graduate of the University of Oxford, and afterwards had charge of a large private school in one of the English counties. Having inherited and acquired a moderate competency, he retired into private life; but later on he lost by the failure of companies wherein his savings had been invested. He then commenced business as a bookseller, did not succeed, and finally decided, at the persuasion of his wife's brother, Mr. William P. Patrick, of Toronto, to emigrate to Canada. Having first satisfied himself of the prudence of the step, by a tour in the United States and Canada, he sent for his family, who arrived here in 1833.

His two sons, Alfred and Alpheus, got the full benefit of their father's classical attainments, and were kept closely to their studies. At an early age, their uncle Patrick took charge of their interests, and placed them about him in the Legislative Assembly, where I recollect to have seen one or both of them, in the capacity of pages, on the floor of the House. From that lowly position, step by step, they worked their way, as we have seen, to the very summit of their respective departments.

Mr. Todd was also an accomplished amateur artist, and drew exquisitely. An etching of the interior of Winchester Cathedral, by him, I have never seen surpassed.

He was fond of retirement and of antiquarian reading, and, while engaged in some learned philological investigation, would shut himself up in his peculiar sanctum and remain invisible for days,even to his own family.

Between the years 1833 and 1840, Mr. Todd published a book, entitled " Notes on Canada and the United States," and I cannot better illustrate his peculiar habits of thought, and mode of expressing them, than by quoting two or three brief passages from that work, and from " Addenda " which I printed for him myself, in 1840 :

" As an acidulated mixture with the purest element will embitter its sweetness, so vice and impurity imported to any country must corrupt and debase it. To this hour, when plunderers no longer feel secure in the scenes of their misdeeds, or culprits would evade the strong arm of the law, to what country do they escape? America— for here, if not positively welcomed (?), they are, at least, safe. If it be asked, did not ancient Rome do the same thing? I answer, slightly so, whilst yet an infant, but never in any shape afterwards; but America, by still receiving, and with open arms, the vicious and the vile from all corners of the earth, does so in her full growth. As she therefore plants, so must she also reap.

* * * " The Episcopal clergy in this country [United States] were originally supported by an annual contribution of tobacco, each male, so tithable, paying 40lbs. ; the regular clergy of the then thinly-settled state of Virginia receiving 16,000 lbs. yearly as salary. In Canada they are maintained by an assignment of lands from the Crown, which moreover extends its assistance to ministers of other denominations; so that the people are not called upon to contribute for that or any similar purpose; and yet, such is the deplorable abandonment to error, and obstinate perversion of fact, amongst the low or radical party here—a small one, it is true, but not on that account less censurable—that this very thing which should ensure their gratitude is a never-ending theme for their vituperation and abuse ; proving to demonstration, that no government on earth, or any concession whatever, can long satisfy or please them.

* * * " The mention of periodicals reminds me, that newspapers on the arrival of a stranger are about the first things he takes up; but on perusing them, he must exercise his utmost judgment and penetration ; for of all the fabrications, clothed too in the coarsest language, that ever came under my observation, many papers here, for low scurrility, and vilifying the authorities, certainly

surpass any I ever met with. It is to be regretted that men without principle and others void of character should be permitted thus to abuse the public ear. * * The misguided individuals in the late disturbance, on being questioned upon the subject, unreservedly admitted, that until reading Mackenzie's flagitious and slanderous newspaper, they were happy, contented, and loyal subjects."

When the seat of Government was removed to Kingston, Mr. Todd's family accompanied it thither; but he remained in Toronto, to look after his property, which was considerable, and died here at the age of 77.

CHAPTER XXVIII.

NEWSPAPER EXPERIENCES.

EARLY in the year 1838, I obtained an engagement as manager of the *Palladium*, a newspaper issued by Charles Fothergill, on the plan of the New York *Albion*. The printing office, situated on the corner of York and Boulton Streets, was very small, and I found it a mass of little better than *pi*, with an old hand-press of the Columbian pattern. To bring this office into something like presentable order, to train a rough lot of lads to their business, and to supply an occasional original article, occupied me during great part of that year. Mr. Fothergill was a man of talent, a scholar, and a gentleman; but so entirely given up to the study of natural history and the practice of taxidermy, that his newspaper received but scant attention, and his personal appearance and the cleanliness of his surroundings still less. He had been King's Printer under the Family Compact régime, and was dismissed for some imprudent criticism upon the policy of the Government. His family sometimes suffered from the want of common necessaries, while the money which should have fed them went to pay for some rare bird or strange fish. This could not last long. The *Palladium* died a natural death, and I had to seek elsewhere for employment.

Amongst the visitors at Mr. Todd's house was John F. Rogers, an Englishman, who, in conjunction with George H. Hackstaff, published the Toronto *Herald*, a weekly journal of very humble pretensions. Mr. Hackstaff was from the United States, and found himself regarded with great distrust, in consequence of the Navy Island and Prescott invasions. He therefore offered to sell me his interest in the newspaper and printing office for a few dollars. I accepted the offer, and thus became a member of the Fourth Estate, with all the dignities, immunities, and profits attaching thereto. From that time until the year 1860, I continued in the same profession, publishing successively the *Herald, Patriot, News of the Week,*

Atlas and *Daily Colonist* newspapers, and lastly the Quebec *Advertiser*. I mention them all now, to save wearisome details hereafter.

I have a very lively recollection of the first job which I printed in my new office. It was on the Sunday on which St. James's Cathedral was burnt owing to some negligence about the stoves. Our office was two doors north of the burnt edifice, on Church Street, where the Public Library now stands; and I was hurriedly required to print a small placard, announcing that divine service would be held that afternoon at the City Hall, where I had then recently drilled as a volunteer in the City Guard.

The *Herald* was the organ, and Mr. Rogers an active member, of the Orange body in Toronto. I had no previous knowledge of the peculiar features of Orangeism, and it took me some months to acquire an insight into the ways of thinking and acting of the order. I busied myself chiefly in the practical work of the office, such as type-setting and press-work, and took no part in editorials, except to write an occasional paragraph or musical notice.

The first book I undertook to print, and the first law book published in Canada, was my young friend Alpheus Todd's " Parliamentary Law," a volume of 400 pages, which was a creditable achievement for an office which could boast but two or three hundred dollars worth of type in all. With this book is connected an anecdote which I cannot refrain from relating :

I had removed my office to a small frame building on Church Street, next door south of C. Clinkinbroomer, the watchmaker's, at the south-west corner of King and Church Streets. One day, a strange-looking youth of fourteen or fifteen entered the office. He had in his hand a roll of manuscript, soiled and dog's-eared, which he asked me to look at. I did so, expecting to find verses intended for publication. It consisted indeed of a number of poems, extending to thirty or forty pages or more, defective in grammar and spelling, and in some parts not very legible.

Feeling interested in the lad, I enquired where he came from, what he could do, and what he wanted. It appeared that his father held some subordinate position in the English House of Commons; that, being put to a trade that he disliked, the boy ran away to Canada, where he verbally apprenticed himself to a shoemaker in Toronto, whom he quitted because his master wanted him to mend shoes, while he wished to spend his time in writing poetry; and that for the last year or so he had been working on a farm. He begged me to give him a trial as an apprentice to the printing business. I had known a fellow-apprentice of my own, who was first taken in as an office-boy, subsequently acquired a little education, became a printer's-devil, and when last I heard of him, was King's printer in Australia.

Well, I told the lad, whose name was Archie, that I would try him. I was just then perplexed with

the problem of making and using composition rollers
in the cold winter of Canada, and in an old frame
office, where it was almost impossible to keep anything from freezing. So I resolved to use a composition ball, such as may be seen in the pictures of
early German printing offices, printing four duo-
decimo pages of book-work at one impression, and
perfecting the sheet—or printing the obverse, as
medallists would say—with other four pages. Archie
was tall and strong—I gave him a regular drilling
in the use of the ball, and after some days' practice,
found I could trust him as beater at the press.
Robinson Crusoe's man Friday was not a more
willing, faithful, conscientious slave than was my
Archie. Never absent, never grumbling, never idle;
if there was no work ready for him, there was
always plenty of mischief at hand. He was very
fond of a tough argument; plodded on with his
press-work; learnt to set type pretty well, before it
was suspected that he even knew the letter boxes;
studied hard at grammar and the dictionary;
acquired knowledge with facility, and retained it
tenaciously. He remained with me many years,
and ultimately became my foreman. After the
destruction of the establishment by fire in 1849, he
was engaged as foreman of the University printing
office of Mr. Henry Rowsell, and left there after a
long term to enter the Toronto School of Medicine,
then presided over by Dr. Rolph, on Richmond

Street, just west of where Knox's Church now stands. After obtaining his license to practise the profession of medicine, he studied Spanish, and then went to Mexico, to practise among the semi-savages of that politically and naturally volcanic republic. There he made a little money.

The country was at the time in a state of general civil war; not only was there national strife between two political parties for the ascendency, but in many of the separate states *pronunciamentos* (proclamations) were issued against the men in power, followed by bloody contests between the different factions. In the "united state" of Coahuila and Nuevo-Leon, in which the doctor then resided, General Vidauri held the reins of power at Monterey, the capital; and General Aramberri flew to arms to wrest the government from him. The opposing armies were no other than bands of robbers and murderers. Aramberri's forces had passed near the town of Salinas, where the doctor lived, plundering everybody on their route. Next day Vidauri's troops came in pursuit, appropriating everything of value which had not been already confiscated. General Julio Quiroga, one of the most inhuman and cruel monsters of the republic—a native of the town, near which he had but recently been a cowherd (gauadéro)—commanded the pursuing force. On the evening previous to his entry, a *peon* (really a slave, though slavery was said to have been abolished in

the republic) had been severely injured in a quarrel
with another of his class, and the doctor was sent
for by the Alcalde to dress his wounds. As the man
was said to belong to a rich proprietor, the doctor
objected unless his fee were assured. An old, rough,
and dirty-looking man thereupon stepped forward
and said he would be answerable for the pay, stating
at the same time that his name was Quiroga, and
that he was the father of Don Julio! When General
Quiroga heard his father's account of the affair, he
had the wounded man placed in the stocks in
the open plaza under a broiling sun; fined the
Alcalde $500 for not having done so himself, as well
as for not having imprisoned the Doctor; had the
Doctor arrested by an armed guard under a lieutenant, and in the presence of a dozen or more officers
ordered him to be shot within twenty minutes for
having insulted his (Quiroga's) father. The execution, however, as may be inferred, did not take
place. The explanation the Doctor gives of his
escape is a curious one. He cursed and swore at the
General so bitterly and rapidly in English (not
being at the time well versed in Spanish expletives)
that Don Julio was frightened by his grimaces, and
the horrible unknown words that issued from his
lips, and fell off his chair in an epileptic fit, to which
he was subject. The Doctor had the clothing about
the General's throat and chest thrown open, and
dashed some cold water in his face. On reviving,
Quiroga told the Doctor to return to his house;

that he need be under no fear ; said he supposed
the difficulty was caused by his (the Doctor's) not
understanding the Spanish language; and added,
that he intended to consult our friend some day
about those *atagues* (fits). Quiroga never returned
to Salinas during the Doctor's stay there, and some
years after these events, like most Mexican generals,
was publicly executed, thus meeting the fate he had
so cruelly dealt out to many better men than himself, and to which he had sentenced our fellow-
citizen.

The Doctor remained in Mexico till the French
invasion in 1863, when, partly on account of the
illness of his wife, and partly because of the disturbed
state of the country, he returned to Toronto. He
practised his profession here and became a well-
known public character, still, he said, cherishing a
warm love for the sunny south, styling the land of
the Montezumas " *Mi Mejico amado* "—my beloved
Mexico—and corresponding with his friends there,
who but very recently offered him some induce-
ments to return.

That truant boy was afterwards known as Dr.
Archibald A. Riddel, ex-alderman, and for many
years coroner for the City of Toronto, which latter
office he resigned so lately as the 30th of June, 1883.
He died in December last, and was buried in the
Necropolis, whither his remains were followed by a
large concourse of sympathizing friends.

L

CHAPTER XXIX.

THE burning of St. James's Cathedral in 1839, marks another phase of my Toronto life, which is associated with many pleasant and some sorrowful memories. The services of the Church of England were, for some months after that event, conducted in the old City Hall. The choir was an amateur one, led by Mr. J. D. Humphreys, whose reputation as an accomplished musician must be familiar to many of my readers. Of that choir I became a member, and continued one until my removal to Carlton in 1853. During those fourteen years I was concerned in almost every musical movement in Toronto, wrote musical notices, and even composed some music to my own poetry. An amateur glee club, of which Mr. E. L. Cull, until lately of the Canada Company's office, and myself are probably the only survivors, used occasionally to meet and amuse ourselves with singing glees and quartettes on Christmas and New Year's Eve, opposite the houses of our several friends. It was then the custom to invite our party indoors, to be sumptuously entertained with the good things provided for the purpose.

Thus the time passed away after the rebellion, and during the period of Sir George Arthur's stay in Canada, without the occurrence of any public event in which I was personally concerned. Lord Durham came; made his celebrated Report: and went home again. Then followed Lord Sydenham, to whom I propose to pay some attention, as with him commenced my first experience of Canadian party politics.

Mackenzie's rebellion had convinced me of the necessity of taking and holding firm ground in defence of monarchical institutions, as opposed to republicanism. It is well known that nearly all Old Country Whigs, when transplanted to Canada, become staunch Tories. So most moderate Reformers from the British Isles are classed here as Liberal Conservatives. Even English Chartists are transformed into Canadian Anti-Republicans.

I had been neither Chartist nor ultra-Radical, but simply a quiet Reformer, disposed to venerate, but not blindly to idolize, old institutions, and by no means to pull down an ancient fabric without knowing what kind of structure was to be erected in its place. Thus it followed, as a matter of course, that I should gravitate towards the Conservative side of Canadian party politics, in which I found so many of the solid, respectable, well-to-do citizens of Toronto had ranged themselves.

CHAPTER XXX.

LORD SYDENHAM'S MISSION.

I HAVE frequently remarked that, although in England any person may pass a life-time without becoming acquainted with his next-door neighbour, he can hardly fall into conversation with a fellow-countryman in Canada, without finding some latent link of relationship or propinquity between them. Thus, in the case of Mr. C. Poulett Thomson, I trace more than one circumstance connecting that great man with my humble self. He was a member—the active member—of the firm of Thomson, Bonar & Co., Russia Merchants, Cannon Street, London, at the same time that my brother-in-law, William Tatchell, of the firm of Tatchell & Clarke, carried on the same business of Russia Merchants in Upper Thames Street. There were occasional transactions between them: and my brother Thomas, who was chief accountant in the Thames Street house, has told me that the firm of Thomson, Bonar &. Co. was looked upon in the trade with a good deal of distrust, for certain sharp practices to which they were addicted.

Again, Sir John Rae Reid, of the East India Company, had been the Tory member of Parliament for

Dover. On his retirement, Mr. Poulett Thomson started as Reform candidate for the same city. I knew the former slightly as a neighbour of my mother's, at Ewell, in Surrey, and felt some interest in the Dover election in consequence. It was in the old borough-mongering times, and the newspapers on both sides rang with accounts of the immense sums that were expended in this little Dover contest, in which Mr. Thomson, aided by his party, literally bought every inch of his way, and succeeded in obtaining his first seat in the House of Commons, at a cost, as his biographer states, of £3,000 sterling. In the matter of corruption, there was probably little difference between the rival candidates.

The Right Hon. Charles Poulett Thomson, it was understood in England, always had the dirty work of the Melbourne Ministry to do; and it was probably his usefulness in that capacity that recommended him for the task of uniting the two Canadas, in accordance with that report of Lord Durham, which his lordship himself disavowed.* That Mr. Thomson did his work well, cannot be denied. He was, in

* On reference to Sir F. B. Head's " Emigrant," pp. 376-8, the reader will find the following letters :—

" 1. *From the Hon. Sir A. N. MacNab.*

" LEGISLATIVE ASSEMBLY,

" Montreal, 28th March, 1846.

" MY DEAR SIR FRANCIS,

" I have no hesitation in putting on paper the conversation which took place between Lord Durham and my-fact, the Castlereagh of Canadian Union. What were the exact means employed by him in Montreal and

---

self, on the subject of the Union. He asked me if I was in favour of the Union ; I said, ' No ;' he replied, ' If you are a friend to your country, *oppose it to the death.*'

"I am, &c.,

"(Signed)   ALLAN N. MACNAB.

"Sir F. B. Head, Bart."

"2. *From W. E. Jervis, Esq.*

"TORONTO, March 12th, 1846.

"DEAR SIR ALLAN,

"In answer to the inquiry contained in your letter of the 2nd inst., I beg leave to state, that, in the year 1838, I was in Quebec, and had a long conversation with the Earl of Durham upon the subject of an Union of the Provinces of Upper and Lower Canada—a measure which I had understood his Lordship intended to propose.

"I was much gratified by his Lordship then, in the most unqualified terms, declaring his strong disapprobation of such a measure, as tending, in his opinion, to the injury of this Province ; and he advised me, as a friend to Upper Canada, *to use all the influence I might possess in opposition to it.*

"His Lordship declared that, in his opinion, no statesman could propose so injurious a project, and authorized me to assure my friends in Upper Canada, *that he was decidedly averse to the measure.*

"I have a perfect recollection of having had a similar enquiry made of me, by the private secretary of Sir George Arthur, and that I made a written reply to the communication. I have no copy of the letter which I sent upon that occasion, but the substance must have been similar to that I now send you.

"I remain, &c.,

"(Signed)   W. E. JERVIS.

"Sir Allan MacNab."

Toronto is not known, but the results were visible enough. Government officials coerced, sometimes

---

"3. *From the Hon. Justice Hagerman.*
"13 ST. JAMES'S STREET,
"LONDON, 12th July, 1846.
"MY DEAR SIR FRANCIS,

"It is well known to many persons that the late Lord Durham, up to the time of his departure from Canada, expressed himself strongly opposed to the Union of the then two Provinces. I accompanied Sir George Arthur on a visit to Lord Durham, late in the autumn, and a very few days only before he threw up his Government and embarked for this country. In a conversation I had with him, he spoke of the Union as *the selfish scheme of a few merchants of Montreal—that no statesman would advise the measure—and that it was absurd to suppose that Upper and Lower Canada could ever exist in harmony as one Province.*

"In returning to Toronto with Sir George Arthur, he told me that Lord Durham had expressed to him similar opinions, and had at considerable length detailed to him reasons and arguments which existed against a measure which he considered would be destructive of the legitimate authority of the British Government, and in which opinion *Sir George declared he fully coincided.*
"I am, Sir,
"(Signed)   C. A. HAGERMAN.
"Sir F. B. Head, Bart."
"4. *From the Earl of Durham.*
"QUEBEC, Oct. 2nd, 1838.
"DEAR SIR,

"I thank you kindly for your account of the meeting [in Montreal], which was the first I received. I fully expected the 'outbreak' about the Union of the two Provinces :—IT IS A PET MONTREAL PROJECT, BEGINNING AND ENDING IN MONTREAL SELFISHNESS.
"Yours, truly,
"(Signed)   DURHAM."

through the agency of their wives, sometimes by direct threats of dismissal; the Legislature overawed by the presence and interference of His Excellency's secretaries and aides-de-camp; votes sought and obtained by appeals to the personal interests of members of Parliament. These and such-like were the dignified processes by which the Union of the Canadas was effected, in spite of the unwillingness of at least one of the parties to that ceremony.

His Excellency did not even condescend to veil his contempt for his tools. When a newly nominated Cabinet Minister waited upon the great man with humility, to thank him for an honour for which he felt his education did not qualify him, the reported answer was—" Oh, I think you are all pretty much alike here."

In Toronto, anything like opposition to His Excellency's policy was sought to be silenced by the threat of depriving the city of its tenure of the Seat of Government. The offices of the principal city journals, the *Patriot* and *Courier*, were besieged by anxious subscribers, entreating that nothing should appear at all distasteful to His Excellency. Therefore it happened, that our little sheet, the *Herald*, became the only mouth-piece of Toronto dissentients; and was well supplied with satires and criticisms upon the politic manœuvres of Government House. We used to issue on New Year's Day a sheet of doggerel verses, styled, " The News Boy's Address to his Patrons," which gave me an opportunity, of which I did not fail to avail myself, of telling His Excellency some wholesome truths in not very complimentary phrase. It is but justice to him to say, that he enjoyed the fun, such as it was, as much as anybody, and sent a servant in livery to our office, for extra copies to be placed on his drawing-room tables for the amusement of New Year's callers, to whom he read them himself. I am sorry that I cannot now treat my readers to extracts from those sheets, which may some centuries hence be unearthed by future Canadian antiquaries, as rare and priceless historical documents.

Whether the course he pursued be thought creditable or the reverse, there is no doubt that Lord Sydenham did Canada immense service by the measures enacted under his dictation. The Union of the Provinces, Municipal Councils, Educational Institutions, sound financial arrangements, and other minor matters, are benefits which cannot be ignored. But all these questions were carried in a high-handed, arbitrary manner, and some of them by downright compulsion. To connect in any way with his name the credit of bestowing upon the united provinces " Responsible Government " upon the British model, is a gross absurdity.

In the Memoirs of his lordship, by his brother, Mr. G. Poulett Scrope, page 236, I find the following plain statements:

"On the subject of 'Responsible Government,' which question was again dragged into discussion by Mr. Baldwin, with a view of putting the sincerity of the Government to the test, he (Lord S.) introduced and carried unanimously a series of resolutions in opposition to those proposed by Mr. Baldwin, distinctly recognising the irresponsibility of the Governor to any but the Imperial authorities, and placing the doctrine on the sound and rational basis which he had ever maintained."

What that "sound and rational basis" was, is conclusively shown in an extract from one of his own private letters, given on page 143 of the same work:

"I am not a bit afraid of the Responsible Government cry. I have already done much to put it down in its inadmissible sense, namely, that the Council shall be responsible to the Assembly, and that the Government shall take their advice, and be bound by it. In fact, this demand has been made much more *for* the people than *by* them. And I have not met with any one who has not at once admitted the absurdity of claiming to put the Council over the head of the Governor. It is but fair too, to say that everything has in times past been done by the different Governors to excite the feelings of the people on this question. First, the Executive Council has generally been composed of the persons most obnoxious to the majority of the Assembly; and next, the Governor has taken extreme care to make every act of his own go forth to the public *on the responsibility* of the Executive Council. So the people have been carefully taught to believe that the Governor is nobody, and the Executive Council the real power, and that by the Governor himself. At the same time they have seen that power placed in the hands of their opponents. Under such a system it is not to be wondered at, if one argument founded on the responsibility of the Governor to the Home Government falls to the ground. I have told the people plainly that, as I cannot get rid of my responsibility to the Home Government, I will place no responsibility on the Council ; that they are *a Council* for the Governor to consult, but no more. And I have yet met with no 'Responsible Government' man, who was not satisfied with the doctrine. In fact, there is no other theory which has common sense. Either the Governor is the Sovereign or the Minister. If the first, he may have ministers, but he cannot be responsible to the Government at home, and all colonial government becomes impossible. He must, therefore, be the Minister, in which case he cannot be under the control of men in the colony."

It is only just that the truth should be clearly established on this question. Responsible Government was not an issue between Canadian Reformers and Tories in any sense; but exclusively between the Colonies and the statesmen of the Mother Country. On several occasions prior to Mackenzie's Rebellion, Tory majorities had affirmed the principle; and Ogle R. Gowan, an influential Orangeman, had published a pamphlet in its favour. Yet some recent historians of Canada have fallen into the foolish habit of claiming for the Reform party all the good legislation of the past forty years, until they seem really to believe the figment themselves.*

---

* I am very glad to see that Mr. Dent, in his " Forty Years — Canada since the Union of 1841," recently pub-

I am surprised that writers who condemn Sir F. B. Head for acting as his own Prime Minister, in strict accordance with his instructions, can see nothing to find fault with in Lord SydenLam's doing the very same thing in an infinitely more arbitrary and offensive manner.　Where Sir Francis persuaded, Lord Sydenham coerced, bribed and derided.

Lower Canada was never consulted as to her own destiny.　Because a fraction of her people chose to strike for independence, peaceable French Canadians were treated bodily as a conquered race, with the

---

lished, has avoided the current fault of those writers who can recognise no historical truth not endorsed by the *Globe*.　In vol. i, p. 357, he says :

"There can be no doubt that the Reform party, as a whole, were unjust to Mr. Draper.　They did not even give him credit for sincerity or good intentions.　The historian of to-day, no matter what his political opinions may be, who contemplates Mr. Draper's career as an Executive Councillor, must doubtless arrive at the conclusion that he was wrong ; that he was an obstructionist —a drag on the wheel of, progress.　But this fact was by no means so easy of recognition in 1844 as it is in 1881; and there is no good reason for impugning his motives, which, so far as can be ascertained, were honourable and patriotic.　No impartial mind can review the acts and characters of the leading members of the Conservative party of those times, and come to the conclusion that they were all selfish and insincere.　Nay, it is evident enough that they were at least as sincere and as zealous for the public good as were their opponents."

I wish I could also compliment Mr. Dent upon doing like justice to Sir Francis B. Head.

undisguised object of swamping their nationality
and language, and over-riding their feelings and
wishes. It is said that the result has justified the
means. But what casuistry is this? What sort of
friend to Responsible Government must he be, who
employs force to back his argument? To inculcate
the voluntary principle at the point of the bayonet,
is a peculiarly Hibernian process, to say the least.

CHAPTER XXXI.

TORIES OF THE REBELLION TIMES.

HAVING, I hope, sufficiently exposed the mis-
representations of party writers, who have
persistently made it their business to calumniate
the Loyalists of 1837-8, I now proceed to the pleas-
anter task of recording the good deeds of some of
those Loyalists, with whom I was brought into personal contact. I begin with—

ALDERMAN GEORGE T. DENISON, SEN.

No Toronto citizen of '37 can fail to recall the
bluff, halc, strongly-built figure of George Taylor
Denison, of Bellevue, the very embodiment of the
English country squire of the times of Addison and

Goldsmith.   Resolute to enforce obedience, generous to the poor, just and fair as a magistrate, hospitable to strangers and friends, a sound and consistent Churchman, a brave soldier and a loyal subject, it seemed almost an anachronism to meet with him anywhere else than at his own birth-place of Dover Court, within sight of the Goodwin Sands, in the old-fashioned County of Essex, in England.

He was the son of John Denison, of Hedon, York-shire, and was born in 1783.   He came with his father to Canada in 1792, and to Toronto in 1796. Here he married the only daughter of Captain Richard Lippincott, a noted U. E. Loyalist, who had fought through the Civil War in the revolted Colo-nies now forming the United States.   In the war of 1812, Mr Denison served as Ensign in the York Volunteers, and was frequently employed on special service.   He was the officer who, with sixty men, cut out the present line of the Dundas Road, from the Garrison Common to Lambton Mills, which was necessary to enable communication between York and the Mills to be carried on without interruption from the hostile fleet on the lake.   During the attack on York, in the following year, he was com-missioned to destroy our vessels in the Bay, to save them from falling into the enemy's hands.   With some he succeeded, but on one frigate the captain refused to obey the order, and while the point was in dispute, the enemy settled the question by capturing the ship, in consequence of which Mr. Denison was held as a prisoner for several months, until exchanged.

Of his services and escapes during the war many amusing stories are told. He was once sent with a very large sum in army bills—some $40,000—to pay the force then on the Niagara River. To avoid suspicion, the money was concealed in his saddle-bags, and he wore civilian's clothing. His destination was the village of St. David's. Within a mile or two of the place, he became aware of a cavalry soldier galloping furiously towards him, who, on coming up, asked if he was the officer with the money, and said he must ride back as fast as possible; the Yankees had driven the British out of St. David's, and parties of their cavalry were spreading over the country. Presently another dragoon came in sight, riding at speed and pursued by several of the enemy's horsemen. Ensign Denison turned at once, and after an exciting chase for many miles, succeeded in distancing his foes and escaping with his valuable charge.

On another occasion, he had under his orders a number of boats employed in bringing army munitions from Kingston to York. Somewhere near Port Hope, while creeping alongshore to avoid the United States vessels cruising in the lake, he observed several of them bearing down in his direction. Immediately he ran his boats up a small stream, destroying a bridge across its mouth to open a passage, and hid them so effectually that the enemy's fleet passed by without suspecting their presence.

About the year 1821, Captain Denison formed the design to purchase the farm west of the city, now known as the Rusholme property. The owner lived at Niagara. A friend who knew of his intention, told him one summer's morning, while he was looking at some goods in a store, that he would not get the land, as another man had left that morning for Niagara, in Oates's sloop, to gain the start of him. The day being unusually fine, Mr. Denison noticed that the sloop was still in sight, becalmed a mile or two off Gibraltar Point. Home he went, put up some money for the purchase, mounted his horse and set out for Niagara round the head of the lake, travelling all day and through the night, and arriving shortly after daybreak. There he saw the sloop in the river, endeavouring with the morning breeze to make the landing. To rouse up the intending vendor, to close the bargain, and get a receipt for the money, was soon accomplished; and when the gentleman who had hoped to forestall him came on the scene, he was wofully chopfallen to find himself distanced in the race.

From the close of the war until the year 1837, Mr. Denison was occupied, like other men of his position, with his duties as a magistrate, the cultivation of his farm, and the rearing of his family. In 1822, he organized the cavalry corps now known as the Governor-General's Body-Guard. When the rebellion broke out, he took up arms again in defence of the Crown, and on the day of the march up Yonge Street, was entrusted with the command of the Old Fort. At about noon a body of men was seen approaching. Eagerly and anxiously the defenders waited, expecting every moment an onset, and determined to meet it like men. The suspense lasted some minutes, when suddenly the Major exclaimed, " Why surely that's my brother Tom ! " And so it was The party consisted of a number of good loyalists, headed by Thomas Denison, of Weston, hastening to the aid of the Government against Mackenzie and his adherents. Of course, the gates were soon thrown open, and, with hearty cheers on .both sides, the new-comers entered the Fort.

For six months Major Denison continued in active service with his cavalry, and in the summer of 1838, was promoted to command the battalion of West York Militia. His eldest son, the late Richard L. Denison, succeeded to the command of the cavalry corps, which was kept on service for six months in the winter of 1838-9.

Mr. Denison was elected an alderman of Toronto in the year 1834, and served in the same capacity up to the end of 1843.

That he was quite independent of the " Family Compact," or of any other official clique, is shown by the fact, that on Mackenzie's second expulsion from

M

the House of Assembly in 1832, Alderman Denison voted for his re-election for the County of York.

Our old friend died in 1853, leaving four sons, viz.: Richard L. Denison, of Dover Court, named above; the late George Taylor Denison, òf Rush-olme; Robert B. Denison, of Bellevue, now Deputy-Adjutant-General for this district; Charles L. Denison, of Brockton: and also one daughter, living. Among his grandchildren are Colonel George T. Denison, commanding the Governor-General's Body Guard, and Police Magistrate; Major F. C. Denison, of the same corps: and Lieutenant John Denison, R. N.   The whole number of the Canadian descendants of John Denison, of Hedon, now living, is over one hundred.

Col. Richard Lippincott Denison, eldest son of the above, was born June 13th, 1814, at the old family estate near Weston, on the Humber River, and followed the occupation of farming all his life. During the troubles of 1837-8, he served his country as captain in command of a troop of the Queen's Light Dragoons.   He took a prominent part in the organization of the Agricultural and Arts Association in 1844, and for twenty-two years was its treasurer. In 1855, he was a commissioner from Canada at the great exposition in Paris, France.. He also held a prominent position in the different county and township agricultural societies for over forty-five years;

was one of the first directors of the Canada Landed
Credit Company, and served on its board for several
years ; was at one time President of the late Beaver
Fire Insurance Company; and at the time of his
death, President of the Society of York Pioneers. For
many years he commanded the Militia in the West
Riding of the City of Toronto; and was alderman
for St. Stephen's Ward in the City Council, which
he represented at the Centennial Exhibition at Philadelphia in 1876.

As a private citizen, Richard L. Denison was generally popular, notwithstanding his strongly-marked
Toryism, and outspoken bluntness of speech. His
portly presence, handsome features, flowing beard,
and kindly smile were universally welcomed; and
when he drove along in his sleigh on a bright winter's
day, strangers stopped to look at him with admiration, and to ask who that fine-looking man was ?
Nor did his personal qualities belie his noble exte-
rior. For many years his house at Dover Court was
one continuous scene of open-handed hospitality.
He was generous to a fault; a warm friend, and an
ever reliable comrade.

He died March 10th, 1878, at the age of sixty-four
years, leaving his widow and eight sons and one
daughter. Few deaths have left so wide a gap as
his, in our social circles.

Colonel George T. Denison, of Rusholme, second son of Alderman George T. Denison, sen., was born 17th of July, 1816, at Bellevue, Toronto. He was educated at Upper Canada College, and became a barrister in 1840.

He was a volunteer in Col. Fitzgibbon's rifle company, prior to the Rebellion of 1837, and attended every drill until it was disbanded. On the Rebellion breaking out, he served for a while as one of the guard protecting the Commercial Bank, and was in the force that marched out to Gallows Hill and dispersed Mackenzie's followers. A few days after, he went as lieutenant in a company of militia, forming part of the column commanded by Col. Sir A. Mac-Nab, to the village of Scotland, in the County of Brant, and from thence to Navy Island, where he served throughout the whole siege. He was one of the three officers who carried the information to Sir Allan, which led to the cutting out and destruction of the steamer *Caroline*.

In November, 1838, he was appointed lieutenant in his father's troop of cavalry, now the Governor-General's Body Guard ; and then just placed under the command of his brother, the late Col. Richard L. Denison. He served for six months in active service that winter, and put in a course of drill for some weeks with the King's Dragoon Guards, at Niagara.

He was alderman for St. Patrick's ward for some years. In 1849, when Lord Elgin, in Toronto, opened the session of Parliament, Col. G. T. Denison escorted His Excellency to and from the Parliament House.

The following account of this affair is copied from the "Historical Record of the Governor-General's Body Guard," by Capt. F. C. Denison :—

"In Montreal, during the riots that followed the passage of the Rebellion Losses bill, the troops of cavalry that had been on regular service for over ten years, forgot their discipline, forgot their duty to their Queen's representative, forgot their *esprit de corps*, and sat on their horses and laughed while the mob were engaged in pelting Lord Elgin with eggs. This Toronto troop acted differently, and established a name then for obedience to orders, that should be looked back to with pride by every man who ever serves in its ranks. Unquestionably there was a great deal politically to tempt them from their duty, and to lead them to remain inactive if nothing worse. But their sense of duty to their Queen, through her representative, was so strong, that they turned out, taking the Governor-General safely to and from the Parliament Buildings, much against the will of a noisy, turbulent crowd. This was an excellent proof of what *esprit de corps* will do, and of the good state the troop must have been in. His Excellency was so pleased with the loyalty, discipline and general conduct of the escort on this occasion, that he sent orders to the officer commanding, to dismount his men, and bring them into the drawing room. By His Excellency's request, Captain Denison presented each man individually to him, and he shook hands with them all, thanking them personally for their services. They were then invited to sit down to a handsome lunch with His Excellency's staff."

In 1855, when the volunteer force was created, Col. Denison took a squadron of cavalry into the

new force, and afterwards organized the Toronto
Field Battery, and in 1860, the Queen's Own Rifles ;
and was appointed commandant of the 5th and 10th
Military Districts, which position he held until his
death.   He was recommended, with Colonel Sewell
and Colonel Dyde, for the order of St. Michael and
St. George; but before the order was granted he had
died, and Col. Dyde, C.M.G., alone of the three, lived
to enjoy the honour.   Col. Denison was the senior
officer in Ontario at the time of his death, and may
be said to have been the father of the volunteer force
of this district.

ALDERMAN DIXON.

Few persons engaged in business took a more
prominent part in the early history of Toronto, and
in the political events of the time, than the subject
of this sketch. For several years he was engaged
in trade in the City of Dublin, being the proprietor
of the most extensive business of the kind, in sad-
dlery and hardware, having the contracts for the
supply of the cavalry in the Dublin garrison, and
also the Viceregal establishment. At that time he
took a very active part in the political warfare of
the day, when Daniel O'Connell was in the zenith
of his power. He and Mr. S. P. Bull—father of the
late Senator Harcourt P. Bull—were active agents
in organizing the " Brunswick Lodges," which played

no inconsiderable part in the politics of that exciting period. The despondency that fell upon Irish Protestant loyalists when the Emancipation Bill became law, induced many to emigrate to America, and among them Mr. Dixon. Though actively employed in the management of his business both in Dublin and Toronto, yet he had found time to lay in a solid foundation of standard literature, and even of theological lore, which qualified him to take a position in intellectual society of a high order. He also possessed great readiness of speech, a genial, good-natured countenance and manner, and a fund of drollery and comic wit, which, added to a strong Irish accent he at times assumed, made him a special favourite in the City Council, as well as at public dinners, and on social festive occasions. I had the privilege of an intimate acquaintance with him from 1838 until his death, and can speak with confidence of his feelings and principles.

Though so thoroughly Irish, his ancestors' came originally from Lanarkshire in Scotland, in the reign of James I., and held a grant of land in the north of Ireland. He felt proud of one of his ancestors, who raised a troop of volunteer cavalry, lost an arm at the Battle of the Boyne, and was rewarded by a captain's commission given under King William's own hand a few days after. His own father served in the "Black Horse," a volunteer regiment of much note in the Irish rebellion.

When Mr. Dixon came to York, his intention was
to settle at Mount Vernon, in the State of Ohio,
where he had been informed there was an Episcopal
College, and a settlement of Episcopalians on the
College territory. In order to satisfy himself of
the truth of these statements, he travelled thither
alone, leaving his family in the then town of York.
Disappointed in the result of his visit, he returned
here, and had almost made up his mind to go back
to Dublin, but abandoned the intention in consequence of the urgent arguments of the Hon. John
Henry Dunn, Receiver-General,* who persuaded him
to remain. His first step was to secure a lease of
the lot of land on King Street, where the Messrs. W. A.
Murray & Co's. warehouses now stand. He built there
two frame shops, which were considered marvels
of architecture at that day, and continued to occupy
one of them until Wellington Buildings, between
Church and Toronto Streets, were erected by himself
and other enterprising tradesmen. Merchants of all
ranks lived over their shops in those times, and very
handsome residences these buildings made.

In 1834, Mr. Dixon was elected alderman for St.
Lawrence Ward, which position he continued to hold
against all assailants, up to the end of 1850. He was

------

* Father of the lamented Lieut.-Col. A. R. Dunn, who
won the Victoria Cross at Balaklava, and died as is believed, by the accidental discharge of a gun in Abys-
sinia.

also a justice of the peace, and did good service in that capacity. In the City Council no man was more useful and industrious in all good works, and none exercised greater influence over its deliberations.

When the troubles of 1837 began, Alderman Dixon threw all his energies into the cause of loyalty, and took so active a part in support of Sir F. B. Head's policy, that his advice was on most occasions sought by the Lieutenant-Governor, and frequently acted upon. Many communications on the burning questions of the day passed between them. This continued throughout the rule of Sir George Arthur, and until the arrival of the Right Hon. C. Poulett Thomson, who cared little for the opinions of other men, however well qualified to advise and inform. Mr. Dixon was too independent and too incorruptible a patriot for that accomplished politician.

Few men in Toronto have done more for the beautifying of our city. The Adelaide Buildings on King Street were long the handsomest, as they were the best built, of their class. His house, at the corner of Jarvis and Gerrard Streets, set an example for our finest private residences. The St. Lawrence Hall, which is considered by visitors a great ornament to the city, was erected from plans suggested by him. And among religious edifices, Trinity Church and St. James's Cathedral are indebted to him, the former mainly and the latter in part, for their complete adaptation in style and convenience, to the services of the Church to which he belonged and which he highly venerated. To Trinity Church, especially, which was finished and opened for divine service on February 14th, 1844, he gave himself up with the most unflagging zeal and watchfulness, examining the plans in the minutest details, supervising the work as it progressed, almost counting the bricks and measuring the stonework, with the eye of a father watching his infant's first footsteps. In fact, he was popularly styled "the father and founder of Trinity Church," a designation which was justly recognised by Bishop Strachan in his dedication sermon.*

As a friend, I had something to say respecting most of his building plans, and fully sympathized with the objects he had in view; one of the fruits of my appreciation was the following poem, which, although of little merit in itself, is perhaps worth preserving as a record of honourable deeds and well employed talents :

THE POOR MAN'S CHURCH.

Wake, harp of Zion, silent long,
  Nor voiceless and unheard be thou

---

* The Building Committee of Trinity Church comprised, besides Alderman Dixon, Messrs. William Gooderham, Enoch Turner, and Joseph Shuter, all since deceased.

While meetest theme of sacred song
    Awaits thy chorded numbers now !

Too seldom, 'mid the sounds of strife
    That rudely ring unwelcome here,
Thy music soothes this fever'd life
    With breathings from a holier sphere.

The warrior, wading deep in crime,
    Desertless, lives in poets' lays ;
The statesman wants not stirring rhyme
    To cheer the chequer'd part he plays :

And Zion's harp, to whom alone,
    Soft-echoing, higher themes belong,
Oh lend thy sweet aërial tone—
    'Tis meek-eyed Virtue claims the song.

———

Beyond the limits of the town
    A summer's ramble, may be seen
A scattered suburb, newly grown,
    Rude huts, and ruder fields between.

Life's luxuries abound not there,
    Labour and hardship share the spot;
Hope wrestles hard with frowning care,
    And lesser wants are heeded not.

Religion was neglected too—
    'Twas far to town—the poor are proud—
They could not boast a garb as new,
    And shunu'd to join the well-drest crowd.

No country church adorned the scene,
    In modest beauty smiling fair,
Of mien so peaceful and serene,
    The poor man feels his home is there.

Oh England ! with thy village chimes,
    Thy church-wed hamlets, scattered wide,
The emigrant to other climes
    Remembers thee with grateful pride ;

And owns that once at home again,
    With fonder love his heart would bless
Each humble, lowly, haloëd fane
    That sanctifies thy loveliness.

But here, alas ! the heart was wrung
    To see so wan, so drear a waste—
Life's thorns and briars rankly sprung,
    And peace and love, its flowers, displaced.

And weary seasons pass'd away,
    As time's fast ebbing tide roll'd by,
To thousands rose no Sabbath-day,
    They lived—to suffer—sin—and die !

Then men of Christian spirit came,
    They saw the mournful scene with grief ;
To such it e'er hath been the same
    To know distress and give relief.

They told the tale, nor vainly told—
    They won assistance far and wide ;
His heart were dull indeed and cold
    Who such petitioner denied.

They chose a slightly rising hill
  That bordered closely on the road,
And workmen brought of care and skill,
  And wains with many a cumbrous load

With holy prayer and chanted hymn
  The task was sped upon its way ;
And hearts beat high and eyes were dim
  To see so glad a sight that day.

And slowly as the work ascends,
  In just proportions strong and fair,
How watchfully its early friends
  With zealous ardour linger near.

'Tis finished now—a Gothic pile,
  —Brave handiwork of faith and love—
In England's ancient hallowed style,
  That pointeth aye, like hope, above :

With stately tower and turret high,
  And quaint-arch'd door, and buttress'd wall,
And window stain'd of various dye,
  And antique moulding over all.

And hark ! the Sabbath-going bell !
  A solemn tale it peals abroad—
To all around its echoes tell
  "This building is the house of God ! "

———

Say, Churchman ! doth no still, small voice
  Within you whisper—" while 'tis day

Go bid the desert place rejoice !"
    Your Saviour's high behest obey :

 :" Say not your pow'rs are scant and weak,
    What hath been done, may be anew ;
    HE addeth strength to all who seek
    To serve Him with affection true."

Alderman Dixon was not only a thorough-going and free-handed Churchman, but was very popular with the ministers and pastors of other religious denominations. The heads of the Methodist Church, and even the higher Roman Catholic clergy of Toronto, frequently sought his advice and assistance to smooth down asperities and reconcile feuds. He was every man's friend, and had no enemies of whom I ever heard. He wrote with facility, and argued with skill and readiness. His memory was exceedingly retentive ; he knew and could repeat page after page from Dryden's "Virgil" and Pope's "Homer." Any allusion to them would draw from him forty or fifty lines in connection with its subject. Mickle's "Lusiad" he knew equally well, and was fond of reciting its most beautiful descriptions of scenery and places in South Africa and India. He was an enthusiastic book-collector, and left a valuable library, containing many very rare and curious books he had brought from Dublin, and to which he made several additions. It is now in the possession of his eldest son, Archdeacon Dixon, of Guelph.

With the Orange body, Alderman Dixon exercised considerable influence, which he always exerted in favour of a Christian regard for the rights and feelings of those who differed from them. On one occasion, and only one, I remember his suffering some indignity at their hands. He and others had exerted themselves to induce the Orangemen to waive their annual procession, and had succeeded so far as the city lodges were concerned. But the country lodges would not forego their cherished rights, and on "the 12th"—I forget the year—entered Toronto from the west in imposing numbers. At the request of the other magistrates, Alderman Dixon and, I think, the late Mayor Gurnett, met the procession opposite Osgoode Hall, and remonstrated with the leaders for disregarding the wishes of the City Council and the example of their city brethren. His eloquence, however, was of no avail, and he and his colleague were rudely thrust aside.

As president of the St. Patrick's Society, he did much to preserve unanimity in that body, which then embraced Irishmen of all creeds among its members. His speeches at its annual dinners were greatly admired for their ability and liberality; and it was a favourite theme of his, that the three nationalities—Irish, Scotch and English—together formed an invincible combination; while if unhappily separated, they might have to succumb to inferior races. He concluded his argument on one

occasion by quoting Scott's striking lines on the
Battle of Waterloo :—

> " Yes—Agincourt may be forgot,
>   And Cressy be an unknown spot,
>   And Blenheim's name be new :
>   But still in glory and in song,
>   For many an age remembered long,
>   Shall live the tow'rs of Hougoumont
>   And Field of Waterloo."

The peals of applause and rapture with which
these patriotic sentiments were received, will not
easily be forgotten by his hearers.

Nor were his literary acquirements limited to such
subjects. The works of Jeremy Taylor and the other
great divines of the Stewart period, he was very familiar with, and esteemed highly.   He was also a
great authority in Irish history and antiquities;
enquiries often came to him from persons in the
United States and elsewhere, respecting disputed
and doubtful questions, which he was generally competent to solve.

Mr. Dixon was long an active member of the committee of the Church Society; and the first delegate
of St. James's Church to the first Diocesan Synod.
In these and all other good works, he was untiring
and disinterested.   Whenever there was any gathering of clergy he received as many as possible in his
house, treating them with warm-hearted hospitality.

Mr. Dixon died in the year 1855, leaving a large family of sons and daughters, of whom several have acquired distinction in various ways. His eldest son, Alexander, graduated in King's College, at the time when Adam Crooks, Judge Boyd, Christopher Robinson, Judge Kingsmill, D. McMichael, the Rev. W. Stennett, and others well known in public life, were connected with that university. Mr. Dixon was university prizeman in History and Belles-Lettres in his third year; took the prize for English oration; and wrote the prize poem two years in succession. He is now Rector of Guelph, and Archdeacon of the northern half of the Niagara diocese. He was also one of the contributors to the " Maple Leaf."

William, second son of Alderman Dixon, was Dominion Emigration Agent in London, England, where he died in 1873. Concerning him, the Hon. J. H. Pope, Minister of Agriculture, stated that he "was the most correct and conscientious administrator he had ever met." He said further in Parliament:—

" The Premier had gone so far as to state that the present Agent General was a person of wonderful ability, and had done more than his predecessors to promote emigration to Canada. He (Mr. Pope) regretted more than he could express the death of Mr. Dixon, the late agent. He was held in high esteem both here and in the old country, and was a gentleman who never identified himself with any political party, but fairly and honestly represented Canada."

Another son, Major Fred. E. Dixon, is well known in connection with the Queen's Own, of Toronto.

N

CHAPTER XXXII.

MORE TORIES OF REBELLION TIMES.

EDWARD G. O'BRIEN.

MY first introduction to this gentleman was on the day after I landed at Barrie, in 1833. He was then living at his log cottage at Shanty Bay, an indentation of the shore near the mouth of Kempenfeldt Bay, at the south-west angle of Lake Simcoe. I was struck with the comparative elegance pervading so primitive an establishment. Its owner was evidently a thorough gentleman, his wife an accomplished lady, and their children well taught and courteous. The surrounding scenery was picturesque and delightful. The broad expanse of the bay opening out to Lake Simcoe—the graceful sweep of the natural foliage sloping down from high banks to the water's edge—are impressed vividly upon my memory, even at this long interval of fifty years. It seemed to me a perfect gem of civilization, set in the wildest of natural surroundings.

I was a commissioner of the Court of Requests at Barrie, along with 'Col. O'Brien, in 1834, and in that capacity had constant opportunities of meeting and appreciating him. He had seen service as midshipman in the Royal Navy, as well as in the Army; was an expert yachtsman of course ; and had ample opportunities of indulging his predilection for the water, on the fine bay fronting his house. At that time it was no unusual thing in winter, to see wolves chasing deer over the thick ice of the bay. On one occasion, being laid up with illness, the Captain was holding a magistrate's court in his dining-room over-looking the bay. In front of the house was a wide lawn, and beyond it a sunken fence, not visible from the house. The case under consideration was pro-bably some riotous quarrel among the inhabitants of a coloured settlement near at hand, who were constantly at loggerheads with each other or with their white neighbours. In the midst of the pro-ceedings, the Captain happened to catch sight of a noble stag dashing across the ice, pursued by several wolves. He beckoned a relative who assisted on the farm, and whispered to him to get out the dogs. A few seconds afterwards the baying of the hounds was heard. The unruly suitors caught the sound, rushed to the window and door, then out to the grounds, plaintiff, defendant, constables and all, helter skelter, until they reached the sunken fence, deeply buried in snow, over which they tumbled *en masse*, amid a chorus of mingled shouts and objurga-tions that baffles description. Whether the hear-ing of the case was resumed that day or not, I cannot say, but it seems doubtful.

His naval and military experience naturally showed itself in Colonel O'Brien's general bearing; he possessed the polished manners and high-bred courtesy of some old Spanish hidalgo, together with a sufficient share of corresponding hauteur when displeased. The first whispers of the Rebellion of 1837, brought him to the front. He called together his loyal neighbours, who responded so promptly that not a single able-bodied man was left in the locality; only women and children, and two or three male invalids, staying behind. With his men he marched for Toronto; but, when at Bond Head, received orders from the Lieutenant-Governor to remain there, and take charge of the district, which had been the head quarters of disaffection. When quiet was restored, he returned to Shanty Bay, and resided there for several years; occupying the position of chairman of the Quarter Sessions for the Simcoe District. After the erection of the County of Simcoe into a municipality, he removed with his family to Toronto, where he entered into business as a land agent; was instrumental in forming a company to construct a railroad to Lake Huron *via* Sarnia, of which he acted as secretary; afterwards organized and became manager of the Provincial Insurance Company, which position he occupied until 1857.

In the year 1840, died Mr. Thos. Dalton, proprietor and editor of the *Toronto Patriot* newspaper; the paper was continued by his widow until 1848, when

Col. O'Brien, through my agency, became proprietor of that journal, which I engaged to manage for him. The editor was his brother, Dr. Lucius O'Brien, a highly educated and talented, but not popular, writer. Col. O'Brien's motive in purchasing the paper was solely patriotic, and he was anxiously desirous that its columns should be closed to everything that was not strictly—even quixotically—chivalrous. His sensitiveness on this score finally led to a difference of opinion between the brothers, which ended in Dr. O'Brien's retirement.

At that time, as a matter of course, the *Patriot* and the *Globe* were politically antagonistic. The *Colonist*, then conducted by Hugh Scobie, represented the Scottish Conservatives in politics, and the Kirk of Scotland in religious matters. Therefore, it often happened, that the *Patriot* and *Colonist* were allied together against the *Globe ;* while at other times, the *Patriot* stood alone in its support of the English Church, and had to meet the assaults of the other two journals—a triangular duel, in fact. A spiteful correspondent of the *Colonist* had raked up some old Edinburgh slanders affecting the personal reputation of Mr. Peter Brown, father of George Brown, and joint publisher of the *Globe.* Those slanders were quoted editorially in the *Patriot,* without my knowledge until I saw them in print on the morning of publication. I at once expressed my entire disapproval of their insertion ; and Col. O'Brien took the matter so much to heart, that, without letting me know his decision, he removed his brother from the editorship, and placed it temporarily in my hands. My first editorial act was, by Col. O'Brien's desire, to disavow the offensive allusions, and to apologize personally to Mr. Peter Brown therefor. This led to a friendly feeling between the latter gentleman and myself, which continued during his lifetime.

On the 25th of May, 1849, the great fire occurred in Toronto, which consumed the *Patriot* office, as well as the cathedral and many other buildings. Soon afterwards Col. O'Brien sold his interest in the *Patriot* to Mr. Ogle R. Gowan.

I have been favoured with the perusal of some "jottings" in the Colonel's own hand-writing, from which I make an extract, describing his first experience of the service at the age of fourteen, as midshipman on board H. M. 36 gun Frigate *Doris*, commanded by his father's cousin, Capt. (afterwards Admiral) Robert O'Brien :

"The *Doris* joined the outward-bound fleet at Portsmouth, where about 1700 vessels of all sizes, from first-class Indiamen of 1400 tons to small fruit-carriers from the Mediterranean of 60 tons, were assembled for convoy. At first, and along the more dangerous parts of the Channel from privateers, the convoy continued to be a large one, including especially many of the smaller men-of-war, but among them were two or three line-of-battle ships and heavy frigates under orders for the Mediterranean. The whole formed a magnificent sight, not often seen. After a while the outsiders dropped off, some to one place, some to another, one large section being the North American trade, another the Mediterranean, until the *Doris* was left commodore of the main body, being the West Indiamen, South American traders, and Cape and East Indiamen, and a stately fleet it was. With the *Doris* was the *Salsette*, a frigate of the same class, and some smaller craft. This convoy, though small apparently for such a fleet in that very active war, was materially strengthened by the heavy armaments of the regular traders in the East India Company's service in the China trade, of which there were twelve, I think. These ships were arranged in two lines, between which all the others were directed to keep their course; the *Doris* leading in the centre between the two lines of Chinamen, and the *Salsette* bringing up the rear, while two or three sloops of war hovered about. My berth on board the *Doris* was that of signal midshipman, which was simply to keep an eye on every individual craft in the fleet. . . . . On reaching the Canaries, the fleet came to an anchor in Santa Cruz roads, at the island of Teneriffe, for the purpose of filling up water, and enabling the Indiamen to lay in a stock of wine for the round voyage. The *Doris* and larger ships outside, and the *Salsette* and smaller ones closer in, and an uncommon tight pack it was. The proper landing place, and only place indeed where casks could be conveniently shipped, was the mole, a long, narrow, high pier or wharf, with a flight of stairs or steps to the water. This was generally one jam from end to end, as well on the pier as on the water, crowded above by casks of all sizes, wine and water, every spare foot or interstice between the casks crammed with idle, lazy, loafing Portuguese, the scum and chief part of the population of the town, assembled there certainly not to work, but amazingly active and busy in looking on, swearing, directing and scolding—terribly in the seamen's way, and by them very unceremoniously kicked and flung aside and into the next man's path. Sometimes there was a scuffle, and then a rare scrimmage caused by a party of soldiers from the mole rushing in to keep the peace. They were immediately pitched into by the blue jackets, who instead of rolling their casks towards their boats, tacked as they called it, and sent the barrels flying among the soldiers' legs. More than one cask of wine in this manner went the wrong way over the pier, down among the boats below, where there was, in its own way, much the same state of confusion, with a good deal more danger. Ships' boats, from the jolly-boat manned by lads, hurried ashore to seek stray pursers' clerks with their small plunder, or stewards and servants with bundles of washed clothing—to the heavy launch loaded with water casks pushing out or striving to get in—each boat's crew utterly reckless, and under no control, intent only on breaking their own way in or out, so that it was marvellous how any escaped damage. And the thing reached its climax, when at daylight on the last day, the signal was made to prepare to weigh anchor. I had been ashore the day before, with a strong working party and three of the frigate's boats, under the command of one of the lieutenants, assisting the Indiamen in getting off their wine and water ; and so, when sent this morning on the same duty, I was somewhat up to the work. I had therefore put on my worst clothes ; all I wanted was to have my midshipman's jacket as conspicuous as possible, having discovered in the previous day's experience the value of the authority of discipline. Our work this day was also increased by the sure precursor of bad weather, a rising sea ; and as the town is situated on an open roadstead, the surf on the beach, which, though always more or less an obstruction, had been hitherto passable, was now insurmountable ; all traffic had to be crowded over the pier, including late passengers, men and women, and more than one bunch of children, with all the odds and ends of clothes-baskets, marketing, curi-

osities, &c., &c. What a scene! We naval mids found ourselves suddenly raised to great importance; and towards
noon I became a very great man indeed. The *Doris* being
outside, she was of course the first under weigh, and
around her were the larger Indiamen, also getting
under sail—the commodore constantly enforcing his
signals by heavy firing. But big as these ships were, and
notwithstanding their superior discipline, they had nearly as many laggards as the smaller fry. . . . All
the forenoon the weather had been getting more and
more threatening, and the breeze and sea rose together.
About 11 o'clock a. m. we all knew that we were in for
something in the shape of a gale, and the *Doris* made
signal for her boats and the working party to return to
the ship; and soon after, for the *Salsette* and the inshore
ships to get under weigh. Our lieutenant, however, seeing the state of things ashore, directed me to remain with
one of the cutters and three or four spare hands; and
if the frigate should be blown off during the night, to get
on board a particular vessel—a fast sailing South Sea
whaler, that had acted as tender to the frigate, and
whose master promised to look after us, as well as any
others of the *Doris's* people who might still be on shore.
Thus I was left in sole command, as the *Salsette* had also
recalled her boats and working parties. Although she
would send no help ashore, she remained still at anchor.
Capt. Bowen, her commander, contenting himself with
sheeting home his top-sails, and repeating the commodore's signal to the inshore ships. We afterwards found
out the secret of all this. Bowen disliked the idea of
playing second fiddle, and wanted to be commodore himself, and this was a beautiful opportunity to divide the
fleet. But as matters got worse, and difficulties increased, we succeeded in getting them more under control.
The crowd, both of casks and live stock on the wharf,
and of boats beneath, gradually diminished. The merchant seamen, and especially the crews of the larger

boats of the Indiamen, worked manfully. The smaller boats were taken outside, and regular gangs formed to pass all small parcels, and especially women and children passengers, across the inner heavy tier to them. This, the moment the seamen caught the idea, became great fun ; and a rousing cheer was raised when a fat, jolly steward's wife was regularly parbuckled over the side of the pier, and passed, decently and decorously (on her back, she dare not kick for fear of showing her legs) like a bale of goods, from hand to hand, or rather from arms to arms, to a light gig outside all. This being successfully achieved, I turned to a party of passengers standing by, and who, though anxious themselves, could not help laughing, and proposed to pass them out in the same manner ; making the first offer to a comely nurse-maid of the party. I was very near getting my ears boxed for my kindness and courtesy, so I turned to the mistress instead, who however contented herself by quietly enquiring whether there was no other way; of course another way was soon found; a few chairs were got, which were soon rigged by the seamen, by means of which, first the children, and then their elders, men and women, were easily passed down to the boats below, and from thence to the boat waiting safely outside.   In all this work I was not only supported in authority by the different ships' officers and mates superintending their own immediate concerns, but also by a number of gentlemen, merchants and others, most of whom came down to the pier to see and assist their friends among the passengers safe off. By their help also I was enabled, not knowing a word of their language myself, to get material help from the Portuguese standing by ; and also got the officer in command of the guard at the mole-head, to clear the pier of all useless hands, and place sentries here and there over stray packages, put down while the owners sought their own proper boats among the crowd. And so at length our work was fairly pushed through, and though late, I managed to get my party safe aboard our friend the whaler, who had kept his signal lights burning for us. Long before, the *Doris* had bore up, and under bare poles had drifted with a large portion of the fleet to the southward; and I saw no more of her, until some months afterwards I joined her in Macao Roads."

This was in the year 1814; soon afterwards the peace with America put an end to our midshipman's prospects of advancement in the navy, to his great and life-long regret. He obtained a commission in the Scots Greys, and exchanged into the 58th Regiment, then under orders for service in the West Indies, where his health failed him, and he was compelled to retire on half-pay. But his love for the sea soon induced him to enter the merchant service, in which he made many voyages to the East. This also, a severe illness obliged him to resign, and to abandon the sea for ever. He then came to Canada, to seek his fortune in the backwoods, where I found him in 1833.

Mr. O'Brien's relations with his neighbours in the backwoods were always kindly, and gratifying to both parties. One evening, some friends of his heard voices on the water, as a boat rowed past his grounds. One man asked " Who lives here ? " " Mr. O'Brien," was the reply. " What is he like ? " " He's a regular old tory." " Oh then, I suppose he's very proud and distant ? " But that he was either proud or distant, his neighbour would not allow, and other voices joined in describing him as the freest and kindest of men—still they all agreed that he was a " regular old tory." The colonel was the last man in the world to object to such an epithet, but those who used it meant probably to describe his sturdy, uncompromising principles, and manly independence. A more utterly guileless, single-hearted man never breathed. Warm and tender-hearted, humble-minded and forgiving, he deplored his hastiness of temper, which was, indeed, due to nervous irritability, the result of severe illness coupled with heavy mental strain when young, from the effects of which he never entirely recovered. He was incapable of a mean thought or dishonourable deed, and never fully realized that there could be others who were unlike him in this respect. Hence, during the long course of his happy and useful, but not wholly prosperous life, he met each such lapse from his own high standard of honour with the same indignant surprise and pain. His habitual reverent-mindedness led him to respect men of all shades of thought and feeling, while to sympathize with sorrow and suffering was as natural to him as the air he breathed.

A neighbour who had had a sudden, sharp attack of illness, meeting one of the colonel's family, said very simply, " I knew you had not heard that I was ill, for Mr. O'Brien has not been to see me ; but please tell him I shall not be about for some time." The man looked upon it as a matter of course that his old friend the colonel would have gone to see him if informed of his illness.

And if Mr. O'Brien's friends and neighbours have kindly recollections of him and of his family, these latter on their part are never tired of recalling unvarying friendliness and countless acts of kindness from all their neighbours.

Before leaving this subject, it may be appropriately added that Mrs. O'Brien (his wife) was his guardian angel—a mother in Israel—the nurse of the sick, the comforter of the miserable; wise, discreet, loving, patient, adored by children, the embodiment of unselfishness. To her Toronto was indebted for its first ragged school.

A few years before the colonel's death, his foreman on the farm, living at the lodge, had five children, of whom three died there of diphtheria. Mrs. O'Brien brought the remainder to her own house—"The Woods,"—to try and save them, the parents being broken-hearted and helpless. It is said to have been a touching spectacle to see the old Colonel carrying about one poor dying child to soothe it, while Mrs. O'Brien nursed the other. Of these two, one died and the other recovered.

The selfish are—happily—forgotten. The unselfish, never. Their memory lives in Shanty Bay as a sweet odour that never seems to pass away. It is still a frequent suggestion, "what would Mrs. O'Brien or the Colonel have done under the circumstances."

In his declining years, failing health, and disease contracted in India, dimmed the cheerfulness of Mr.

O Brien's nature.   But none so chivalrously anxious to repair an unintentional injury or a hasty word.

He and his wife lie side by side in the burial ground of the church he was mainly instrumental in building. Over them is a simple monument in shape of an Irish cross—on it these words :—

"In loving remembrance of Edward George O'Brien, who died September 8, 1875, age 76 : and of Mary Sophia his wife, who died October 14, 1876, age 78 : This stone is raised by their children. He, having served his country by sea and land, became A.D. 1830 the founder of the settlement and mission of Shanty Bay. She was a true wife and zealous in all good works. Faithful servants, they rest in hope."

* * *

JOHN W. GAMBLE.

"Squire Gamble"—the name by which this gentleman was familiarly known throughout the County of York—was born at the Old Fort in Toronto, in 1799. His father, Dr. John Gamble, was stationed there as resident surgeon to the garrison. The family afterwards removed to Kingston, where the boy received his education. It was characteristic of him, that when about to travel to York, at the age of fifteen, to enter the store of the late Hon. Wm. Allan, he chose to make the journey in a canoe, in which he coasted along by day, and by night camped on shore. In course of time, he entered extensively into the business of a miller and country merchant, in which he continued all his life with some intervals.

In manner and appearance Mr. Gamble was a fine specimen of a country magistrate of half a century ago. While the rougher sort of farming men looked up to him with very salutary apprehension, as a stern represser of vice and evil doing, they and everybody else did justice to his innate kindness of heart, and his generosity towards the poor and suffering. He was, in the best sense of the phrase, a popular man. His neighbours knew that in every good work, either in the way of personal enterprise, in the promotion of religious and educational objects, or in the furtherance of the general welfare, Squire Gamble was sure to be in the foremost place. His farm was a model to all others; his fields were better cleared; his fences better kept; his home- stead was just perfection, both in point of orderly management and in an intellectual sense—at least, such was the opinion of his country neighbours, and they were not very far astray. Add to these merits, a tall manly form, an eagle eye, and a commanding mien, and you have a pretty fair picture of Squire Gamble.

As a member of parliament, to which he was three times elected by considerable majorities, Mr. Gamble was hard-working and independent. He supported good measures, from whichever side of the House they might originate, and his vote was always safe for progressive reforms. His toryism was limited entirely to questions of a constitutional character, particularly such as involved loyalty to the throne and the Empire. And in this, Mr. Gamble was a fair representative of his class. And here I venture to assert, that more narrowness of political views, more rigidity of theological dogma, more absolutism in a party sense, has been exhibited in Canada by men of the Puritan school calling themselves Reformers, than by those who are styled Tories.

Perhaps the most important act of Mr. Gamble's political life, was the part he took in the organization of the British American League in 1849. Into that movement he threw all his energies, and the ultimate realization of its views affords the best proof of the correctness of his judgment and foresight. About it, however, I shall have more to say in another chapter.

Mr. Gamble, as I have said, was foremost in all public improvements. To his exertions are chiefly due the opening and construction of the Vaughan plank road, from near Weston, by St. Andrew's, to Woodbridge, Pine Grove, and Kleinburg; which gave an easy outlet to a large tract of country to the north-west of Toronto, and enabled the farmers to reach our market to their and our great mutual advantage.

He was a man who made warm friends and active enemies, being very outspoken in the expression of his opinions and feelings. But even his strongest political foes came to him in full confidence that they were certain to get justice at his hands. And occasionally his friends found out, that no inducement of personal regard could warp his judgment in any matter affecting the rights of other men. In this way he made some bitter adversaries on his own side of politics.

Among Mr. Gamble's public acts was the erection of the church at Mimico, and that at Pine Grove; in aid of which he was the chief promoter, giving freely both time and means to their completion. For years he acted as lay-reader at one or other of those churches, travelling some distance in all weathers to do so. His whole life, indeed, was spent in benefiting his neighbours in all possible ways.

He died in December, 1873, and was buried at Woodbridge.

CHAPTER XXXIII.

A CHOICE OF A CHURCH.

I HAVE mentioned that I was educated as a Swedenborgian, or rather a member of the New Jerusalem Church, as the followers of Emanuel

o

Swedenborg prefer to be called. As a boy, I was well read in his works, and was prepared to tilt with all comers in his cause. But I grew less confident as I became more conversant with the world and with general literature. At the age of fifteen I was nominated a Sunday-school teacher in a small Swedenborgian chapel in the Waterloo road, and declined to act because the school was established with the object of converting from the religion of their parents the children of poor Roman Catholic families in that neighbourhood, which I thought an insidious, and therefore an evil mode of disseminating religious doctrine. Of course, this was a sufficiently conceited proceeding on the part of so young a theologian. But the same feeling has grown up with me in after life. I hold that Christians are ill-employed, who spend their strength in missionary attempts to change the creed of other branches of the Christian Church, while their efforts at conversion might be much better utilised in behalf of the heathen, or, what is the same thing in effect, the untaught multitudes in our midst who know nothing whatever of the teachings of the Gospel of Christ.

It will, perhaps, surprise some of my readers to hear that Swedenborg never contemplated the founding of a sect. He was a civil engineer, high in rank at the Swedish court, and was ennobled for the marvellous feat of transporting the Swedish fleet from sea to sea, across the kingdom and over a formidable chain of mountains. He was also what would now be called an eminent scientist, ranking with Buffon, Humboldt, Kant, Herschel, and others of the first men of his day in Europe, and even surpassing them all in the extent and variety of his philosophical researches. His " Animal Kingdom " and " Physical Sciences " are wonderful efforts of the human mind, and still maintain a high reputation as scientific works.

At length Swedenborg conceived the idea that he enjoyed supernatural privileges—that he had communings with angels and archangels—that he was permitted to enter the spiritual world, and to record what he there saw and heard. Nay, even to approach our Saviour himself, in His character of the Triune God, or sole impersonation of the Divine Trinity. Unlike Mahomet and most other pretenders to inspired missions, Swedenborg never sought for power, honour or applause. He was to the day of his death a quiet gentleman of the old school, unassuming, courteous, and a good man in every sense of the word.

I remember that one of my first objections to the writings of Swedenborg, was on account of his declaring the Church of France to be the most spiritual of all the churches on earth ; which dogma immensely offended my youthful English pride. His first " readers " were members of various churches— clergymen of the Church of England, professors in universities, literary students, followers of Wesley, and generally devout men and women of all denominations. In time they began to assemble together for " reading meetings ; " and so at length grew into a sect—a designation, by the way, which they still stoutly repudiate. I remember one clergyman, the Rev. John Clowes, rector of a church in Manchester, who applied to the Bishop of Lichfield for leave to read and teach from the works of Swedenborg, and was permitted to do so on account of their entirely harmless character.

When still young, I noticed with astonishment, that the transcendental virtues which Swedenborg inculcated were very feebly evidenced in the lives of his followers ; that they were not by any means free from pride, ostentation, even peculation and the ordinary trickery of trade—in fact, that they were no better than their fellow-Christians generally. When I came to Toronto, I of course mixed with all sorts of people, and found examples of thoroughly consistent Christian life amongst all the various denominations—Roman Catholics, English Churchmen, Methodists, Presbyterians, Congregationalists, Baptists, and many others—which taught me the lesson, that it is not a man's formal creed that is of importance, so much as his personal sincerity as a follower of Christ's teachings and example.

I was at the same time forcibly impressed with another leading idea—that no where in the Scriptures have we any instance of a divinely regulated government, in which the worship of God did not occupy a chief place. I thought—I still think—that the same beneficent principle which makes Christianity a part of the common law of England, and of all her colonies, including the United States, should extend to the religious instruction of every soul in the community, gentle or simple, and more especially to what are called the off-scourings of society.

Looking around me, I saw that of all the churches within my purview, the Church of England most completely met my ideal—that she was the Church by law established in my motherland—that she allowed the utmost latitude to individual opinion—in fine, that she held the Bible wide open to all her children, and did her best to extend its knowledge to all mankind. Had I been a native of Scotland, upon the same reasoning I must have become a Presbyterian, or a Lutheran in Holland or Germany, or a Roman Catholic in France or Spain. But that contingency did not then present itself to me.

So I entered the Church of England ; was confirmed by Bishop Strachan, at St. James's Cathedral, in the year 1839, if I remember rightly, and have never since, for one instant, doubted the soundness of my conclusions.

On this occasion, as on many others, my emotions shaped themselves in a poetical form. The two fol-

lowing pieces were written for the *Church* newspaper, of which I was then the printer, in partnership with the Messrs. Rowsell :—

HYMN FOR EASTER.

"CHRIST IS RISEN."*

" Christ is risen from the dead and become the first fruits of them
that slept.
" For since by man came death; by man came also the resurrection
of the dead.
" For as in Adam all die ; even so in Christ shall all be made alive."

Christ is risen ! Jesu lives;
   He lives His faithful ones to bless ;
The grave to life its victim gives—
   Our grief is changed to joyfulness.

The sleeping Saints, whom Israel slew,
   Waking, shall list the joyful sound ;
He—their first fruits—doth live anew,
   Hell hath a mighty conqueror found.

Paschal offering ! spotless Lamb !
   For us was heard thy plaintive cry ;
For us, in agony and shame,
   Thy blood's sweet incense soar'd on high.

By erring man came woe—the grave—
   The ground accurs'd—the blighted tree—
Jesus, as man, for ransom gave
   Himself, from death to set us free.

---

* Easter salutation of the Primitive Church.

Christ is risen ! saints, rejoice !
Your hymns of praise enraptured pour—
Ye heavenly angels, lend your voice—
Jesus shall reign for evermore !
Hallelujah ! Amen.

THE SINNER'S COMPLAINT AND CONSO-LATION.

Oh for a conscience free from sin !
Oh for a breast all pure within—
A soul that, seraph winged, might fly
'Mid heav'n's full blaze unshrinkingly,
And bask in rays of wisdom, bright
From HIS own throne of life and light.

Peace, pining spirit ! know'st thou not that JESUS died
for thee—
For thee alone His last sigh breathed upon th' accursed
tree ;
For thee His Omnipresence chain'd within a mortal
" clod "—
And bore *thy* guilt, to be as well thy Saviour as thy GOD :
Aye, suffered anguish more—far more—than thou canst
e'en conceive,
Thy sins to cleanse—*thy* self-earnt condemnation to relieve.

And did He suffer so for me ?
Did HE endure upon the tree
A living death—a mortal's woe,
With pangs that mortals *cannot* know !

> Oh triumph won most wofully !
> My SAVIOUR died for me—for *me !*

And have I basely wish'd to make this wondrous off'ring
    vain ;
Shall love so vast, be unrepaid by grateful love again ?
Oh ! true affection never chafes at obligation's chain,
But hugs with joy the gracious yoke whose guidance is its
    gain ;
And such the Saviour's ardent love—His suff'ring pa-
    tience—these
Most unlike human bonds, are cancell'd by their own
    increase.

> Rejoice, my soul ! though sin be thine,
> Thy refuge seek in grace divine :
> And mark His Word—more joy shall be
> In heav'n for sinners such as thee
> Repenting, than can e'er be shown
> For scores whom guilt hath never known.

In explanation of my having become, in 1840,
printer of the *Church* newspaper, I must go back to
the date of Lord Sydenham's residence in Toronto.
The Loyalist party, as stated already, became
grievously disgusted with the iron grasp which that
nobleman fastened upon each and every person in
the remotest degree under government control. Not
only the high officers of the Crown, such as the Provincial Treasurer and Secretary, the Executive

Councillors, the Attorney-General and the Sheriff, but also the editors of newspapers publishing the government advertisements, in Toronto and elsewhere, were dictated to, as to what measures they should oppose, and what support. It was "my government,"—"my policy"—not "the policy of my administration," before which they were required to bow down and blindly worship. There were, however, still men in Toronto independent enough to refuse to stoop to the dust; and they met together and taking up the *Toronto Herald* as their mouthpiece, subscribed sufficient funds for the payment of a competent editor, in the person of George Anthony Barber, English Master of Upper Canada College, now chiefly remembered as the introducer and fosterer of the manly game of cricket in Toronto. He was an eloquent and polished writer, and created for the paper a wide reputation as a conservative journal.

About the same time, Messrs. Henry and William Rowsell, well-known booksellers, undertook the printing of the *Church* newspaper, which was transferred from Cobourg to Toronto, under the editorship of Mr. John Kent,—a giant in his way—and subsequently of the Rev. A. N. Bethune, since, and until lately, Bishop of Toronto.

Being intimate friends of my own, they offered me the charge of their printing office, with the position of a partner, which I accepted; and made over my interest in the *Herald* to Mr. Barber.

CHAPTER XXXIV.

THE CLERGY RESERVES.

I HAVE lately astonished some of my friends with the information, that William Lyon Mackenzie was originally an advocate of the Clergy Reserves—that is, of state endowment for religious purposes—a fact which makes his fatal plunge into treason the more to be regretted by all who coincide with him on the religious question.

In Lindsey's " Memoirs " we read (vol. 1, p. 46):

" A Calvinist in religion, proclaiming his belief in the Westminster Confession of Faith, and a Liberal in politics, yet was Mr. Mackenzie, at that time, no advocate of the voluntary principle. On the contrary, he lauded the British Government for making a landed endowment for the Protestant clergy in the Provinces, and was shocked at the report that, in 18J.2, voluntaryism had robbed three millions of people of all means of religious ordinances. ' In no part of the constitution of the Canadas,' he said, ' is the wisdom of the British Legislature more apparent than in its setting apart a portion of the country, while yet it remained a wilderness, for the support of religion.'

. . . " Mr. Mackenzie compared the setting apart of one-seventh of the public lands for religious purposes to a like dedication in the time of the [early] Christians. But he objected that the revenues were monopolized by one church, to which only a fraction of the population belonged. The envy of the non-recipient denominations made the favoured Church of England unpopular.

. . . "Where the majority of the present generation of Canadians will differ from him, is that on the Clergy Reserves question, he did not hold the voluntary view. At that time, he would have denounced secularization as a monstrous piece of sacrilege."*

How much to be regretted is it, that instead of splitting up the Clergy Reserves into fragments, the friends of religious education had not joined their forces for the purpose of endowing all Christian denominations with the like means of usefulness. We are now extending across the entire continent what I cannot help regarding as the anti-Christian practice of non-religious popular education. We are, I believe, but smoothing the road to crime in the majority of cases. Cannot something be done now, while yet the lands of the vast North-West are at our disposal ? Will no courageous legislator raise his voice to advocate the dedication of a few hundred thousand acres to unselfish purposes ? Have we wiled away the Indian prairies from their aboriginal owners, to make them little better than a race-course for speculating gamblers ?

Even if the jealousy of rival politicians—each bent upon self-aggrandizement at the expense of

---

* Mackenzie afterwards drew up petitions which prayed, amongst other things, for the secularization of the Clergy Reserves, but I judge that on that question these petitions rather represented the opinions of other men than his own, and were specially aimed at the Church of England monopoly.

more honourable aims—should defeat all efforts in behalf of religious endowments through the Dominion Legislature, cannot the religious associations amongst us bestir themselves in time? Cannot the necessity for actual settlement be waived in favour of donations by individuals for Church uses? Cannot the powerful Pacific Railway Syndicate themselves take up this great duty, of setting apart certain sections in favour of a Christian ministry?

The signs of the times are dark—dark and fearful. In Europe, by the confession of many eminent public writers, heathenism is overspreading the land. In the United States, a community of the sexes is shamelessly advocated; and there is no single safeguard of public or private order and morality, that is not openly scoffed at and set at nought.

Oh, men! men! preachers, and dogmatists, and hierarchs of all sects! see ye not that your strifes and your jealousies are making ye as traitors in the camp, in the face of the common enemy? See ye not the multitudes approaching, armed with the fell weapons of secular knowledge—cynicism, self-esteem, greed, envy, ambition, ill-regulated passions unrestrained!

One symptom of a nobler spirit has shown itself in England, in the understanding lately suggested, or arrived at, that the missions of any one Protestant Church in the South Sea Islands shall be entirely undisturbed by rival missionaries. This is right;

and if right in Polynesia, why not in Great Britain? why not in Canada? Why cultivate half-a-dozen contentious creeds in every new township or village? Would it not be more amiable, more humble, more self-denying, more exemplary—in one word, more like our Master and Saviour—if each Christian teacher were required to respect the ministrations of his next neighbour, even though there might be some faint shade of variety in their theological opinions; provided always that those ministrations were accredited by some duly constituted branch of the Christian Church.

I profess that I can see no reason why an endowment should not be provided in every county in the North-West, to be awarded to the first congregation, no matter how many or how few, that could secure the services of a missionary duly licensed, be he Methodist, Presbyterian, Baptist, Congregationalist, Disciple—aye, even Anglican or Roman Catholic. No sane man pretends, I think, that eternal salvation is limited to any one, or excluded from any one, of those different churches. That great essential, then, being admitted, what right have I, or have you, dear reader, to demand more? What right have you or I to withhold the Word of God from the orphan or the outcast, for no better reason than such as depends upon the construction of particular words or texts of Holy Scripture, apart from its general tenor and teaching?

Again I say, it is much to be deplored that Canada had not more Reformers, and Conservatives too, as liberal-minded as was W. L. Mackenzie, in regard to the maintenance and proper use of the Clergy Reserves.

It was not the Imperial Government, it was not Lord John Russell, or Sir Robert Peel, or Lords Durham and Sydenham, that were answerable for the dispersion of the Clergy Reserves. What they did was to leave the question in the hands of the Canadian Legislature. It was the old, old story of the false mother in the " Judgment of Solomon," who preferred that the infant should be cut in twain rather than not wrested from a rival claimant.

I would fain hope that the future may yet see a reversal of that disgrace to our Canadian Statute Book. Not by restoring the lands to the Church of England,or the Churches of England and Scotland— they do not now need them—but by endowing all Christian churches for the religious teaching of the poorer classes in the vast North-West.

CHAPTER XXXV.

A POLITICAL SEED-TIME.

FROM the arrival of Sir Charles Bagot in January, 1842, up to the departure of Lord Metcalfe in November, 1844, was a period chiefly remarkable for the struggles of political leaders for power, without any very essential difference of principle between them. Lord Cathcart succeeded as Administrator, but took no decided stand on any Canadian question. And it was not until the Earl of Elgin arrived, in January, 1847, that anything like violent party spirit began again to agitate the Provinces.

In that interval, some events happened of a minor class, which should not be forgotten. It was, I think, somewhere about the month of May, 1843, that there walked into my office on Nelson Street, a young man of twenty-five years, tall, broad-shouldered, somewhat lantern-jawed, and emphatically Scottish, who introduced himself to me as the travelling agent of the New York *British Chronicle*, published by his father. This was George Brown, afterwards publisher and editor of the *Globe* newspaper. He was a very pleasant-mannered, courteous, gentlemanly young fellow, and impressed me favourably. His father, he said, found the political atmosphere of New York hostile to everything British, and that it was as much as a man's life was worth to give expression to any British predilections whatsoever (which I knew to be true). They had, therefore, thought of transferring their publication to Toronto, and intended to continue it as a thoroughly Conservative journal. I, of course, welcomed him as a co-worker in the same cause with ourselves; little expecting how his ideas of conservatism were to develop themselves in subsequent years. The publication of the *Banner*—a religious journal, edited by Mr. Peter Brown—commenced on the 18th of August following, and was succeeded by the *Globe*, on March 5th, 1844.

About the same time, there entered upon public life, another noted Canadian politician, Mr. John A. Macdonald, then member for Kingston, with whom I first became personally acquainted at the meeting of the British American League in 1849, of which I shall have occasion to speak more fully in its order; as it seems to have escaped the notice of Canadian historians, although an event of the first magnitude in our annals.

CHAPTER XXXVI.

"THE MAPLE LEAF."

IT was in the year 1841, that the Rev. Dr. John McCaul entered upon his duties as Vice-President of King's College, after having been Principal of Upper Canada College since 1838. With this gentleman are closely connected some of the most pleasurable memories of my own life. He was a zealous promoter of public amusement, musical as well as literary. Some of the best concerts ever witnessed in Toronto were those got up by him in honour of the Convocation of the University of Toronto, October 23rd, 1845, and at the several public concerts of the Philharmonic Society, of which he was president, in that and following years. As a member of the managing committee, I had the honour of conducting one of the Society's public concerts, which happened, being a mixed concert of sacred and secular music, to be the most popular and profitable of the series, greatly to my delight.

In 1846, 1847 and 1848, Dr. McCaul edited the *Maple Leaf, or Canadian Annual,* a handsomely illustrated and bound quarto volume, which has not since been surpassed, if equalled, in combined beauty and literary merit, by any work that has issued from the Canadian press.

P

Each volume appeared about Christmas day, and was eagerly looked for. The principal contributors were Dr. McCaul himself; the Hon. Chief Justice Hagarty; the late Rev. R. J. McGeorge, then of Streetsville, since of Scotland; the late Hon. Justice Wilson, of London; Miss Page, of Cobourg; the Rev. Dr. Scadding; the late Rev. J. G. D. McKenzie; the late Hon. J. Hillyard Cameron; the Rev. Alex. (now Archdeacon) Dixon, of Guelph; the Rev. Walter Stennett, of Cobourg; C. W. Cooper, Esq., now of Chicago; the late T. C. Breckenridge; the late Judge Cooper, of Goderich; and myself; besides a few whose names are unknown to me.

My own connection, as a writer, with the "Maple Leaf" originated thus: While printing the first volume, I had ventured to send to Dr. McCaul, through the post-office, anonymously, a copy of my poem entitled "Emmeline," as a contribution to the work. It did not appear, and I felt much discouraged in consequence. Some months afterwards, I happened to mention to him my unsuccessful effusion, when he at once said that he had preserved it for the second volume. This was the first ray of encouragement I had ever received as a poet, and it was very welcome to me. He also handed me two or three of the plates intended for the second volume, to try what I could make of them, and most kindly gave me carte-blanche to take up any subject I pleased. The consequence of which was, that I set to work

with a new spirit, and supplied four pieces for the
second and five for the third volume. Two of my
prose pieces—" A Chapter on Chopping," and " A
First Day in the Bush "—with two of the poems, I
have incorporated in these " Reminiscences: " my
other accepted poems, I give below. After this explanation, the reader will not be surprised at the
affection with which I regard the " Maple Leaf." I
know that the generous encouragement which
Dr. McCaul invariably extended to even the humblest rising talent, in his position as head of our Toronto University, has been the means of encouraging
many a youthful student to exertions, which have
ultimately placed him in the front rank among our
public men. Had I met with Dr. McCaul thirty
years earlier, he would certainly have made of me a
poet by profession.

———

EMMELINE.

The faynt-rayed moone shynes dimme and hoar,
The nor-wynde moans with fittful roare,
The snow-drift hydes the cottage doore,
Emmeline,
I wander lonelie on the moore,
Emmeline.

Thou sittest in the castle halle
In festal tyre and silken palle,
'Mid smylinge friendes—all hartes thy thrall,
Emmeline,

My best-beloved—my lyfe—my all,
                        Emmeline.

I marke the brightness quit thy cheeke,
I knowe the thought thou dost not speake,
Some absent one thy glances seeke,
                        Emmeline,
I pace alone the mooreland bleake,
                        Emmeline.

Thy willfull brother—woe the daye !
Why did hee cross mee on my waye ?
I slewe him that I would not slaye,
                        Emmeline,
I cannot washe his bloode awaye,
                        Emmeline.

Oh, why, when stricken from his hande,
Far flew his weapon o'er the strande—
Why did hee rush upon my brande ?
                        Emmeline,
Colde lyes his corse upon the sande,
                        Emmeline.

Thou'rt too, too younge—too younge and fayre
To learne the wearie rede of care—
My bitter griefe thou must not share,
                        Emmeline,
I could not bidde thee wedde despaire,
                        Emmeline.

Through noisome fenne and tangled brake,
Where crawle the lizard and the snake,

My mournfull hopelesse way I take,

Emmeline,

To live a hermitt for thy sake,

Emmeline.

Thy buoyaunt spirit may forgett
The happie houre when last we mett—
My sunne of hope is darklie sett,

Emmeline,

I'll bee thy guardian-angell yett,

Emmeline.

CHANGES OF AN HOUR

ON LAKE ERIE.

Smiles the sunbeam on the waters—
  On the waters glad and free ;
Sparkling, flashing, laughing, dancing—
  Emblem fair of childhood's glee.

Ruddy on the waves reflected,
  Deeper glows the sinking ray ;
Like the smile of young affection
  Flushed by fancy's changeful play.

Mist-enwreathing, chill and gloomy,
  Steals grey twilight o'er the lake—
Ah ! to days of autumn sadness
  Soon our dreaming souls awake.

Night has fallen, dark and silent,
  Starry myriads gem the sky ;
Thus, when earthly hopes have failed us,
  Brighter visions beam on high.

A CANADIAN ECLOGUE.

An aged man sat lonesomely within a rustic porch,
His eyes in troubled thoughtfulness were bent upon the ground:
Why pondered he so mournfully, that venerable man ?
He dreamt sad dreams of early days, the happy days of youth.

He dreamt fond dreams of early days, the lightsome days of youth;
He saw his distant island home—the cot his fathers built—
The bright green fields their hands had tilled—the once accus-
    tomed haunts;
And, dearer still, the old churchyard where now their ashes lie.

Long, weary years had slowly passed—long years of thrift and
    toil—
The hair, once glossy brown, was white, the hands were rough
    and hard;
Deep-delving care had plainly marked its furrows on the brow;
The form, once tall and lithe and strong, now bent and stiff and
    weak.

His many kind and duteous sons, his daughters, meek and good,
Like scattered leaves from autumn gales, were reft the parent tree;
Tho' lands, and flocks, and rustic wealth, an ample store he owned,
They seemed but transitory gains—a coil of earthly care.

Old neighbours, from that childhood's home, have paused before
    his door;
Oh, gladly hath he welcomed them, and warmly doth he greet;
They bring him—token of old love—a little cage of birds,
The songsters of his native vale, companions of his youth.

Those warbled notes, too well they tell of other, happier hours,
Of joyous, childish innocence, of boyhood's gleeful sports,
A mother's tender watchfulness, a father's gentle sway—
The silent tear rolls stealthily adown his furrowed cheek.

Sweet choristers of England's fields, how fondly are ye prized!
Your melody, like mystic strains upon the dying ear,
Awakes a chord that, all unheard, long slumbered in the breast,
That vibrates but to one loved sound—the sacred name of "Home,"

ZAYDA.

" Come lay thy head upon my breast,
And I will kiss thee into rest."
—*Byron.*

Wherefore art thou sad, my brother? why that shade upon thy
　　brow,
Like yon clouds each other chasing o'er the summer landscape
　　now ?
What hath moved thy gentle spirit from its wonted calm the
　　while ?
Shall not Zayda share thy sorrow, as she loves to share thy smile?

Tell me, hath our cousin Hassan passed thee on a fleeter steed ?
Hath thy practised arm betrayed thee when thou threwst the
　　light jereed ?
Hath some rival, too ungently, taunted thee with scoffing pride ?
Tell me what hath grieved thee, Selim—ah, I will not be denied.

Some dark eye, I much mistrust me, hath too brightly answered
　　thine;
Some sweet voice hath, all too sweetly, whispered in the Bezestein.
Nay, doth sadder, deeper feeling dim the gladness of thine eye?
Tell me, dearest, tell me truly, why thou breath'st that mournful
　　sigh ?

Oh, if thou upon poor Zayda cast one look of cold regard,
Whither shall she turn for comfort in a world unkind and hard ?
Since our tender mother, dying, gave me trustfully to thee,
Selim, brother, thou hast always been far more than worlds to me.

Take this rose—upon my bosom I have worn it all the day ;
Like thy sister's true affection, never can its scent decay :
As the pure wave, murm'ring fondly, lingers round some lonely
　　isle,
Life-long shall my love enchain thee, Selim, asking but a smile.

THE TWO FOSCARI.*

Ho ! gentlemen of Venice !
  Ho ! soldiers of St. Mark !
Pile high your blazing beacon-fire,
  The night is wild and dark,
Behoves us all be wary,
  Behoves us have a care
No traitor spy of Austria
  Our watch is prowling near.

Time was, would princely Venice
  No foreign tyrant brook ;
Time was, before her stately wrath
  The proudest Kaiser shook ;
When o'er the Adriatic
  The Wingéd Lion hurled
Destruction on his enemies—
  Defiance to the world.

'Twas when the Turkish crescent
  Contended with the cross,
And many a Christian kingdom rued
  Discomfiture and loss ;

---

* This and the preceding poem were written as illustrations of two beautiful plates which appeared in the Maple Leaf. One, Zayda presenting a rose to her supposed brother, Selim ; the other, the Doge Foscari passing sentence of exile upon his son. The incidents in the Venetian story are all historical facts.

We taught the turban'd Paynim—
  We taught his boastful fleet,
Venetian freemen scorned alike
  Submission or retreat.

Alas, for fair Venezia,
  When wealth and pomp and pride
—The pride of her patrician lords—
  Her freedom thrust aside :
When o'er the trembling commons
  The haughty nobles rode,
And red with patriotic blood
  The Adrian waters flowed.

'Twas in the year of mercy
  Just fourteen fifty two
—When Francis Foscari was Doge,
  A valiant prince and true—
He won for the Republic
  Ravenna—Brescia bright—
And Crema—aye, and Bergamo
  Submitted to his might :

Young Giacopo, his darling,
  —His last and fairest child—
A gallant soldier in the wars,
  In peace serene and mild—
Woo'd gentle Mariana,
  Old Contarini's pride,
And glad was Venice on that day
  He claimed her for his bride,

The Bucentaur showed bravely
    In silks and cloth of gold,
And thousands of swift gondolas
    Were gay with young and old;
Where spann'd the Canalazo
    A boat-bridge wide and strong,
Amid three hundred cavaliers
    The bridegroom rode along.

Three days were joust and tourney,
    Three days the Plaza bore
Such gallant shock of knight and steed
    Was never dealt before,
And thrice ten thousand voices
    With warm and honest zeal,
Loud shouted for the Foscari
    Who loved the Commonweal.

For this the Secret Council—
    The dark and subtle Ten—
Pray God and good San Marco
    None like may rule again !
Because the people honoured
    Pursued with bitter hate,
And foully charged young Giacopo
    With treason to the state.

The good old prince, his father—
    Was ever grief like his !—
They forced, as judge, to gaze upon
    His own child's agonies !

No outward mark of sorrow
  Disturb'd his awful mien—
No bursting sigh escaped to tell
  The anguish'd heart within.

Twice tortured and twice banish'd,
  The hapless victim sighed
To see his old ancestral home,
  His children and his bride :
Life seem'd a weary burthen
  Too heavy to be borne,
From all might cheer his waning hours
  A hopeless exile torn.

In vain—no fond entreaty
  Could pierce the ear of hate—
He knew the Senate pitiless,
  Yet rashly sought his fate ;
A letter to the Sforza
  Invoking Milan's aid,
He wrote, and placed where spies might see—
  'Twas seen, and was betrayed.

Again the rack—the torture—
  Oh ! cruelty accurst !—
The wretched victim meekly bore—
  They could but wreak their worst ;
So he but lay in Venice,
  Contented, if they gave
What little space his bones might fill—
  The measure of a grave.

The white-haired sire, heart-broken,
   Survived his happier son,
To learn a Senate's gratitude
   For faithful service done ;
What never Doge of Venice
   Before had lived to tell,
He heard for a successor peal
   San Marco's solemn bell.

When, years before, his honours
   Twice would he fain lay down,
They bound him by his princely oath
   To wear for life the crown ;
But now, his brow o'ershadow'd
   By fourscore winters' snows,
Their eager malice would not wait
   A spent life's mournful close.

He doff'd his ducal ensigns
   In proud obedient haste,
And through the sculptured corridors
   With staff-propt footsteps paced ;
Till on the giant's staircase,
   Which first in princely pride
He mounted as Venezia's Doge,
   The old man paused—and died.

Thus govern'd the Patricians
   When Venice owned their sway,
And thus Venetian liberties
   Became a helpless prey :

They sold us to the Teuton,
   They sold us to the Gaul—
Thank God and good San Marco,
   We've triumph'd over all!

Ho! gentlemen of Venice!
   Ho! soldiers of St. Mark!
You've driven from your palaces
   The Austrian, cold and dark!
But better for Venezia
   The stranger ruled again,
Than the old patrician tyranny,
   The Senate and the Ten!

CHAPTER XXXVII.

ST. GEORGE'S SOCIETY.

MY new partner, Mr. William Rowsell, and Mr. Geo. A. Barber, are entitled to be called the founders of the St. George's Society of Toronto. Mr. Barber was appointed secretary at its first meeting in 1835, and was very efficient in that capacity. But it was the enthusiastic spirit and the galvanic energy of William Rowsell that raised the society to the high position it has ever since maintained in Toronto. Other members, especially George P.

Ridout, William Wakefield, W. B. Phipps, Jos. D. Ridout, W. B. Jarvis, Rev. H. Scadding, and many more, gave their hearty co-operation then and afterwards. In those early days, the ministrations of the three national societies of St. George, St. Andrew, and St. Patrick, were as angels' visits to thousands of poor emigrants, who landed here in the midst of the horrors of fever and want. Those poor fellows, who, like my companions on board the *Asia*, were sent out by some parochial authority, and found themselves, with their wives and half a dozen young children, left without a shilling to buy their first meal, must have been driven to desperation and crime but for the help extended to them by the three societies.

The earliest authorized report of the Society's proceedings which I can find, is that for the year 1843-4, and I think I cannot do better than give the list of the officers and members entire:

ST. GEORGE'S SOCIETY OF TORONTO.

Officers for 1844.

PATRON—His Excellency the Right Hon. Sir CHARLES T. METCALFE, Bart., K. G. B., Governor-General of British North America, &c.

PRESIDENT—William Wakefield. VICE-PRESIDENTS —W. B. Jarvis, G. P. Ridout, W. Atkinson. CHAPLAIN —The Rev. Henry Scadding, M. A. PHYSICIAN—Robt. Hornby, M. D. TREASURER—Henry Rowsell. MANAGING COMMITTEE—G. Walton, T. Clarke, J. D. Ridout,

F. Lewis, J. Moore, J. G. Beard, W. H. Boulton. SECRETARY—W. Rowsell. STANDARD BEARERS—G. D. Wells, A. Wasnidge, F. W. Coate, T. Moore.

List of Members, March, 1844.

E. H. Ades, E. S. Alport, Thos. Armstrong, W. Atkinson.

Thos. Baines, G. W. Baker, Jr. ; G. A. Barber, F. W. Barron, Robert Barwick, J. G. Beard, Robt. Beard, Edwin Bell, Matthew Betley, J. C. Bettridge, G. Bilton, T. W. Birchall, W. H. Boulton, Josh. Bound, W. Bright, Jas. Brown, Jno. Brown, Thos. Brunskill, E. C. Bull, Jas. Burgess, Mark Burgess, Thos. Burgess.

F. C. Capreol, W. Cayley, Thos. Champion, E. C. Chapman, Jas. Christie, Edw. Clarke, Jno. Clarke, Thos. Clarke, Thos. Clarkson, D. Cleal, F. W. Coate, Edw. Cooper, C. N. B. Cozens.

Jno. Davis, Nath. Davis, G. T. Denison, Sen., Robt. B. Denison, Hon. W. H. Draper.

Jno. Eastwood, Jno. Elgie, Thos. Elgie, Jno. Ellis, Christopher Elliott, J. P. Esten, Jas. Eykelbosch.

C. T. Gardner, Jno. Garfield, W. Gooderham, G. Gurnett.

Chas. Hannath, W. Harnett, Josh. Hill, Rich. Hockridge, Joseph Hodgson, Dr. R. Hornby, G. C. Horwood, J. G. Howard.

Æ. Irving, Jr.

Hon. R. S. Jameson, W. B. Jarvis, H. B. Jessopp.

Alfred Laing, Jno. Lee, F. Lewis, Henry Lutwych, C. Lynes, S. G. Lynn.

Hon. J. S. Macaulay, Rich. Machell, J. F. Maddock, Jno. Mead, And. Mercer, Jas. Mirfield, Sam. Mitchell, Jno. Moore, Thos. Moore, Jas. Moore, Jas. Morris, W. Morrison, J. G. Mountain, W. Mudford.

J. R. Nash.

Thos. Pearson, Jno. E. Pell, W. B. Phipps, Sam. Phillips, Hiram Piper, Jno. Popplewell, Jno. Powell.

M. Raines, J. D. Ridout, G. P. Ridout, Sam. G. Ridout, Ewd. Robson, H. Rowsell, W. Rowsell, F. Rudyerd.

Chas. Sabine, J. H. Savigny, Hugh Savigny, Geo. Sawdon, Rev. H. Scadding, Jas. Severs, Rich. Sewell, Hon. Henry Sherwood, Jno. Sleigh, I. A. Smith, L. W. Smith, Thos. Smith (Newgate Street), Thos. Smith, (Market Square), J. G. Spragge, Jos. Spragge, W. Steers, J. Stone.

Leonard Thompson, S. Thompson, Rich. Tinning, Enoch Turner.

Wm. Wakefield, Jas. Wallis, Geo. Walton, W. Walton, Alf. Wasnidge, Hon. Col. Wells, G. D. Wells, Thos. Wheeler, F. Widder, H. B. Williams, J. Williams, W. Wynn.

Thos. Young.

The list of Englishmen thus reproduced, may well raise emotions of love and regret in us their survivors. Most of them have died full of years, and rich in the respect of their compatriots of all nations. There are still living some twenty out of the above one hundred and thirty-seven members.

The following song, written and set to music by me for the occasion, was sung by the late Mr. J. D. Humphreys, the well-known Toronto tenor, at the annual dinner held on the 24th April, 1845 :—

THE ROSE OF ENGLAND.

The Rose, the Rose of England,
 The gallant and the free !
Of all our flow'rs the fairest,
 The Rose, the Rose for me !

Our good old English fashion
  What other flow'r can show ?
Its smiles of beauty greet its friends,
  Its thorns defy the foe !
Chorus—The Rose, the Rose of England,
    The gallant and the free !
  Of all our flow'rs the fairest,
    The Rose, the Rose for me !

Though proudly for the Thistle
  Each Scottish bosom swell,
The Thistle hath no charms for me
  Like the Rose I love so well.
And Erin's native Shamrock,
  In lonely wilds that grows,
Its modest leaflet would not strive
  To vie with England's Rose.
      Chorus—The Rose, the Rose, etc.

Yet Scotia's Thistle bravely
  Withstands the rudest blast,
And Erin's cherished Shamrock
  Keeps verdant to the last ;
And long as British feeling
  In British bosoms glows,
Right joyfully we'll honour them,
  As they will England's Rose.
      Chorus—The Rose, the Rose, etc.

Before closing my reminiscences of the St. George's
Society, it may not be out of place to give some ac-

Q

count of its legitimate congener, the North America
St. George's Union.   Englishmen in the United
States, like those of Canada, have formed themselves
into societies for the relief of their suffering brethren
from the Fatherland, in all their principal cities.
The necessity of frequent correspondence respecting
cases of destitution, naturally led the officers of those
societies to feel an interest in each other's welfare
and system of relief, which at length gave rise to a
desire for formal meeting and consultation, and that
finally to the establishment of an organized association.

In 1876, the fourth annual convention of the St.
George's Union was for the first time held in Canada, at the City of Hamilton; in 1878 at Guelph;
in 1880 at Ottawa; and in August, 1883, at Toronto
—the intervening meetings taking place at Philadelphia, Bridgeport and Washington, U. S., respectively.

To give an idea of what has been done, and of the
spirit which actuates this great representative body
of Englishmen, I avail myself of the opening speech
of the President, our fellow-citizen and much esteemed friend, J. Herbert Mason, Esq., which was
delivered at the City Hall here, on the 29th of August last. After welcoming the delegates from other
cities, he went on to say :—

" Met together to promote objects purely beneficent,
for which, in the interests of humanity, we claim the

support of all good citizens, of whatever flag or origin,
we may here give expression to our sentiments and opinions without reserve, and with confidence that they will
be received with respect, even by those who may not be
able to share in the glorious memories, and vastly more
glorious anticipations, with which we, as Englishmen and
the descendants of Englishmen, are animated.

"And in the term Englishmen, I wish to be understood as including all loyal Irishmen, Scotchmen, and
Welshmen. There need be no division among men of
British origin in regard to the objects we are banded together to promote.

"The city of Toronto is in some respects peculiarly
suitable as a place for holding a convention of representative men of English blood. Its Indian name, Toronto,
signifies a place of meeting. Ninety years ago its site
was selected as that of the future capital of Upper Canada, by General Simcoe, a Devonshire man, distinguished
both as a soldier and a statesman, who, in the following
year, founded the city.

"At that time the shore of our beautiful bay, and
nearly the entire country from the Detroit river to Montreal, was a dense forest, the home of the wolf, the beaver
and the bear. In earlier years the surrounding country
had been inhabited by powerful Indian tribes; but after
a prolonged contest, carried on with the persistence and
ferocity which distinguished them, the dreaded Iroquois
from the southern shores of Lake Ontario had exterminated or driven away the Hurons, their less warlike
kinsmen, and at the time I speak of, the only human
beings that were found here was a single family of the
Mississaga Indians. The story of the contest which ended
in the supremacy of the Iroquois Confederacy, taken from
the records of the Jesuit fathers, who shared in the destruction of their Huron converts, so graphically described
by Parkman, the New England historian, furnishes one
of the most interesting and romantic chapters of Ameri-

can history.   In the names and general appearance of its streets, the style of its habitations, in its social life, and the characteristics of its people (if the opinions of tourists and visitors may be accepted), Toronto recals to Englishmen vivid impressions of home in a greater degree than any other American city.

" The opening up of the Canadian North-West, and the increased tendency of English emigration towards this Continent, instead of, as formerly, towards those great English communities in the Southern hemisphere, proportionately increases the responsibility thrown upon their kindred living here, to see that all reasonable and necessary counsel and assistance are afforded to them on their arrival. One of the most suitable agencies for effecting this object is the formation of St. George's Societies in every city and town where Englishmen exist. To the friendless immigrant, suddenly placed in a new and unknown world, not understanding the conditions of success, and, in many cases, suffering in health from change of climate, the familiar tones, the kindly hand, and the brotherly sympathy of a fellow-countryman, are most welcome. It supplies to the stranger help of the right kind when most needed, and is one of those acts of divine charity which covers a multitude of sins. One of the chief objects of the St. George's Union is to increase the number and usefulness, and enlarge the membership of such societies, and if, under its fostering influence and encouraging example, Englishmen generally, and their descendants, are aroused to a more faithful discharge of their duty in this respect, the Union is surely well worth maintaining. In this connection, and for the information and example of younger societies, permit me to point out some features of the work of the St. George's Society of this city. It was organized in 1835, when the population of the city was only 8,000. In the nearly fifty years of its existence, it has had enrolled among its chief officers, men of distinguished position and high moral excellence. It is a notable circumstance, that at the time of the meeting of this Union in Toronto, the Lieutenant-Governor of Ontario, whose official residence is here, as well as the Mayor, the Police Magistrate, the Treasurer, the Commissioners, the Acting Engineer, and the Chairman of the Free Library Board of Toronto, are all members of the St. George's Society, and two of them past-presidents of it. It has a membership of about six hundred, an annual income of about $2,400, and invested funds to the amount of nearly $9,000. The office of the Society is open daily, where cases requiring immediate advice or assistance are promptly attended to by its indefatigable Secretary, Mr. J. E. Pell. The Committee for General Relief meets weekly. Every case is investigated and treated on its merits. Efforts are made to secure employment for those who are able to work, and all tendencies towards pauperism, or the formation of a pauper class, are severely discouraged. One feature in the work of this society I invite special attention to, which is its annual distribution of 'Christmas Cheer' to the English poor. Last Christmas Eve there were given away 7,500 pounds of excellent beef ; 4,400 pounds of bread ; 175 pounds of tea, and 650 pounds of sugar. Each member of the society had, therefore, the satisfaction of knowing when he sat down to his Yule-tide table, loaded with the good things of this life, and surrounded by the happy faces of those he loved best, that every one of his needy fellow-countrymen was, on that day, bountifully supplied with the necessaries of life."

From the Annual Report of the Committee I gather a few items :

"Reports from nineteen societies (affiliated to the Union) show the following results :—

Membership (excluding honorary members)   3,247
Receipts during the year -   -   -   - $19,618

<pre>
Expended for charity during the year (ex-
   cluding private donations)   -   -   - $12,003
Value of investments, furniture and fixtures   96,568
</pre>

" The Society of St. George, of London, England, has intimate relations with the Union. The General Committee embraces such eminent names as those of the Duke of Manchester, Lord Alfred Churchill, Sir Philip Cunliffe Owen; Messrs. Beresford-Hope and Puleston, of the House of Commons ; Blanchard Jerrold and Hyde Clarke, while death has removed from the Committee Messrs. W. Hepworth Dixon and Walter Besant. St. George's Day has been publicly celebrated ever since the institution of the Society in 1879. A new history of the titular saint, by the Rev. Dr. Barons, has been promoted by the Society, and by its efforts appropriate mortuary honours were paid to Colonel Chester, the Anglo-American antiquarian, who died while prosecuting in England his researches concerning the genealogy of the Pilgrim Fathers. Through the industry and zeal of the chairman of the Executive Committee there has been much revival of interest, at home and abroad, respecting England's patron saint and the ancient celebrations of his legendary natal day."

After the official business of the convention had been disposed of, the American and Canadian visitors were hospitably entertained, on Wednesday the 30th, at " Ermeleigh," the private residence of the President, on Jarvis street ; on Thursday afternoon at Government House, as guests of the Lieutenant-Governor and Mrs. Robinson ; and in the evening at the Queen's Hotel, where a handsome entertainment was provided.

CHAPTER XXXVIII.

A GREAT CONFLAGRATION.

THE 7th of April, 1849, will be fresh in the memory of many old Torontonians. It was an unusually fine spring day, and a large number of farmers' teams thronged the old market, then the only place within the city where meat was allowed to be sold. The hotel stables were crowded, and among them those of Graham's tavern on King and George Streets. At two o'clock in the afternoon, an alarm of fire was heard, occasioned by the heedlessness of some teamster smoking his after-dinner pipe. It was only a wooden stable, and but little notice was taken at first. The three or four hand-engines which constituted the effective strength of the fire brigade of that day, were brought into play one by one; but the stable, and Post's stable adjoining, were soon in full blaze. A powerful east wind carried the flames in rear of a range of brick stores extending on the north side of King Street from George to Nelson (now Jarvis) Street, and they attacked a small building on the latter street, next adjoining my own printing office, which was in the third story of a large brick building on the corner of King and Nelson Streets, afterwards well-known as Foy & Austin's corner. The *Patriot* newspaper was printed there, and the compositors and pressmen not only of that office, but of nearly all the newspaper offices in the city, were busily occupied in removing the type and presses downstairs. Suddenly the flames burst through our north windows with frightful strength, and we shouted to the men to escape, some by the side windows, some by the staircase. As we supposed, all got safely away; but unhappily it proved otherwise. Mr. Richard Watson was well known and respected as Queen's Printer since the rebellion times. He was at the head of the profession, universally liked, and always foremost on occasions of danger and necessity. He had persisted in spite of all remonstrance in carrying cases of type down the long, three-story staircase, and was forgotten for a while. Being speedily missed, however, cries were frantically raised for ladders to the south windows; and our brave friend, Col. O'Brien, was the first to climb to the third story, dash in the window-sash—using his hat as a weapon—but not escaping severe cuts from the broken glass—and shouting to the prisoner within. But in vain. No person could be seen, and the smoke and flames forcing their way at that moment through the front windows, rendered all efforts at rescue futile.

In the meantime, the flames had crossed Nelson Street to St. James's buildings on King Street; thence across King Street to the old city hall and the market block, and here it was thought the destruction would cease. But not so. One or two men noticed a burning flake, carried by the fierce gale, lodge itself in the belfry of St. James's Cathedral, two or three hundred yards to the west. The men of the fire brigade were all busy and well-nigh exhausted by their previous efforts, but one of them was found, who, armed with an axe, hastily rushed up the tower-stairs and essayed to cut away the burning woodwork. The fire had gained too much headway. Down through the tower to the loft over the nave, then through the flat ceiling in flakes, setting in a blaze the furniture and prayer-books in the pews; and up to the splendid organ not long before erected by May & Son, of the Adelphi Terrace, London, at an expense of £1200 sterling, if I recollect rightly. I was a member of the choir, and with other members stood looking on in an agony of suspense, hoping against hope that our beloved instrument might yet be saved; but what the flames had spared, the intense heat effected. While we were gazing at the sea of fire visible through the wide front doorway, a dense shower of liquid silvery metal, white hot, suddenly descended from the organ loft. The pipes had all melted at once, and the noble organ was only an empty case, soon to be consumed with the whole interior of the building, leaving nothing but ghostly-looking charred lime-stone walls.

Next morning there was a general cry to recover the remains of poor Watson. The brick walls of our office had fallen in, and the heat of the burning mass in the cellar was that of a vast furnace. But nothing checked the zeal of the men, all of whom knew and liked him. Still hissing hot, the burnt masses were gradually cleared away, and after long hours of labour, an incremated skeleton was found, and restored to his sorrowing family for interment, with funeral obsequies which were attended by nearly all the citizens.

Shortly afterwards, Col. O'Brien's interest in the *Patriot* newspaper was sold to Mr. Ogle R. Gowan, and it continued to be conducted by him and myself until, in 1853, we dissolved partnership by arbitration, he being awarded the weekly, and I the daily edition.

CHAPTER XXXIX.

THE REBELLION LOSSES BILL.

ON the 25th of the same month of April, 1849, the Parliament Houses at Montreal were sacked and burnt by a disorderly mob, stirred up to riot by the unfortunate act of Lord Elgin, in giving the royal assent to a bill for compensating persons whose property had been destroyed or injured during the rebellion in Lower Canada in 1837-8. That the payment of those losses was a logical consequence of the general amnesty proclaimed earlier in the same year, and that men equally guilty in Upper Canada, such as Montgomery and others, were similarly compensated, is indisputable. But in Upper Canada there was no race hatred, such as Lord Durham, in the Report written for him by Messrs. C. Buller & E. G. Wakefield, describes as existing between the French and British of Lower Canada.* The rebels of Gallows Hill and the militia of Toronto were literally brothers and cousins; while the rival factions of Montreal were national enemies, with their passions aroused by long-standing mutual injuries and insults. Had Lord Elgin reserved the bill for imperial consideration, no mischief would probably have followed. What might have been considered magnanimous generosity if voluntarily accorded by the conquerors, became a stinging insult when claimed by conquered enemies and aliens. And so it was felt to be in Montreal and the Eastern Town-

---

* As originally introduced by the Lafontaine-Baldwin Ministry, the bill recognised no distinction between the claims of men actually in arms and innocent sufferers, nor was it until the last reading that a pledge not to compensate actual criminals was wrested from the Government.

ships.   But the opportunity of putting in force the
new theory of ministerial responsibility to the Canadian commons, seems to have fascinated Lord Elgin's mind, and so he " threw a cast " which all but
upset the loyalty of Lower Canada, and caused that
of the Upper Province almost to hesitate for a brief
instant.

In Toronto, sympathy with the resentment of the
rioters was blended with a deep sense of the necessity for enforcing law and order. To the passionate
movement in Montreal for annexation to the English race south of the line, no corresponding sentiment gained a hold in the Upper Province. And
in the subsequent interchange of views between
Montreal and Toronto, which resulted in the convention of the British American League at Kingston in
the following July, it was sternly insisted by western men, that no breath of disloyalty to the Empire
would be for a moment tolerated here. By the loss
of her metropolitan honours which resulted, Montreal paid a heavy penalty for her mad act of law-
lessness.

CHAPTER XL.

THE BRITISH AMERICAN LEAGUE.

THE Union of all the British American colonies now forming the Dominion of Canada, was discussed at Quebec as long ago as the year 1815; and at various times afterwards it came to the surface amid the politics of the day. The Tories of 1837 were generally favourable to union, while many Reformers objected to it. Lord Durham's report recommended a general union of the five Provinces, as a desirable sequel to the proposed union of Upper and Lower Canada.

But it was not until the passage of the Rebellion Losses Bill, that the question of a larger confederation began to assume importance. The British population of Montreal, exasperated at the action of the Parliament in recognising claims for compensation on the part of the French Canadian rebels of 1837 —that is, on the part of those who had slain loyalists and ruined their families—were ready to adopt any means—reasonable or unreasonable—of escaping from the hated domination of an alien majority. The Rebellion Losses Bill was felt by them to imply a surrender of all those rights which they and theirs had fought hard to maintain. Hence the burning of the Parliament buildings by an infuriated populace. Hence the demand in Montreal for annexation to the United States. Hence the attack upon Lord Elgin's carriage in the same city, and the less serious demonstration in Toronto. But wiser men and cooler politicians saw in the union of all the British-American Provinces a more constitutional, as well as a more pacific remedy.

The first public meetings of the British American League were held in Montreal, where the movement early assumed a formal organization; auxiliary branches rapidly sprang up in almost every city, town and village throughout Upper Canada, and the Eastern Townships of Lower Canada. In Toronto, meetings were held at Smith's Hotel, at the corner of Colborne Street and West Market Square, and were attended by large numbers, chiefly of the Tory party, but including several known Reformers. In fact, from first to last, the sympathies of the Reformers were with the League; and hence there was no serious attempt at a counter demonstration, notwithstanding that the Government and the *Globe* newspaper—at the time—did their best to ridicule and contemn the proposed union.

The principal speakers at the Toronto meetings were P. M. Vankoughnet, John W. Gamble, Ogle R. Gowan, David B. Read, E. G. O'Brien, John Duggan and others. They were warmly supported.

After some correspondence between Toronto and Montreal, it was arranged that a general meeting of the League, to consist of delegates from all the town and country branches, formally accredited, should be held at Kingston, in the new Town Hall, which had been placed at their disposal by the city authorities. Here, in a lofty, well-lighted and commodiously-seated hall, the British American League assembled on the 25th day of July, 1849. The number of delegates present was one hundred and forty, each representing some hundreds of stout yeomen, loyal to the death, and in intelligence equal to any constituency in the Empire or the world. The number of people so represented, with their families, could not have been less than half a million.

The first day was spent in discussion (with closed doors) of the manner in which the proceedings should be conducted, and in the appointment of a committee to prepare resolutions for submission on the morrow. On the 26th, accordingly, the public business commenced.*

---

* Although no notice of the annexation movement in Montreal was taken publicly at the meeting, it was well known that in the discussions with closed doors, all violence, and all tendencies towards disloyalty were utterly condemned and repudiated. The best possible testimony on this point is contained in the following extract from the Kingston correspondence of the *Globe* newspaper, of July 31st, 1849, the perusal of which now

The proceedings were conducted in accordance with parliamentary practice. The chairman, the Hon. George Moffatt, of Montreal, sat on a raised platform at the east end of the hall; at a table in front of him were placed the two secretaries, W. G. Mack, of Montreal, and Wm. Brooke, of Shipton, C. E. On either side were seated the delegates, and outside a rail, running transversely across the room, benches were provided for spectators, of whom a large number attended. A table for reporters stood on the south side, near the secretaries' table. I was present both as delegate and reporter.

The business of the day was commenced with prayer, by a clergyman of Kingston.

Mr. John W. Gamble, of Vaughan, then, as chairman of the committee nominated the previous day,

---

must, I think, rather astonish the well-known writer himself, should he happen to cast his eye upon these pages :

"The British Anglo-Saxons of Lower Canada will be most miserably disappointed in the League. They have held lately that they owed no allegiance to the crown of England, even if they did not go for annexation. *The League is loyal to the backbone* ; many of the Lower Canadians are Free Traders, at least they look to Free Trade with the United States as the great means for promoting the prosperity of the Province—*the League is strong for protection as the means of reviving our trade.* * * * * Will the old Tory compact party, with protection and vested rights as its cry, ever raise its head in Upper Canada again, think you ? "

introduced a series of resolutions, the first of which was as follows :—

" That it is essential to the prosperity of the country that the tariff should be so proportioned and levied, as to give just and adequate protection to the manufacturing and industrial classes of the country, and to secure to the agricultural population a home market with fair and remunerative prices for all descriptions of farm produce."

Resolutions in favour of economy in public expenditure, of equal justice to all classes of the people, and condemnatory of the Government in connection with the Rebellion Losses Bill, were proposed in turn, and unanimously adopted, after discussions extending over two or three days. The principal speakers in support of the resolution were J. W. Gamble, Ogle R. Gowan, P. M. Vankoughnet, Thos. Wilson, of Quebec, Geo. Crawford, A. A. Burnham, —. Aikman, John Duggan, Col. Frazer, Geo. Benjamin, and John A. Macdonald.

At length, the main object of the assemblage was reached, and embodied in the form of a motion introduced by Mr. Breckenridge, of Cobourg.

·THAT DELEGATES BE APPOINTED TO CONSULT WITH SIMILAR DELEGATES FROM NOVA SCOTIA AND NEW BRUNSWICK, CONCERNING THE PRACTICABILITY OF A UNION OF ALL THE PROVINCES.

This resolution was adopted unanimously after a full discussion. Other resolutions giving effect there-

R

to were passed, and a committee appointed to draft an address founded thereon, which was issued immediately afterwards.

On the 1st November following, the League reassembled in the City Hall, Toronto, to receive the report of the delegates to the Maritime Provinces, which was altogether favourable. It was then decided, that the proper course would be to bring the subject before the several legislatures through the people's representatives; and so the matter rested for the time.

In consequence of the removal of the seat of government to Toronto, I was appointed secretary of the League, with Mr. C. W. Cooper as assistant secretary. Meetings of the Executive Committee took place from time to time. At one of these Mr. J. W. Gamble submitted a resolution, pledging the League to join its forces with the extreme radical party represented by Mr. Peter Perry and other Reformers, who were dissatisfied with the action of the Baldwin-Lafontaine-Hincks administration, and the course of the *Globe* newspaper in sustaining the same. This proposition I felt it my duty to oppose, as being unwarranted by the committee's powers; it was negatived by a majority of two, and never afterwards revived. ———

I subjoin Mr. Gamble's speech on Protection to Native Industry, reported by myself for the *Patriot*, July 27, 1849, as a valuable historical document, which the *Globe* of that day refused to publish:

J. W. Gamble, Esq., in rising to support the motion said :—He came to this convention to represent the views and opinions of a portion of the people of the Home District, and to deliberate upon important measures necessary for the good of the country, and not to subserve the interests of any party whatever ; to consider what it was that retarded the onward progress of this country in improvement, in wealth, in the arts and amenities of life; why we were behind a neighbouring country in so many important respects. Unless we made some great change, unless we learnt speedily how to overtake that country, it followed in the natural course of events that we should be inevitably merged in that great republic, which he (Mr. G.) wished to avoid. The political questions which would engage the attention of the convention, embracing gross violations of our constitution and involving momentous consequences, were yet of small importance when compared with the great question of protection to native industry. A perusal of the statutes enacted by the Parliament of Great Britain from the time of the conquest of Canada to the abolition of the corn laws, for the regulation of the commercial intercourse of this colony, leads to the unavoidable conviction, that the first object of the framers of those statutes was to protect and advance the interests of the people of England and such of them as might temporarily resort to the colony for the purpose of trade ; and that when their tendency was to promote colonial interests, that tendency was more incidental than their chief purpose. That such a course of legislation was to be expected in the outset it was but reasonable to suppose, and that a continuation of enactments in the same spirit should be suffered by the British Canadians, with but few and feeble remonstrances on their part, might be accounted for and even anticipated when we remember the material of which a large portion of the original population of Canada was composed. Ten thousand U. E. Loyalists had emigrated from the United States to Upper Canada in 1783, rather than surrender their allegiance to the British throne ; their enthusiastic attachment to the Crown of Great Britain had made them ever prone to sacrifice their own, to what had been improperly termed the *interests of the empire.* He (Mr. G.) was himself a grandson of one of those U. E. Loyalists, and might be said to have imbibed his British feelings with his mother's milk. He remembered the time well, when the utterance of a word disrespectful of the Sovereign was looked upon as an insult to be resented on the spot. Remembering all this, and that these same people, Canada's earliest settlers, rather than live under a foreign government, though the people of that government were their own countrymen, yea, their very kinsmen and relatives—that they had forsaken their cultivated farms, their lands and possessions, to take up their abode with their families in a wilderness ; remembering these circumstances, it need excite no surprise that the old colonial commercial system was allowed to continue without any very weighty remonstrance from the colonists, until it expired in Britain's free trade policy. Although that same system, primarily intended for Britain's benefit, was not calculated to advance the settlement, the improvement, or the wealth of Canada, with equal rapidity to that of the adjoining country, whose inhabitants enacted their own commercial regulations with a view to their own immediate benefit and without reference to that of others. The United States had legislated solely for their own interests. Our commercial legislation, instead of consulting exclusively our good, had been directed for the benefit of England. If that same policy were continued hereafter, to overtake our neighbours would be hopeless, and he reiterated that the consequences would be fatal to our connexion with Great Britain.

We must protect the industry of our country. The people of this country surely are the first entitled to the benefits of the markets of their country. He had been brought up a commercial man, and until lately held to the free trade principles of commercial men. From his youth, Smith's " Wealth of Nations " had been almost as familiar to him as his Catechism, and was regarded with almost equal deference; but practical experience had of late forced upon him the conviction, that that beautiful theory was not borne out by corresponding benefits ; he had looked at its practical results, and was constrained to acknowledge, in spite of early predilections, that that theory was a fallacy. He had adopted the views of the American Protectionists as those most consonant with sound reason and common sense. Their arguments he looked upon as unanswerable ; with them he believed that economists and free trade advocates had overlooked three principles which to him appeared like economic laws of nature, and the disregard of which alone was sufficient to account for the present position of our country. They say, and he believed with them, that the earth, the only source of all production, requires the refuse of its products to be returned to its soil, or productiveness diminishes and eventually ceases. That the expense of carriage to distant markets not only wastes the manure of animals on the road, but that the expenses of freight and commissions, of charges to carriers and exchangers, are in themselves a *waste*, avoided by a home market whenever the *consumer* is not separated from the *producer* ; and that those productions fitted for distant markets, such as wheat and other grains, are only *yielded by bushels*, while those adapted for the use of the home consumer, and unsuited for distant transportation, as potatoes, turnips, cabbages, are yielded by tons. These were facts well worthy the attention of our agriculturists —eight-tenths of our whole population—and which could not be too often or too plainly placed before them. It is essential to the prosperity of every agricultural country that the consumer should be placed side by side with the producer, the loom and anvil side by side with the plough and harrow. The truth of these principles is well known in England, and practically carried out there by her agriculturists every day. She possesses within herself unlimited stores of lime, chalk and, marl, besides animal manures, valued in McQueen's Statistics in 1840 at nearly sixty millions of pounds, more than the then value of the whole of her cotton manufactures. Yet England employs whole fleets in conveying manure, guano and animal bones to her shores ; yes, has ransacked the whole habitable globe for materials to enrich her fields, and yet, forsooth, her economists and hosts of other writers would fain persuade all nations and make the world believe, that all countries are to be enriched by sending their food, their raw produce, their wheat, their rye, their barley, their oats and their grains to her market, to be eaten upon her ground, which thus receives the benefit of the refuse of the food of man, while that of animals employed in its carriage is wasted on the road, and the grower's profits are reduced by freight to her ship-owners and commission to her merchants. Behold the inconsistency, behold the practice of England and the preaching of England; behold how it is exemplified in the countries most closely in connection with her : look at Portugal, " our ancient ally." By the famous Methuen treaty she surrendered her manufactures for a market for her wines, and thus separated the *producer* from the consumer. From that hour Portugal declined, and is now—what ?—the least among the nations of the earth. Next, let us direct our attention to the West India Islands. They do not even refine their own sugar, but import what they consume of that article from England, whither they send the raw material from which it is made, in order, he supposed, to enrich the British ship-owner with two voyages across the Atlantic, and the British refiner in England, instead of bringing him and his property within their own islands. Such is their commercial policy ; and with free trade the West India planter has been ruined, the prospects of the country are blighted, and discord and discontent pervade the land. Next comes the East Indies : partial free trade with England has destroyed her manufactures. He (Mr. G.) could well recollect when Indian looms supplied the nation with cottons ; here in Canada they were the only cottons used : he appealed to the chairman, who could corroborate his statement, and must remember the Salampores and Baftas of India. But Arkwright's invention of the spinning jenny enabled England to import the raw material from India, and send back the finished article better and cheaper than the native operatives could furnish it. It was forced into their markets in spite of their earnest protests, which only sought for the imposition on British goods in India of like duties to those levied upon Indian products in Britain, and which was denied them. Now, mark the result. The agriculture of India is impoverished, many tracts of her richest soil have relapsed into jungle, and both her import and export trade are now in a most unsatisfactory state—at least so says the " Economist," the best free trade journal in England. India was prosperous while clothed in fabrics the work of her own people. What country can compare with her in the richness of her raw products ? But England forced her to separate the producer and consumer, and bitter fruits—the inevitable results of the breach of that economic law of nature which requires they should be placed side by side—have been the consequence. Turn next to Nova Scotia, New Brunswick and our own Canada. Are those countries in a prosperous condition ? (No, No !) Are we prosperous in Canada ? The meeting of this convention tells another story. Canada exports the sweat of her sons ; she sends to England her wheat, her flour, her timber, and other raw produce, the product of manual labour, and receives in return England's cottons, woollens and hardwares, the product of labour-saving, self-acting and inexpensive machinery.   We separate the consumer and the producer ; we seek in distant markets a reward for our labour ; it is denied us, and this suicidal policy must exist no longer.   Behold its effects in our currency ; not a dollar in specie can we retain, unless it is circulated at a greater value than it bears in the countries of our indebtedness, while our government is obliged to issue shin-plasters to eke out its revenue. The true policy for Canada is to consult her own interests, as the people of the United States have consulted theirs, irrespective of the interests of any other country.   Leave others to take care of themselves.   Our present system has inundated us with English and Foreign manufactures, and has swept away all the products of our soil, all the products of our forests, all the capital brought into the country by emigration, all the money expended by tbe British Government for military purposes, and leaves us poor enough. Why does not Canada prosper equally with the adjacent republic ?   He had often asked the question. " Oh, the Americans have more enterprise, more capital, and more emigration than Canada," is the universal answer.   It is true, these are causes of prosperity in the Union, but they are secondary causes only ; in the first instance, they are effects, the legitimate effects of her commercial code, which protects the industry of her citizens, stimulates enterprise and largely rewards labour.   Why does the poor western emigrant leave Canada?—because in the union he gets better reward for his labour. * * * * This was strictly a labour question.   He desired not to see the wages of labour reduced until a man's unremitting toil procured barely sufficient for the supply of his animal wants—he desired to behold our labourers, mechanics, and operatives a well fed, well clothed and well educated part of the community.   The country must support its labour ; is it not then far preferable to support it in the position of an independent, intelligent body, than as a mass of paupers—you may bring it down, down, down, until, as in Ireland, the man will be forced to do his daily work for his daily potatoes. He had forgotten Ireland, a case just in point ; she exports to England vast quantities of food, of raw produce—who has not heard in the English markets of Irish wheat, Irish oats, Irish pork, beef and butter. Ireland has but few manufactures— she has separated the producer and consumer, and has reaped the consequence of exporting her food, in poverty, wretchedness and rags. Ireland has denied the earth the refuse of its productions, and the earth has cast out her sons. Ask the reason—it is the con-acre system, says one ; it is the absentee landlords, says another. But if the absenteeism invariably produced such results, why is it not the case in Scotland ? Scotland, since the union, has doubled, trebled, aye, quadrupled her wealth, he knew not how often. Since the union, Scotland exports but little food, the food produced by the soil is there consumed upon the soil, and to her absentee landlords, she pays the rent of that soil in the produce of her looms and her furnaces. This led him to consider the policy of those countries that support the greatest number of human beings in proportion to their area. First, Belgium, the battle field of Europe ; that country had suffered immeasurably from the effects of war, yet her people were always prosperous, quiet and contented, amid the convulsions of Europe, for there the consumer and producer were side by side. In Normandy, China, the North of England, and South of Scotland, in the Eastern States, the same system prevailed. The speaker that preceded him (Mr. Gowan), had said that under the present system we were led to speculate in human blood, upon the chance of European wars ; it was too true, it was horrible to contemplate ; but he would say, was it not more horrible still, to speculate upon the chance of famine ? Had we never looked, never hoped, for a famine in Ireland, England or the continent of Europe, that we might increase our store thereby ! ! ! put money in our pockets ! ! !

to such dreadful shifts, dreadful to reflect upon, had the disregard of the great principle he had enunciated reduced us. The proper remedy was to protect our native industry, to protect it from the surplus products of the industry of other countries—surplus products sold in our markets without any reference to the cost of production. Manufacturers look at home consumption in the first place for their profits ; that market being filled, they do not force off their surplus among their own people —that might injure their credit, or permanently lower the value of their manufactures at home. They send their surplus abroad to sell for what it will bring. Another view of the question was, that in the exchanging produce for foreign manufactures, one half of the commodities is raised by native industry and capital, and one half by foreign. One half goes to promote native industry and capital, and the other half foreign industry and capital, but if the exchange is made at home, it stands to common sense, that all the commodities are raised by native industry and capital, and the benefit of the barter if retained *at home*, to promote and support them. Where the raw material produced in any country is worked up in that country, the difference between the value of the material and the finished article is retained in the country.

*   *   *   *

He would be met, he supposed, with a stale objection that protection is a tax imposed for the benefit of one class upon the rest of the community. Never was any assertion more fallacious. Admitting that the value of an article was enhanced by protection, which he (Mr. G) did not admit, the rest of the community were benefited a thousand fold by that very protection ; for instance, if a farmer paid a little more for his coat, was he not doubly, quadruply compensated for his wool, to say nothing of the market, also at his own door, for his potatoes, turnips, cabbages, eggs, and milk. But he denied that increase of price invariably followed a protective policy; that policy furnished the manufacturer a market at home *for quantity and quantity only,* while home competition, stimulated by a system securing a fair reward for industrial pursuits, soon brought down the manufactured article as low as it ought to be. He might be answered, your system will destroy our foreign trade altogether. The fact was the very reverse; the saving made by home consumption of food and raw produce on the soil where it was grown, to the producer, enabled that producer to purchase a greater quantity of articles brought from a distance, and made him a greater consumer of those very articles than when the value of the produce of his own farm was diminished by carriage to, and by charges in a distant market. He had now in his possession statistical tables of the United States, for successive periods, sufficient to convince the most sceptical, that during the periods their manufacturers had been most strongly protected, the average prices of such manufactures had been less, while the amount of imported goods had exceeded that of similar periods under low duties. Mr. Gowan had alluded to a case in which the very sand of the opposite shore was turned into a source of wealth by a glass manufactory, and also to the rocks of New Hampshire. He had also visited the Eastern States, and was delighted with the industry, the economy and intelligence of the people; but as to the country, he believed it would be a hard matter to induce a Canadian to take up his abode among its granite rocks and ice, yet those very rocks and that ice were by that thrifty people converted into wealth, and formed no small item in their resources.

Such are the results, the legitimate results of a protective policy, but the United States have not always followed that policy. The revolution did not do away with their prejudices in favour of British goods; for a long period after, nothing would go down but British cloths, cottons, and hardware. Then came the war of 1812, which showed them that they were but nominally independent while other nations supplied their wants ; the war forced them to manufacture for themselves. After that war, excepting in some coarse goods, low *ad valorem* duties were imposed ; the consequence was, a general prostration of the manufacturing interests, followed by low prices in all agricultural staples. In 1824 recourse was again had to protection ; national prosperity was soon visible ; but why should he further detail the experiments made by that country ? Suffice it to say, three times was the trial of free trade made, and three times had they to retrace their steps and return to the protective system, now so successfully in operation. England herself, with above one hundred millions of unprotected subjects, now declares the partially protected United States her best customer ; in 1844 the amount of her exports to that country was eight millions, a sum equal to the whole of her exports to all her colonies. In 1846 the amount of cotton goods imported into the United States was one-fifth of their whole consumption, the amount of woollens likewise a fifth, and the amount of iron imported one-eighth of the entire quantity consumed. What proportion our importation of these articles in Canada bears to our consumption he had not been able to ascertain ; but his conviction was, that if we adopted a similar commercial policy to that of the United States, the time would come when we should only import one-fifth of our cottons, one-fifth of our woollens, one-eighth of our iron ; and when that time did come, and not till then, might we hope to cast our eye upon our republican neighbour without envying her greater prosperity.

CHAPTER XLI.

RESULTS OF THE B. A. LEAGUE.

THE very brief summary which I have been able to give in the preceding chapter, may suffice to show, as I have desired to do, that no lack of progressiveness, no lack of patriotism, no lack of energy on great public occasions, is justly chargeable against Canadian Tories. I could produce page after page of extracts, in proof that the objects of the League were jeered at and condemned by the Reform press, led by the *Globe* newspaper. But in that instance Mr. George Brown was deserted by his own party. I spoke at the time with numbers of Reformers who entirely sympathized with us.; and it was not long before we had our triumph, which was in the year 1864, when the Hon. George Brown and the Hon. John A. Macdonald clasped hands together, for the purpose of forming an administration expressly pledged to effect the union of the five Provinces of Upper and Lower Canada, Nova Scotia, New Brunswick, and Prince Edward Island.

In the importance of the object, the number and intelligence of the actors, and, above all, in the determined earnestness of every man concerned, the meetings of the British American League may well claim to rank with those famous gatherings of the people, which have marked great eras in the world's progress both in ancient and modern times. In spite of every effort to dwarf its importance, and even to ignore its existence, the British American League fulfilled its mission.

By the action of the League, was Canada lifted into a front rank amongst progressive peoples.

By the action of the League, the day was hastened, when our rivers, our lakes, our canals, our railroads, shall constitute the great highway from Europe to Eastern Asia and Australasia.

By the action of the League, a forward step was taken towards that great future of the British race, which is destined to include in its heaven-directed mission, the whole world—east, west, north and south !

CHAPTER XLII.

TORONTO CIVIC AFFAIRS.

MY first step in public life was in 1848. I had leased from the heirs of the late Major Hartney (who had been barrack-master of York during its siege and capture by the American forces under Generals Pike and Dearborn in 1813) his house on Wellington street, opposite the rear of Bishop Strachan's palace. I thus became a resident ratepayer of the ward of St. George, and in that capacity contested the representation of the ward as councilman, in opposition to the late Ezekiel F. Whittemore, whose American antecedents rendered him unpopular just then. As neither Mr. Whittemore nor myself resorted to illegitimate means of influencing votes, we speedily became fast friends—a friendship which lasted until his death. I was defeated after a close contest. Before the end of the year, however, Mr. Whittemore resigned his seat in the council and offered me his support, so that I was elected councilman in his stead, and held the seat as councilman, and afterwards as alderman, continuously until 1854, when I removed to Carlton, on the Davenport Road, five miles north-west of the city. The electors have since told me that I taught them how to vote without bribery, and certainly I never purchased a vote. My chief outlay arose from a custom—not bad, as I think—originated by the late Alderman Wakefield, of providing a hearty English dinner at the expense of the successful candidates, at the Shades Hotel, in which the candidates and voters on both sides were wont to participate. Need I add, that the company was jovial, and the toasts effusively loyal.

The members of the council, when I took my seat, were: George Gurnett, Mayor, who had been conspicuous as an officer of the City Guard in 1837-38; aldermen, G. Duggan, jr., Geo. P. Ridout, Geo. W. Allan, R. Dempsey, Thos. Bell, Jno. Bell, Q.C., Hon. H. Sherwood, Q.C., Robt. Beard, Jas. Beatty, Geo. T. Denison, jr., and Wm. A. Campbell; also, councilmen Thos. Armstrong, Jno. Ritchey, W. Davis, Geo. Coulter, Jas. Ashfield, R. James, jr., Edwin Bell, Samuel Platt, Jno. T. Smith, Jno. Carr and Robt. B. Denison. My own name made up the twenty-four that then constituted the council. The city officers were: Chas. Daly, clerk; A. T. McCord, chamberlain; Clarke Gamble, solicitor; Jno. G. Howard, engineer; Geo. L. Allen, chief of police; Jno. Kidd, governor of jail; and Robt. Beard, chief engineer of fire brigade.

During the years 1850, '1, '2 and '3, I had for colleagues, in addition to those of the above who were re-elected: aldermen John G. Bowes, Hon. J. H. Cameron, Q.C., R. Kneeshaw, Wm. Wakefield, E. F. Whittemore, Jno. B. Robinson, Jos. Sheard, Geo. Brooke, J. M. Strachan, Jno. Hutchison, Wm. H. Boulton, John Carr, S. Shaw, Jas. Beaty, Samuel Platt, E. H. Rutherford, Angus Morrison, Ogle R. Gowan, M. P. Hayes, Wm. Gooderham and Hon. Wm. Cayley; and councilmen Jonathan Dunn, Jno. Bugg, Adam Beatty, D. C. Maclean, Edw. Wright, Jas. Price, Kivas Tully, Geo. Platt, Chas. E. Romain, R. C. McMullen, Jos. Lee, Alex. Macdonald, Samuel Rogers, F. C. Capreol, Samuel T. Green, Wm. Hall, Robert Dodds, Thos. McConkey and Jas. Baxter.

The great majority of these men were persons of high character and standing, with whom it was both a privilege and a pleasure to work; and the affairs of the city were, generally speaking, honestly and disinterestedly administered. Many of my old colleagues still fill conspicuous positions in the public service, while others have died full of years and honours.

My share of the civic service consisted principally in doing most of the hard work, in which I took a delight, and found my colleagues remarkably willing to cede to me. All the city buildings were re-erected or improved under my direct charge, as chairman of the Market Block and Market committees. The St. Lawrence Hall, St. Lawrence Market, City Hall, St. Patrick's Market, St. Andrew's Market, the Weigh-House, were all constructed in my time. And lastly, the original contract for the esplanade was negotiated by the late Ald. W. Gooderham and myself, as active members of the Wharves and Harbours committee. The by-laws for granting £25,000 to the Northern Railway, and £100,000 to the Toronto & Guelph Railway, were both introduced and carried through by me, as chairman of the Finance committee, in 1853.

The old market was a curiously ugly and ill-contrived erection. Low brick shops surrounded three sides of the square, with cellars used for slaughtering sheep and calves; the centre space was paved with

s

rubble stones, and was rarely free from heaps of cabbage leaves, bones and skins. The old City Hall formed the fourth or King Street side, open underneath for fruit and other stalls. The owners of imaginary vested rights in the old stalls raised a small rebellion when their dirty purlieus were invaded; and the decision of the Council, to rent the new stalls by public auction to avoid charges of favouritism, brought matters to a climax. On the Saturday evening when the new arcade and market were lighted with gas and opened to the public, the Market committee walked through from King to Front Street to observe the effect. The indignation of the butchers took the form of closing all their shutters, and as a last expression of contempt nailing thereon miserable shanks of mutton! Dire as this omen was meant to be, it does not seem to have prevented the St. Lawrence Market from being a credit to the city ever since.

There is a historical incident connected with the old market, of a very tragic character. One day towards the latter end of 1837, William Lyon Mackenzie held there a political meeting to denounce the Family Compact. There was a wooden gallery round the square, the upright posts of which were full of sharp hooks, used by the butchers to expose their meat for sale, as were also the cross beams from post to post. A considerable number of people—from three to four hundred—were present, and the great agitator spoke from an auctioneer's desk placed near the western stalls. Many young men of Tory families, as well as Orangemen and their party allies, attended to hear the speeches. In the midst of the excitement—applauding or derisive, according to the varying feelings of the crowd—the iron stays of the balcony gave way and precipitated numbers to the ground. Two or three were caught on the meat-hooks, and one—young Fitzgibbon, a son of Col. Fitzgibbon who afterwards commanded at Gallows Hill—was killed. Others were seriously wounded, amongst whom was Charles Daly, then stationer, and afterwards city clerk, whose leg was broken in the fall. I well remember seeing him carried into his own shop insensible, and supposed to be fatally hurt.

The routine of city business does not afford much occasion for entertaining details, and I shall therefore only trouble my readers with notices of the principal civic events to which I was a party, from 1849 to 1853.

CHAPTER XLIII.

LORD ELGIN IN TORONTO.

ON the 9th day of October, 1849, Lord Elgin made his second public entry into Toronto. The announcement of his intention to do so, communicated to the mayor, Geo. Gurnett, Esq., by letter signed by his lordship's brother and secretary, Col. Bruce, raised a storm of excitement in the city, which was naturally felt in the city council. The members were almost to a man Tories, a large proportion of whom had served as volunteers in 1837-8. The more violent insisted upon holding His Excellency personally responsible for the payment of rebels for losses arising out of the rebellion in Lower Canada; while moderate men contended, that as representative of the Queen, the Governor-General should be received with respect and courtesy at least, if not with enthusiasm. So high did party feeling run, that inflammatory placards were posted about the streets, calling on all loyal men to oppose His Excellency's entrance, as an encourager and abettor of treason. A special meeting of the council was summoned in consequence, for September 13th, at which the Hon. Henry Sherwood, member for the city, moved a resolution declaring the determination of the council to repress all violence, whether of word or deed, which was carried by a large majority.

The draft of an address which had been prepared by a committee of the citizens, and another by Ald. G. T. Denison, were considered at a subsequent meeting of the council held on the 17th, and strongly objected to—the first as too adulatory, the second as too political. As I had the readiest pen in the council, and was in the habit of helping members on both sides to draft their ideas in the form of resolutions, the mayor requested me to prepare an address embodying the general feelings of the members. I accordingly did so to the best of my ability, and succeeded in writing one which might express the loyalty of the citizens, without committing them to an approval of the conduct of the Hincks-Taché government in carrying through Parliament the Rebellion Losses Bill. The other addresses having been either defeated or withdrawn, I submitted mine, which was carried by a majority of seventeen to four. And thus was harmony restored.

His Excellency arrived on the appointed day, being the 9th of October. The weather was beautiful, and the city was alive with excitement, not unmingled with apprehension. Lieut.-Col. and Ald. G. T. Denison had volunteered the services of the Governor-General's Body Guard, which were graciously accepted. A numerous cortege of officials and promi-

nent citizens met and accompanied the Vice-regal
party from the Yonge St. wharf to Ellah's Hotel, on
King St. west.   As they were proceeding up Yonge
street, one or two rotten eggs were thrown at the
Governor-General's carriage, by men who were immediately arrested.

On arriving at Ellah's Hotel, His Excellency took
his stand on the porch, where the City Address was
presented, which with the reply I give in full :—

ADDRESS.

*To His Excellency the Right Hon. James Earl of Elgin and
Kincardine, Governor-General, &c., &c.*

MAY IT PLEASE YOUR EXCELLENCY,

We, the Mayor, Aldermen, and Commonalty of the
City of Toronto, in Common Council assembled, beg leave
to approach Your Excellency as the representative of our
Most Gracious and beloved Sovereign, with renewed as-
surances of our attachment and devotion to Her Majesty's
person and government.

We will not conceal from Your Excellency, that great
diversity of opinion, and much consequent excitement,
exists among us on questions connected with the political
condition of the Province; but we beg to assure Your
Excellency, that however warmly the citizens of Toronto
may feel on such subjects, they will be prepared on all
occasions to demonstrate their high appreciation of the
blessings of the British Constitution, by according to the
Governor-General of this Province that respect and consideration which are no less due to his exalted position,
than to the well tried loyalty and decorum which have
ever distinguished the inhabitants of this peaceful and
flourishing community.

The City of Toronto has not escaped the commercial depression which has for some time so generally prevailed. We trust, however, that the crisis is now past, and that the abundant harvest with which a kind Providence has blessed us, will ere long restore the commerce of the country to a healthy tone.

We watch with lively interest the prospect which the completion of our great water communications with the ocean, will open to us; and we fervently hope that the extension of trade thus opened to Her Majesty's North American Provinces will tend to strengthen the union between these Provinces and the Parent State.

We congratulate Your Excellency and Lady Elgin upon the birth of an heir to Your Excellency's house ; and we truly sympathise with Her Ladyship upon her present delicate and weak state, and venture to hope that her tour through Upper Canada will have the effect of restoring her to the enjoyment of perfect health.

REPLY.

GENTLEMEN,—I receive with much satisfaction the assurance of your attachment and devotion to Her Majesty's person and government.

That the diversities of opinion which exist among you, on questions connected with the political condition of the Province, should be attended with much excitement, is greatly to be regretted, and I fully appreciate the motives which induce you at the present time, to call my attention to the fact. I am willing, nevertheless, to believe that however warmly the citizens of Toronto may feel on such subjects, they will be prepared, on all occasions, to demonstrate their high appreciation of the blessings of the British Constitution, by according to the Governor-General that respect and consideration which are no less due to his position than to their own well-tried loyalty and decorum.

It is my firm conviction, moreover, that the inhabitants of Canada, generally, are averse to agitation, and
that all communities as well as individuals, who as-
pire to take a lead in the affairs of the Province, will
best fit themselves for that high avocation, by exhibiting
habitually in their demeanour, the love of order and of
peaceful progress.

I have observed with much anxiety and concern the
commercial depression from which the City of Toronto,
in common with other important towns in the Province,
has of late so seriously suffered. I trust, however, with
you, that the crisis is now past, and that the abundant
harvest, with which a kind Providence has blessed the
country, will ere long restore its commerce to a healthy
tone.

The completion of your water communications with
the ocean must indeed be watched with a lively interest
by all who have at heart the welfare of Canada and the
continuance of the connection so happily subsisting between the Province and the Parent State. These great
works have undoubtedly been costly, and the occasion of
some financial embarrassment while in progress. But I
firmly believe that the investment you have made in
them has been judicious, and that you have secured thereby for your children, and your children's children, an
inheritance that will not fail them so long as the law of
nature endures which causes the waters of your vast in-
land seas to seek an outlet to the ocean.

I am truly obliged to you for the congratulations which
you offer me on the birth of my son, and for the kind interest which you express in Lady Elgin's health : I am
happy to be able to inform you, that she has already
derived much benefit from her sojourn in Upper Canada.

As not a little fictitious history has been woven
out of these events, I shall call in evidence here the

Globe newspaper of the 11th, the following day, in which I find this editorial paragraph :—

" It is seldom we have had an opportunity of speaking in terms of approbation of our civic authorities, but we cannot but express our high sense of the manly, independent manner in which all have done their duty on this occasion. The grand jury* is chiefly composed of Conservatives, the Mayor, Aldermen and the police are all Conservatives, but no men could have carried out more fearlessly their determination to maintain order in the community."

Of all the Governors-General who have been sent out to Canada, Lord Elgin was by far the best fitted, by personal suavity of manners, eloquence in speech, and readiness in catching the tone of his hearers, to tide over a stormy political crisis. He had not been long in Toronto before his praises rang from every tongue, even the most embittered. Americans who came in contact with him, went away charmed with his flattering attentions.

----

* The grand jury, who happened to be in session, had presented some thirteen young men as parties to an attempt to create a riot. Some months afterwards, the persons accused were brought to trial, and three of them found guilty and sentenced to short terms of imprisonment.

CHAPTER XLIV.

TORONTO HARBOUR AND ESPLANADE.

THE number of citizens is becoming few indeed, who remember Toronto Bay when its natural surroundings were still undefaced and its waters pure and pellucid. From the French Fort to the Don River, curving gently in a circular sweep, under a steep bank forty feet high covered with luxuriant forest trees, was a narrow sandy beach used as a pleasant carriage-drive, much frequented by those residents who could boast private conveyances. A wooden bridge spanned the Don, and the road was continued thence, still under the shade of umbrageous trees, almost to Gibraltar Point on the west, and past Ashbridge's Bay eastward. At that part of the peninsula, forming the site of the present east entrance, the ground rose at least thirty feet above high-water mark, and was crested with trees. Those trees and that bank were destroyed through the cupidity of city builders, who excavated the sand and brought it away in barges to be used in making mortar. This went on unchecked till about the year 1848, when a violent storm—almost a tornado —from the east swept across the peninsula, near

Ashbridge's Bay, where it had been denuded of sand nearly to the ordinary level of the water. This aroused public attention to the danger of further neglect.

The harbour had been for some years under the charge of a Board of Commissioners, of which the chairman was nominated by the Government, two members by the City Council, and two by the Board of Trade. The Government, through the chairman, exercised of course the chief control of the harbour and of the harbour dues.

In the spring of 1849, the chairman of the Harbour Commission was Col. J. G. Chewett, a retired officer I think of the Royal Engineers; the other members were Ald. Geo. W. Allan and myself, representing the City Council; Messrs. Thos. D. Harris, hardware merchant, and Jno. G. Worts, miller, nominees of the Board of Trade. I well remember accompanying Messrs. Allan, Harris and Worts round the entire outer beach, on wheels and afoot, and a very pleasant trip it was. The waters on retiring had left a large pool at the place where they had crossed, but no actual gap then existed. Our object was to observe the extent of the mischief, and to adopt a remedy if possible. Among the several plans submitted was one by Mr. Sandford Fleming, for carrying out into the water a number of groynes or jetties, so as to intercept the soil washed down from the Scarboro' heights, and thus gradually widen

the peninsula as well as resist the further erasion of
the existing beach.   At a subsequent meeting of the
Harbour Commission, this suggestion was fully discussed.   The chairman, who was much enfeebled by
age and ill-health, resented angrily the interference
of non-professional men, and refused even to put a
motion on the subject.   Thereupon, Mr. Allan, who
was as zealously sanguine as Col. Chewett was the
reverse, offered to pay the whole cost of the groynes
out of his own pocket.   Still the chairman continued
obdurate, and became so offensive in his remarks,
that the proposition was abandoned in disgust.*

In following years, the breach recurred again and
again, until it produced an established gap.   Efforts
were made at various times to have the gap closed,
but always defeated by the influence of eastern property owners, who contended that a free current
through the Bay was necessary to the health of the
east end of the city.   The only thing accomplished
from 1849 to 1853, was the establishment of buoys

---

*After I had left the Council, the question of harbour
preservation was formally taken up at Mayor Allan's instance, and three premiums offered for the best reports
on the subject.   The first prize was adjudged to the joint
report of Mr. Sandford Fleming and Mr. H. Y. Hind, in
which the system of groynes was recommended.   The
reports were printed, but the Council—did nothing.   Mr.
Allan again offered to put down a groyne at his own expense, Mr. Fleming agreeing to superintend the work.
The offer, however, was never accepted.

at the western entrance of the harbour, and a light-house and guide light on the Queen's wharf; also the employment of dredges in deepening the channel between the wharf and the buoys, in which Mr. T. D. Harris took a lively interest, and did great service to the mercantile community.

Beyond the erection of wharves at several points, no attempt was made to change the shore line until 1853, when it became necessary to settle the mode in which the Northern and Grand Trunk Railways should enter the city. An esplanade had been determined upon so long ago as 1838; and in 1840 a by-law was passed by the City Council, making it a condition of all water-lot leases, that the lessees should construct their own portion of the work. In May, 1852, the first active step was taken by notifying lessees that their covenants would be enforced. The Mayor, John G. Bowes, having reported to the Council that he had made verbal application to members of the government at Quebec, for a grant of the water-lots west of Simcoe Street, then under the control of the Respective Officers of Her Majesty's Ordnance in Upper Canada, a formal memorial applying for those lots was adopted and transmitted accordingly.

The Committee on Wharves, Harbours, etc., for 1852, consisted of the Mayor, Councilmen Tully and Lee, with myself as chairman. We were actively engaged during the latter half of the year and the following spring, in negotiations with the Northern and Grand Trunk Railway boards, in making surveys and obtaining suggestions for the work of the Esplanade, and in carrying through Parliament the necessary legislation. Messrs. J. G. Howard, city engineer; William Thomas, architect; and Walter Shanly, chief engineer of the Grand Trunk Railway, were severally employed to prepare plans and estimates; and no pains were spared to get the best advice from all quarters. The Mayor was indefatigable on behalf of the city's interests, and to him undoubtedly, is mainly due the success of the Council in obtaining the desired grant from Government, both of the water-lots and the peninsula.

The chairman of the Committee on Wharves and Harbours, etc., for 1853, was the late Alderman W. Gooderham, a thoroughly respected and respectable citizen, who took the deepest interest in the subject. I acted with and for him on all occasions, preparing reports for the Council, and even went so far as to calculate minutely from the soundings the whole details of excavation, filling in, breastwork, etc., in order to satisfy myself that the interests of the city were duly protected.

In September, 1853, tenders for the work were received from numerous parties, and subjected to rigorous examination, the opinions of citizens being freely taken thereon. In the meantime, it was necessary, before closing the contract, to obtain authority from the Government with respect to the western water lots, and I was sent to Quebec for that purpose, in which, but for the influence of the Grand Trunk Company, and of Messrs. Gzowski & Macpherson, I might have failed. The Hon. Mr. Hincks, then premier, received me rather brusquely at first, and it was not until he was thoroughly satisfied that the railway interests were fairly consulted, that I made much progress with him. I did succeed, however, and brought back with me all necessary powers both as to the water lots and the peninsula.

Finally, the tender of Messrs. Gzowski & Co. was very generally judged to be most for the interests of the city. They offered to allow £10,000 for the right of way for the Grand Trunk Railway along the Esplanade; and engaged for the same sum to erect five bridges, with brick abutments and stone facings, to be built on George, Church, Yonge, Bay, and either York or Simcoe Streets, to the wharves.* The contract also provided that the cribwork should be of sufficient strength to carry stone facing hereafter.†

---

* The necessary plans and specifications for these five bridges were prepared by Mr. Shanly accordingly,—their value when completed, being put at fully £15,000.

† The same year, I was chairman of the Walks and Gardens Committee, and in that capacity instructed Mr. John Tully, City Surveyor, to extend the surveys of all streets leading towards the Bay, completely to the water

When canvassing St. George's Ward in December, 1852, for re-election as alderman, I told my constituents that nothing but my desire to complete the Esplanade arrangements could induce me to sacrifice my own business interests by giving up more than half my time for another year : and it was with infinite satisfaction that on the 4th of January, 1854— the last week but one of my term in the Council—I saw the Esplanade contract "signed, sealed and delivered" in the presence of the Wharves and Harbours Committee. On the 11th January, a report of the same committee, recommending the appointment of a proper officer to take charge of the peninsula, and put a stop to the removal of sand, was adopted in Council.

I heartily wish that my reminiscences of the Esplanade contract could end here. I ceased to have any connection with it, officially or otherwise ; but in 1854, an agitation was commenced within the Council and out of doors, the result of which was, the cancellation by mutual consent of the contract made with Messrs. Gzowski & Co., and the making a new contract with other parties, by which it was understood the city lost money to the tune of some $50,-000, while Messrs. Gzowski & Co. benefited to the

line of the Esplanade. This was before any concession was made to the Northern, or any other railway. I mention this by way of reminder to the city authorities, who seem to me to have overlooked the fact.

extent of at least $16,000, being the difference be-
tween the rates of wages in 1853 and 1855. The
five bridges were set aside, to which circumstance is
due the unhappy loss of life by which we have all
been shocked of late years. Of the true cause of all
these painful consequences, I shall treat in my next
chapter.

CHAPTER XLV.

MAYOR BOWES—CITY DEBENTURES.

OF all the members of the City Council for 1850,
and up to 1852, John G. Bowes was the most
active and most popular. In educational affairs, in
financial arrangements, and indeed, in all questions
affecting the city's interests, he was by far the ablest
man who had ever filled the civic chair. His acquirements as an arithmetician were extraordinary;
and as a speaker he possessed remarkable powers.
I took pleasure in seconding his declared views on
nearly all public questions; and in return, he showed
me a degree of friendship which I could not but
highly appreciate. By his persuasion, and rather
against my own wish, I accepted, in 1852, the secre-
taryship of the Toronto and Guelph Railway Com-

T

pany, which I held until it was absorbed by the Grand Trunk Company in 1853.*

In the same year, rumours began to be rife in the city, that Mr. Bowes, in conjunction with the Hon. Francis Hincks, then premier, had made $10,000 profits out of the sale of city debentures issued to the Northern Railway Company. Had the Mayor admitted the facts at once, stating his belief that he was right in so doing, it is probable that his friends would have been spared the pain, and himself the loss and disgrace which ensued. But he denied in the most solemn manner, in full Council, that he had any interest whatever in the sale of those debentures, and his word was accepted by all his friends there. When, in 1854, he was compelled to admit in the Court of Chancery, that he had not only sold the debentures for his own profit to the extent of $4,800, but that the Hon. Francis Hincks was a partner in the speculation, and had profited to the same amount, the Council and citizens were alike astounded. Not so much at the transaction itself, for it must be remembered that more than one judge in chancery held the dealing in city debentures to be perfectly legal both on the part of Mr. Bowes and

---

* I was offered by Sir Cusack Roney, chief secretary of the G. T. R. Co., a position worth $2,000 a year in their Montreal office, but declined to break up my connections in Toronto. On my resigning the secretaryship, the Board honoured me with a resolution of thanks, and a gratuity of a year's salary.

Sir Francis Hincks, but at the palpable deception which had been perpetrated on the Finance Committee, and through them on the Council.

While the sale of the $50,000 Northern Railway debentures was under consideration, Mr. Bowes as Mayor had been commissioned to get a bill passed at Quebec to legalize such sale. On his return it was found that new clauses had been introduced into the bill, and particularly one requiring the debentures to be made payable in England, to which Alderman Joshua G. Beard and myself took objection as unnecessarily tying the hands of the Council. Mr. Bowes said, " Mr. Hincks would have it so." Had the committee supposed that in insisting upon those clauses Mr. Hincks was using his official powers for his own private profit, they could never have consented to the change in the bill, but would have insisted upon the right of the Council to make their own debentures payable wheresoever the city's interests would be best subserved.*

---

* The judgment given by the Judicial Committee of the Privy Council expressly stated that " the evidence of Ald. Thompson and Councilman Tully was conclusive as to the effect of their having been kept in ignorance of the corrupt bargain respecting the sale of the city debentures issued for the construction of the Northern Railway ; and that they would not have voted for the proposed bill for the consolidation of the city debt, if they had been aware of the transaction."

It is matter of history, that the suit in Chancery resulted in a judgment against Mr. Bowes for the whole amount of his profits, and that in addition to that loss he had to pay a heavy sum in costs, not only of the suit, but of appeals both here and in England. The consequence to myself was a great deal of pain, and the severance of a friendship that I had valued greatly. In October, 1853, a very strong resolution denouncing his conduct was moved by Alderman G. T. Denison, to which I moved an amendment declaring him to have been guilty of "a want of candour," which was carried, and which was the utmost censure that the majority of the Council would consent to pass. For this I was subjected to much animadversion in the public press. Yet from the termination of the trial to the day of his death, I never afterwards met Mr. Bowes on terms of amity. At an interview with him, at the request and in presence of my partner, Col. O. R. Gowan, I told the Mayor that I considered him morally responsible for all the ill-feeling that had caused the cancellation of the first Esplanade contract, and for the loss to the city which followed. I told him that it had become impossible for any man to trust his word. And afterwards when he became a candidate for a seat in parliament, I opposed his election in the columns of the *Colonist*, which I had then recently purchased; for which he denounced me personally, at his election meetings, as a man capable of assassination.

Notwithstanding, I believe John G. Bowes to have been punished more severely than justice required ; that he acted in ignorance of the law ; and that his great services to the city more than outweighed any injury sustained. His subsequent election to Parliament, while it may have soothed his pride, can hardly have repaid him for the forfeiture of the respect of a very large number of his fellow-citizens.

CHAPTER XLVI.

CARLTON OCEAN BEACH.

IN 1853, I removed to the village of Carlton West, on the gravel road to Weston, and distant seven miles north-west of the city. My house stood on a gravel ridge which stretches from the Carlton station of the Northern Railway to the River Humber, and which must have formed the beach of the antediluvian northern ocean, one hundred and eighty feet above the present lake, and four hundred and thirty above the sea. This gravel ridge plainly marks the Toronto Harbour at the mouth of the Humber, as it existed in those ancient days, before the Niagara River and the Falls had any place on our world's surface. East of Carlton station, a high bluff of clay continues the old line of coast, like the modern, to Scarboro' Heights, showing frequent depressions caused by the ice of the glacial period. In corroboration of this theory, I remember that for the first house built on the Avenue Road, north of Davenport Road, the excavations for a cellar laid bare great boulders of granite, limestone, and other rock, evidently deposited there by icebergs, which had crossed the clay bluff by channels of their own dredging, and melted away in the warmer waters to the south. I think it was Professor Chapman, of Toronto University, who pointed this out to me, and mentioned a still more remarkable case of glacial action which occurred in the Township of Albion, where a limestone quarry which had been worked profitably for several years, turned out to the great disappointment of its owner to be neither more nor less than a vast glacial boulder, which had been transported from its natural site at a distance of at least eighty miles. This locomotive rock is said to have been seventy feet in thickness and as much in breadth.

While speaking of the Carlton gravel ridge, it is worth while to note that, in taking gravel from its southern face, at a depth of twenty feet, I found an Indian flint arrow-head; also a stone implement similar to what is called by painters a muller, used for grinding paint. Several massive bones, and the horns of some large species of deer, were also found

in the same gravel pit, and carried or given away by
the workmen.   The two articles first named are still
in my possession.   Being at the very bottom of the
gravel deposit, they must have lain there when no
such beach existed, or ever since the Oak Ridges
ceased to be an ocean beach.

My house on the Davenport Road was a very
pleasant residence, with a fine lawn ornamented with
trees chiefly planted by my own hands, and was supplied with all the necessaries for modest competence.
It is worth recording, that some of the saplings—
silver poplars (abeles) planted by me, grew in twelve
years to be eighteen inches thick at the butt, and
sixty feet in spread of branches ; while maples and
other hardwoods did not attain more than half that
size.   Thus it would seem, that our North-West
prairies might be all re-clothed with full-grown ash-
leaved maples—their natural timber—in twenty-
five years, or with balm of Gilead and abele poplars
in half that time.   Would it not be wise to enact
laws at once, having that object in view ?

I have been an amateur gardener since early
childhood ; and at Carlton indulged my taste to the
full by collecting all kinds of flowers cultivated and
wild.   I still envy the man who, settling in the new
lands, say in the milder climates of Vancouver's
Island or British Columbia, may utilize to the full
his abundant opportunities of gathering into one
group the endless floral riches of the Canadian wil-

derness. We find exquisite lobelias, scarlet, blue and lilac; orchises with pellucid stems and fairy elegance of blossom; lovely prairie roses; cacti of infinite delicacy and the richest hues. Then as to shrubs—the papaw, the xeranthemum of many varieties, the Indian pear (or saskatoon of the North-West), spiræa prunifolia of several kinds, shrubby St. John's-wort, œnothera grandiflora, *cum multis aliis.*

Now that the taste for wild-flower gardens has become the fashion in Great Britain, it will doubtless soon spread to this Continent. No English park is considered complete without its special garden for wild flowers, carefully tended and kept as free from stray weeds as the more formal parterre of the front lawn. Our wealthier Canadian families cannot do better than follow the example of the Old Country in this respect, and assuredly they will be abundantly repaid for the little trouble and expenditure required.

CHAPTER XLVII.

CANADIAN POLITICS FROM 1853 to 1860.

IN May, 1853, I sold out my interest in the *Patriot* to Mr. Ogle R. Gowan, and having a little capital of my own, invested it in the purchase of the *Colonist* from the widow of the late Hugh Scobie, who died December 6th, 1852. It was a heavy undertaking, but I was sanguine and energetic, and—as one of my friends told me—thorough. The *Colonist*, as an organ of the old Scottish Kirk party in Canada, had suffered from the rivalry of its Free Kirk competitor, the *Globe*; and its remaining subscribers, being, as a rule, strongly Conservative, made no objection to the change of proprietorship; while I carried over with me, by agreement, the subscribers to the daily *Patriot*, thus combining the mercantile strength of the two journals.

I had hitherto confined myself to the printing department, leaving the duties of editorship to others. On taking charge of the *Colonist*, I assumed the whole political responsibility, with Mr. John Sheridan Hogan as assistant editor and Quebec correspondent. My partners were the late Hugh C. Thomson, afterwards secretary to the Board of Agriculture, who acted as local editor; and James Bain, now of the firm of Jas. Bain & Son, to whom the book-selling and stationery departments were committed. We had a strong staff of reporters, and commenced the new enterprise under promising circumstances. Our office and store were in the old brick building extending from King to Colborne Street, long previously known as the grocery store of Jas. F. Smith.

The ministry then in power was that known as the Hincks-Taché Government. Francis Hincks had parted with his old radical allies, and become more conservative than many of the Tories whom he used to denounce. People remembered Wm. Lyon Mackenzie's prophecy, who said he feared that Francis Hincks could not be trusted to resist temptation. When Lord Elgin went to England, it was whispered that his lordship had paid off £80,000 sterling of mortgages on his Scottish estates, out of the proceeds of speculations which he had shared with his clever minister. The St. Lawrence and Atlantic purchase, the £50,000 Grand Trunk stock placed to Mr. Hincks' credit—as he asserted without his consent—and the Bowes transaction, gave colour to the many stories circulated to his prejudice. And when he went to England, and received the governorship of Barbadoes, many people believed that it was the price of his private services to the Earl of Elgin.

Whatever the exact truth in these cases may have been, I am convinced that from the seed then sown, sprang up a crop of corrupt influences that have since permeated all the avenues to power, and borne their natural fruit in the universal distrust of public men, and the wide-spread greed of public money, which now prevail. Neither political party escapes the imputation of bribing the constituencies, both personally at elections, and by parliamentary grants for local improvements. The wholesale expenditure at old country elections, which transferred so much money from the pockets of the rich to those of the poor, without any prospect of pecuniary return, has with us taken the form of a speculative investment to be "re-couped" by value in the shape of substantial government favours.

Could I venture to enter the lists against so tremendous a rhetorical athlete as Professor Goldwin Smith, I should say, that his idea of abolishing party government to secure purity of election is an utter fallacy; I should say that the great factor of corruption in Canada has been the adoption of the principle of coalitions. I told a prominent Conservative leader in 1853, that I looked upon coalitions as essentially immoral, and that the duty of either political party was to remain contentedly " Her Majesty's Loyal Opposition," and to support frankly all good measures emanating from the party in office, until the voice of the country, fairly expressed, should call the Opposition to assume the reins of power legitimately. I told the late Hon. Mr. Spence, when he joined the coalition ministry of 1854, that we (of the *Colonist*) looked upon that combination as an organized attempt to govern the country through its vices; and that nothing but the violence of the *Globe* party could induce us to support any coalition whatsoever. And I think still that I was right, and that the Minister who buys politicians to desert their principles, resembles nothing so much as the lawyer who gains a verdict in favour of his client by bribing the jury.

The union of Upper and Lower Canada is chargeable, no doubt, with a large share of the evils that have crept into our constitutional system. The French Canadian *habitans*, at the time of the Union, were true scions of the old peasantry of Normandy and Brittany, with which their songs identify them so strikingly. All their ideas of government were ultra-monarchical; their allegiance to the old French Kings had been transferred to the Romish hierarchy and clergy, who, it must be said, looked after their flocks with undying zeal and beneficent care. But this formed an ill preparation for representative institutions. The *Rouge* party, at first limited to lawyers and notaries chiefly, had taken up the principles of the first French revolution, and for some years made but little progress; in time, however, they learnt the necessity of cultivating the assistance, or at least the neutrality of the clergy, and in this they were aided by ties of relationship. As in Ireland, where almost every poor family emaciates itself to provide for the education of one of its sons as a " counsellor " or a priest, so in Lower Canada, most families contain within themselves both priest and lawyer. Thus it came to pass, that in the Lower Province, a large proportion of the people lived in the hope that they might sooner or later share in " government pap," and looked upon any means to that end as unquestionably lawful. It is not difficult to perceive how much and how readily this idea would communicate itself to their Upper Canadian allies after the Union ; that it did so, is matter of history.

In fact, the combination of French and British representatives in a single cabinet, itself constitutes a coalition of the most objectionable kind ; as the result can only be a perpetual system of compromises. For example, one of the effects of the Union, and of the coalition of 1854, was the passage of the bill secularizing the Clergy Reserves, and abolishing all connection between church and state in Upper Canada, while leaving untouched the privileges of the Romish Church in the Lower Province. That some day, there will arise a formidable Nemesis spawned of this one-sided act, when the agitation for disendowment shall have reached the Province of Quebec, who can doubt ?

In 1855 and subsequently, followed a series of struggles for office, without any great political object in view, each party or clique striving to bid higher than all the rest for popular votes, which went on amid alternate successes and reverses, until the denouement came in 1859, when neither political party could form a Ministry that should command a majority in parliament, and they were fain

to coalesce *en masse* in favour of confederation. At
one time, Mr. George Brown was defeated by Wm.
Lyon Mackenzie in Halton ; at another, he voted
with the Tories against the Hincks ministry ; again,
he was a party to a proposed coalition with Sir
Allan MacNab. I was myself present at Sir Allan's house in Richey's Terrace, Adelaide Street,
where I was astonished to meet Mr. Brown himself
in confidential discussion with Sir Allan. I recollect a member of the Lower House—I think Mr.
Hillyard Cameron—hurrying in with the information that at a meeting of Conservative members
which he had just left, they had chosen Mr. John
A. Macdonald as their leader in place of Sir Allan,
which report broke up the conference, and defeated
the plans of the coalitionists. This was, I think, in
1855. Then came on the " Rep. by Pop." agitation
led by the *Globe*, in 1856.*　In 1857, the great
business panic superseded all other questions. In
1858, the turn of the Reform party came, with

---

* The same year occurred the elections for members of
the Legislative Council. I was a member of Mr. G. W.
Allan's committee, and saw many things there which
disgusted me with all election tactics. Men received
considerable sums of money for expenses, which it was
believed never left their own pockets. Mr. Allan was in
England, and sent positive instructions against any kind
of bribery whatsoever, yet when he arrived here, claims
were lodged against him amounting to several thousand
dollars, which he was too high-minded to repudiate.

Mr. Brown again at their head, who held power for precisely four days.

In 1858, also, the question of protection for native industry, which had been advocated by the British-American League, was taken up in parliament by the Hon. Wm. Cayley and Hon. Isaac Buchanan separately. In 1859, came Mr. Brown's and Mr. Galt's federal union resolutions, and Mr. Cayley's motion for protection once more.

All these years—from 1853 to 1860—I was in confidential communication with the leaders of the Conservative party, and after 1857 with the Upper Canadian members of the administration personally; and I am bound to bear testimony to their entire patriotism and general disinterestedness whenever the public weal was involved. I was never asked to print a line which I could not conscientiously endorse; and had I been so requested, I should assuredly have refused.

CHAPTER XLVIII.

BUSINESS TROUBLES.

UP to the year 1857, I had gone on prosperously, enlarging my establishment, increasing my subscription list, and proud to own the most enterprising newspaper published in Canada up to that day. The *Daily Colonist* consisted of eight pages, and was an exact counterpart of the *London Times* in typographical appearance, size of page and type, style of advertisements, and above all, in independence of editorial comment and fairness in its treatment of opponents. No communication courteously worded was refused admission, however caustic its criticisms on the course taken editorially. The circulation of the four editions (daily, morning and evening, bi-weekly and weekly) amounted to, as nearly as I can recollect, 30,000 subscribers, and its readers comprised all classes and creeds.

In illustration of the kindly feeling existing towards me on the part of my political adversaries, I may record the fact that, when in the latter part of 1857, it became known in the profession that I had suffered great losses arising out of the commercial panic of that year, Mr. George Brown, with whom I was on familiar terms, told me that he was authorized by two or three gentlemen of high standing in the Liberal party, whom he named, to advance me whatever sums of money I might require to carry on the *Colonist* independently, if I would accept their aid. I thanked him and replied, that I could publish none other than a Conservative paper, which ended the discussion.

The Hon. J. Hillyard Cameron, being himself embarrassed by the tremendous pressure of the money market, in which he had operated heavily, counselled me to act upon a suggestion that the *Colonist* should become the organ of the Macdonald-Cartier Government, to which position would be attached the right of furnishing certain of the public departments with stationery, theretofore supplied by the Queen's Printer at fixed rates. I did so, reserving to myself the absolute control of the editorial department, and engaging the services of Mr. Robert A. Harrison (of the Attorney-General's office, afterwards Chief Justice), as assistant editor. Instead, however, of alleviating, this change of base only intensified my troubles.

I found that, throughout the government offices, a system had been prevalent, something like that described in *Gil Blas* as existing at the Court of Spain, by which, along with the stationery required for the departments, articles for ladies' toilet use, etc., were included, and had always theretofore been charged in the government accounts as a matter of course. I directed that those items should be supplied as ordered, but that their cost be placed to my own private account, and that the parties be notified, that they must thereafter furnish separate orders for such things. I also took an early opportunity of pointing out the abuse to the Attorney-General, who said his colleagues had suspected the practice before, but had no proof of misconduct; and added, that if I would lay an information, he

U

would send the offenders to the Penitentiary; as in fact he did in the Reiffenstein case some years afterwards. I replied, that were I to do so, nearly every man in the public service would be likely to become my personal enemy, which he admitted to be probable. As it was, the apparent consequence of my refusal to make fraudulent entries, was an accusation that I charged excessive prices, although I had never charged as much as the rate allowed the Queen's Printer, considering it unreasonable. My accounts were at my request referred to an expert, and adjudged by him to be fair in proportion to quality of stationery furnished. Gradually I succeeded in stopping the time-honoured custom as far as I was concerned.

Years after, when I had the contract for Parliamentary printing at Quebec, matters proved even more vexatious. When the Session had commenced, and I had with great outlay and exertion got every thing into working order, I was refused copies of papers from certain sub-officers of the Legislature, until I had agreed upon the percentage expected upon my contract rates. My reply, through my clerk, was, that I had contracted at low rates, and could not afford gratuities such as were claimed, and that if I could, I would not. The consequence was a deadlock, and it was not until I brought the matter to the attention of the Speaker, Sir Henry Smith, that I was enabled to get on with the work. These things happened a quarter of a century ago, and although I suffer the injurious consequences myself to this day, I trust no other living person can be affected by their publication now.

The position of ministerial organist, besides being both onerous and unpleasant, was to me an actual money loss. My newspaper expenses amounted to over four hundred dollars per week, with a constantly decreasing subscription list.* The profits on the government stationery were no greater than those realized by contractors who gave no additional *quid pro quo;* and I was only too glad, when the opportunity of competing for the Legislative printing presented itself in 1858, to close my costly newspaper business in Toronto. I sold the goodwill of the *Colonist* to Messrs. Sheppard & Morrison,† and on my removal to Quebec next year, established a cheap journal there called the *Advertiser*, the history of which in 1859–60, I shall relate in a chapter by itself.

---

* The late Mr. George Brown has often told me, that whenever the *Globe* became a Government organ, the loss in circulation and advertising was so great as to counterbalance twice over the profits derived from government advertising and printing.

† On my retirement from the publication of the *Colonist*, the Attorney-General offered me a position under Government to which was attached a salary of $1,400 a year, which I declined as unsuited to my tastes and habits.

CHAPTER XLIX.

BUSINESS EXPERIENCES IN QUEBEC.

WHEN I began to feel the effects of official hostility in Quebec, as above stated, I was also suffering from another and more vital evil. I had taken the contract for parliamentary printing at prices slightly lower than had before prevailed. My knowledge of printing in my own person gave me an advantage over most other competitors. The consequence of this has been, that large sums of money were saved to the country yearly for the last twenty-four years. But the former race of contractors owed me a violent grudge, for, as they alleged, taking the contract below paying prices. I went to work, however, confident of my resources and success. But no sooner had I got well under weigh, than my arrangements were frustrated, my expenditure nullified, my just hopes dashed to the ground, by the action of the Legislature itself. A joint committee on printing had been appointed, of which the Hon. Mr. Simpson, of Bowmanville, was chairman, which proceeded deliberately to cut down the amount of printing to be executed, and particularly the quantity of French documents to be printed, to such an extent as to reduce the work for which I had contracted by at least one-third. And this without the smallest regard to the terms of my contract. Thus were one-half of all my expenditures—one-half of my thirty thousand dollars worth of type—one-half of my fifteen thousand dollars worth of presses and machinery—literally rendered useless, and reduced to the condition of second-hand material. I applied to my solicitor for advice. He told me that, unless I threw up the contract, I could make no claim for breach of conditions. Unfortunately for me, the many precedents since established, of actions on "petition of right" for breach of contract by the Government and the Legislature, had not then been recorded, and I had to submit to what I was told was the inevitable.

I struggled on through the session amid a hurricane of calumny and malicious opposition. The Queen's Printers, the former French contractor, and, above all, the principal defeated competitor in Toronto, joined their forces to destroy my credit, to entice away my workmen, to disseminate but too successfully the falsehood, that my contract was taken at unprofitable rates, until I was fairly driven to my wits' end, and ultimately forced into actual insolvency. The cashier of the Upper Canada Bank told me very kindly, that everybody in the Houses and the Bank knew my honesty and energy, but the combination against me was too strong, and it was useless for me to resist it, unless my Toronto friends would come to my assistance.

I was not easily dismayed by opposition, and determined at least to send a Parthian shaft into my enemies' camp. The session being over, I hastened to Toronto, called my creditors together at the office of Messrs Cameron & Harman, and laid my position before them. All I could command in the way of valuable assets was invested in the business of the contract. I had besides, in the shape of nominal assets, over a hundred thousand dollars in newspaper debts scattered over Upper Canada, which I was obliged to report as utterly uncollectable, being mainly due by farmers who—as was generally done throughout Ontario in 1857—had made over their farms to their sons or other parties, to evade payment of their own debts. All my creditors were old personal friends, and so thoroughly satisfied were they of the good faith of the statements submitted by me, that they unanimously decided to appoint no assignee, and to accept the offer I made them to conduct the contract for their benefit, on their providing the necessary sinews of war, which they undertook to do in three days.

What was my disappointment and chagrin to find, at the end of that term, that the impression which had been so industriously disseminated in Quebec, that my contract prices were impracticably low, had reached and influenced my Toronto friends, and that it was thought wisest to abandon the undertaking. I refused to do so.

Among my employees in the office were four young men, of excellent abilities, who had grown into experience under my charge, and had, by marriage and economy, acquired means of their own, and could besides command the support of monied relatives. These young men I took into my counsels. At the bailiff's sale of my office which followed, they bought in such materials as they thought sufficient for the contract work, and in less than a month we had the whole office complete again, and with the sanction of the Hon. the Speaker, got the contract work once more into shape. The members of the new firm were Samuel Thompson, Robert Hunter, George M. Rose, John Moore, and François Lemieux.

CHAPTER L.

QUEBEC IN 1859-60.

I RESIDED for eighteen months in the old, picturesque and many-memoried city. My house was a three-story cedar log building known as the White House, near the corner of Salaberry Street and Mount Pleasant Road. It was weather-boarded outside, comfortably plastered and finished within, and was the most easily warmed house I ever occupied. The windows were French, double in winter, opening both inwards and outwards, with sliding panes for ventilation. It had a good garden, sloping northerly at an angle of about fifteen degrees, which I found a desolate place enough, and left a little oasis of beauty and productiveness. One of my amusements there was to stroll along the garden paths, watching for the sparkle of Quebec diamonds, which after every rainfall glittered in the paths and flower-beds. They are very pretty, well shaped octagonal crystals of rock quartz, and are often worn in necklaces by the Quebec demoiselles. On the plains of Abraham I found similar specimens brilliantly black.

Quebec is famous for good roads and pleasant shady promenades. By the St. Foy Road to Spencer Wood, thence onward to Cap Rouge, back by the St. Louis Road or Grande Allée, past the citadel and through the old-fashioned St. Louis Gate, is a charming stroll; or along the by-path from St. Louis Road to the pretty Gothic chapel overhanging the Cove, and so down steep rocky steps descending four hundred feet to the mighty river St. Lawrence; or along the St. Charles river and the country road to Lorette; or by the Beauport road to the old chateau or manor house of Colonel Gugy, known by the name of "Darnoc." The toll-gate on the St. Foy

Road was quite an important institution to the simple *habitans*, who paid their shilling toll for the privilege of bringing to market a bunch or two of carrots and as many turnips, with a basket of eggs, or some cabbages and onions, in a little cart drawn by a little pony, with which surprising equipage they would stand patiently all morning in St. Anne's market, under the shadow of the old ruined Jesuits' barracks, and return home contented with the three or four shillings realized from their day's traffic.

One of the specialties of the city is its rats. In my house-yard was a sink, or rather hole in the rock, covered by a wooden grating. A large cat, who made herself at home on the premises, would sit watching at the grating for hours, every now and then inserting her paw between the bars and hooking out leisurely a squeaking young rat, of which thirty or forty at a time showed themselves within the cavity. I was assured that these rats have underground communications, like those of the rock of Gibraltar, from every quarter of the city to the citadel, and so downward to the quays and river below. Besides the cat, there was a rough terrier dog named Cæsar, also exercising right of occupancy. To see him pouncing upon rats in the pantry, from which they could not be easily excluded by reason of a dozen entrances through the stone basement walls, was something to enchant sporting characters. I was

not of that class, so stopped up the rock with broken
bottles and mortar, and provided traps for stray in-
truders.

The Laurentine mountains, distant a few miles
north of the city, rise to a height of twenty-five
hundred feet. By daylight they are bleak and barren enough ; but at night, seen in the light of the
glorious Aurora Borealis which so often irradiates
that part of Canada, they are a vision of enchanting
beauty. This reminds me of a conversation which
I was privileged to have with the late Sir William
Logan, who most kindly answered my many inqui-
sitive questions on geological subjects. He explained that the mountains of Newfoundland, of
Quebec, of the height of land between the St. Lawrence and Lake Nipissing, and of Manitoba and Kee-
watin in the North-West, are all links of one continuous chain, of nearly equal elevation, and marked
throughout that vast extent by ancient sea-beaches
at an uniform level of twelve hundred feet above the
sea, with other ancient beaches seven hundred feet
above the sea at various points; two remarkable examples of which latter class are the rock of Quebec
and the Oak Ridges eighteen miles north of Toronto.
He pointed out further, that those two points indicate precisely the level of the great ocean which covered North America in the glacial period, when
Toronto was six hundred feet under salt water, and
Quebec was the solitary rock visible above water

for hundreds of miles east,west and south—the Laurentides then, as now, towering eighteen hundred feet higher, on the north.

In winter also, Quebec has many features peculiar to itself. Close beside, and high above the little steep roofed houses—crowded into streets barely wide enough to admit the diminutive French carts without crushing unlucky foot-passengers,—rise massive frowning bastions crowned with huge cannon, all black with age and gloomy with desperate legends of attack and defence. The snow accumulates in these streets to the height of the upper-floor windows, with precipitous steps cut suddenly down to each doorway, so that at night it is a work of no little peril to navigate one's way home. Near the old Palace Gate are beetling cliffs, seventy feet above the hill of rocky debris which forms one side of the street below. It is high carnival with the Quebec *gamins,* when they can collect there in hundreds, each with his frail handsleigh, and poising themselves on the giddy edge of the " horrent summit," recklessly shoot down in fearful descent, first to the sharp rocky slope, and thence with alarming velocity to the lower level of the street. Outside St. John's Gate is another of these infantile race-grounds. Down the steep incline of the glacis, crowds of children are seen every fine winter's day, sleighing and tobogganing from morning till night, not without occasional accidents of a serious nature.

But the crowning triumph of Quebec scenery, summer and winter, centres in the Falls of Montmorenci, a seven mile drive, over Dorchester bridge, along the Beauport road, commanding fine views of the wide St. Lawrence and the smiling Isle of Orleans, with its pilot-inhabited houses painted blue, red and yellow—all three colours at once. occasionally—(the paints wickedly supposed to be perquisites acquired in a professional capacity from ships' stores)—and so along shady avenues varied by brightest sunshine, we find ourselves in front and at the foot of a cascade four hundred feet above us, broken into exquisite facets and dancing foam by projecting rocky points, and set in a bordering of lovely foliage on all sides. This is of course in summer. In winter how different. Still the descending torrent, but only bare tree-stems and icy masses for the frame-work, and at the base a conical mountain of snow and ice, a hundred and fifty feet high, sloping steeply on all sides, and with the frozen St. Lawrence spread out for miles to the east. He who covets a sensation for life, has only to climb the gelid hill by the aid of ice-steps cut in its side, and commit himself to the charge of the habitant who first offers his services, and the thing is soon accomplished. The gentleman adventurer sits at the back of the sleigh,—which is about four feet long—tucks his legs round the habitant, who sits in front and steers with his heels; for an instant the steersman manœuvres into position on the edge of the cone, which slightly overhangs—then away we go, launching into mid-air, striking ground—or rather ice—thirty feet below, and down and still down, fleet as lightning, to the level river plain, over which we glide by the impetus of our descent fully half-a-mile further. I tried it twice. My companion was severely affected by the shock, and gave in with a bad headache at the first experiment. The same day, several reckless young officers of the garrison would insist upon steering themselves, paying a guinea each for the privilege. One of them suffered for his freak from a broken arm. But with experienced guides no ill-consequences are on record.

An appalling tragedy is related of this ice-mountain. An American tourist with his bride was among the visitors to the Falls one day some years back. They were both young and high-spirited, and had immensely enjoyed their marriage trip by way of the St. Lawrence. Standing on the summit of the cone, in raptures with the cataract, the cliffs ice-bedecked, the trees ice-laden, their attention was for an instant diverted from each other. The young man, gazing eastward across the river, talking gaily to his wife, was surprised at receiving no reply, and looking round found himself alone. Shouting frantically, no answering cry could be distinguished,—the roaring of the cascade was loud enough to drown any human voice. Hanging madly over the edge next the Falls, which is quite precipitous, there was nothing to be seen but a boiling whirlpool of angry waters. The poor girl had stepped unconsciously backward,—had slipped down into the boiling surf, —had been instantaneously carried beneath the ice of the river.

Another peculiarity of Quebec is its ice-freshets in spring. Near the vast tasteless church of St. John, on the road of that name, a torrent of water from the higher level crosses the street, and thunders down the steep ways descending to the Lower Town. At night it freezes solidly again, and becomes so dangerously slippery, that I have seen ladies piloted across for several hundred feet, by holding on to the courteously extended walking stick of the first gentlemanly stranger to whom they could appeal for help in their utter distress and perplexity. These freshets flood the business streets named after St. Peter and St. Paul on the level of the wharves. To cross them at such times, floating planks are put in requisition, and no little skill is required to escape a wetting up to the knees.

The social aspects of the city are as unique as its natural features. The Romish hierarchy exercises an arbitrary, and I must add a beneficial, rule over the mixed maritime and crimping elements which form its lowest stratum. Private charity is universal on the part of the well-to-do citizens. It is an interesting sight to watch the numbers of paupers who are supplied weekly from heaps of loaves of bread piled high on the tradesmen's counters, to which all comers are free to help themselves.

The upper classes are divided into castes as marked as those of Hindostan. French Canadian seigniors, priestly functionaries of high rank, government officials of the ruling race, form an exclusive, and it is said almost impenetrable coterie by themselves. The sons or nephews of Liverpool merchants having branch firms in the city, and wealthy Protestant tradesmen, generally English churchmen, constitute a second division scarcely less isolated. Next to these come the members of other religious denominations, who keep pretty much to themselves. I am sorry to hear from a respected Methodist minister whom I met in Toronto lately, that the last named valuable element of the population has been gradually diminishing in numbers and influence, and that it is becoming difficult to keep their congregations comfortably together. This is a consequence, and an evil consequence, of confederation.

Another characteristic singularity of Quebec life arises from the association, without coalescing, of two distinct nationalities having diverse creeds and habits. This is often ludicrously illustrated by the system of mixed juries. I was present in the Recorder's Court on one occasion, when a big, burly Irishman was in the prisoner's dock, charged with violently ejecting a bailiff in possession, which I believe in Scotland is called a deforcement on the premises. It appeared that the bailiff, a little habitant, had been riotously drunk and disorderly, having helped himself to the contents of a number of bottles of ale which he discovered in a cupboard. The prisoner, moved to indignation, coolly took up the drunken offender in his arms, tossed him down a flight of steps into the middle of the street, and shut the door in his face. The counsel for the complainant, a popular Irish barrister, lamented privately that he was on the wrong side, being more used to defending breaches of the laws than to enforcing them—that there was no hope of a verdict in favour of authority—and that the jury were certain to disagree, however clearly the facts and the law were shown. And so it proved. The French jurors looked puzzled—the English enjoyed the fun —the judge charged with a half smile on his countenance—and the jury disagreed—six to six. On leaving the court, one of the jurors whispered to the ·discharged prisoner, " Did you think we were agoing to give in to them French fellows ? "

CHAPTER LI.

DEPARTURE FROM QUEBEC.

I SUPPOSE it is in the very nature of an autobiography to be egotistical, a fault which I have desired to avoid; but find that my own personal affairs have been often so strangely interwoven with public events, that I could not make the one intelligible without describing the other. My departure from Quebec, for instance, was caused by circumstances which involved many public men of that day, and made me an involuntary party to important political movements.

I have mentioned that, with the sanction of the Upper Canadian section of the Ministry, I had commenced the publication in Quebec of a daily newspaper with an evening edition, under the title of the *Advertiser*. I strove to make it an improvement upon the style of then existing Quebec journals, but without any attempt at business rivalry, devoting my attention chiefly to the mercantile interests of the city, including its important lumber trade. I wrote articles describing the various qualities of Upper Canadian timber, which I thought should be made known in the British market. This was to some degree successful, and as a consequence I gained the friendship of several influential men of business. But I did not suspect upon how inflammable a mine I was standing. A discourteous remark in a morning contemporary, upon some observations in the *Courrier du Canada*, in which the ground was taken by the latter that French institutions in Europe exceeded in liberality, and ensured greater personal freedom than those of Great Britain, and by consequence of Canada, induced me to enter into an amicable controversy with the *Courrier* as to the relative merits of French imperial and British monarchical government. About the same time, I gave publicity to some complaints of injustice suffered by Protestant—I think Orange—workmen who had been dismissed from employment under a local contractor on one of the wharves, owing as was asserted to their religious creed. Just then a French journalist, the editor of the *Courrier de Paris*, was expelled by the Emperor Louis Napoleon for some critique on " my policy." This afforded so pungent an opportunity for retort upon my Quebec friend, that I could not resist the temptation to use it. From that moment, it appears, I was considered an enemy of French Canadians and a hater of Roman Catholics, to whom in truth I never felt the least antipathy, and never even dreamt of enquiring either the religious or political principles of men in my employment.

I was informed, that the Hon. Mr. Cartier desired that I should discontinue the *Advertiser*. Astonished at this, I spoke to one of his colleagues on the subject. He said I had been quite in the right; that the editor of the *Courrier* was a d—d fool; but I had better see Cartier. I did so; pointed out that I had no idea of having offended any man's prejudices; and could not understand why my paper should be objectionable. He vouchsafed no argument; said curtly that his friends were annoyed; and that I had better give up the paper. I declined to do so, and left him.

This was subsequent to the events related in Chapter xlix. I spoke to others of the Ministers. One of them—he is still living—said that I was getting too old [I was fifty], and it was time I was superannuated—but that—they could not go against Cartier! My pride was not then subdued, and revolted against such treatment. I was under no obligations to the Ministry; on the contrary, I felt they were heavily indebted to me. I waited on the Hon. L. V. Sicotte, who was on neutral terms with the government, placed my columns at his disposal, and shortly afterwards, on the conclusion of an understanding between him and the Hon. J. Sandfield Macdonald, to which the Hon. A. A. Dorion was a party, I published an article prepared by them, temperately but strongly opposed to the policy of the existing government.   This combination ultimately resulted in the formation of the Macdonald-Sicotte Ministry in 1862.

But this was not all.   The French local press took up the quarrel respecting French institutions—told me plainly that Quebec was a " Catholic city," and that I would not be allowed to insult their institutions with impunity—hinted at mob-chastisement, and other consequences.   I knew that years before, the printing office of a friend of my own—since high in the public service—had been burnt in Quebec under similar circumstances.   I could not expose my partners to absolute ruin by provoking a similar fate.   The Protestants of the city were quite willing to make my cause a religious and national feud, and told me so.   There was no knowing where the consequences might end.   For myself, I had really no interest in the dispute; no prejudices to gratify ; no love of fighting for its own sake, although I had willingly borne arms for my Queen ; so I gave up the dispute ; sold out my interest in the printing contract to my partners for a small sum, which I handed to the rightful owner of the materials, and left Quebec with little more than means enough to pay my way to Toronto.

CHAPTER LII.

JOHN A. MACDONALD AND GEORGE BROWN.

IN Chapter xxxv. I noticed the almost simultaneous entrance of these two men into political life. Their history and achievements have been severally recorded by friendly biographers, and it is unnecessary for me to add anything thereto. Personally, nothing but kindly courtesy was ever shown me by either. In some respects their record was much alike, in some how different. Both Scotchmen, both ambitious, both resolute and persevering, both carried away by political excitement into errors which they would gladly forget—both unquestionably loyal and true to the empire. But in temper and demeanour, no two men could be more unlike. Mr. Brown was naturally austere, autocratic, domineering. Sir John was kindly, whether to friends or foes, and always ready to forget past differences.

A country member, who had been newly elected for a Reform constituency, said to a friend of mine, " What a contrast between Brown and Macdonald ! " I was at the Reform Convention the other day, " and there was George Brown dictating to us all, " and treating rudely every man who dared to make

"a suggestion. Next day, I was talking to some
"fellows in the lobby, when a stranger coming up
"slapped me on the shoulder, and said in the heartiest
"way 'How d'ye do, M———? shake hands—glad to
"see you here—I'm John A.!'"

Another member, the late J. Sheridan Hogan—
who, after writing for the *Colonist*, had gone into
opposition, and was elected member for Grey—told
me that it was impossible to help liking Sir John—
he was so good-natured to men on both sides of the
House, and never seemed to remember an injury, or
resent an attack after it was past.

Hence probably the cause of the differing careers
of these two men. Standing together as equals during the coalition of 1862, and separating again after
a brief alliance of eighteen months' duration, the
one retained the confidence of his party under very
discouraging circumstances, while the other gradually lapsed into the position of a governmental impossibility, and only escaped formal deposition as a
party leader by his own violent death.

I am strongly under the impression that the assassination of George Brown by the hands of a dismissed employee, in May, 1880, was one of the consequences of his own imperious temper. Many
years ago, Mr. Brown conceived the idea of employing females as compositors in the *Globe* printing
office, which caused a "strike" amongst the men.
Great excitement was created, and angry threats

were used against him ; while the popular feeling
was intensified by his arresting several of the workmen under an old English statute of the Restora-
tion. The ill-will thus aroused extended among the
working classes throughout Ontario, and doubtless
caused his party the loss of more than one constituency. It seems highly probable, that the bitterness
which rankled in the breast of his murderer, had its
origin in this old class-feud.

Sir John is reported to have said, that he liked
supporters who voted with him, not because they
thought him in the right, but even when they believed him to be in the wrong. I fancy that in so
saying, he only gave candid expression to the secret
feeling of all ambitious leaders. This brusque candour is a marked feature of Sir John's character,
and no doubt goes a great way with the populace.
A friend told me, that one of our leading citizens
met the Premier on King Street, and accosted him
with—" Sir John, our friend —— says that you are
" the d—st liar in all Canada !" Assuming a very
grave look, the answer came—" I dare say it's true
" enough !"

Sir John once said to myself. " I don't care for
" office for the sake of money, but for the sake of
" power, and for the sake of carrying out my own
" views of what is best for the country." And I believe he spoke sincerely. Mr. Collins, his biographer,
has evidently pictured to himself his hero some day

taking the lead in the demand for Canadian independence. I trust and think he is mistaken, and that the great Conservative, leader would rather die as did his late rival, than quit for a moment the straight path of loyalty to his Sovereign and the Empire.

CHAPTER LIII.

JOHN SHERIDAN HOGAN.

I HAVE several times had occasion to mention this gentleman, who first came into notice on his being arrested, when a young man, and temporarily imprisoned in Buffalo, for being concerned in the burning of the steamer *Caroline*, in 1838. He was then twenty-three years old, was a native of Ireland, a Roman Catholic by religious profession, and emigrated to Canada in 1827. I engaged him in 1853, as assistant-editor and correspondent at Quebec, then the seat of the Canadian legislature. He had previously distinguished himself at college, and became one of the ablest Canadian writers of his day. He was the successful competitor for the prize given for the best essay on Canada at the Universal Exhibition of 1856, and had he lived, might have proved a strong man in political life.

In 1858, Mr. Hogan suddenly disappeared, and it was reported that he had gone on a shooting expedition to Texas. But in the following spring, a partially decomposed corpse was found in the melting snow near the mouth of the Don, in Toronto Bay. Gradually the fearful truth came to light through the remorse of one of the women accessory to the crime. A gang of loose men and women who infested what was called Brooks's Bush, east of the Don, were in the habit of robbing people who had occasion to cross the Don bridge at late hours of the night. Mr. Hogan frequently visited a friend who resided east of the bridge, on the Kingston Road, and on the night in question, was about crossing the bridge, when a woman who knew him, accosted him familiarly, while at the same moment another woman struck him on the forehead with a stone slung in a stocking; two or three men then rushed upon him, while partially insensible, and rifled his pockets. He recovered sufficiently to cry faintly, " Don't murder me !" to a man whom he recognised and called by name. This recognition was fatal to him. To avoid discovery, the villains lifted him bodily, in spite of his cries and struggles, and tossed him over the parapet into the stream, where he was drowned. In 1861, some of the parties were arrested; one of them, named Brown, was convicted and hanged for the murder; two others managed to prove an *alibi*, and so escaped punishment.

CHAPTER LIV.

DOMESTIC NOTES.

THE Rev. Henry C. Cooper was the eldest of a family of four brothers, who emigrated to Canada in 1832, and settled in what is known as the old Exeter settlement in the Huron tract. He was accompanied to Canada by his wife and two children, afterwards increased to nine, who endured with him all the hardships and privations of a bush life. In 1848 he was appointed to the rectory of Mimico, in the township of Etobicoke, to which was afterwards added the charge of the church and parish of St. George's, Islington, including the village of Lambton on the Humber.

In 1863, his eldest daughter, Elizabeth, became my wife. Our married life was in all respects a happy one, saddened only by anxieties arising from illness, which resulted in the death of one child, a daughter, at the age of six months, and of two others prematurely. These losses affected their mother's health, and she died in November, 1868, aged 36 years. To express my sense of her loss, I quote from Tennyson's "In Memoriam";

"The path by which we twain did go,
    Which led by tracts which pleased us well,
    Through four sweet years arose and fell,
From flower to flower, from snow to snow :

" And we with singing cheer'd the way,
    And crown'd with all the season lent,
    From April on to April went,
And glad at heart from May to May :

" But where the path we walked began
    To slant the fifth autumnal slope,
    As we descended, following Hope,
There sat the Shadow fear'd of man ;

. " Who broke our fair companionship,
    And spread his mantle dark and cold,
    And wrapt thee formless in the fold,
And dull'd the murmur on thy lip ;

" And bore thee where I could not see
    Nor follow, tho' I walk in haste,
    And think that somewhere in the waste
The Shadow sits and waits for me."

For the following epitaph on our infant daughter,
I am myself responsible. It is carved on a tomb-
stone where the mother and her little ones lie together in St. George's churchyard :

We loved thee as a budding flow'r
    That bloomed in beauty for awhile ;
We loved thee as a ray of light
    To bless us with its sunny smile ;

We loved thee as a heavenly gift
　So rich, we trembled to possess,—
A hope to sweeten life's decline,
　And charm our griefs to happiness.

The flower, the ray, the hope is past—
　The chill of death rests on thy brow—
But ah ! our Father's will be done,
　We love thee as an angel now !

Mr. Cooper died Sept. 10, 1877, leaving behind him the reputation of an earnest, upright life, and a strong attachment to the evangelical school in the English Church. His widow still resides at St. George's Hill, with one of her daughters. Two of her sons are in the ministry, the Rev. Horace Cooper, of Lloydtown, and the Rev. Robert St. P. O. Cooper, of Chatham.

One of Mr. H. C. Cooper's brothers became Judge Cooper, of Huron, who died some years since. Another, still living, is Mr. C. W. Cooper, barrister, formerly of Toronto, now of Chicago. He was recording secretary to the B. A. League, in 1849, and is a talented writer for the press.

CHAPTER LV.

THE BEAVER INSURANCE COMPANY.

IN 1860, soon after my return to Toronto, I was asked by my old friend and former partner, Mr. Henry Rowsell, to take charge of the Beaver Mutual Fire Insurance Company, which had been organized a year or two before by W. H. Smith, author of a work called " Canada—Past, Present, and Future," and a Canadian Gazetteer. Of this company I became managing director, and continued to conduct it until the year 1876, when it was legislated out of existence by the Mackenzie government. I do not propose to inflict upon my readers any details respecting its operations or fortunes, except in so far as they were matters of public history. Suffice it here to say, that I assumed its charge with two hundred members or policy holders ; that, up to the spring of 1876, it had issued seventy-four thousand policies, and that not a just claim remained unsatisfied. Its annual income amounted to a hundred and fifty thousand dollars, and its agencies numbered a hundred. That so powerful an organization should have to succumb to hostile influences, is a striking example of the ups and downs of fortune.

CHAPTER LVI.

THE OTTAWA FIRES.

THE summer of 1870 will be long remembered as the year of the Ottawa fires, which severely tried the strength of the Beaver Company. On the 17th August in that year, a storm of wind from the south-west fanned into flames the expiring embers of bush-fires and burning log-heaps, throughout the Counties of Lanark, Renfrew, Carleton and Ottawa, bordering on the Ottawa River between Upper and Lower Canada. No rain had fallen there for months previously, and the fields were parched to such a degree as seemingly to fill the air with inflammable gaseous exhalations, and to render buildings, fences, trees and pastures so dry, that the slightest spark would set them in a blaze. Such was the condition of the Townships of Fitzroy, Huntley, Goulburn, March, Nepean, Gloucester, and Hull, when the storm swept over them, and in the brief space of four hours left them a blackened desert, with here and there a dwelling-house or barn saved, but every-thing else—dwellings, out-buildings, fences, bridges, crops, meadows—nay, even horses, horned cattle, sheep, pigs, poultry, all kinds of domestic and wild animals, and most deplorable of all, twelve human beings—involved in one common destruction. Those farmers who escaped with their lives did so with extreme difficulty, in many cases only by driving their waggons laden with their wives and children into the middle of the Ottawa or some smaller stream, where the poor creatures had to remain all night, their flesh blistered with the heat, and their clothing consumed on their bodies.

The soil in places was burned so deeply as to render farms worthless, while the highways were made impassable by the destruction of bridges and corduroy roads. To the horrors of fire were added those of starvation and exposure ; it was many days before shelter could be provided, or even food furnished to all who needed it. The harvest, just gathered, had been utterly consumed in the barns and stacks ; and the green crops, such as corn, oats, turnips and potatoes, were so scorched in the fields as to render them worthless.

The number of families burnt out was stated at over four.hundred, of whom eighty-two were insurers in the Beaver Company to the extent of some seventy thousand dollars, all of which was satisfactorily paid.

The government and people of Canada generally took up promptly the charitable task of providing relief, and it is pleasant to be able to add that, within two years after, the farmers of the burnt district themselves acknowledged that they were better off than before the great fire—partly owing to a succession of good harvests, but mainly to the thorough cleansing which the land had received, and the perfect destruction of all stumps and roots by the fervid heat.

One or two remarkable circumstances are worth recording. A farmer was sitting at his door, having just finished his evening meal, when he noticed a lurid smoke with flames miles off. In two or three minutes it had swept over the intervening country, across his farm and through his house, licking up everything as it went, and leaving nothing but ashes behind it. He escaped by throwing himself down in a piece of wet swamp close at hand. His wife and children were from home fortunately. Every other living thing was consumed. Another family was less fortunate. It consisted of a mother and several children. Driven into a swamp for shelter, they became separated and bewildered. The calcined skeletons of the poor woman and one child were found several days afterward. The rest escaped.

The fire seems to have resembled an electric flash, leaping from place to place, passing over whole farms to pounce upon others in rear, and again vaulting to some other spot still further eastward.

CHAPTER LVII.

SOME INSURANCE EXPERIENCES.

IN the course of the ordinary routine of a fire
insurance office, circumstances are frequently
occurring that may well figure in a sensational novel.
One or two such may not be uninteresting here. I
suppress the true names and localities, and some
of the particulars.

One dark night, in a frontier settlement of the
County of Simcoe, a young man was returning
through the bush from a township gathering, when
he noticed loaded teams passing along a concession
line not far distant. As this was no unusual occurrence, he thought little of it, until some miles
further on, he came to a clearing of some forty
acres, where there was no dwelling-house apparently, but a solitary barn, which, while he was looking
at it, seemed to be lighted up by a lanthorn, and
after some minutes, by a flickering flame which
gradually increased to a blaze, and shortly enve-
loped the whole building. Hastening to the spot,
no living being was to be seen there, and he was
about to leave the place; but giving a last look at
the burning building, it struck him that there was

W

very little fire inside, and he turned to satisfy his curiosity. There was nothing whatever in the barn.

In due course, a notice was received at our office, that on a certain night the barn of one Dennis ——, containing one thousand bushels of wheat, had been burnt from an unknown cause, and that the value thereof, some eight-hundred dollars, was claimed from the company. At the same time, an anonymous letter reached me, suggesting an inquiry into the causes of the fire. The inquiry was instituted accordingly. The holder of the policy, an old man upwards of sixty years of age, a miser, reputed worth ten thousand dollars at least, was arrested, committed to —— gaol, and finally tried and found guilty, without a doubt of his criminality being left on any body's mind who was present. Through the skill of his counsel, however, he escaped on a petty technicality; and considering his miserable condition, the loss he had inflicted on himself, and his seven months' detention in gaol, we took no further steps for his punishment.

A country magistrate of high standing and good circumstances at ————, had a son aged about twenty-seven, to whom he had given the best education that grammar-school and college could afford, and who was regarded in his own neighbourhood as the model of gallantry and spirited enterprise. His father had supplied him with funds to erect substantial farm buildings, well stocked and furnished, in anticipation of his marriage with an estimable and well-educated young lady. Amongst the other buildings was a cheese-factory, in connection with which the young man commenced the business of making and selling cheese on an extensive scale. So matters went on for some months, until we received advices that the factory which we had insured, had been burnt during the night, and that the owner claimed three-thousand dollars for his loss. Our inspector was sent to examine and report, and was returning quite satisfied of the integrity of the party and the justice of the claim, when just as he was leaving the hotel where he had staid, a bystander happened to remark how curious it was that cheese should burn without smell. "That is impossible," said the landlord. "I am certain," said the former speaker, "that this had no smell, for I remarked it to Jack at the time."

The inspector reported this conversation, and I sent a detective to investigate the case. He remained there, disguised of course, for two or three weeks, and then reported that large shipments of cheese to distant parts had taken place previously to the fire; but he could find nothing to criminate any individual, until accidentally he noticed what looked like a dog's muzzle lying in a corner of the stable. He picked it up, and untying a string that was wound around it, found it to be the leg of a new pair of pantaloons of fine quality. Watching his opportunity the same evening, while in conversation with the claimant, he produced the trowser-leg quietly, and enquired where the fellow-leg was? Taken by surprise, the young man slunk silently away. He had evidently cut off a leg of his own pants, and used it to muzzle his house-dog, to silence its barking while he set the factory afire. He left the country that night, and we heard no more of the claim.

A letter was received one day from a Roman Catholic priest, which informed me that a woman whose dying confession he had received, had acknowledged that several years before she had been accessary to a fraud upon our company of one hundred dollars. Her husband had insured a horse with us for that amount. The horse had been burnt in his stable. The claim was paid. Her confession was, that the horse had died a natural death, and that the stable was set on fire for the purpose of recovering the value of the horse. In this case, the woman's confession becoming known to her husband, he left the country for the United States. The woman recovered and followed him.

CHAPTER LVIII.

A HEAVY CALAMITY.

IN the year 1875, the blow fell which destroyed the Beaver Insurance Company, and well nigh ruined every man concerned in it, from the president to the remotest agent. In April of that year, a bill was passed by the Dominion Legislature relative to mutual fire insurance companies. It so happened that the Premier of Canada was then the Hon. Alexander Mackenzie, for whose benefit, it was understood, the Hon. George Brown had got up a stock company styled the Isolated Risk Insurance Co., of which Mr. Mackenzie became president. There was a strong rivalry between the two companies, and possibly from this cause the legislation of the Dominion took a complexion hostile to mutual insurance. Be that as it may, a clause was introduced into the Act without attracting attention, which required the Beaver Company to deposit with the Government the sum of fifty-thousand dollars, being the same amount as had been customary with companies possessing a stock capital. For eighteen months this clause remained unobserved, when the Hon. J. Hillyard Cameron, being engaged as counsel in an insurance case, happened to light upon it, and mentioned it to me at the last meeting of the Board which he attended before his death, which took place two or three weeks afterwards. At the following Board meeting, I stated the facts as reported by him, and was instructed to take the opinion of Mr. Christopher Robinson, the eminent Queen's counsel, upon the case. I did so at once, and was advised by him to submit the question to Professor Cherriman, superintendent of insurance, by whom it was referred to the law officers of the Crown at Ottawa. Their decision was, that the Beaver Company had been required by the new Act to make a deposit of fifty thousand dollars before transacting any new business since April, 1876, and that nothing but an Act of Parliament could relieve the company and its agents from the penalties already incurred in ignorance of the statute.

On receipt of this opinion, immediate notice was sent by circular to all the company's agents, warning them to suspend operations at once. A bill was introduced at the following session, in February, 1877, which received the royal assent in April, remitting all penalties, and authorizing the company either to wind up its business or to transmute itself into a stock company. But in the meantime, fire insurance had received so severe a shock from the calamitous fire at St. John, N. B., by which many companies were ruined, and all shaken, that it was found impossible to raise the necessary capital to resume the Beaver business.

Thus, without fault or error on the part of its Board of Management, without warning or notice of any kind, was a strong and useful institution struck to the ground as by a levin-bolt. The directors, who included men of high standing of all political parties, lost, in the shape of paid-up guarantee stock and promissory notes, about sixty thousand dollars of their own money, and the officers suffered in the same way. The expenses of winding up, owing to vexatious litigation, have amounted to a sum sufficient to cover the outside liabilities of the company.

These particulars may not interest the majority of my readers, but I have felt it my duty to give them, as the best act of justice in my power to the public-spirited and honourable men, with whom for twenty-three years I have acted, and finally suffered. That the members of the company—the insured—have sustained losses by fire since October, 1876, to the amount of over $45,000, which remain unpaid in consequence of its inability to collect its assets, adds another to the many evils which are chargeable to ill-considered and reckless legislation, in disregard of the lawful vested rights of innocent people, including helpless widows and orphans.

CHAPTER LIX.

THE HON. JOHN HILLYARD CAMERON.

ON the 20th day of April, 1844, I was standing outside the railing of St. James's churchyard, Toronto, on the occasion of a very sad funeral. The chief mourner was a slightly built, delicate-looking young man of prepossessing appearance. His youthful wife, the daughter of the late Hon. H. J. Boulton, at one time Chief Justice of Newfoundland, had died, and it was at her burial he was assisting. When the coffin had been committed to the earth, the widowed husband's feelings utterly overcame him, and he fell insensible beside the still open grave.

This was my first knowledge of John Hillyard Cameron. From that day, until his death in November, 1876, I knew him more or less intimately, enjoyed his confidence personally and politically, and felt a very sincere regard for him in return. I used at one time to oppose his views in the City Council, but always good-naturedly on both sides. I was chairman of the Market Committee, and it was my duty to resist his efforts to establish a second market near the corner of Queen and Yonge

Streets, in the rear of the buildings now known as the Page Block. He was a prosperous lawyer, highly in repute, gaining a considerable revenue from his profession, and being of a lively, sanguine temperament, launched out into heavy speculations in exchange operations and in real estate.

As an eloquent pleader in the courts, he excelled all his contemporaries, and it was a common saying among solicitors, that Cameron ruled the Bench by force of argument, and the jury by power of persuasion. In the Legislature he was no less influential. His speeches on the Clergy Reserve question, on the Duval case, and many others, excited the House of Assembly to such a degree, that on one occasion an adjournment was carried on the motion of the ministerial leader, to give time for sober reflection. So it was in religious assemblies. At meetings of the Synod of the Church of England, at missionary meetings, and others, his fervid zeal and flowing sentences carried all before them, and left little for others to say.

In 1849, Mr. Cameron married again, this time a daughter of General Mallett, of Baltimore, who survives him, and still resides in Toronto. After that date, and for years until 1857, everything appeared to prosper with him. A comfortable residence, well stored with valuable paintings, books and rarities of all kinds. The choicest of society and hosts of friends. An amiable growing family of sons and daughters.   Affluence and elegance, popular favour, and the full sunshine of prosperity.   Honours were showered upon him from all sides.   Solicitor-General in 1846, member of Parliament for several constituencies in turn, Treasurer of the Law Society, and Grand Master of the Orange Association.   Judgeships and Chief-Justiceships were known to be at his disposal, but declined for personal reasons.

My political connection with Mr. Cameron commenced in 1854, when, having purchased from the widow of the late Hugh Scobie the *Colonist* newspaper, I thought it prudent to strengthen myself by party alliances.   He entered into the project with an energy and disinterestedness that surprised me. It had been a semi-weekly paper; he offered to furnish five thousand dollars a year to make it a daily journal, independent of party control; stipulated for no personal influence over its editorial views, leaving them entirely in my discretion, and undertaking that he would never reclaim the money so advanced, as long as his means should last.   I was then comparatively young, enterprising, and unembarrassed in circumstances, popular amongst my fellow-citizens, and mixed up in nearly every public enterprise and literary association then in existence in Toronto.   Quite ready, in fact, for any kind of newspaper enterprise.

My arrangement with Mr. Cameron continued, with complete success, until 1857.   The paper was acknowledged as a power in the state ; my relations with contemporary journals were friendly, and all seemed well.

In the summer of 1857 occurred the great business panic, which spread ruin and calamity throughout Canada West, caused by the cessation of the vast railway expenditure of preceding years, and by the simultaneous occurrence of a business pressure in the United States. The great house of Duncan Sherman & Co., of New York, through which Mr. Cameron was in the habit of transacting a large exchange business with England, broke down suddenly and unexpectedly. Drafts on London were dishonoured, and Mr. Cameron's bankers there, to protect themselves, sold without notice the securities he had placed in their hands, at a loss to him personally of over a hundred thousand pounds sterling.

Mr. Cameron was for a time prostrated by this reverse, but soon rallied his energies. Friends advised him to offer a compromise to his creditors, which would have been gladly accepted ; but he refused to do so, saying, he would either pay twenty shillings in the pound or die in the effort. He made the most extraordinary exertions, refusing the highest seats on the judicial bench to work the harder at his profession ; toiling day and night to retrieve his fortunes ; insuring his life for heavy sums by way of security to his creditors ; and felt confident of final success, when in October, 1876, while attending the assize at Orillia, he imprudently refreshed himself after a night's labour in court, by bathing in the cold waters of the Narrows of Lake Couchiching, and contracted a severe cold which laid him on a sick bed, which he never quitted alive.

I saw him a day or two before his death, when he spoke of a heavy draft becoming due, for which he had made provision. In this he was disappointed. He tried to leave his bed to rectify the error, but fell back from exhaustion, and died in the struggle —as his friends think—from a broken heart.

<hr>

CHAPTER LX.

TORONTO ATHENÆUM.

ABOUT the year 1843, the first effort to establish a free public library in Toronto, was made by myself. Having been a member of the Birkbeck Institute of London, I exerted myself to get up a similar society here, and succeeded in enlisting the sympathies of several of the masters of Upper Canada College, of whom Mr. Henry Scadding (now the Rev. Dr. Scadding) was the chief. .He became president of the Athenæum, a literary association, of which I was

secretary and librarian. In that capacity I corres
ponded with the learned societies of England and
Scotland, and in two or three years got together
several hundred volumes of standard works, all in
good order and well bound. Meetings for literary
discussion were held weekly, the principal speakers
being Philip M. Vankoughnet (since chancellor),
Alex. Vidal (now senator), David B. Read (now Q.C.),
J. Crickmore, — Martin, Macdonald the younger
(of Greenfield), and many others whose names I
cannot recall. I recollect being infinitely amused
by a naïve observation of one of these young men—
"Remember, gentlemen, that we are the future legislators of Canada !" which proved to be prophetic,
as most of them have since made their mark in some
conspicuous public capacity.

We met in the west wing of the old City Hall.
The eastern wing was occupied by the Commercial
News room, and in course of time the two associations were united. As an interesting memento of
many honoured citizens, I copy the deed of transfer
in full :

" We, the undersigned shareholders of the Commercial
News Room, do hereby make over, assign, and transfer
unto the members, for the time being, of the Toronto
Athenæum, all our right, title, and interest in and to
each our share in the said Commercial News Room, for
the purposes and on the terms and conditions mentioned
in the copy of a Resolution of the Committee of the said
Commercial News Room, hereunto annexed.

"In witness whereof we have hereunto placed our hands and seals this 3rd day of September, 1847."

Thos. D. Harris.	W. Allan.
Jos. D. Ridout.	J. Mitchell.
W. C. Ross.	James F. Smith.
A. T. McCord.	W. Gamble.
D. Paterson.	Richard Kneeshaw.
Wm. Proudfoot.	John Ewart.
F. W. Birchall.	George Munro.
Geo. Perc. Ridout.	Thos. Mercer Jones.
Alexander Murray.	Joseph Dixon.

Signed, sealed and delivered
   in the presence of
      Samuel Thompson.

After the destruction by fire of the old City Hall, the Athenæum occupied handsome rooms in the St. Lawrence Hall, until 1855, when a proposition was received to unite with the Canadian Institute, then under the presidency of Chief Justice Sir J. B. Robinson. Dr. Wilson (now President Toronto University) was its leading spirit. It was thereupon decided to transfer the library and some minerals, with the government grant of $400, to the Canadian Institute. In order to legalize the transfer, application was made to Parliament, and on the 19th May, 1855, the Act 18 Vic., c. 236, received the royal assent. The first clause reads as follows:—"The members of the Toronto Athenæum shall have power to transfer and convey to the Canadian Institute, such and so much of the books, minerals, and other property of the said Toronto Athenæum, whether held absolutely or in trust, as they may decide upon so conveying, and upon such conditions as they may think advisable, which conditions, if accepted by the said Canadian Institute, shall be binding."

Accordingly a deed of transfer was prepared and executed by the two contracting parties, by which it was provided :

"That the library formed by the books of the two institutions, with such additions as may be made from the common funds, should constitute a library to which the public should have access for reference, free of charge, under such regulations as may be adopted by the said Canadian Institute in view of the proper care and management of the same."

The books and minerals were handed over in due time, and acknowledged in the *Canadian Journal*, vol. 3, p. 394, old series. On the 9th February, 1856, Professor Chapman presented his report as curator, " on the minerals handed over by the Toronto Athenæum," which does not appear to have been published in the *Journal*. The reading room was subsequently handed over to the Mechanics' Institute, which was then in full vigour.

It will be seen, therefore, that the library of the Canadian Institute is, to all intents and purposes, a public library by statute, and free to all citizens for ever. I am sorry to add, that for many years back the conditions of the trust have been very indifferently carried out—few citizens know their rights respecting it, and still fewer avail themselves thereof,

The Institute now has a substantial building, very comfortably fitted up, on Richmond Street east; has a good reading room in excellent order, and very obliging officials; gives weekly readings or lectures on Saturday evenings, and has accumulated a valuable library of some eight thousand volumes.

I have thus been identified with almost every movement made in Toronto, for affording literary recreation to her citizens, and rejoice to see the good work progressing in younger and abler hands.

CHAPTER LXI.

THE BUFFALO FETE.

IN the month of July, 1850, the Mayor and citizens of Buffalo, hearing that our Canadian legislators were about to attend the formal opening of the Welland Canal, very courteously invited them to extend their trip to that city, and made preparations for their reception. Circumstances prevented the visit, but in acknowledgment of the good will thus shown, a number of members of the Canadian Parliament, then in session here, acting in concert with our City Council, proposed a counter-invitation, which was accordingly sent and accepted, and a joint committee formed to carry out the project.

The St. Lawrence Hall, then nearly finished, was hurriedly fitted up as a ball-room for the occasion, under the volunteered charge chiefly of Messrs. F. W. Cumberland and Kivas Tully, architects. The hall was lined throughout, tent-fashion, the ceiling with blue and white, the walls with pink and white calico, in alternate stripes, varied with a multitude of flags, British and American, mottoes and other showy devices. The staircase was decorated with evergreens, which were also utilized to convert the unfinished butchers' arcade into a bowery vista 500 feet long, lighted with gas laid for the occasion, and extending across Front Street to the entrance of the City Hall, then newly restored, painted and papered.

Lord Elgin warmly seconded the hospitable views of the joint committee, and Colonel Sir Hew Dalrymple promised a review of the troops then in garrison. All was life and preparation throughout the city.

On Friday, August 8th, the steamer *Chief Justice* was despatched to Lewiston to receive the guests from Buffalo. On her return, in the afternoon, she was welcomed with a salute of cannon, the men of the Fire Brigade lining the wharf and Front Street, along which the visitors were conveyed in carriages to the North American Hotel.

Soon after nine o'clock, the Hall began to fill with a brilliant and joyous assemblage of visitors and citizens with their ladies. Lord and Lady Elgin

x

arrived at about ten o'clock, and were received with the strains of "God Save the Queen," by the admirable military band, which was one of the city's chief attractions in those times.

The day was very wet, and the evening still rainy. The arcade had been laid with matting, but it was nevertheless rather difficult for the fair dancers to trip all the way to the City Hall, in the council chamber of which supper had been prepared. However, they got safely through, and seemed delighted with the adventure. Never since, I think, has the City Hall presented so distinguished and charming a scene. Of course there was a lady to every gentleman. The fair Buffalonians were loud in their praises of the whole arrangements, and thoroughly disposed to enjoy themselves.

On a raised dais at the south side of the room was a table, at which were seated Mayor Gurnett as host, with Lady Elgin; the Governor-General and Mrs. Judge Sill, of Buffalo; Mayor Smith, of Buffalo, and Madame Lafontaine; the Speakers of the two Houses of Parliament, with Mrs. Alderman Tiffany of Buffalo, and the Hon. Mrs. Bruce. Four long tables placed north and south, and two side tables, accommodated the rest of the party, amounting to about three hundred. All the tables were tastefully decorated with floral and other ornaments, and spread with every delicacy that could be procured.

The presiding stewards were the Hon. Mr. Bourret, Hon. Sir Allan N. McNab, Hon. Messrs. Hincks, Cayley, J. H. Cameron, S. Taché, Drummond and Merritt.

Toasts and speeches followed in the usual order, after which everybody returned to the St. Lawrence Hall, where dancing was resumed and kept up till an early hour next morning.

The next day, being the 9th, the promised review of the 71st Regiment took place, with favourable weather, and was a decided success.

In the afternoon, Lord Elgin gave a fête champêtre at Elmsley Villa, where he then resided, and which has since been occupied as Knox's College. The grounds then extended from Yonge Street to the University Park, and an equal distance north and south. They were well kept, and on this occasion charmingly in unison with the bright smiles and gay costumes of the ladies who, with their gentlemen escorts, made up the most joyous of scenes.

Having paid my respects at the Government House on New Year's day, I was present as an invited guest at the garden party. His Excellency showed me marked attention, in recognition probably of my services as a peacemaker. The corporation, as a body, were not invited, which was the only instance in which Lord Elgin betrayed any pique at the unflattering reception given him in October,

1849.*   While conversing with him, I was amused at the enthusiasm of a handsome Buffalo lady, who came up, unceremoniously exclaiming, " Oh, my lord, I heard your beautiful speech (in the marquee), you should come among us and go into politics.   If you would only take the stump for the Presidency, I am confident you would sweep every state of the Union !"

An excellent déjeuner had been served in a large tent on the lawn.   Speeches and toasts were numerous and complimentary.   The conservatory was cleared for dancing, which was greatly enjoyed, and the festivities were wound up by a brilliant display of fireworks.

The guests departed next morning, amid hearty handshaking and professions of friendship.   Before leaving the wharf, the Mayor of Buffalo expressed in warm and pleasing terms, his high sense of the hospitality shown himself and his fellow-citizens. And so ended the Buffalo Fête.

---

* Some members of the corporation were much annoyed at their exclusion, and inclined to resent it as a studied insult, but wiser counsels prevailed.

CHAPTER LXII.

THE BOSTON JUBILEE.

THE year 1851 is memorable for the celebration, at Boston, of the opening of the Ogdensburg Railway, to connect Boston with Canada and the Lakes, and also of the Grand Junction Railway, a semicircular line by which all the railways radiating from that city are linked together, so that a passenger starting from any one of the city stations can take his ticket for any other station on any of those railways, either in the suburbs or at distant points. I am not aware that so perfect a system has been attempted elsewhere. The natural configuration of its site has probably suggested the scheme. Boston proper is built on an irregular tri-conical hill, with its famous bay to the east; on the north the wide Charles River, with the promontory and hills of Charlestown and East Cambridge; on the south Dorchester Heights. Between the principal elevations are extensive salt marshes, now rapidly disappearing under the encroachments of artificial soil, covered in turn by vast warehouses, streets, railway tracks, and all the various structures common to large commercial cities.

It was in the month of July, that a deputation from the Boston City Council visited our principal Canadian cities, as the bearers of an invitation to Lord Elgin and his staff, with the government officials, as well as the mayors and corporations and leading merchants of those cities, and other principal towns of Upper and Lower Canada, to visit Boston on the occasion of a great jubilee to be held in honour of the opening of its new railway system.

Numerous as were the invited Canadian guests, however, they formed but a mere fraction of the visitors expected. Every railway staff, every municipal corporation throughout the Northern States, was included in the list of invitations; free passes and free quarters were provided for all; and it would be hard to conceive a more joyous invasion of merry travellers, than those who were pouring in by a rapid succession of loaded trains on all the numerous lines converging upon " the hub of the universe."

Our Toronto party was pretty numerous. Mr. J. G. Bowes was mayor, and among the aldermen present were Messrs. W. Wakefield (who was a host of jollity in himself), G. P. Ridout, R. Dempsey, E. F. Whittemore, J. G. Beard, Robt. Beard, John B. Robinson, Jos. Sheard and myself; also councilmen James Ashfield, James Price, M. P. Hayes, S. Platt, Jonathan Dunn, and others. There were besides, of leading citizens, Messrs. Alex. Dixon, E. G. O'Brien, Alex. Manning, E. Goldsmith, Kivas Tully, Fred.

Perkins, Rice Lewis, George Brown, &c. We had a delightful trip down the lake by steamer, and at Ogdensburg took the cars for Lake Champlain. We arrived at Boston about 10 a.m. Waiting for us at the Western Railroad Depot were the mayor and several of the city council of Boston, with carriages for our whole party. But we were too dusty and tired with our long journey to think of anything but refreshments and baths, and all the other excellent things which awaited us at the American Hotel. Here we were confidentially informed that the Jubilee was to be celebrated on temperance principles, but that in compliment to the Canadian guests, a few baskets of champagne had been provided for our especial delectation; and I am compelled to add, that on the strength thereof, two or three worshipful aldermen of Toronto got themselves locked up for the night in the police stations.

It is but justice to explain here, that a very small offence is sufficient to procure such a distinction in Boston. Even the smoking of a cigar on the side-walks, or the least symptom of unsteadiness in gait, is enough to consign a man to durance vile. The police were everywhere.

The first day of the Jubilee was occupied by the members of the committee in receiving their visitors, providing them with comfortable and generally luxurious quarters, and introducing the principal guests to each other—also in exhibiting the local lions.

On the second day there was an excursion down the harbour, which is many miles long and broad. Six steamboats and two large cutters, gay with flags and streamers, conveyed the party; champagne was in abundance (always for the Canadian visitors!)— each boat had its band of music—very fine German bands too. Then, as the flotilla left the wharf and passed in succession the fortifications and other prominent points, salvoes of cannon boomed across the bright waters, re-echoing far and wide amid the surrounding hills. President Fillmore and his suite were on board the leading vessel, and to him, of course, these honours were paid. On every boat was spread a banquet for the guests; toasts and sentiments were given and duly honoured; and to judge by the noise and excited gesticulations of the banqueters, nothing could be more complete than the fusion of Yankees and Canadians.

At noon, a regatta was held, which, the weather being fine, with a light breeze, was pronounced by yachtsmen a distinguished success. At five o'clock the citizens crowded in vast numbers to the Western Railway Station, there to meet His Excellency the Earl of Elgin and Kincardine, with his brother Colonel Bruce and a numerous staff. He was welcomed by Mayor Bigelow, a fine venerable old man of the Mayflower stock. Mutual compliments were exchanged, and the new comers escorted to the Revere House, a very handsome hotel, the best in Boston. Everywhere the streets were lined with throngs of people, who cheered our Governor-General to the uttermost extent of their lung-power.

On the third day took place a monster procession, at least a mile and a-half in length, and modelled after the plan of the German trades festivals. Besides the long line of carriages filled with guests, from the President and the Governor-General down to the humblest city officer, there was an immense array of "trades expositions" or pageants, that is, huge waggons drawn by four, six, eight and sometimes ten horses, each waggon serving as a model workshop, whereon printers, hatters, bootmakers, turners, carriage-makers, boat-riggers, stone-cutters, silversmiths, plumbers, market-men, piano-forte makers, and many other handicraftsmen worked at their respective callings.

The finest street of private residences was Dover Street, a noble avenue of cut stone buildings, occupied by wealthy people of old Boston families. The decorations here were both costly and tasteful; and the hospitality unbounded. As each carriage passed slowly along, footmen in livery presented at its doors silver trays loaded with refreshments, in the shape of pastry, bon-bons, and costly wines. The ladies of each house, richly dressed, stood on the lower steps and welcomed the visitors with smiles and waving of handkerchiefs. At two or three places in the line of procession, were platforms handsomely festooned, occupied by bevies of fair girls in white, or by hundreds of children of both sexes, belonging to the common schools, prettily dressed, and bearing bouquets of bright flowers which they presented to the occupants of the carriages.

I could not help remarking to my companion, one of the members of the Boston City Council, that more aristocratic-looking women than these Dover Street matrons, were not, I thought, to be found in all Europe.   He told me not to whisper such a sentiment in Boston, for fear it might expose the objects of my complimentary remark to being mobbed by the democracy.

At length the procession came to an end.   But it was only a prelude to a still more magnificent demonstration, which was the great banquet given to four thousand people under one vast tent covering half an acre of ground on the Common.   Thither the visitors were escorted in carriages, with the usual attention and solicitude for their every comfort, and when within, and placed according to their several ranks and localities, it was truly a sight to be remembered.   The tent was two hundred and fifty feet in length by ninety in width.   The roof and sides were all but hidden by the profusion of flags and bunting festooned everywhere.   A raised table for the visitors extended around the entire tent. For the citizens proper were placed ten rows of parallel tables running the whole length of the inner area ; altogether providing seats for three thousand six hundred people, besides smaller tables at convenient spots. There were present also a whole army of waiters, one to each dozen guests, and indefatigable in their duties.

The repast included all kinds of cold meats and temperance drinks. Flowers for every person and great flower trophies on the tables ; abundance of huge water and musk melons, and other fruits in great variety and perfection, especially native grown peaches and Bartlett pears, which Boston produces of the finest quality. Also plenty of pastry of many tempting kinds. It took scarcely twenty minutes to seat the entire " dinner party " comfortably, so excellent were the arrangements.

Before dinner commenced, Mayor Bigelow, who presided, announced that President Fillmore was required to leave for Washington on urgent state business ; which he did after his health had been proposed and acknowledged. A little piece of dramatic acting was noticeable here, when the President and Lord Elgin, one on each side of the Mayor, shook hands across his worshipful breast, the President retaining his lordship's hand firmly clasped in his own for some time ; a tableau which gave rise to a tumultuous burst of applause from the whole assemblage.

Then commenced in earnest the play of knives and forks, four thousand of each, producing a unique and somewhat droll effect. After the President had gone, Lord Elgin became the chief lion of the day, and right well did his lordship play his part, entering thoroughly into the prejudices of his auditors while disclaiming all flattery, pouring out witticism after witticism, sometimes of the broadest, and altogether carrying the audience with him until they were worked up into a perfect frenzy of applause.

"The health of Her Majesty the Queen of the United Kingdom of Great Britain and Ireland" having been proposed by His Honour Mayor John P. Bigelow, was received, as the Boston account of the Jubilee says, " with nine such cheers as would have made Her Majesty, had she been present, forget that she was beyond the limits of her own dominions; and the band struck up 'God save the Queen,' as if to complete the illusion." The compliment was acknowledged by Lord Elgin, who said :

" Allow me, gentlemen, as there seems to be in America some little misconception on these points, to observe, that we, monarchists though we be, enjoy the advantages of self-government, of popular elections, of deliberative assemblies, with their attendant blessings of caucuses, stump orators, lobbyings and log-rollings—(Laughter)— and I am not sure but we sometimes have a little pipe-laying—(renewed laughter)—almost, if not altogether, in equal perfection with yourselves. I must own, gentlemen, that I was exceedingly amused the other day, when one of the gentlemen who did me the honour to visit me at Toronto, bearing the invitation of the Common Council and Corporation of the City of Boston, observed to me, with the utmost gravity, that he had been delighted to find, upon entering our Legislative Assembly at Toronto, that there was quite as much liberty of speech there as in any body of the kind he had ever visited. (Laughter.) I could not help thinking that if my kind friend would only favour us with his company in Canada for a few weeks, we should be able to demonstrate, to his entire satisfaction, that the tongue is quite as 'unruly' a 'member' on the north side of the line as on this side. (Renewed laughter.)

"Now, gentlemen, you must not expect it, for I have not the voice for it, and I cannot pretend to undertake to make a regular speech to you. I belong to a people who are notoriously slow of speech. (Laughter.) If any doubt ever existed on this point, it must have been set at rest by the verdict which a high authority has recently pronounced. A distinguished American—a member of the Senate of the United States, who has lately been in England, informed his countrymen, on his return, that sadly backward as poor John Bull is in many things, in no one particular does he make so lamentable a failure as when he tries his hand at public speaking. (Laughter.) Now, gentlemen, deferring, as I feel bound to do, to that high authority, and conscious that in no particular do I more faithfully represent my countrymen than in my stammering tongue and embarrassed utterance (continued laughter), you may judge what my feelings are when I am asked to address an assembly like this, convened under the hospitable auspices of the Corporation of Boston, I believe to the tune of some four thousand, in this State of Massachusetts, a State which is so famous for its orators and its statesmen, a State that can boast of Franklins, and Adamses, and Everetts, and Winthrops and Lawrences, and Sumners and Bigelows, and a host of other distinguished men ; a State, moreover, which is the chosen home, if not the birthplace of the illustrious Secretary of State of the American Union. (Applause.)

" But, gentlemen, although I cannot make a speech to you, I must tell you, in the plain and homely way in which John Bull tries to express his feelings when his heart is full—that is to say, when they do not choke him and prevent his utterance altogether (sensation)—in that homely way I must express to you how deeply grateful I and all who are with me (hear, hear), feel for the kind and gratifying reception we have met with in the City of Boston. For myself, I may say that the citizens of Boston could not have conferred upon me a greater favour than that which they have conferred, in inviting me to this festival, and in thus enabling me not only to receive the hand of kindness which has been extended to me by the authorities of the City and of the State, but also giving me the opportunity, which I never had before, and perhaps may never have again, of paying my respects to the President of the United States. (Applause.) And although it would ill become me, a stranger, to presume to ^eulogise the conduct or the services of President Fillmore, yet as a bystander, as an observer, and by no means an indifferent or careless observer, of your progress and prosperity, I think I may venture to affirm that it is the opinion of all impartial men, that President Fillmore will occupy an honourable place on the roll of illustrious men on whom the mantle of Washington has fallen. (Applause and cheers.)

" Somebody must write to the President, and tell him how that remark about him was received. (Laughter.)

" Gentlemen : I have always felt a very deep interest in the progress of the lines of railway communication, of which we are now assembled to celebrate the completion. The first railway that I ever travelled upon in North America, forms part of the iron band which now unites Montreal to Boston. I had the pleasure, about five years ago, of travelling with a friend of mine, whom I see now present—Governor Paine—I think as far as Concord, upon that line.

" Ex-Governor Paine, of Vermont—It was Franklin.

" Lord Elgin—He contradicts me ; he says it was not Concord, but Franklin ; but I will make a statement which I am sure he will not contradict ; it is this—that although we travelled together two or three days—after leaving the cars, over bad roads, and in all sorts of queer conveyances, we never reached a place which we could with any propriety have christened Discord. (Laughter and applause.)

*　　*　　*　　*　　*　　*　　*

" As to the citizens of Boston, I shall not attempt to detail their merits, for their name is Legion ; but there is one merit, which I do not like to pass unnoticed, because they always seem to have possessed it in the highest perfection.　It is the virtue of courage.　Upon looking very accurately into history, I find one occasion, and one only upon which it appears to me that their courage entirely failed them.　I see a great many military men present, and I am afraid that they will call me to account for this observation (laughter)—and what do you think that occasion was ?　I find, from the most authentic records, that the citizens of Boston were altogether carried away by panic, when it was first proposed to build a railroad from Boston to Providence, under the apprehension that they themselves, their wives and their children, their stores and their goods, and all they possessed, would be swallowed up bodily by New York. (Laughter.)

" I hope that Boston has wholly recovered from that panic. I think it is some evidence of it, that she has laid out fifty millions in railways since that time."

After his lordship, followed Edward Everett, whose speech was a complete contrast in every respect.　Eloquent exceedingly, but chaste, terse and poetical ; it charmed the Canadian visitors as much as Lord Elgin's had delighted the natives.　Here are a few extracts :—

" It is not easy for me to express to you the admiration with which I have listened to the very beautiful and appropriate speech with which his Excellency, the Governor-General of Canada, has just delighted us. You know, sir, that the truest and highest art is to conceal art ; and I could not but be reminded of that maxim, when I heard that gentleman, after beginning with disabling himself, and cautioning us at the onset that he was slow of speech, proceed to make one of the happiest, most appropriate and eloquent speeches ever uttered. If I were travelling with his lordship in his native mountains of Gael, I should say to him, in the language of the natives of those regions, *sma sheen*—very well, my lord. But in plain English, sir, that which has fallen from his lordship has given me indeed new cause to rejoice that 'Chatham's language is my mother tongue.' (Great cheering.)

  * * * * * *

"'We have, Sir, in this part of the country long been convinced of the importance of this system of communication ; although it may be doubted whether the most sagacious and sanguine have even yet fully comprehended its manifold influences. We have, however, felt them on the sea board and in the interior. We have felt them in the growth of our manufactures, in the extension of our commerce, in the growing demand for the products of agriculture, in the increase of our population. We have felt them prodigiously in transportation and travel. The inhabitant of the country has felt them in the ease with which he resorts to the city markets, whether as a seller or a purchaser. The inhabitant of the city has felt them in the facility with which he can get to a sister city, or to the country ; with which he can get back to his native village ;—to see the old folks, aye, Sir, and some of the young folks—with which he can get a mouthful of pure mountain air—or run down in dog days to Gloucester or Phillips' beach, or Plymouth, or Cohassett, or New Bedford.

" I say, Sir, we have felt the benefit of our railway system in these and a hundred other forms, in which, penetrating far beyond material interests, it intertwines itself with all the concerns and relations of life and society; but I have never had its benefits brought home to me so sensibly as on the present occasion. Think, Sir, how it has annihilated time and space, in reference to this festival, and how greatly to our advantage and delight !

" When Dr. Franklin, in 1754, projected a plan of union for these colonies, with Philadelphia as the metropolis, he gave as a reason for this part of the plan, that Philadelphia was situated about half way between the extremes, and could be conveniently reached even from Portsmouth, New Hampshire, in eighteen days ! I believe the President of the United States, who has honoured us with his company at this joyous festival, was not more than twenty-four hours actually on the road from Washington to Boston ; two to Baltimore, seven more to Philadelphia, five more to New York, and ten more to Boston.

" And then Canada, sir, once remote, inaccessible region—but now brought to our very door. If a journey had been contemplated in that direction in Dr. Franklin's time, it would have been with such feelings as a man would have now-a-days, who was going to start for the mouth of Copper Mine River, and the shores of the Arctic Sea. But no, sir; such a thing was never thought of— never dreamed of. A horrible wilderness, rivers and lakes unspanned by human art, pathless swamps, dismal forests that it made the flesh creep to enter, threaded by nothing more practicable than the Indian's trail, echoing with no sound more inviting than the yell of the wolf and the warwhoop of the savage ; these it was that filled the space between us and Canada. The inhabitants of the British Colonies never entered Canada in those days but as provincial troops or Indian captives ; and lucky he that got back with his scalp on. (Laughter.) This state of things existed less than one hundred years ago ; there are men living in Massachusetts who were born before the

Y

last party of hostile Indians made an incursion to the banks of the Connecticut river.

" As lately as when I had the honour to be the Governor of the Commonwealth, I signed the pen ion warrant of a man who lost his arm in the year 1757, in a conflict with the Indians and French in one of the border wars, in those dreary Canadian forests. His Honour the Mayor will recollect it, for he countersigned the warrant as Secretary of State. Now, Sir, by the magic power of these modern works of art, the forest is thrown open— the rivers and lakes are bridged—the vallesy rise, the mountains bow their everlasting heads; and the Governor-General of Canada takes his breakfast in Montreal, and his dinner in Boston ;—reading a newspaper leisurely by the way which was printed a fortnight ago in London. [Great Applause.] In the excavations made in the construction of the Vermont railroads, the skeletons of fossil whales and palœozoic elephants have been brought to light. I believe, Sir, if a live spermaciti whale had been seen spouting in Lake Champlain, or a native elephant had walked leisurely into Burlington from the neighbouring woods, of a summer's morning, it would not be thought more wonderful than our fathers would have regarded Lord Elgin's journey to us this week, could it have been foretold to them a century ago, with all the circumstances of despatch, convenience and safety. [Applause.]

" I recollect that seven or eight years ago there was a project to carry a railroad into the lake country in England—into the heart of Westmoreland and Cumberland. Mr. Wordsworth, the lately deceased poet, a resident in the centre of this region, opposed the project. He thought that the retirement and seclusion of this delightful region would be disturbed by the panting of the locomotive, and the cry of the steam whistle. If I am not mistaken, he published one or two sonnets in deprecation of the enterprise. Mr. Wordsworth was a kind-hearted man, as well

as a most distinguished poet, but he was entirely mistaken, as it seems to me, in this matter. The quiet of a
few spots may be disturbed ; but a hundred quiet spots
are rendered accessible. The bustle of the station house
may take the place of the Druidical silence of some shady
dell ; but, Gracious Heavens ! sir, how many of those
verdant cathedral arches, entwined by the hand of God in
our pathless woods, are opened to the grateful worship of
man by these means of communication. (Cheers).

" How little of rural beauty you lose, even in a country
of comparatively narrow dimensions like England—how
less than little in a country so vast as this—by works of
this description. You lose a little strip along the line of
the road, which partially changes its character ; while, as
the compensation, you bring all this rural beauty—

> " The warbling woodland, the resounding shore,
> The pomp of groves, the garniture of fields,"

within the reach, not of a score of luxurious, sauntering
tourists, but of the great mass of the population, who
have senses and tastes as keen as the keenest. You throw
it open, with all its soothing and humanizing influences, to
thousands who, but for your railways and steamers, would
have lived and died without ever having breathed the
life giving air of the mountains ; yes, sir, to tens of thousands, who would have gone to their graves, and the sooner
for the privation, without ever having caught a glimpse of
the most magnificent and beautiful spectacle which nature
presents to the eye of man—that of a glorious combing
wave, a quarter of a mile long, as it comes swelling and
breasting towards the shore, till its soft green ridge bursts
into a crest of snow, and settles and dies along the whis-
pering sands !" (Immense cheering.)

" But even this is nothing compared with the great
social and moral effects of this system, a subject admir-
ably treated, in many of its aspects, in a sermon by Dr.

Gannett, which has been kindly given to the public. All important also are its political effects in binding the States together as one family, and uniting us to our neighbours as brethren and kinsfolk. I do not know, Sir, [turning to Lord Elgin,] but in this way, from the kindly seeds which have been sown this week, in your visit to Boston, and that of the distinguished gentlemen who have preceded and accompanied you, our children and grandchildren, as long as this great Anglo-Saxon race shall occupy the continent, may reap a harvest worth all the cost which has devolved on this generation. [Cheers.]

Other speeches followed, which would not now interest my readers. In due time the assemblage broke up, and the guests streamed away over the lovely Common in all directions, forming even in their departure a wonderful and pleasing spectacle.

We Canadians remained in Boston several days, visiting the public institutions, presenting and receiving addresses, and participating in a series of civic pageants, the more enjoyable because to us altogether novel and unprecedented. Our hosts informed us, that they were quite accustomed to and always prepared for such gatherings.

CHAPTER LXIII.

VESTIGES OF THE MOSAIC DELUGE.

IN chapters xlvi. and l. of this book, I have referred to certain conversations I had with Sir Wm. Logan, on the existence of ocean beaches, extending from Newfoundland to the North-West Territory, at an altitude of from twelve to fifteen hundred feet above the present sea level. Also of a secondary series of beaches, seven hundred feet above Lake Ontario, at Oak Ridges, eighteen miles north of Toronto; and a third series, one hundred and eighty to two hundred feet above the Lake, which I believe also occur at many points on the opposite lake-shore. In chapter xlvi. I mentioned the fact of my finding evidences of human remains at the very base of one of these lower beaches, at Carlton, on the Weston and Davenport Roads, near Toronto.

When I wrote those chapters, and until this present month of January, 1884, I was doubtful whether I should not be regarded as fanciful or unreliable. I have now, however, just seen in *Good Words* for this month, an article headed " Geology and the Deluge," from the pen of the Duke of

Argyle, which appears to me conclusive on the points to which I· allude, namely, first, that there was spread over the whole northern portion of this continent, a sea fifteen hundred feet above the land; secondly, that the depth of water was reduced to a thousand feet, and remained so during the formation of our Oak Ridges; and lastly, that a further subsidence of eight hundred feet took place, reducing the sea to the height of the Carlton beach; and that the latest of these subsidences must have occurred after our earth had been long peopled, and within historic times—probably at the date of the deluge recorded by Moses.

His Grace says :—

" I think I could take any one, however unaccustomed he might be to geological observation or to geological reasoning, to a place within a few miles of Inverary, and point out a number of facts which would convince him that the whole of our mountains, the whole of Scotland, had been lying deeper in the sea than it does now to a depth of at least 2,000 feet. . . . I believe that the submergence of the land towards the close of what is called the Glacial Period, was to a considerable extent a sudden submergence, probably more sudden to the south of the country than it was here, and that the Deluge was closely connected with that submergence. . . . The enormous stretch of country which lies between Russia and Behring's Straits is very little known, and almost uninhabited.   It is frozen to within a very few feet of the surface all the year round.   In that frozen mud the Mammoth has been preserved untouched.   There have been numerous carcases found with the flesh, the skin, the hair and the eyes complete. . . . Has this great catastrophe of the submergence of the land to the depth of at least two or three thousand feet, taken place since the birth of Man? In answer to this question I must refer to the fact now clearly ascertained, that Man co-existed with the Mammoth, and that stone implements are found in numbers in the very gravels and brick earths which contain the bones of those great mammalia."

I should be glad to quote more, but this is enough to account for the circumstances I have myself noted, and to explain also, I think, the vast deposit of mud which forms the prairies of the Western States, and of the Canadian North-West; which has its counterpart in the European prairie countries of Moldavia and Wallachia. But the Duke appears to me to overlook the circumstance, that the vast accumulation of animal remains in Siberia, mostly of southern varieties, to which he refers, must have been swept there, not by an upheaval, but by a depression in the northern hemisphere, and a corresponding rise in the southern, whence all these mammoths, lions and tigers, are supposed to have been swept. To account for their present elevated position, a second convulsion restoring the depressed parts to their original altitude, must apparently have occurred—at least that is my unscientific conclusion. It would seem that we ought to look for similar accumulations of animal matter in our own Hudson's Bay territory, where, also, it is stated, the ground remains frozen throughout summer to within three feet of the surface, as in Siberia.

CHAPTER LXIV.

THE FRANCHISE.

WHILE I was a member of the City Council, the question of the proper qualification for electors of municipal councils and of the legislature, was much under discussion. I told my Reform opponents, who advocated an extremely low standard, that the lower they fixed the qualification for voters, the more bitterly they would be disappointed; that the poorer the electors the greater the corruption that must necessarily prevail. And so it has proved.

In thinking over the subject since, I have been led to compare the body politic to a pyramid, the stones in every layer of which shall be more numerous than the aggregate of all the layers above it. And this comparison is by no means strained, as I believe it will be found, that each and every class is indeed numerically greater than all the classes higher in social rank—the idlers than the industrious—the workers than the employers—the children than the parents—the illiterate than the instructed—and so on. Thus it follows as a necessary consequence, that the adoption of the principle of manhood suffrage, now so much advocated, must necessarily place all political power in the hands of the worst offscourings of the community—law-breakers, vagrants, and outcasts of all kinds. This would be equivalent to inverting the pyramid, and expecting it to remain poised upon its apex—which is a mere impossibility.

Whether the capstone of the social pyramid ought to be king or president, is not material to my argument. On republican principles—and with the French King, Louis Philippe, I hold that the British constitutional monarchy is "the best of all republics" —the true theory of representative institutions must be, that each class of the electors should have a voice in the councils of the country equal to, and no greater than, each of the several classes (or strata) above. This would greatly resemble the old Scandinavian storthings, in which there were four orders of legislators—king, nobles, clergy, and peasants, each of which had a veto on all questions brought before any one of them.

Thus, the election of members of local municipal councils would be vested in the rate-payers, much as at present. The district (not county) councils would be elected by the local municipalities; and would themselves be entitled to elect members of the provincial legislatures. These latter again might properly be entrusted with the election of the Dominion House of Commons. And to carry the idea a step further, the Dominion Legislature itself would be a fitting body to nominate representatives to a great council of the Empire, which should decide all questions of peace or war, of commerce, and other matters affecting the whole body politic. To make the analogy complete, and bind the whole structure together, each class should be limited in its choice to the class next above it, by which process, it is to be presumed, " the survival of the fittest " would be secured, and every man elected to the higher bodies must have won his way from the municipal council up through all the other grades.

I should give each municipal voter such number of votes as would represent his stake in the municipality, say one vote for every four hundred dollars of assessable property, and an additional vote for every additional four hundred dollars, up to a maximum of perhaps ten votes, and no more, which would sufficiently protect the richer ratepayers without neutralizing the wishes of the poorer voters.

On such a system, every voter would influence the entire legislation of the country to the exact extent of his intelligence, and of his contributions to the general expenditure. Corruption would be almost, and intimidation quite, impracticable.

To meet the need for a revisory body or senate, the retired judges of the Upper Courts, and retired members of the House of Commons, after ten or twenty years' service, should form an unexceptionable tribunal for any of the colonies.

I am aware that the election of legislators by the county councils has been already advocated in Canada, and that in other respects this chapter may be considered not a little presumptuous; but I conclude, nevertheless, to print it for what it is worth.

CHAPTER LXV.

FREE TRADE AND PROTECTION.

I HAVE, I believe, in the preceding pages, established beyond contradiction the historical fact, that the Conservative party, whatever their other faults may have been, are not justly chargeable with making use of the Protection cry as a mere political manœuvre, only adopted immediately prior to the general elections of 1878.

I have mentioned, that when I was about eighteen years of age, the Corn-Law League was in full blast in England. I was foreman and proof-reader of the printing office whence all its principal publications issued, and was in daily communication with Col. Peyronnet Thompson, M. P., and the other free-trade leaders. I was even then struck with the circumstance, that while loudly professing their disinterested desire for the welfare of the whole human race, the authors of the movement urged as their main argument with the manufacturers and farmers, that England could undersell the whole world in cheap goods, while her agriculturists could never be undersold in their own markets. This reasoning appeared to me both hypocritical and fraudulent; and I hold that it has proved so, and that for England and Scotland, the day of retribution is already looming in the near future. As righteously might a single shop-keeper build his hopes of profit upon the utter ruin of all his trade competitors, as a single country dare to speculate, as the British free-trader has done, on the destruction of the manufacturing industries of all other nations.

The present troubles in Ireland, are they not the direct fruit of the crushing out of its linen industry? The Scindian war in India, was it not caused by the depopulation of a whole province of a million and a half of people, through the annihilation of its nankeen manufacture. And if Manchester and Birmingham had their way, would not France and Germany, and Switzerland and America—including Canada—become the mere bond-slaves of the Cobdens and the Brights—*et hoc genus omne?*

But there is a Power above all, that has ordered events otherwise. I assume it to be undeniable, that according to natural laws, the country which produces any raw material, must ultimately become its cheapest manipulator. England has no inherent claim to control any manufactures but those of tin, iron, brass and wool; and with time, all or most of these may be wrested from her. Her cotton mills must ultimately fade away before those of India, the Southern States, and Africa. Her grain can never again compete with that of Russia and the Canadian North-West. Her iron-works with difficulty now hold their own against Germany and the United States. Birmingham and Sheffield are threatened by Switzerland, by the New England States, and—before many decades—by Canada. And so on with all the rest of England's monopolies. Dear labour, dear farming, dear soil, will tell unfavourably in the end, in spite of all trade theories and *ex parte* arguments.

Yet more. It would not be hard to show, I think, that the tenant-right and agrarian agitations of the present day are due to Free Trade; that the cry, "the land belongs to the labourer," is the direct offspring of the Cobden teaching; and that the issue will but too probably be, a disastrous revulsion of labour against capital, and poverty against wealth. They who sow the wind, must reap the whirlwind! God send that it may not happen in our day!

CHAPTER LXVI.

THE FUTURE OF CANADA.

I MAY venture, I hope, to put down here some of the conclusions to which my fifty years' experience in Canada, and my observation of what has been going on during the same term in the United States, have led me. It is a favourite boast with our neighbours, that all North America must ultimately be brought under one government, and that the manifest destiny of Canada will irresistibly lead her on to annexation. And we have had, and still have amongst us, those who welcome the idea, and some who have lately grown audacious enough to stigmatize as traitors those who, like myself, claim to be citizens, not of the Dominion only, but of the Empire.

To say nothing of the semi-barbarous population of Mexico, who would have to be consulted, there is a section of the Southern States which may yet demand autonomy for the Negro race, and which will in all probability seize the first opportunity for so doing. Then in Canada, we have a million of French Canadians, who make no secret of their preference for French over British alliance; and who will surely claim their right to act upon their convictions the moment British authority shall have become relaxed. Nor can they be blamed for this, however we may doubt the soundness of their conclusions. Then we have the Acadians of Nova Scotia, who would probably follow French Canada wheresoever she might lead; nor could the few British people of New Brunswick and Prince Edward Island—unaided by England—escape the same fate. (Even Eastern Ontario might have to fight hard to escape a French Republican régime.

There remain Middle and Western Ontario, and the North-West—two naturally isolated territories, neither of which could be expected to incur the horrors of war for the sake of the other. It is not, I think, difficult to foresee, that, given independence, Ontario must inevitably cast her lot in with the United States. But with the North-West, the case is entirely different.

From Liverpool to Winnipeg, *via* Hudson's Bay, the distance is less by eleven hundred miles than by way of the St. Lawrence. From Liverpool to China and Japan, *via* the same northern route, the distance is—as a San Francisco journal points out—a thousand miles shorter than by any other trans-American line. It is really *two thousand miles* shorter than *via* San Francisco and New York. From James's Bay as a centre, the cities of Quebec, Montreal, Kingston, Toronto, Hamilton, London, and

Winnipeg, are pretty nearly equidistant. How immense, then, will be the power which the possession of the Hudson's Bay, and of the railway route through to the Pacific, must confer upon Great Britain, so long as she holds it under her sole control. And where is the nation that can prevent her so holding it, while her fleets command the North Atlantic Ocean. Is it not utterly inconceivable, that English statesmen can be found so mad or so unpatriotic, as to throw away the very key of the world's commerce, by neglecting or surrendering British interests in the North-West; or that Manchester and Birmingham—Sheffield and Glasgow—should sustain for a moment any government that could dream of so doing. I firmly believe, in fine, that either by the St. Lawrence or the Hudson's Bay route, or both, British connexion with Canada is destined to endure, all prognostications to the contrary notwithstanding. England may afford to be shut out of the Suez canal, or the Panama canal, or the entire of her South African colonies, better than she can afford to part with the Dominion, and notably the Canadian North-West. If there be any two countries in the world whose interests are inseparable, they are the British Isles and North-Western Canada—the former being constrained by her food necessities, the latter by her want of a secure grain market. Old Canada, some say, has her natural outlet in the United States—which is only very partially true, as the reverse might be asserted with equal force. Not so the North-West. She has her natural market in Great Britain ; and Great Britain, in turn, will find in the near future her best customer in Manitoba and the North-Western prairies.

So mote it be !

CHAPTER LXVII.

THE TORONTO MECHANICS' INSTITUTE.

THE following account of the rise and progress of this institution, has been obligingly furnished me by one of its earliest and best friends, Mr. William Edwards, to whom, undoubtedly, more than to any other man, it has been indebted for its past success and usefulness :

The Toronto Mechanics' Institute was established in January, 1831, at a meeting of influential citizens called together by James Lesslie, Esq., now of Eglinton. Its first quarterly meeting of members was held in Mr. Thompson's school-room ; the report being read by Mr. Bates, and the number of enrolled members being fifty-six. Dr. W. W. Baldwin (father of the Hon. Robert Baldwin), Dr. Dunlop, Capt. Fitzgibbon, John Ewart, Wm. Lawson, Dr. Rolph, James Cockshutt, James and James G. Worts, John Harper, E. R. Denham, W. Musson, J. M. Murchison, W. B. Jarvis, T. Carfrae, T. F. (the late Rev. Dr.) Caldicott, James Cull, Dr. Duns-

Z

combe, C. C. Small, J. H. Price, Timothy Parsons, A. Thomson, and others, were active workers in promoting the organization and progress of the Institute.

Where the institute was at first located, the writer has not been able to ascertain ; but meetings were held in the " Masonic Lodge " rooms in Market (now Colborne) Street, a wooden building, on the ground floor of which was the common school taught by Thomas Appleton. A library and museum were formed, lectures delivered, and evening classes of instruction carried on for the improvement of its members.

During the year 1835, a grant of £200 was made by the legislature, for the purchase of apparatus. The amount was entrusted to Dr. Birkbeck, of London, and the purchases were made by him or by those to whom he committed the trust. The apparatus was of an expensive character, and very incomplete, and was never of much value to the Institute.

The outbreak of the rebellion of Upper Canada in December, 1837, and the excitement incident thereto, checked the progress of the Institute for awhile ; but in 1838, the directors reported they had secured from the city corporation a suite of rooms for the accommodation of the Institute, in the south east corner of the Market Buildings —the site of the present St. Lawrence Market.

In the year 1844, the Institute surrendered the rooms in the Market Buildings, and occupied others above the store No. 12 Wellington Buildings, just east of the Wesleyan Book-room ; and, through the kindness of the late sheriff, W. B. Jarvis, had the use of the county court-room for its winter lectures. During this year the city corporation contracted to erect a two-story fire-hall on the site of the present fire-hall and police-court buildings. On the memorial of the Institute, the council extended its ground plan, so as to give all necessary accommodation to the fire department in the lower story, and the Institute continued the building of the second story for its accommodation, and paid to the contractors the difference between the cost of the extended building and the building first contracted for, which amounted to £465 5s. 6d.— this sum being raised by voluntary subscriptions of from 1s. to £1 each.

The foundation stone of the building was laid on the 27th of August, 1845, and the opening of the rooms took place (John Ewart, Esq., in the chair), on the 12th of February, 1846 ; when the annual meeting of the Institute was held, and the Hon. R. B. Sullivan delivered an eloquent address, congratulatory to the Institute on its possession of a building so convenient for its purposes.

The statute for the incorporation of the Institute was assented to on the 28th July, 1847, and a legislative grant of money was made to the Institute during the same year.

In 1848, the Institute inaugurated the first of a series of exhibitions of works of art and mechanism, ladies' work, antiquities, curiosities, &c. This was kept open for two weeks, and was a means of instruction and amusement to the public, and of prcfit to the Institute funds. Similar exhibitions were repeated in 1849, 1850, 1851, 1861, and 1866 ; and in 1868 an exclusively fine arts exhibition was held, of upwards of 700 paintings and drawings—many of them being copies of the old masters. In obtaining specimens for, and in the management of nearly all these exhibitions, as well as in several other departments of the Institute's operations, Mr. J. E. Pell was always an indefatigable worker.

In 1851, the members of the Institute began to realize the fact that their hall accommodation was too limited ; and in September, 1853, the site at the corner of Church and Adelaide Streets was purchased by public auction, for £1,632 5s. 0d., and plans for a new building were at once prepared, and committees were appointed to canvas for subscriptions. The appeal to the citizens was nobly responded to, and before the close of the year the sum of £1,200 was contributed. The president of the Institute,

the late F. W. Cumberland, Esq., generously presented
the plans and specifications and superintendence, free of
charge.   A contract for the erection of the new building
was entered into in November, and the chief corner stone
was laid with Masonic honours on the 17th of April,
1854.

During the year 1855, the Provincial Government
leased the unfinished building for four years, for depart-
mental purposes, the Government paying at the time
$5,283.20 to enable the Institute to discharge its then lia-
bilities thereon.   At the expiration of the lease, the Government paid to the Institute the sum of $16,000, to
cover the expense of making the necessary changes in
the building, and to finish it as nearly as possible in accordance with the original plans.   The building had a
frontage of eighty feet on Church Street, and of 104 feet
on Adelaide Street, and its cost to the Institute when
finished was $48,380.78.   The amount received by sub-
scription was $8,190.49 ; sale of old hall, $2,000 ; sale of
old building on the new site, $14.50 ; from Government,
to meet building fund liabilities, $5,283.20 ; by loans
from the U. C. College funds, $18,400 ; and from the
Government for completion of the building, $16,000 ;
leaving a balance to be expended for general purposes of
$1,507.41.   This commodious building was finished and
occupied during the year 1861.   A soiree was held as a
suitable entertainment for the inauguration ; and this
was followed by a bazaar—the two resulting in a profit
of about $400 to the funds of the Institute.

During the year 1862, the very successful annual series
of literary and musical entertainments was instituted.
From the first organization of the Institute, evening class
instruction, in the rudimentary and more advanced studies, had been a special feature of its operations ; but the
session of 1861-2 inaugurated a more complete system
than had before been carried out.   These classes were
continued annually with marked success until the winter

of 1879-80 ; when the Institute gave up this portion of
its work in consequence of the Public School Board establishing evening classes in three of its best city school-
houses.

In 1868, the Institute purchased a vacant lot on the
east of its building, on Adelaide Street, with the intention of erecting thereon a larger music hall than it possessed. The contemplated improvement was not carried
out by the Institute ; but the Free Library Board has
now made the extension very much as at first intended,
but for library purposes only.

In the year 1871, the Ontario Government purchased
the property from the Institute for the sum of $36,500,
for the purposes of a School of Technology, then being
established. The sale left in the Institute treasury upwards of $11,000, after paying off all its liabilities ; and
owing to the liberality of the Government in allowing the
Institute to occupy the library, reading-room, and board-
room free of rent during its tenancy, it was placed in a
very favourable position, and considerably improved its
finances. In 1876, the Government resolved to erect a
more suitable building for the School of Technology (then
named "School of Science"), in the University Park,
and re-sold the property it had purchased to the Institute
for $28,000. Many alterations were made in the build-
ing when the Institute got possession. A ladies' reading-
room was established, the music hall was made a recrea-
tion-room, with eleven billiard tables, chess-boards, &c.,
for the use of the members. This latter feature was a
success, both financially and otherwise.

In the year 1882, the "Free Libraries Act" was
passed, which provided that if adopted in any municipality, the Mechanics' Institute situated therein may transfer to such municipality all its property for the purposes
of the Act. The ratepayers of Toronto having, by a large
majority, decided to establish a Free Library, the members of the Institute in special general meeting held on

29th March, 1883, by an almost unanimous vote, resolved to make over all its property, with its assets and
liabilities, to the City Corporation of Toronto for such
library purposes; and both the parties having agreed
thereto, the transfer deed giving legal effect to the same,
was executed on the 30th day of June, in the said year
1883.

With the adoption of the Free Library system in this
city, the usefulness of the Institute as an educator would
have passed away.   It was better for it to go honourably
out of existence, than to die a lingering death, of debt
and starvation.   During its fifty-three years of existence
it had done a good work.   Thousands of the young men
of this city, by its refining and educating influences, had
their thoughts and resolves turned into channels of industry and usefulness, that might otherwise have run
in directions far less beneficial to themselves and to society.   Its courses of winter lectures in philosophy, mechanics, and historical and literary subjects, inaugurated
with its earliest life and provided year by year in the face
of great difficulties until the year 1875, led many of its
members to study the useful books in the library, to join
with their fellows in the class-rooms, and in after years
to take responsible positions in the professions and in
the workshops, that only for the Institute they would not
have attained to.

Until the Canadian Institute—which was nursed into
existence in the Mechanics' Institute, through the energy
and activity of Sandford A. Fleming, Esq., one of its
members—the Institute had the lecture field in Toronto
to itself.   Next came the Young Men's Christian Association, with its lectures, and free reading-room and
library.   In the face of all these noble and better sustained associations, it would have been but folly to have
endeavoured to keep the Mechanics' Institute in existence.

This notice of the Institute in some of the leading events in its history, is necessarily brief; but it would be unjust to close without noticing some of those who have for extended periods been its active workers. They have been so many, that I fear to name any when I cannot name them all. I give, however, the names of those who served the Institute in the various positions of president, vice-presidents, treasurer, secretaries, librarians and directors, for periods of from eight to thirty years in all, as follows :—

W. Edwards (30 years consecutively), W. Atkinson (17), J. E. Pell (15), Hiram Piper, R. Edwards, Thos. Davison (each 13), John Harrington, M. Sweetnam (each 12), Francis Thomas, W. H. Sheppard, Charles Sewell (each 11), F. W. Cumberland, R. H. Ramsay, J. J. Withrow, John Taylor, Lewis Samuel, Walter S. Lee (each 10), Daniel Spry, Prof. Croft, Patrick Freeland, Rice Lewis (each 9), James Lesslie, H. E. Clarke, Dr. Trotter (each 8 years).

Except for the years 1833, 5, 8, 9 and 1840, of which no records have been found, the successive presidents of the Institute have been as follows : John Ewart, (1831, 1844), Dr. Baldwin (1832, 4, 7), Dr. Rolph (1836), R. S. Jameson (1841), Rev. W. T. Leach (1842), W. B. Jarvis (1843), T. G. Ridout, 1845, 6, 8), R. B. Sullivan (1847), Professor Croft (1849, 1850), F. W. Cumberland (1851, 2, 1865, 6), T. J. Robertson, (1853), Patrick Freeland (1854, 9), Hon. G. W. Allan (1855, 1868, 9), E. F. Whittemore (1856), J. E. Pell (1857), John Harrington (1858), J. D. Ridout (1860), Rice Lewis (1861, 2), W. Edwards (1863), F. W. Coate (1864), J. J. Withrow (1867), James McLennan (part of 1870), John Turner (part of 1870), M. Sweetnam (1871, 2, 3, 4), Thos. Davison (1875, 6, 8), Lewis Samuel (1877), Donald C. Ridout (1879), W. S. Lee (1880, 1), James Mason (1882, 3).

The recording secretaries have been in the following order and number of years' service: Jos. Bates (1831), T.

Parson (1832, 3, 4, 5, 6), C. Sewell (1837, 8 and 1841), J. F. Westland (1840 and 1842), W. Edwards (1843, 4, 5, 6, 7, 8, 9, 1850, 1859, 1860), R. Edwards (1851, 2, 3, 4, 5, 6, 7, 8), G. Longman (1861, 2, 3, 4, 5, 6), John Moss (1867), Richard Lewis (1868), Samuel Brodie (1869, 1870, 1), John Davy (1872, 3, 4, 5, 6, 7, 8, 9, 1880, 1, 2, 3).

The corresponding secretaries have been A. T. McCord (1836), C. Sewell (1842, 3, 4, 5), J. F. Westland (1841), W. Steward (1846), Alex. Christie (1847, 8, 9, 1850, 3), Patrick Freeland (1851, 2), M. Sweetnam (1854, 5), J. J. Woodhouse (1856), John Elliott (1857), J. H. Mason (1858, 9, 1860). From this date the office was not continued.

The treasurers have been, James Lesslie (1831, 4, 5, 6), H. M. Mosley (1832), T. Carfrae (1833), W. Atkinson (1840, 1, 2, 3, 4, 5, 6), John Harrington (1847, 8, 9, 1850, 1, 2, 3, 4, 5, 6), John Paterson (1857, 8, 9, 1860, 1, 2), John Cowan (1863), W. Edwards (1864, 5, 6, 7, 8, 9, 1870), John Hallam (1871), Thos. Maclear (1872, 3, 4, 5), W. B. Hartill (1876), R. H. Ramsay (1877, 1881, 2, 3), G. B. Morris (1878, 9), John Taylor (1880).

CHAPTER LXVIII.

THE FREE PUBLIC LIBRARY.

THE establishment of Free Libraries, adapted to meet the wants of readers of all classes, has made rapid progress within the last few years. Some, such as the Chetham Library of Manchester, owe their origin to the bequests of public-spirited citizens of former days; some, like the British Museum Library, to national support; but they remained comparatively unused, until the modern system of common school education, and the wonderful development of newspaper enterprise, made readers of the working classes. I remember when London had but one daily journal, the *Times*, and one weekly, the *News*, which latter paper was sold for sixpence sterling by men whom I have seen running through the streets on Sunday morning, blowing tin horns to announce their approach to their customers.

The introduction of Mechanics' Institutes by the joint efforts of Lord Brougham and Dr. Birkbeck, I also recollect; as a lad I was one of the first members. They spread over all English-speaking communities, throve for many years, then gradually waned. Scientific knowledge became so common, that lectures on chemistry, astronomy, &c., ceased to attract audiences. But the appetite for reading did not diminish in the least, and hence it happened that Free Libraries began to supersede Mechanics' Institutes.

Toronto has heretofore done but little in this way, and it remained for a few public-spirited citizens of the present decade, to effect any marked advance in the direction of free reading for all classes. In August, 1880, the Rev. Dr. Scadding addressed a letter to the City Council, calling its attention to the propriety of establishing a Public Library in Toronto.

In the following December, Alderman Taylor, in an address to his constituents, wrote—" In 1881 the nucleus of a free Public Library should be secured by purchase or otherwise, so that in a few years we may boast of a library that will do no discredit to the educational centre of the Dominion. Cities across the lake annually vote a sum to be so applied, Chicago alone voting $39,000 per annum for a similar purpose. Surely Toronto can afford say $5,000 a year for the mental improvement of her citizens." In the City Council for 1881, the subject was zealously taken up by Aldermen Hallam, Taylor and Mitchell. Later in the year, Alderman Hallam presented to the council an interesting report of his investigations among English public libraries, describing their system and condition.

Early in 1882, an Act was passed by the Ontario Legislature, giving power to the ratepayers of any municipality in Ontario to tax themselves for the purchase or erection and maintenance of a Free Public Library, limiting the rate to be so levied to one half mill on the dollar on taxable property.*

---

* " Whatever may be its fate, the friends of progress will remember that the Province is indebted for this bill (the Free Libraries Act) to the zeal and public spirit of an alderman of the City of Toronto, Mr. John Hallam. With a disinterested enthusiasm and an assurance that the inhabitants of the towns and villages of Ontario would derive substantial benefits from the introduction of free public libraries, Mr. Hallam has spared no pains

The Town of Guelph was the first to avail itself of the privilege, and was followed by Toronto, which, on 1st January, 1883, adopted a by-law submitted by the City Council in accordance with the statute, the majority thereon being 2,543, the largest ever polled at any Toronto city election for raising money for any special object.

This result was not obtained without very active exertions on the part of the friends of the movement, amongst whom, as is admitted on all hands, Alderman Hallam is entitled to the chief credit. But for his liberal expenditure for printing, his unwearied activity in addressing public meetings, and his successful appeals through the children of the common schools to their parents, the by-law might have failed. Ald. Taylor and other gentlemen gave efficient aid. Professor Wilson, President of Toronto University, presided at meetings held in its favour; and Messrs. John Hague, W. H. Knowlton and other citizens supported it warmly through the press. The editors of the principal city papers also doing good service through their columns.

---

to stimulate public opinion in their favour. He has freely distributed a pamphlet on the subject, which embodies the result of much enquiry and reflection, gathered from various sources, and he seems to be very sanguine of success."—See Dr. ALPHEUS TODD'S paper "*On the Establishment of Free Libraries in Canada*," read before the Royal Society of Canada, 25th May, 1882.

In Toronto, as elsewhere, the Mechanics' Institute
has had its day.   But times change, and the public
taste changes with them.   A library and reading-
room supported by subscription, could hardly hope
to compete with an amply endowed rival, to which
admission would be absolutely free.   So the officers
of the Mechanics' Institute threw themselves heartily
into the new movement, and after consultation with
their members, offered, in accordance with the statute, to transfer their property, valued at some
twenty thousand dollars, exclusive of all encum-
brances, to the City Council for the use of the Free
Library, which offer was gladly accepted.

The first Board of Management was composed as
follows :—The Mayor, A. R. Boswell (ex-officio);
John Hallam, John Taylor and George D'Arcy Boulton,* nominated by the City Council; Dr. George
Wright, W. H. Knowlton and J. A. Mills, nominees
of the Public School Board ; and James Mason and
Wm. Scully, representing the Board of Separate
School Trustees.   At their first meeting, held February 15th, 1883, the new Board elected John
Hallam to be their chairman for the year, and myself as secretary *pro tem.*

The following extract from the Chairman's opening address, illustrates the spirit in which the library is to be conducted :

* Mr. Boulton retired January 1st, 1884, and Alderman Bernard Saunders was appointed in his stead.

" Toronto is pre-eminently a city of educational institutions. We all feel a pride in her progress, and feel
more so now that it is possible to add a free public library to her many noble and useful institutions. I feel
sure that the benefit to the people of a reference and
lending library of carefully selected books, is undisputed
by all who are interested in the mental, moral, and social
advancement of our city. The books in such a library
should be as general and as fascinating as possible. I
would have this library a representative one, with a grand
foundation of solid, standard fact literature, with a choice,
clear-minded, finely-imaginative superstructure of light
reading, and avoid the vulgar, the sensuously sensational,
the garbage of the modern press. A rate-supported library should be practical in its aims, and not a mere curiosity shop for a collection of curious and rare books—
their only merit being their rarity, their peculiar binding,
singular type, or quaint illustrations. It is very nice to
have these literary rare-bits ; but the taxes of the people
should not be spent in buying them. A library of this
kind, to be valuable as far as our own country is concerned, should contain a full collection of—

" 1. Manuscript statements and narratives of pioneer
settlers ; old letters and journals relative to the early history and settlement of Ontario, Quebec, Manitoba, Nova
Scotia, New Brunswick, Newfoundland, and Prince Edward Island, and the wars of 1776 and 1812 ; biographi-
cal notes of our pioneers and of eminent citizens deceased,
and facts illustrative of our Indian tribes, their history,
characteristics, sketches of their prominent chiefs, orators,
and warriors.

2. " Diaries, narratives, and documents relative to the
U. E. Loyalists, their expulsion from the old colonies, and
their settlement in the Maritime Provinces.

3. " Files of newspapers, books, pamphlets, college cata-
logues, minutes of ecclesiastical conventions, associations,
conferences, and synods, and all other publications relating to this and other provinces.

" 4. Indian geographical names of streams and localities, with their signification, and all information generally respecting the condition, language, and history of different tribes of the Indians.

" 5. Books of all kinds, especially such as relate to Canadian history, travels, and biography in general, and Lower Canada or Quebec in particular, family genealogies, old magazines, pamphlets, files of newspapers, maps, historical manuscripts and autographs of distinguished persons.

" I feel sure such a library will rank and demand recognition among the permanent institutions in the city for sustaining, encouraging and stimulating everything that is great and good.

" Free libraries have a special claim on every ratepayer who desires to see our country advance to the front, and keep pace with the world in art, science, and commerce, and augment the sum of human happiness. This far-reaching movement is likely to extend to every city and considerable town in this Province. The advantages are many. They help on the cause of education. They tend to promote public virtue. Their influence is on the side of order, self-respect, and general enlightenment. There are few associations so pleasant as those excited by them. They are a literary park where all can enjoy themselves during their leisure hours. To all lovers of books and students, to the rich and poor alike, the doors of these institutions are open without money and without price."

The year 1883 was employed in getting things into working order. The City Council did their part by voting the sum of $50,000 in debentures, for the equipment and enlargement of the Mechanics' Institute building for the purposes of the main or central library and reading room ; the opening of branch libraries and reading rooms in the north and west ;

and for the purchase of 25,000 volumes of books, of which 5,000 each were destined for the two branches.

On the 3rd July, the Board of Management appointed Mr. James Bain, jr., as librarian-in-chief, with a staff of three assistant librarians, and four junior assistants (females). The duties of secretary were at the same time attached to the office of first assistant-librarian, which was given to Mr. John Davy, former secretary and librarian to the Mechanics' Institute. I was relegated to the charge of the Northern Branch, at St. Paul's Hall; while the Western Branch, at St. Andrew's Market, was placed in the hands of Miss O'Dowd, an accomplished scholar and teacher.

The Chairman and Librarian, Messrs. Hallam and Bain, proceeded in October to England for the purchase of books, most of which arrived here in January. *The Week* for December 13th last says of the books selected, that they " would make the mouth water of every bibliophile in the country." While I am writing these lines they are being catalogued and arranged for use, and the Free Library of Toronto will become an accomplished fact, almost simultaneously with the publication of these "Reminiscences."

CHAPTER LXIX.

Postscript.

AFTER having spent the greater part of half a century in various public capacities—after having been the recipient of nearly every honorary distinction which it was in the power of my fellow-citizens to confer—there now remains for me no further object of ambition, unless to die in harness, and so escape the taunt—

> " Unheeded lags the veteran on the stage."

Three times have I succeeded in gaining a position of reasonable competence; and as often—in 1857, 1860 and 1876—the " great waterfloods " have swept over me, and left me to begin life anew. It is too late now, however, to scale another Alp, so let us plod on in the valley, watching the sunshine fading away behind the mountains, until the darkness comes on ; and aye singing—

> " Night is falling dark and silent,
>   Starry myriads gem the sky ;
> Thus, when earthly hopes have failed us,
>   Brighter visions beam on high."